"A mix of magic realism and Southern Gothic, this stunning collaboration between King and McDowell . . . moves at a hypnotic pace, like an Alabama water moccasin slipping through black water."

—*Publishers Weekly* (starred review)

"Spooky . . . Supernatural elements, complicated schemes, and a neatly portrayed sense of place—was the sunny Gulf beach ever so threatening?—make this a shivery fun novel for summer." —*The Tampa Tribune*

"[A] lightly supernatural confection . . . King completes it beautifully as to tone, aura, and flavor, and it's funny and intriguing, magnetically readable." —*Booklist*

"A superb paranormal gothic thriller that grips readers from start to finish . . . Tabitha King completes the late Michael McDowell's tale so that no one will be able to ascertain who wrote what nor care as the growing suspense to an anticipated High Noon showdown is what the audience will appreciate." —Alternative-worlds.com

Candles Burning

A Novel

Tabitha King *and* Michael McDowell

BERKLEY BOOKS, NEW YORK

THE BERKLEY PUBLISHING GROUP
Published by the Penguin Group
Penguin Group (USA) Inc.
375 Hudson Street, New York, New York 10014, USA
Penguin Group (Canada), 90 Eglinton Avenue East, Suite 700, Toronto, Ontario M4P 2Y3, Canada
(a division of Pearson Penguin Canada Inc.)
Penguin Books Ltd., 80 Strand, London WC2R 0RL, England
Penguin Books Ireland, 25 St. Stephen's Green, Dublin 2, Ireland (a division of Penguin Books Ltd.)
Penguin Group (Australia), 250 Camberwell Road, Camberwell, Victoria 3124, Australia
(a division of Pearson Australia Group Pty. Ltd.)
Penguin Books India Pvt. Ltd., 11 Community Centre, Panchsheel Park, New Delhi—110 017, India
Penguin Group (NZ), 67 Apollo Drive, Rosedale, North Shore 0745, Auckland, New Zealand
(a division of Pearson New Zealand Ltd.)
Penguin Books (South Africa) (Pty.) Ltd., 24 Sturdee Avenue, Rosebank, Johannesburg 2196,
South Africa

Penguin Books Ltd., Registered Offices: 80 Strand, London WC2R 0RL, England

This is a work of fiction. Names, characters, places, and incidents either are the product of the author's imagination or are used fictitiously, and any resemblance to actual persons, living or dead, business establishments, events, or locales is entirely coincidental.

CANDLES BURNING

A Berkley Book / published by arrangement with the authors

PRINTING HISTORY
Berkley hardcover edition / June 2006
Berkley mass-market edition / May 2007

Copyright © 2006 by Tabitha King and Michael McDowell.
"You Are My Sunshine" by Jimmie Davis copyright © 1940 by Peer International Corporation.
Cover illustration and design by Gene Mollica. *Tree:* Stephen Wolf/Images.com
Reference: courtesy of The New York Public Library Picture Collection.

ISBN: 978-0-425-21570-8

BERKLEY®
Berkley Books are published by The Berkley Publishing Group,
a division of Penguin Group (USA) Inc.,
375 Hudson Street, New York, New York 10014.
BERKLEY is a registered trademark of Penguin Group (USA) Inc.
The "B" design is a trademark belonging to Penguin Group (USA) Inc.

PRINTED IN THE UNITED STATES OF AMERICA

10 9 8 7 6 5 4 3 2 1

For Michael

This novel is a collaboration. Michael McDowell began it a decade ago. He died before he could finish it. His editor, Susan Allison, approached me through my agent, Ralph Vicinanza, with the idea of completing it. I was immediately intrigued. The manuscript and the notes that Michael left were incomplete, but he had carried the story forward several hundred pages. The story as I completed it is not the story that Michael set out to tell, or the one that he would have told, had he lived to finish it. Every novelist knows the difference. This is the story that I drew from Michael's manuscript.

I hope that it would have pleased and amused him, and that it pleases Laurence Senelick, Michael's longtime companion, and Michael's sister, Ann, and brother, James, who survive him. Laurence has given me generous support and approval for this project and provided notes and fragments of the original manuscript that had gone astray. He has my deep gratitude.

Thanks to Julie Ann Eugley, Marsha DeFillippo, Barbara Ann McIntyre, Margaret Morehouse, Marcella Spruce, and Diane Ackerly, providers of logistical support, research, scheduling, and lunches; to Dave Higgins, who maintains our Macs. As always, to my first readers, Nora K., Kelly B., Owen, Joey, Steve, Sarah Jane, M., my oldest sister, and M., my youngest sister. Thanks to my family also, for the humor with which they have tolerated my antisocial prickliness when I am working. Thanks to Douglas Winter, who knows for what, and shrieks to Lyn.

Thanks to Ralph and to Susan.

But most of all, thank you, Michael. It was fun. And I miss you.

One

MY father died unpleasantly.

Mama put it that way. "My husband died," she used to say, letting her voice catch before concluding, "unpleasantly."

Stepping on a wasp barefoot—that's unpleasant. A mouthful of sour milk—that's unpleasant. What happened to Daddy was no mere unpleasance. It was murder. And not a cozy one. Not the butler in the library with the revolver, not a bloodless, painless, game of clues with a polite high-class suicide to avoid the common gallows at the end.

I was seven years old when Daddy died. I did not entirely understand the nature of Daddy's death nor did I accept its finality. His death was an event that had happened to me, and to Mama, and to my brother, Ford; the realization that it had happened to Daddy came only with the passage of time. The pictures of the bloody footlocker that made the cover of what turned out to be the last issue of *True Sex Crimes*, the stories that appeared in that grimy little scandal sheet and its trashy ilk—*Savage Real Crimes, Twentieth-Century Grue*—were successfully kept from my eyes until much later.

Recently I have read or reread all the newspaper and periodical clippings and the popular psychological forensics farragoes, such as Dr. Meyers's 1975 publication, *Sexual Pathology and the Homicidal Impulse,* which included a chapter entitled "Footlocker, Broomstick and Cleaver." The unspeakably cruel details of Daddy's death quickly defeated the cynical attitude with which I had armored myself. Mama's once ludicrous euphemism now lodges sharp as a fishbone in my throat.

The women who actually murdered Daddy were caught. They were tried. They were judged guilty and sentenced to die in the electric chair. Even in Louisiana in 1958, it was rare for women to be executed but what they did to my father was, in the opinion of the judge, "an unimaginably heinous atrocity against nature."

But the two guilty women did not die by electrocution.

Judy DeLucca was murdered in the prison laundry—slit open from throat to crotch with a razor blade embedded in the handle of a toothbrush. When Janice Hicks, housed in a different wing of the same prison in Baton Rouge, heard of her friend's death, she began to gasp frantically. She was dead before a doctor could be summoned. The autopsy showed that her lungs were full of water.

Seawater.

Two

MY name is Calley Dakin.

I was christened Calliope Carroll Dakin. Every time I ever asked Mama why she named me Calliope, she spun a new and blatant lie, from the lackadaisical to the sadistic: Calliope was the name of the best friend in college who had proved to be treacherous, or of the childhood doll that had always had an odd smell, or the forbidden creek where a naughty child was bitten by a water moccasin and when the body was recovered, the snake was inside the child's mouth.

I discovered for myself that a calliope is a nineteenth-century steam organ associated with circuses, and that Calliope is the classical Greek muse of epic poetry. At my first opportunity, I informed Mama of these facts.

"I had no idea," said Mama, in a flat sarcastic tone. "If only I had had an inkling."

From my earliest babyhood, Daddy took me to the circus as often as one showed up within reasonable reach so that I came to know the range of sounds of the calliope. No one could call it a delicate instrument but I did admire its great rowdy wind. Mama never went with us. She had an allergy to hokum, she said. It was some years before I was disabused of the notion that hokum was some kind of plant like ragweed that provoked people to sneeze and swell up.

Mama was born Roberta Ann Carroll. The Carrolls were a very old Alabama family, very high in Alabama, as high as you could get without actually being the current governor or so rich that people in other states had heard of you. Mama never let me forget that I was a Carroll, or that I was failing to measure up to being one.

But my last name was Dakin.

The Dakins were very low in Alabama, as low as you could get without being colored. The Dakins had never amounted to anything, Mama always said. They were not quality. Without history, without standing, they might as well have hailed from the backside-of-the-moon.

The only things they did have were hillbilly accents and boys. There were no Dakin girls, just family after family of Mama Dakin, Daddy Dakin, and four, five, six, or in the case of Daddy's mama and daddy, seven little boy Dakins.

So why did Roberta Carroll marry Joe Cane Dakin?

Because, unlike all the other Dakins in Alabama, Daddy was rich.

Though his name actually was Joe, Mama called him Joseph. She asserted that it was typically ignorant of the Dakins to put a nickname on a birth certificate. Daddy's brothers were Jimmy Cane Dakin, Timmy Cane Dakin, Tommy Cane Dakin, Lonny Cane Dakin, Dickie Cane Dakin, and Billy Cane Dakin. Mama claimed that the middle name was because they were all born in a cane field.

Daddy told me that it was his mama's lesson to them all, so they would not forget the stain of Cain upon the human race. The misspelling was of no import. The idea of spelling as a strict science never penetrated very deeply among the barely literate like Daddy's mama, or the illiterate like his daddy. Indeed, it is an idea that begins now to seem a quaint affectation. I have seen the signature of Daddy's father, on county documents, signed variously Cyrus, Cyris, Syris, and even Sires Dakin. He had the Dakin down cold; it was his Christian name that was a speculation every time. Daddy's mama signed the family Bible in neat printing: Burmah Moses. Daddy's mama was herself an orphan, raised in an orphanage operated by The Daughters of the Pharaoh. They were a peculiar, and now extinct, offshoot of the Eastern Star, but while they existed, they sent all their charges out into the world bearing the last name of Moses. No doubt her orphan soul, like the too-large shoes she was given to wear away from the orphanage, could hardly avoid picking up the odd pebble of a religious enthusiasm.

I never knew Cyrus or Burmah Moses Dakin or Daddy's brother Tommy Cane Dakin, who died of whooping cough when he was four, or his other dead brother, Timmy Cane Dakin, who died in his late twenties from a mule kick in the head—not before he had a chance to leave a widow and four boys under the age of seven.

Daddy was the youngest. He started out with nothing, and as little education as rural Alabama could in those days provide. Daddy had a knack for fixing cars. From his early teens, he would have six or seven broke-down Model T's or baling-wired farm trucks in the yard of his widowed mama's dogtrot. He scrounged parts from junkyards and cannibalized hopeless wrecks. Nobody in rural Alabama had much by way of currency or coin in the middle of the Depression, so the owners of the rattletraps he put back on the road paid him as often in barter—a chicken, a sack of sweet potatoes, a ham, a bundle of firewood—as cash. The quarters and fifty-cent pieces and dollars came sweaty and slow, but once won, they did not escape his grasp.

An automobile dealer from Montgomery, Mr. Horace H. Fancy, heard of him and offered him a job as a mechanic. With Burmah Moses Dakin recently gone to Glory, Daddy did not have any reason to stick where he was. Mr. Fancy discovered that Daddy was more than a natural-born grease monkey. Joe Cane Dakin was a natural-born salesman too—and as honest as an August noon in Alabama is hot. People liked him. They came away feeling that for once they were not being cheated. Mr. Fancy realized that he had found the man for whom he had been looking, the very one to take over his business so he could retire. Mr. Fancy taught Daddy the automobile business.

And not just the business. Mr. Fancy saw to it that Daddy got a library card and educated himself. Mr. Fancy's wife was dead but he had a widowed sister, Miz Lulu Taylor, keeping house for him, and she took it on herself to teach Daddy proper manners and diction and everything else that he needed to pass for a country gentleman. Mama liked to tease Daddy that Miz Lulu must have been sweet on him but Daddy said she was just an old retired schoolteacher who missed the schoolroom.

In a very few years, Daddy bought Mr. Fancy's dealership and made it the biggest Ford dealership in Alabama. It was so successful Henry Ford II called up personally from Detroit one day and asked Daddy to establish a dealership in Birmingham because nobody there seemed to know how to sell Fords right. So Daddy went and did it. By the time he was thirty-two—a decade before he married Mama—Daddy owned three dealerships—in Birmingham, in Montgomery, and in Mobile—and was worth three million dollars and change.

A mild bout of polio in the summer of 1939 left Daddy with a slow stiff walk and a weak left arm. He had no choice but to fight the war at home. When the National Guard got federalized, Alabama organized itself a State Guard as a substitute. Daddy joined it, along with all the old men and boys and lame and halt fellows the military wouldn't take. They were supposed to protect Alabama from being invaded by the enemy that actually was bold enough to blow up shipping in the Gulf of Mexico. Daddy sat on the State Defense Board that coordinated all the civil defense activities. He did his turn as an ordinary warden too. When the war came to a close and the factories shifted back to domestic consumption, Daddy started making money again, hand over fist.

Mama and Daddy met right after the war, in Boyer's Drugstore in Mama's hometown, Tallassee, not far from Montgomery. Daddy was buying a pack of Wrigley's gum, to be polite, while checking on whether Mr. Boyer was still thinking about trading his old Ford for a new one. Mama went into Boyer's to buy a lipstick she didn't need. Mama knew who Daddy was. He didn't know her, but it wasn't ten minutes before she had him assuring her that that shade of lipstick was just right on her. She always made it seem like once she uncapped that new lipstick, he never had a chance.

As he built his businesses, Daddy put his brothers to work in them.

Uncle Jimmy Cane Dakin worked for Daddy in Birmingham, Uncles Lonny Cane and Dickie Cane worked for Daddy in Mobile, and Uncle Billy Cane and his wife, Aunt Jude, worked for Daddy in Montgomery.

Mama declined to have anything much to do with his side

of the family. He tolerated her ignoring the Dakins but snuck me out to see his people. If he ever took my brother, Ford, to see them, he had stopped doing it by the time I came along.

I liked Billy Cane best, mostly because Uncle Billy and Aunt Jude doted on me. Being Dakins, they had nothing but a pack of boys. Aunt Jude was one of a flock of girls who all had girl children of their own and she missed not having a girl child for herself. I was special to them also on account of my being the first female Dakin child in memory. I reckon too that it didn't trouble them any to aggravate Mama and her mama, whom Ford and I were taught to call Mamadee. I doubt that my Dakin relations minded making a few dead Carrolls groan in their graves.

In photographs now, Daddy seems unfamiliar to me, someone I recognize not because I ever knew him but because, in looking for him, I have studied those photographs so intently. A man of middling size and height, his blond, thinning hair slicked back with Brylcreem, his light eyes, guarded in his long-jawed, sunburned face, look back at me. His nose was large and aquiline and crooked, as if it had been broken. Probably it had, but he never got around to telling me how. His ears were large too, and narrowed his face between them like a single book between unnecessarily large bookends. I recall him wearing both suspenders and a belt. His voice, though, I have never forgotten: a country tenor, softened by his Alabama drawl. His favorite song was "You Are My Sunshine." He said, "gone" for "going," and left off the "to," as we were all apt to do, though, of course, we were taught better.

Just as he never got around to telling me how his nose got broke, Daddy never had a chance to tell me why he married Mama.

I could speculate that he thought that he loved her. She was a young and beautiful woman and she wanted him to marry her. Between illness and the war and not being able to join up and fight in it, maybe he was looking to recover some of his fading youth and vigor. He may have begun to feel there should be more to life than money and the making of it. If he had not been a Dakin—if he had been born into a family like the Carrolls—he would have had a mama or a sister to look out for a suitable mate. But he was a sisterless Dakin and by

the time he met Roberta Ann Carroll, Burmah Moses Dakin
was long dead of poverty and overwork. If he had not married
Mama, I wouldn't ever have been born, nor would Ford. And
Joe Cane Dakin would not have been murdered in New Orleans in 1958.

Three

NATURALLY, Daddy drove anything he had a mind to drive, right off the lot. He put Mama in the model he wanted to promote in any given year. The sight of Mama behind the wheel might make a husband imagine that if he bought a car like that, his wife would maybe look a little like Mama. The wife might imagine herself looking a little more like Mama than she did.

At that time in her life, Mama was not only the best-looking woman in Alabama, she was Miz Joe Cane Dakin, and that meant she was rich. Her looks had earned her position; she deserved it. Being Miz Joe Cane Dakin and driving a Ford was as far as she was willing to go in the direction of working for a living.

In 1958 Daddy was promoting the Edsel, so Mama drove a four-door hardtop Edsel Citation, which had the big engine and wheelbase, a tri-tone gold-metallic, jonquil-yellow–jet-black paint job, gold upholstery with little flecks of metallic gold in it, and marshmallow-creme leather trim. Daddy knew the Edsel was an ungainly looking thing and Mama knew it too, but Daddy had his loyalty to the Ford Motor Company. The Ford Motor Company, he declared, paid the bills.

Mama didn't bother to hold an opinion on that. It was enough for her that Joe Cane Dakin paid the bills. The least Mama could do was to pretend to like the Edsel. She always derived a certain satisfaction from playing a role. Mama believed that being movie-star beautiful was the equivalent of having movie-star talent, though she would never, of course, be so common as to stoop to the hard work of becoming a real actress.

When Daddy wanted to attend a convention of Ford dealers in New Orleans, he drove us the three-hundred-some miles from Montgomery in Mama's Edsel: Mama in the front seat, Ford and I in the back. The convention was due to start on Friday the fourteenth and run into the next week, permitting the dealers to treat themselves to Mardi Gras on the eighteenth. And the very next day, Ash Wednesday, would be my seventh birthday. I was promised not only a birthday cake but also the *specialité du maison* of the Hotel Pontchartrain, a concoction called Mile-High Pie.

Ford was able to make the trip because the convention fell during the February school vacation. I could have gone anyway, as my presence in Miz Dunlap's first grade was not as strictly demanded as Ford's was in Miz Perlmutter's sixth grade. Whenever Daddy wanted me to keep him company on some drive to Birmingham or Mobile or wherever, I was allowed to play hooky. Miz Dunlap never said boo. Since Mama liked to pretend that Daddy never did anything that she did not tell him to do, when he took me with him, she always made it her idea; she would declare that if she didn't get some relief from me, Joe Cane Dakin was gone have a wife in the mental hospital.

While Mama and Daddy were gone be in New Orleans, Ford and I might have stayed with Mamadee in Tallassee. But Daddy said ever'body ought to go to Mardi Gras once in their life. Unsaid but understood by us all was that Daddy wanted to be with me to celebrate my birthday. If he had to be away, he would just have to take me with him. Mama wasn't very happy about having us in tow but she was gone find something to make her unhappy anyway and Daddy knew it.

In the car, Mama remarked that she had been to Mardi Gras and if she was gone go again, she would rather she did not have kids with her to fret about. She smoked Kools, one every half hour or so, and turned the pages of the latest *Vogue* as she told Daddy everything she had already told him before all over again. He smoked Lucky Strikes, one every fifteen minutes or so, and said not much of anything.

Just the day before the Gulf Coast had gotten cold enough so that snow fell in the Florida panhandle, which, if the lines on the map were drawn straight, would be southeast Alabama.

*

WITH the windows up against the cold, it was harder for me to hear the world outside of the Edsel, but that made me more aware of the workings of the Edsel itself, and of its occupants. Knowing them too well, I did my best to block them out.

We stopped at Daddy's dealership in Mobile. He could not very well drive though Mobile and *not* stop. Mama harried me into the ladies' room and out again and back into the Edsel, not because she cared if I wet myself or not or because I was dawdling; she just used me for an excuse to sweep in and out without having to converse much with the people who worked for Daddy.

Ford left the car only long enough to help himself to a Co'Cola. Daddy always called Co'Cola dope. Every time that he did, Mama said "dope" was slang, and A Man In His Position ought to know that using slang made him look like a country fool.

Uncle Lonny Cane Dakin came out, in his greasy overalls and with a big streak of black grease on his left cheek. Lonny Cane looked a lot like Daddy, if Daddy were for sale in a thrift shop.

Despite the cold, Daddy lowered all the windows before he went inside to air the cigarette smog out of the Edsel. When Uncle Lonny Cane started to lean in the open window next to Mama, she flinched away, glaring at his fingernails.

"My Lord, Lonny Cane Dakin, don't you touch my car with those fingers!" she hissed. "You'll get that grease ever'where."

Uncle Lonny Cane froze with his hands clawed up, before shrinking back and tucking them behind his back like a kid who don't want to admit to not washing up before dinner. His face shone red under the grease. He grinned so hard with embarrassment, I could see all the gaps between his few remaining crooked, poor boy's teeth.

"Beg pardon, Miz Roberta," he mumbled. Then he craned his leathery neck and squinted into the backseat at Ford and me.

Ford was closest to Lonny Cane, so I threw myself on top of him and let a rebel yell out Ford's window. Mama flinched. Ford about choked on his Co'Cola. He threw me off him onto the floor. Uncle Lonny Cane's guffaw was like circus music to my ears; it had the rude blat of a clown's bulb horn.

"I'm getting a sick headache," Mama wailed. "Calley Dakin, you hush your mouth right now. I do not want to hear from you again in this lifetime! Ford, go tell your daddy to hurry up, and bring me a BC!"

Ford took care to step on my right hand as he got out of the car again.

Mama covered her eyes with her hands and moaned.

I whispered into the back of Mama's seat, "You want me to sing you a song, Mama?"

She drove her elbow back into the seat. That meant she didn't want me to sing a song. I could sing like anybody but she never cared for my voice however I sang.

Ford came back and flung himself into the backseat.

Daddy opened the driver's door and peered in. "I brang you some aspirin, Bobbie Ann, and a dope." He had three open bottles between his big fingers by their necks.

"Don't call me Bobbie Ann," Mama said. "And don't use slang, Joseph. Make that child sit in her seat and be still! I told you we should have left her at home."

"With your mama? Over my dead body. And you wouldn't hear of calling on Ida Mae," Daddy said.

Mama stiffened right up like I give her a poke. My used-to-be nursemaid, Ida Mae, was a delicate subject between them, months and months after Mama had fired her.

Daddy hesitated. He seemed to be on the edge of saying more. But he didn't.

Ford cocked his eyebrows at me mockingly as he took a long swallow of his Co'Cola. He was eleven then, mostly legs, and mean as cat-dirt. Mama doted on Ford because he was a real Carroll—so much a Carroll that Ford already looked down his nose at Daddy for being a Dakin. But Ford took the Carroll character a step further—he looked down on Mama for having married a Dakin. Mama doted on Ford all the more for this.

Daddy settled in behind the wheel and handed back one of the open bottles to me. "I heard that yell, Sunshine. Had to make you thirsty."

I did not know how thirsty I was until then. Co'Cola makes

me burp though, and I did, which made Mama moan again and Ford snigger.

What with Mama having a sick headache, there was even less than no chance of radio music. When Daddy and I were on one of our road trips, I could sit in the front seat, and he would let me ramble up and down the dial, listening wherever I wanted, at as much volume as I could get out of the radio. But when Mama was with us, we were hardly ever allowed to have the radio. I had to sing to myself, inside my head, and a blessing it was that I could. Ida Mae Oakes had taught me to look for the blessings.

Though I had been allowed to bring a shoebox of my paper dolls with me, with Ford within reach, I could not play with them in the backseat of the Edsel. They were in my suitcase in the trunk, alongside my red Elvis Autograph Phonograph that Daddy had given me for Christmas, and some of my 45s, and the Valentine card that I had made for Daddy at school. I particularly wished that I could play with my Rosemary Clooney paper doll. Mama did not care for me singing Rosemary Clooney songs when I played with the paper doll, so I had to whisper them.

Since Ford would not be caught dead touching an actual doll, I did have my Betsy McCall doll with me. She was little, just the right size for me to clutch in my hand. If I touched him with her, he would shudder and shrink away and threaten to tear her limb from limb.

Mamadee subscribed to *McCall's* magazine. She brought it to Mama every month after she had perused it. "Perused" was her word. Mama did not want it, which is why Mamadee brought it to her. Mama took it because she was not gone let Mamadee think anything Mamadee did was significant enough to irritate her. They managed to insult each other more with courtesies than they could have with a whole dictionary of cuss words.

Betsy McCall paper dolls appeared in every issue of *McCall's*. Betsy McCall's face was plain and sweet as a sugar cookie, with great big widespread eyes like root-beer balls. She had a little smiling rosebud mouth and no chin to speak of, and a proper little girl hairstyle with curls, and on the rare occasions that they showed, elfin little ears. Every month, Betsy McCall Did *Something*. She Went To A Picnic or

Started School or Helped Her Mother Bake Cookies. What she did, she did it first and last name, always in capital letters, and it always required a wardrobe.

Every month, I cut out Betsy McCall and her dog and her friends and relations and played with them in sight of Mamadee and Mama. Mama told Daddy that I loved Betsy McCall so much that he should buy me a Betsy McCall doll for Christmas. So he did, all unknowing that Mama knew that I wanted a baby doll. I had a name all picked out: Ida Mae. And knowing that Mama had been so mean, I made a great fuss over Betsy McCall. I took that Betsy McCall doll everywhere with me and sniveled if I were made to leave her behind. Since I was deprived of the privilege of naming my own doll by the fact that Betsy McCall already had a name, I gave her a secret middle name: Cane.

After a while, Daddy started talking to Ford about the new bridge in New Orleans. I settled back to listen to the sound of the tires on the road and sounds of the engine and the air conditioner and the satisfying tautness of the fan belt. With the windows closed, I could not hear the birds or animals or people outside. The speed of the Edsel spun all the sounds outside behind it; those separate sounds got all slurried together like drops of water forced out of a hose hard enough to bruise.

I slept some of that long ride, dreaming of

swishzapswishzapswishzapswishzap

loud rain that kept getting louder until there was nothing else but the sound of it. A hard rain makes what one day I would discover is called "white noise." It is better than cotton balls in my ears.

I heard Daddy singing, the way he did sometimes when we took a drive together or when I was going to sleep.

> *The other night, dear*
> *As I lay sleeping*
> *I dreamed I held you in my arms.*
> *When I awoke, dear*
> *I was mistaken*
> *And I hung my head and cried;*

You are my sunshine
My only sunshine
You make me happy
When skies are grey
You'll never know dear
How much I love you
Please don't take my sunshine away.

It seemed to me that Daddy was singing it to me as I slept, making a joke between the two of us, because it was raining. Rain so hard it scared me in my sleep. I felt as if I were drowning in that relentless rain, the rain itself, the dying breaths of thousands of other people hanging round my neck, drawing me down into the city of the dead.

Half an hour outside of New Orleans, I woke up when Ford slid over to pinch me.

"Wake up, Dumbo. We're getting there. You got drool all over yourself," Ford said.

Ford was lying; the corners of my mouth were a little wet but that was all. I knew it was

swishzapshlurrup

raining before I tried to look out the window. I could smell the rain, even over the ever-present cigarette smog. We were inside my dream, inside the car, and for all I could see, we might as well have been under water.

Ford looked bored. It was about his favorite thing to do when he was not up to actual no-good, and he did it a lot. He had not wanted to come on this trip nor had he wanted to stay home, and like Mama he was not gone have a good time no matter what. He tried real hard to stay bored as we began to see New Orleans but I could tell from the way he straightened up taller that it was drawing his attention. Mama was paying attention too. She paused for a second or two, taking out a new cigarette.

I knelt on the seat and stared out the window on my side, and past Daddy, out his window and the span of the windshield. Most of what I saw and heard was rain. The lights of other vehicles on the road wobbled past in blurred yellow and red, like candle flames wavering in a draft behind a wet window.

There was a lot more to New Orleans than Mobile or Birmingham or Montgomery, never-you-mind Tallassee—though Tallassee could claim a big league second baseman, Fred Hatfield. I reckoned that New Orleans could probably claim so many big league players that nobody there bothered to boast of it. There were ever so many more people, of which we were hardly more than four drops in the rain, but I couldn't see them. I knew they were there because when I found out we were going to New Orleans, I looked it up in Daddy's atlas that gave the population of ever'where. It wasn't that I couldn't hear them through the rain, so much as what I heard of them was diluted to not much more than a shiver at the nape of my neck. I was frightened. Not for me. For all those people I couldn't see but whose distant voices under the downpour sang to me not in words but in their terror.

Four

THE Hotel Pontchartrain loomed twelve stories over St. Charles Avenue and we were staying on the very top floor, in Penthouse B. Penthouse sounded like some kind of jail to me, but Daddy said that meant it was the best. I was still scared when the hotel manager took us up in the elevator. I believe that I was born hating elevators. The minute I enter one, I just want to sit down on the floor and hug my knees and squinch my eyes tight, so I won't see the doors close. It's bad enough to have to listen to the machinery work and see in my head the *push-pull-yank-thump-clank* of the belts and chains and gears that could go awry anytime with nary a doorknob or sesame in sight.

Penthouse B turned out to be a patch of big rooms with high ceilings and a baby grand piano with a key in it that Mama snatched away when I reached for it. There was a color television console and a bar with cut-glass bottles, heavily carved dark furniture, turkey rugs, and damask draperies over swagged and bellied sheers on the windows. Except for the baby grand, our home in Montgomery was much the same, only bigger, and Mamadee's in Tallassee was even more so.

The manager opened some draperies and shutters to show us French doors. We went out on the balcony and looked down. St. Charles Avenue was a black ditch of rain, so far down, it made me a little dizzy. I backed off the balcony and into the parlor of the Penthouse. The piano was still locked. A piano is an echo chamber, a sounding board, and I was not ever gone make this one tell me its secrets. Mama was gone keep that key for the whole time we were at Hotel Pontchartrain. I could see my face like a sick melting ghost in the mirror of its glossy black finish. I looked like I was in a grown-up coffin, way too big for me.

Mama ordered supper for Ford and me. I helped her unpack and hang her clothes and watched her change to go to dinner with Daddy. She used the dressing room while Daddy did his changing in the bedroom. Mama's dress was a wasp-waisted horizontal-striped strapless sheath, with a filmy overskirt in the back like a short train. She put up her hair like Grace Kelly and made herself up like a movie star, with emphatically arched brows and plenty of mascara and dark lipstick. When Daddy whistled at her and shook his fingers to put out the fire, she pretended to ignore him, but her eyes shone.

After they left, Ford turned on the TV to watch Sergeant Preston arrest criminals in the name of the Crown. In my bedroom, I plugged in my Elvis Autograph Phonograph. As I was deciding, shuffling through "Jailhouse Rock," "Teddy Bear," "The Twelfth of Never," "The Yellow Rose of Texas," "The Banana Boat Song," "Blueberry Hill," and "How Much Is That Doggie in the Window," I heard a chink and gurgle, glass on glass, and then a gulp: Ford, getting himself a drink from the cut-glass bottles. He did it at home whenever Mama and Daddy went out but was careful to take only a little so as not to get caught. Ford was born even more devious than most Carrolls.

I sat on the floor, listening to my records and playing with my paper dolls. It was not easy to get a story going on account of the 45s hardly went three minutes or so, and then I had to start them again or change them. Concentrating was hard work. At seven though, I had more than an inkling of self-discipline. I was grateful for Betsy McCall. She was what Ida Mae Oakes called a focus.

The January Betsy McCall had been a disappointment. Betsy McCall Made A Calendar, which for once did not require any special wardrobe. But Mamadee had presented the February issue in time for me to take it with me on our trip. I was allowed a pair of those crinky little scissors that are made for small children. They were too small for my fingers and the edge on their blades was about fit to cut Jell-O. So one day when Mama's seamstress, Rosetta, was in the house, I wheedled a small pair of real shears out of her from her workbasket. With those, I cut out Betsy McCall Has A Valentine Picnic and then sent Betsy McCall To New Orleans On The Banana Boat For Her Picnic On Blueberry Hill.

In the silence after Elvis finished offering to make Betsy McCall his Teddy Bear, the Zorro theme song came on the television. I was moved by the music to try out the small shears as a sword. They proved a poor substitute, as the very first slash of my *Z* took off Betsy McCall's head. I dropped Betsy McCall's bits into the box and the shears after them. Since Betsy McCall Came To Calliope Carroll Dakin's House every month, I viewed her as disposable and often cut her up and rearranged her parts. With more cutouts from the advertisements in *McCall's,* a sheet of paper and some paste, I could turn her into a clown or a circus freak, stuff her into a dryer so it looked like her bits were churning around behind the porthole door, or mix her up with peas and corn and mashed potatoes in a TV dinner. My collages horrified Mamadee, who said that they were sure evidence of degeneracy and mental disturbance, and proof that not only was I more Dakin than Carroll, but that Mama had allowed the influence of Ida Mae Oakes over me for far too long. Mamadee's pronouncements just naturally inspired me to greater efforts.

The television went abruptly silent. The elevator was coming up.

By the time it wheezed to a stop, I was in bed. Daddy came in and gave me a quick kiss on the cheek.

He whispered, "Sunshine, your lamp here is still warm and I can see your pajamas in your suitcase over there. After I close the door, you hop out and get into them, okay? Say your bedtime prayer too."

I opened one eye and winked at him. He kissed my head and went out.

Daddy might have been a Dakin, he might walk a little stiffly and have a weak left arm, but his eyes and ears and brains worked just fine.

I was seven years old: All I knew was the way things were.

I could only reckon that was the way they were supposed to be. I expected them to stay that way. I had enough to do, coping with being Calliope Carroll Dakin.

Sometimes I pretended that I was Ford and when I glanced in a mirror with my Bored Ford face on, I thought I looked more than a little bit like him, no matter how much Mama and Mamadee said I didn't have a bit of Carroll visible in me, that I was hopeless pure-D backside-of-the-moon Dakin.

They were right.

I looked just like my bony, graceless, goofy boy Dakin cousins, except for the twin ponytails that were meant to hide my ears. Ford said that they looked like somebody left the car doors open. I could waggle my ears as if they were the stumps of an extra set of limbs that had failed to grow. Despite the pleasure this parlor trick gave to others, I was forbidden to do it, particularly in Mamadee's presence. To Mamadee, my ears were the definitive proof of Dakin degeneracy.

Without intending it, I left breakage like a trail of crumbs behind me. If I was very still, I could minimize the possible damage, and the unwelcome attention that I might draw. I worked at it diligently. Ida Mae Oakes used to tease me, saying, *Diligent is your middle name, Calliope Dakin,* and *Calliope Diligent Dakin, I swear.*

Because I had a difficult birth and was a troublesome infant—I screamed all the livelong day and night—and Mama had to recuperate a long time, Daddy hired Ida Mae Oakes to be my nursemaid. She stood in high repute in Montgomery for how well she took care of troublesome babies. My secret pride was that Ida Mae stayed with me longer than any other child in her career, at least until me.

Daddy paid Ida Mae's wages, and Mama ordered her around, but Ida Mae made it clear that *I* was her job. Not Ford, and not housemaid's work, kitchen work, or running errands for Mama. For a long time, Mama was too relieved not to have to take care of me herself to want to bend Ida Mae to her will. Whenever Mamadee got started on how insolent Ida Mae Oakes was, not to bring her sweet tea when she wanted it, or polish Ford's shoes, because Ida Mae was too busy taking care of me, and how Mama didn't understand how to be firm with those people, Mama would point out that it was Ida Mae Oakes who had stopped me crying all the time.

Mamadee and Mama didn't care how Ida Mae did it, though Mamadee suspected Ida Mae of having spiked the diluted canned milk formula with moonshine. They agreed that if she hadn't taken me out of the house and quieted me enough to live with normal people, they would both have been driven to the mental hospital and would probably still be there. Of course, if they were ever driven to the mental hospital, they would not let themselves go and sit around in bathrobes with their hair undone, like some people did.

Mama fired Ida Mae Oakes between my fifth and sixth birthdays, and there I was with my seventh near upon me, and I missed Ida Mae some time or other about every day. Mama didn't know that I wrote letters to Ida Mae Oakes or that Daddy mailed them for me. The letters that came back for me, Daddy let me read when we were driving around, and then he would take them and hide them in his desk at the Montgomery dealership. It was highly deceitful, of course, but Daddy was some angry with Mama for firing Ida Mae, and I was too. Daddy said that we had to keep the peace in the house, Mama had her reasons and I would understand when I was older. Looking each other right in the eye, we both knew that he was saying that lying was gone save him some trouble with Mama. He was shamefaced and diminished, and I hated Mama for driving him to lies because it cost him so much more than it ever did her. I would lie the crows out of the sky for Daddy.

While I missed Ida Mae Oakes, I don't expect that she missed me. Ida Mae Oakes was a professional. My letters to her were more like report cards, to let her know that I hadn't forgotten all she taught me. Her return letters were prompt and polite but no more personal than a note brought home from the teacher. Nobody reading them could accuse her of encouraging me to defy Mama.

The way Ida Mae stopped me crying all the time was simple. She sang to me.

Five

VALENTINE'S Day, Daddy left a bee-you-tee-full store-bought card on my pillow. The one I left on his pillow had a paper-lace-doily-edged heart on it and as much glitter as the glue would take. The one he gave me had drawings of candy hearts, the kind with Be Mine and Sweetheart and mush like that on them, and inside the envelope was a good dozen of the actual real candy. It was a joke between us: Daddy knew my opinion that nothing tastes cheaper or nastier than those little candy hearts, except for candy lipsticks.

Mama found a little box all wrapped up in gold foil paper and red ribbon on her pillow, along with a card from Daddy. It was pearl earrings. She gave him a kiss that left him laughing and wiping lipstick off his face with a big white cotton handkerchief.

Of course she had to put them on right away to see how they looked on her.

While she was admiring herself and the earrings in the mirror, Mama said, "I don't know how you did it, Joseph, but I believe you must have read my mind. I have been longing for these earrings since the day I first saw them in the window at Cody's." Then she glanced up at his reflection looking at her in the mirror and added, "Don't think this fixes anything, Joseph. I do you the honor of believing that you would never try to bribe me with baubles. I take these as a gift of the heart."

Daddy stopped smiling and looked away. Embarrassment, anger, and weariness stiffened his face. I never saw him look sadder. It made me angry with Mama, her taking away his pleasure in giving her a gift.

Daddy was in meetings all that day. Ford went with him to most of them. Daddy listened to speeches, he shook hands, he gave a couple of talks, he shook more hands, and he said, "No thanks, I just had one," when someone offered him a drink or a girl. This is what Ford reported to me. Ford thought it was funny. I caught on to the part about the drink but I couldn't figure out why anybody at a convention would offer Daddy a girl, and why he would say "just had," when he must have meant "already have," meaning me.

Mama went with Daddy to the convention lunch. I stayed in the Penthouse with Ford. He tried to feed me half a sandwich all at once. I gritted my teeth tightly while he mashed my lips against them with the sandwich. When I shoved a pointer finger into the hollow at the base of his throat, he made a *gakking* noise and jumped up and slammed out. I reckoned that I had better than held my own, which made the ice I sucked to stop my mouth swelling up taste all the sweeter.

When Mama came back, she never even asked where he was. I volunteered nothing. He had not told me that he was going out or where or why, and after all, he was eleven and had gone to meetings with Daddy. I certainly did not care where Ford was, so long as he was not plaguing me.

Mama did not need to do anything else until it was time to dress for the big Valentine's Day dinner, so she took me shopping.

And that was why Daddy got murdered.

It was still

Plashplotzplashplotz

raining.

The water bouncing off the pavement made a mist around our ankles. It was like standing in a cold shower with clothes on. I kept my glasses in my coat pocket to keep them dry. The droplets beaded on my light wool coat and then began to seep through the weave. The rain did not matter to Mama. She had an umbrella and she hardly cared whether I got wet or not. More than once, she had told me that I would not melt.

Mama rarely shopped for clothes in stores back then—she turned her nose up at most everything off the rack. She had Rosetta copy fashions out of *Vogue* magazine. Elsa Schiaparelli was her favorite designer. Besides wearing copies of Schiaparelli designs, Mama bought real Schiaparelli hats and bags and gloves and silk stockings. Daddy had given her a real Schiaparelli karakul coat, with the label inside it to prove it.

Mostly she shopped in antique stores. Mama liked being rich and buying things that other rich people were now too poor or too dead to hold on to, and buying them cheap. Bargains indeed were to be had, for it was one of those times when the antiques trade languished. The fifties were about the new things that could be mass-produced. Mama bought small things: old jewelry, old perfume bottles, and candlesticks.

She was very fond of candlelight, which flattered her skin. I knew from the way she checked the mirrors after she lit candles. At home, she always had candles lighted on the table when we ate our evening meal. Decades before candles became a decorating fad, Mama set them out in her bathroom and her boudoir. Naturally the candles had to be *in* something.

Along with ashtrays, candlesticks made excellent hissy-fit projectiles. Mama was no athlete but she could always summon strength enough to pitch a candlestick or an ashtray. Fortunately, she rarely hit anything or anyone who might be too far away to grab her wrist and arrest her throw. Her habits did maim or destroy quite a few ashtrays and candlesticks, as well as the walls and furniture and windows, making replacements in kind welcome. Her ashtrays never came from antique stores. She ordered cut-crystal ones that fit the palm of her hand, by the dozen, from the best downtown jeweler, the one where Daddy bought her the pearl earrings.

We traipsed from one antique shop to another. Each shop was a single room, cramped with enormous pieces of mahogany furniture, every piece dark with wax, every piece laden with old lamps and old porcelain figurines and old odd pieces of brass. On the walls were old bad paintings of saints, old good portraits of the formerly rich and old mildewed prints behind glass that sweated with Louisiana moisture. Even in Montgomery or Mobile or Birmingham, each shop was always still and damp and the proprietor was always an old woman with paper-white skin, or sometimes a middle-aged man with pomade-shiny hair, who was likely the son or nephew of the old woman with narcissus-petal skin. The light was dim and dusty in those shops and my only occupation, while Mama poked about and the old proprietor kept a wary watch on me, was to try to catch stray gleams of sunlight as they were refracted through the dusty dangling prisms of old chandeliers and lamps.

As soon as we entered a shop, Mama would order me to touch nothing and be still and silent, on pain of some gaudy punishment. The proprietor would then stare at me for fear that I would seize a poker from a fender set and run wildly through the shop, screaming like a maniac, smashing everything I could. Sometimes I longed to do just that. Knowing my own clumsiness, I usually found a spot out of the way and pretended to be a big dead doll, imagining what bits of me were broke and how messy my hair was and that my eyeballs were all popped out and looking in different directions.

In the last shop but one, the proprietor reacted to Mama's warning with a violent hiss and shooing gestures directed at me. Mama sent me outside, where I stood on a corner and dripped and listened to the sounds a steady rain makes on all the different surfaces around a person standing in it. I wondered what snow would sound like. Someday I meant to see snow in the flesh and hear it and feel its cold kiss upon my upturned face but, of course, I could hardly expect it in New Orleans. I wondered if it had ever snowed in New Orleans. Snow would sound not like a leaf falling but like a downy feather. I would have liked to hear the birds in New Orleans. Hadn't Daddy said that there were wild parrots in New Orleans? I would have liked to hear the voices of whatever other critters lived there. Surely there were chipmunks or squirrels or both, and certainly as wet a place as it is, there must be rats. There had to be mice and cats and dogs, and someone in New Orleans surely had a monkey. There must be a zoo. But the rain drowned out any hint of any of those enchanting possibilities. A sudden swoop of wind threw rain into my face and down the back of my neck and the downpour intensified, so I shivered. I tipped back my head and opened my mouth to the rain, and got a face-wash as well as a drink.

The next shop we approached ticked. I heard it distinctly from outside and around the corner. As the jangle of the brass bell on the door announcing our entry subsided and the ticking again dominated, I took my glasses out of my coat pocket where they been safe and dry and put them on. A whole wall of old clocks, none of them with their hands pointed at the same hours or minutes or seconds as the others, ticked and tocked and clicked and thocked and pecked and clucked like an aviary of mechanical birds.

This shop also seemed to have more candlesticks than most, though candlesticks are by nature reticent and usually more numerous than at first impression. Stand still and look around any old antique or junque shoppe and they are everywhere: prickets and chambersticks; chandeliers never converted for electric lights; three-, five-, and seven-branched candelabra; wall sconces in brass and glass; girandoles; glass candleholders in ruby, cobalt, and crystal; old dented candlesticks in pewter; old blotched candlesticks in brass; and old silver candlesticks, tarnished black as a lost soul. The servants of light in the centuries before whale-oil lamps, gaslights, and electricity, the holders of candles are no longer necessities, but are reduced to bric-a-brac, nicknack-paddywhack, bring the dog a bone. Occasionally one might still become a blunt object and make a dent in a wall or extract a little blood. Colonel Mustard, in the library. Mama, in her boudoir.

Mama spent a lot of time in this particular shop. If she spent more than five minutes in a shop, she always bought something lest the proprietor think his prices were too rich for her financial blood or that she was not the sort of woman truly to appreciate rare and beautiful objects.

Because of the rain, no sun refracted through the prisms in the shop. The ticking shop was empty except for me and Mama and the middle-aged man behind the high schoolmaster's desk that served for a counter. He didn't seem to care one way or the other that Mama and I were in his shop. When Mama had been his only customer for ten minutes, the shop door opened with the ring of the brass bell.

The proprietor smiled and said to the lady coming through the door, "Oh, I'm very glad to see *you*."

The lady smiled back at him.

I do not remember what she looked like. Well. Sometimes I think I do, but wonder if my memory is trustworthy. Perhaps I have given the lady the face that suited her, or me. I do remember the knife-pleat of her skirt, though not the color or print, and the filmy plastic galoshes she wore over her shoes, which were pumps with low heels. In that era, most women had a pair of those galoshes; Mama did. They were supposed to be see-through so the shoe inside was visible but they never were—shoes visible nor galoshes truly transparent, I mean. Her hands were gloved, as indeed Mama's were, gloves being like hats a commonplace accessory.

And I do remember the way the lady looked at me.

Just once at first, and for only a few seconds. She was looking *at* me. She was not looking at a gawky little girl who was wet and trying not to drip on anything. She was looking at Calliope Carroll Dakin, whoever she was at the age of seven years. She looked at me a moment and then she looked at Mama.

Then she said to the proprietor, "There's a wet little girl standing behind your door, Mr. Rideaux. Does she belong to you?"

"She's mine," Mama said.

The lady turned abruptly to the proprietor. "I'm looking for a candlestick, Mr. Rideaux."

The atmosphere of the shop was suddenly very precarious. Anything might happen. Mama picked up the nearest candlestick—just a dollar-and-a-half of cobalt glass—and took it back to the proprietor's desk.

That was when Mama discovered that she no longer had her pocketbook.

Mama was embarrassed, and more. She was flustered. Somehow she had managed to misstep repeatedly. She assured Mr. Rideaux that her handbag was *somewhere*, that she really did have the money for the candlestick (even though she probably did not really want it at all), and pleaded for him to put it aside for her until she came back with the money.

"Did you have your pocketbook with you earlier?" he asked politely, but in an easy tone that suggested he hardly cared much one way or the other.

"I don't remember."

The strange lady had been moving slowly about, looking at and picking up this candlestick or that, and putting it down and smiling to herself. She paused by a magnificent stuffed macaw that had escaped my notice until she ran her gloved fingers over its scarlet crown and down its back. A parrot in New Orleans, after all, but as dumb as any candlestick. She looked at me again—a clean, swift, prompting look.

"You must have, Mama, because you bought that little cameo pin and I saw you take out your change purse," I said.

Mama glared at me. I was not supposed to speak in public unless it was to make my manners to someone or to say something nice about her.

"Probably you left it there, last place you were in," Mr. Rideaux suggested.

"Probably I did," Mama agreed. "Come on, Calley."

A look passed between the strange lady and the proprietor.

"Oh, leave the little girl here, she is being an angel," the proprietor said.

Mama looked at him and then at me. She was trying to decide whether this might be a treat for me, in which case she was not about to allow it. But I looked as wet and miserable and bored as I could, so she relented.

"You hit her if she breaks anything and I'll pay double for it when I get back," Mama said.

So Mama went out with her umbrella and the satisfaction that Mr. Rideaux knew that she had money enough to pay twice the price of anything he had in his store.

No one else came into the shop. Mr. Rideaux sat at his desk, writing in a ledger. The lady glanced at me. I must have looked like I was about to drop because she made a little noise in her throat that provoked Mr. Rideaux to look at her again.

He pointed his pen at me. "Young lady, go sit yourself down on that little chair over there."

I sat on the very edge of the tapestry seat of the little mahogany chair. My hair, my dress and coat dried while I watched and listened to the wall of clocks telling all their false times. An excitement bloomed in me. I laughed aloud. The clocks had nothing to do with time but were merely instruments, the clicking and ticking of silver and gold and bronze and pinchbeck arrows, a droll and slapstick rhapsody of lies.

And the odd music became odder, less chaotic, more complicated; it came to me that a new timepiece had entered the song and transformed it.

Entranced as I was, I saw the lady's mouth quiver and the proprietor's left eyebrow jig as they exchanged looks. I felt their gazes on me from time to time but there was in them no censure or disapproval but contrariwise, a quiet pleasure.

The jangle of the bell on the door broke the spell as Mama opened it. I gasped as if my heart had come to a stop in my chest. And just at that instant, all the clocks on the wall stopped, so that the shop was suddenly as still as the dead old things it sheltered.

"Calley, what do you mean, plopping yourself down on Mr. Rideaux's antique chair?" Mama said.

She marched back to the proprietor's desk.

"Mr. Rideaux, I could not find my pocketbook anywhere, but I will have my husband write you a check for that chair Calley has probably *ruined,* and of course I still want the candlestick."

Mr. Rideaux smiled at Mama. I did not believe his smile but Mama did.

"The young lady did not ruin that chair. I reserve that chair for wet little girls who come into my shop and I would not sell it for the world. And I am not one bit surprised that you did not find your pocketbook because it was here all the time," said Mr. Rideaux.

He got up, fingered a key out from the watch pocket of his vest, and used it to open his filing cabinet. From the top drawer of his filing cabinet he pulled out Mama's pocketbook, her brown Hermès Kelly bag.

My view from the chair of Mr. Rideaux had been full. At no time had I seen him find Mama's pocketbook, and at no time did he even get up from his desk, much less unlock the filing cabinet and stick Mama's pocketbook into it. I felt the strange lady's gaze on me. I said nothing, and it came into my mind that I hardly knew how much real time had passed while the clocks had entranced me. It was what Daddy would call a conundrum.

The lady spoke suddenly, making Mama start. "I found it, right over here."

She pointed to a little petticoat table—five hundred pounds of mahogany and Georgia marble that had been carved and glued and polished in order to support a little mirror, six inches off the floor, so the ladies of the 1850s could check the fall of their crinolines. Mamadee had one, of which she was sinfully proud. Mama and Mamadee often informed me of instances of sinful pride on the part of the other. I myself was so often hell-bound from my sinful pride that I was sinfully proud of it.

Mama smiled and held her pocketbook against her breast and hugged it.

"Thank you for saving my life," Mama said to the lady.

"I was going to steal it, and your little girl too, but I was afraid I would get caught," the lady said.

"Who would want Calley?" Mama said.

The lady gave me a warm smile. "Well, wet little girls must be good for *something*." Then she turned back to the proprietor and said, "You've got so much new stock, Mr. Rideaux, and I'm just not sure *what* I want. I think I'll have to come back one day when it's not raining."

She left with a tinkle of the little brass bell, and without looking at me again.

"Can you change a fifty?" Mama asked Mr. Rideaux. Before he could answer, Mama cried, "Oh, no wait, I think I have two singles."

Mr. Rideaux smiled and started to take the bills.

Mama held on to them. "Then all I can buy is this little piece of cobalt?"

"That's all you can buy *today*," he said, delicately plucking the two bills out of her hand. "But you come back tomorrow, and I promise I won't let you out for under that fifty you're putting back in your purse."

Mama laughed delicately too, at this proof that Mr. Rideaux knew that she had money. "Then I guess I'll have to come back."

But of course we never went back.

Six

THE elevator jerked and sighed and thumped to a stop like somebody getting hanged. Mama tiptoed into the Penthouse in her stocking feet, holding her high heels in one hand by their ankle straps. She crept into my room and grabbed my foot under the blanket and shook it.

"Calley, wake up and come unzip me," she whispered.

I sat up and knuckled my eyes as if I had been asleep, though the only time my eyes had been closed since she and Daddy went out was just before she reached my room. The more I tried not to think about the strange time in the shop that ticked, the more it troubled me. It was a relief to have Mama back. Putting on my glasses and grabbing Betsy Cane McCall from under my pillow, I hopped out of bed and followed Mama to the big bedroom and its dressing room.

Mama had gone out in a strapless copper taffeta with an iridescent peach half-skirt. She dropped her heels on the carpet and simultaneously reached for one of her earrings. I watched her replace her jewelry in its velvet-lined boxes. She tipped her chin toward the vanity bench. When I knelt on it, she backed up to me so I could reach the hidden zipper running down the back of the dress to her waist. Another one, meant to prevent any stress on the waistline or hip, ran down from under one armpit past the waist about six inches. She could have done that one herself but she turned sideways with her arm up, so I did it. The taffeta slipped in a luxuriant rustle to the carpet; she stepped daintily out of it.

I zipped the dress onto its padded hanger and returned it to the rod in the closet. "Where's Daddy?"

Mama shucked her half-slip over her head, flung it aside, and turned to the vanity to light a Kool. "Having a last drink and cigar with the boys."

I watched her unhook her silk stockings from her garters. Mama loved her silk stockings.

"Hands and nails," she said.

I held out my hands.

"Calley, have you been shucking oysters while I was out? Get some cream onto those claws."

Obediently, I rubbed some of her cold cream into my hands.

Mama sat down at the vanity to raise one foot while I slipped the stockings off as I had been taught, rolling them carefully from top to toe. I tucked them into her lingerie bag.

When she had unpainted her face and was nearly finished putting on her skin food, I asked for something. "Mama, come sleep with me tonight. Please."

She looked at me hard. "Why?"

"I just want you to."

"You do not just want me to, Calliope Dakin. You have always got a reason for asking a favor."

"I'm scared."

"Scared of what?"

I shrugged.

"A great big girl like you. Scared. You are a crazy girl. I am gone be one of those poor women saddled with a mental case for a child for the rest of my life."

"Please, Mama."

She glanced at the clock on the bedside table. I could not bring myself to look at another clock face just yet.

"I go to bed in here, your daddy will come bumbling in and wake me up."

After grinding out her cigarette in the ashtray, she followed me to my room.

There she dropped wearily onto my bed. "Get down at the foot and rub my feet. They are killing me." The foot of the bed, she meant.

Mama often wanted me to rub her feet. Mama would lie

down with her head on the pillow and I would huddle at the end of the bed, cradling her feet and rubbing them. And if I rubbed her feet long enough, she would fall asleep in my bed. I loved sleeping with Mama. I wasn't ready to stop being a little girl yet. The sound of her heartbeat was my best lullaby.

I paused once when her eyes were closed and she hadn't said anything for a long while, but she spoke right up: "Keep on it, Calley, or I might as well go on back to my own bed and wait there for your philandering father."

But when I stopped again later, Mama did not speak. I collected Betsy Cane McCall from the floor where I had dropped her, crawled back up to the head of the bed, turned my pillow over to get the cool side, and fell into a sweaty doze. I didn't feel as if I were asleep. Instead, I was trapped in the panicky darkness beneath the surface of sleep. The darkness was a sea of keening and lamentations and loss. I was under that dark water again, the rain spattering desperately against the glass. I was breathing that woe and misery, my mouth, my ears, my eyes stinging with its bitterness.

Some time later Mama shook me awake. She was out of bed, evidently having checked the bedroom she shared with Daddy.

"It's one o'clock, Calley, and your daddy is not back. He's drinking, or else he has run off with some New Orleans floozy with Negro blood in her veins."

Having heard similar speculations from her on other occasions when Daddy was late, and not really understanding them, I took her remarks indifferently.

She slipped back into the bed and I snugged up to her. We went back to sleep.

I woke up before Mama, about seven o'clock, and wiggled out of bed to run to the bathroom.

Mama yanked the covers tight over herself so I could not get back in under them.

"I'm sorry, Mama. I had to *go*."

"That's what comes of drinking water in the night. Be quiet now and let me sleep."

I went to check the master bedroom of the suite. The big bed was just as the chambermaid had left it, turned down for expected occupants, and unused.

It was my turn to shake Mama's shoulder. "Daddy's still not here."

She rolled toward me a little and lifted her head to look at me. Her eyes narrowed. She flung off the covers and jumped up.

"Joe Cane Dakin," she said, "you are a dead man!"

When she stalked off to the master bedroom, I decided it was time for Ford to wake up. I gooched Ford in the nape of his neck with two fingers. He rolled over with a pillow clutched in one hand and hurled it at me. I batted it away.

"Daddy's been out all night. Drinking or run off with a Negro floozy, Mama says."

"That's hooey, Dumbo." Ford flopped back on his bed and closed his eyes.

I went looking for Mama again and found her in the dressing room.

"He was in a wreck, I just know it," Mama whispered, with a quick tearful glance at me.

She disappeared into the bathroom. The pipes clanked and the water crashed in the shower directly to the tiles, unimpeded by Mama's body, as she ran it until it was really hot. I sat at the vanity and moved things around, but I did not use any of her makeup. I knew better, right down to the knuckles on which she would use the spine of a comb if I messed with any of it. In the bathroom, Mama stepped into the shower.

She came out all pink and soft and shooed me off the vanity bench, where she sat down to do her face. I studied her the way I did most mornings when she was putting on her face. The intensity of her concentration fascinated me as much as what she did. In the middle of it, she came to a sudden stop, her mascara wand in her hand. She stared at herself.

"I'm gone be old," she said, "and nobody's gone care what happens to me."

"I will!"

Her expression went from bleak self-pity to irritation and she made scatting motions with her hands.

I was in my room, pulling up my underpants, when the doorbell chimed. I ran to get the door.

Ford glanced out of his door and informed me what I already knew perfectly well: that I was in my underpants. It occurred to me that when I was fully dressed, I could still be said to be in my underpants, but Ford closed his door before I could advance the argument.

It was only the maid bringing the tray with the coffee and brioche that Mama needed to face the day. I recognized the maid as the one from the previous morning. A disconcerted look came over her when she beheld me half-naked. Realizing that I was embarrassing her, I went into reverse, backing toward Mama's room.

"Please leave it on the table," I told her, as if I were Mama, and the instant I did so, I realized how ludicrous I was, a seven-year-old girl in her underpants instructing a chambermaid as if I was a grown-up lady.

I retreated to Mama's dressing room to tell that her coffee and brioche had arrived. She was particularly fond of the brioche, for which the Hotel Pontchartrain was as famous as it was for its Mile-High Pie.

She was still at the vanity, angrily smoking a Kool. I reckoned when Daddy finally showed up, he was gone be in for it.

"Mama."

"Calley, stop parading around naked this minute and make yourself decent!"

"I'm not naked—" I began.

She slapped me.

I would not give her the satisfaction of making me cry, especially not over a little slap. She turned back to the mirror.

I marched back to my room, ready to give Betsy Cane McCall a whipping that she would never forget.

Betsy Cane McCall was sitting on top of a pink envelope, on one of the pillows of my unmade bed. With a mother who wore Schiaparelli pink and Schiaparelli Shocking perfume, I knew tasteful pink and tasteful scent from—as Mama and Mamadee would put it—*vulgar*. The pink of that envelope could not be more vulgar. The paper itself reeked with a scent that was even worse. It crossed my mind that it was another Valentine, maybe from Daddy. Or Ford might have made me a joke one, something that would be hurtful or spring something nasty in my face. The envelope was unaddressed and unsealed. Inside was a sheet of matching paper. It was printed in green ink and read:

Joe Cane Dakin is a Dead Man if
You Don't Give Us
$$$ 1,000,000.00 in Mony
Judy + Janice

Seven

JUDY was Judy DeLucca, the chambermaid who brought the breakfast tray up to the room that morning. She was twenty-two, with brown eyes and brown hair. Her nose tilted to the left as if somebody right-handed had given her a very hard slap.

Janice was Janice Hicks, twenty-seven years of age, brown eyes and brown hair. Her whole face looked flat because her cheeks were fat and stuck out and her nose was a tiny bump between those fat cheeks. She had so many chins there was no telling where her jaw ended and her neck began. She weighed three hundred and ninety-seven pounds. Janice worked in the kitchen of the Hotel Pontchartrain, baking the brioche that Judy brought up to the room every morning.

Mama raised her newly penciled eyebrows when I held out the folded note to her. She took it and sniffed at it.

"Cheap, darling, vulgar. You ever catch me using perfume like this, shoot me."

She opened it and quickly scanned the words. Her eyes narrowed.

"Calley, I do not like jokes."

As if I didn't know.

Her fingers crushed the note into a sharp-edged ball and she flung it at me. It stung against my cheek.

Mama stared at me. The red of her anger drained from her face.

"Oh—my—God," she whispered. She scrambled for the note, spread it open and studied it. "You did not write this, did you?" Her eyes were wide now and suddenly tearful. The note shook in her hands. Her lips quivered and then she screamed like somebody just tore off her arm.

Ford came running. Mama was incoherent and hysterical. Ford poured a glass of something from one of the decanters, closed her hands around it and brought it to her lips. It did calm her in another few moments—enough for her to go scrabbling around the room, looking for her cigarettes and lighter.

Ford read the note hastily and then shoved me out of the room. "Did you write this?"

I yanked my hand from his clasp. "Creep! My letters are perfect!"

My writing was—and is—extremely neat, each small letter carefully spaced and equal in size. It looks typed, as well it might, since I learned myself when I was five by tracing the letters Ida Mae Oakes typed on an old Corona. Ida Mae said that I could do it if I concentrated and that I *had* to concentrate. Learning to concentrate was more important even than learning to write.

My first-grade teacher, Miz Dunlap, wanted me to learn to connect up the letters. Script, she called it. I pretended to be too stupid to get the hang of it. Stupid is something else I learned from Ida Mae Oakes, who told me if a person just stands there silent, paying attention but not reacting, a lot of folks, the rackety kind, would jump to the conclusion that the person was stupid, which was sometimes a very useful thing to be. A person might get yelled at or punished or even fired, but if a person didn't want to do something, being stupid might be the way not to do it. Or maybe a person would get the time to figure out what to do next, just by being stupid.

Ford had one hand fisted, ready to punch me. "Liar!"

"Jerk!"

"If it turns out you did this, I am gone drown you head first in the toilet!"

Then he came to a sudden halt. His anger wavered. For once he seemed unsure of himself.

"What do we do now?" His whisper revealed a degree of shock and fear that, like a pebble making rings in water, acted to enlarge my own emotions.

After bringing Mama more of whatever it was from the decanter, from which he took a good knock on the way, Ford persuaded her to summon Mr. Richard, the hotel manager. While we were waiting, Ford ordered breakfast.

I finished dressing. I remember that I hurried, because it seemed suddenly important that I be dressed and not just because mere underpants made me vulnerable to slaps or suspicions. I felt as if I had been caught unprepared by some great emergency, like a fire, a flood, a tornado.

Mr. Richard emerged from the Penthouse B elevator in a high state of managerial calm, exuding reassurance and confidence that all would be well. He announced himself, as if we had never met him before, in order to remind us that his name was said the French way: *Ree-shard.*

Mama stubbed out her Kool. She picked up the note from the dining table and thrust it at him as if it were on fire. Mr. Ree-shard examined it, before replacing it carefully on the table. Ford stood a little behind Mama's chair, with one hand on her shoulder, that now and again she would cover briefly with her left hand.

I hung about the periphery, trying to be invisible—easy enough, given Mama and Ford ignored me. Only Mr. Ree-shard ever glanced at me and that uneasily. He tried not to look again but could not help himself. A certain fear was in his eyes, and pity too. His reaction to me was not particularly unusual, so I was unperturbed. I had other causes for anxiety.

Mama assured Mr. Ree-shard that Ford and I were not a couple of kids playing a silly game. He in turn reassured Mama that he was totally at her service. Then Mr. Ree-shard made some calls to other people attending the convention—high pooh-bahs in the dealers' association—and, having determined that Daddy was not drunk on the floor behind the sofa in somebody else's room or suite, he called the police. By then he was somewhat chagrined—for Mama, I think, and only a little for himself, given his standard procedure had so far proved fruitless.

The chambermaid brought our full breakfast, which none of us ate. A number of folks came and went. Most of the visitors were Daddy's fellow automobile dealers. Some had a wife in tow and all were worried, solemn, consoling.

On the arrival of the police, Mr. Ree-shard herded all the

concerned callers into the elevator so that a New Orleans police detective could interview Mama in relative privacy.

The detective told Mama that kidnappers never signed their real names to a ransom note. What could be stupider than that? So there was no point in looking for a couple of female criminals named Janice and Judy. His immediate opinion was that Ford and I were playing a rotten prank and needed a good whipping. When neither of us burst into tears and confessed, Mama shooed us out of the room.

Ford conjectured to me that the detective was working on convincing Mama that the two of us could have made the whole thing up and that Daddy was in all probability drunk somewhere outside the hotel, or maybe in a whorehouse.

"What's a whorehouse?" I asked.

"Where the floozies are." Ford used the tone he employed to imply that I was mentally enfeebled.

I was not in fact very clear what floozies were, other than potential mothers of Daddy's other children, or possibly the sort of woman who smoked cigarettes on the street. The word "whore" I heard as h-o-a-r, as in "Hoar-frost twinkles on the trees," from a poem by Winnie-the-Pooh that Ida Mae Oakes had read to me when I was littler. Ida Mae told me that hoar-frost was ice. A hoarhouse must be something like an ice palace to me, where an Ice Queen might reign. I could make no connection between floozies and ice palaces. The big word Mama used so often when Daddy was late—philandering—I had been unable to find in the dictionary due to the fact that I was misspelling it as *fil*andering. My best guess was that philandering meant inexcusably late.

Somebody's wife—the name is long forgotten, if I ever knew it—looked in on us. She advised us that our mama was prostrate and that in this trying moment, we must be very, very good children. She told us that Mama had sent for Mamadee. The Dixie Hummingbird was making a special stop at Tallassee for her. Likely she would take us home. Then she had us kneel down and pray for Mama and for Daddy's safe return.

It was a prayer about me, not Daddy. Prayer, as I understood it, was in the same class of mundane magic as spells and step-on-a-crack-break-your-mama's-back and tossing a pinch of spilled salt over my shoulder. For all the churchgoing we did, I only knew the Lord's Prayer and the bedtime prayer by heart. I thought of the bedtime prayer as the One Long Word Prayer and said it as fast as possible to annoy Mama:

> *Now-I-lay-me-down-to-sleep-*
> *I-pray-the-Lord-my-soul-to-keep-*
> *If-I-should-die-before-I-wake-*
> *I-pray-the-Lord-my-soul-to-take.*

Lacking a more specific hocus-pocus, I shut my eyes tightly and tried to say the Lord's Prayer as I had it memorized, adapting the beginning to apply to Daddy.

> *My Daddy, witch art in heaven*
> *Halloween be thy name*
> *thy king dumb come*
> *thy will be done*
> *asset issin heavn*
> *giveusthisday hourdailybred*
> *and forgiveus ourdetz*
> *aswe forgive our deaders*
> *and lead us snot into temtayshun but*
> *deliverus fromevil*
> *forthineistheking dumb*
> *and thepowr and thegory*
> *forever*
> *amen.*

I mumbled so that Miz Someone would not notice any errors on my part.

Ford hid his disgust until Miz Someone went away again and then muttered, "Goddamn it, I am not going home until Daddy comes back."

I did not need to tell him that I did not want to go home to Montgomery, and not with Mamadee, and not to her big house, Ramparts, in Tallassee.

Ford tried to give me orders. "Dumbo, you have to be invisible. You have to keep your mouth shut. If Mamadee decides she's got to run the show here, she'll ignore us."

I knew sense when I heard it, even if it came out of Ford's usually lying trap.

Ford had his own strategy for himself. He stayed at Mama's side, holding her hand, or fetching her cooling drinks, cool cloths for her brow, dry handkerchiefs when she wept, BC or Goody's when she had a headache. She ate it up.

Eight

MAMADEE did not arrive alone. With her was Daddy's lawyer, Winston Weems. Lawyer Weems was even older than Mamadee, who had once in my hearing pronounced him the soul of rectitude. He certainly looked it. He was a grey man, all the way through. For no reason I have ever understood, people associate the dour, the humorless, the anemic and the old with rectitude.

Mamadee tried grimly to take the situation in hand. Her first demand was that we be sent home. She would have Tansy, her housekeeper, come for us.

Mama recovered enough to spar with her. "I will not send my children away, Mama." She pulled Ford close and he let her, something he would normally never permit. "Ford has been my little man!"

What with Ford being so much more Carroll than Dakin, Mamadee could hardly disagree.

"Well, Calley's just underfoot. Surely you do not want the nuisance of her, do you?"

Mama had to think about it. Ford said nothing, provoking me out of my discretion.

I laid out what I felt was compelling evidence of how utterly unjust it would be send me away before we got Daddy back.

"I am not underfoot! I am not a nuisance! I found the ransom note!"

Lawyer Weems fixed me in his toadish glare.

"You see?" Mamadee asked Mama. Then she frowned. "Did you say it was on Calley's bed?"

The four of them looked at me. Mamadee's eyes got cold and scary. I backed away.

"Stop that ridiculous cringing, Calley!" Mama said sharply. And then to Mamadee, "Mama, you know that Calley prints like a little typewriter. And where would she get that horrible paper and a green ink pen?"

Mamadee pointed out that anyone, even a child, could obtain such items at the nearest dime store. As always, she was more than willing to credit my intelligence for no-good.

The house phone rang, saving me from incipient conviction of all charges against me. Ford answered. Uncle Billy Cane Dakin and Aunt Jude were in the lobby of the Hotel Pontchartrain.

Mamadee and Ford and Mama couldn't figure out how they had learned that Daddy was missing, as there had been no reports on the radio or in the papers.

Later, Mamadee would discover in the hotel bill the record of a call made from Penthouse B to Uncle Billy Cane's home number. She accused me of making it but I never owned up.

If anybody was to try shipping me anywhere, I was not gone just go along with it. If I had had a phone number for Ida Mae Oakes, I would have called her too. I needed somebody—if not Ida Mae, then Uncle Billy and Aunt Jude. The three of us cared more about Daddy than anybody else did. In my heart, I was convinced that the combined strength of our desire for his return would somehow make that wish come true. I cannot remember now if I had seen *Peter Pan* or not at that time, or even if Disney had released it yet, but to a certainty I had lived my going-on seven years among people who believed as a matter of faith beyond religion that if they wished or willed anything hard enough, it would have to be so.

Mamadee ordered Uncle Billy and Aunt Jude to go home and stay out of the way.

Much to Mamadee's shock, Aunt Jude planted her splayed and knobby feet. Uncle Billy settled his shoulders and looked grim and immovable.

Lawyer Weems tried to bully them away too but he was no more successful than Mamadee.

"You stay," Mama said abruptly to Uncle Billy and Aunt Jude.

I do not know if she really wanted them but maybe she thought she might need some allies against Mamadee and Lawyer Weems too. Maybe she just wanted to be contrary. She had Mr. Ree-shard find a cheap room for them and after that largely ignored them, except to send them on errands.

On the second day of Daddy's disappearance, when the New Orleans police had been unable to find him in bar, brothel, hospital or morgue, Mama and Mamadee and Lawyer Weems agreed with the police that they must act as if the ransom note were real. Mr. Weems departed for Montgomery, to fetch the million dollars. He would return late on Monday with the cash, in small bills.

That was the day the FBI came into the case. By then I had determined the best listening post. The agents told Mama and Mamadee and Lawyer Weems, and Uncle Billy and Aunt Jude, that the signing of the note by "Judy" and "Janice" was just a subterfuge to make everybody think there were two female kidnappers. In the vast experience of the FBI, women occasionally kidnapped infants or small children, but they never, never kidnapped grown men. The agents assured Mama and Mamadee and the New Orleans police detectives (who seemed less than grateful for the vast expertise of the FBI) that, very definitely, the kidnappers, if there were kidnappers, were male. And just because two names were signed to the ransom note, the vast expertise of the FBI could assure all parties that that didn't mean that there were two kidnappers—a gang of five had been operating in St. Louis the year before, for instance, or it might just be one man.

Mamadee had one question of the vastly expert FBI agents. "What do you mean, *if*?"

"It may yet prove to be a hoax, ma'am," said one agent. While another cleared his throat and added, "And sometimes what looks like a kidnapping is French leave."

"What's 'French leave'?" I asked Ford later.

"Running away to Rio de Janeiro to start a new life, without getting a divorce or anything. Usually the person that leaves takes all the money, and maybe his secretary."

The thought that Daddy might leave us willingly was more than I could imagine. The idea that he would take his secretary, Miz Twilley, with him, was incomprehensible. Why his secretary? Would she place the long-distance phone calls home to us for him? Take down the letters that he would write to us on her steno pad in the shorthanded, secret code she used? And why was it French leave? French was a busy word, attached to a number of oddly assorted objects and processes. For instance, I could throw a spitball to the French Quarter from the balcony of Penthouse B.

Something was making my eyes sting and water.

"You snivel, I am not telling you anything else!" Ford threatened.

"I am not sniveling! What else?"

"The other thing is, sometimes kidnapping is a disguise for murdering somebody."

My throat tightened; my stomach felt kicked back to my backbone. Murder was a common enough threat in our house, but as on television, it was bloodlessly make-believe. *True Sex Crimes* and its kindred were as sub rosa as girly magazines. The idea that anybody real would kill some other real person was a genuine shock to me. At that moment, I felt foolish and, worse, that my foolishness might be lethal. I was old enough to grasp at least some of the wickedness of human beings. And it was my daddy who was at stake. I have never told anyone before, but I peed myself. It ran down my legs into my socks. My overalls hid it just long enough for me to escape Ford.

But first he asked a superior rhetorical question to which he, of course, did know the answer. "You know who the first suspect always is?"

I shook my head.

"The wife. Or the husband, if the wife is missing."

"Mama?" I whispered.

Ford nodded. Something about the idea pleased him, or else he was just enjoying scaring me.

I gave him a violent shove and ran for my room.

In the meantime, Janice Hicks baked brioche in the hotel kitchen, and Judy DeLucca brought them up to our room every morning with Mama's coffee.

Nine

JUDY DeLucca and Janice Hicks both got off work at two o'clock in the afternoon, when they went home and tortured Daddy.

Janice lived with her baby brother, Jerome, who also weighed more than three hundred pounds, in a house owned by an aunt and uncle no one had seen in years. Judy rented a room in the house next door to the Hicks. Judy's landlady was eighty-two years and deaf, so she never heard Daddy's screams.

Nobody knows why the two women were in the hotel at night, when Daddy was last seen, or how they got him out of the hotel without being noticed. Judy's testimony was at best sketchy.

Judy said, "I hit him over the head and I pushed him into a taxi and I told the driver that he was my uncle who had a plate in his head since the war and sometimes he got dizzy and to take us to my house."

Janice only said, "It was Judy got him to her house. I hardly had a thing to do with that part. I was out buying stuff."

The stuff Janice Hicks bought was a sturdy metal footlocker, two bottles of rubbing alcohol, five rolls of bandages, a pair of cuticle scissors, and a new broom. She gave a colored man fifteen cents to carry the bulky footlocker to Judy's.

The two women cut off all Daddy's clothes. He must have been unconscious, because Judy patiently used the cuticle scissors—though there were other, much larger pairs of scissors in the house—and that must have taken a long time. With strips of the cloth of his trousers, jacket, and shirt—and employing intact his belt and his tie—they tied him to Judy's bed.

"I poured the rubbing alcohol in his eyes," Janice said, "but it didn't make him blind."

That was the first day.

The second day, when Judy and Janice came home from work, Judy's landlady complained about a smell.

The smell was from Daddy, who had been tied to the bed all night and morning long with no provision for his bodily functions.

"I cleaned it up that time," Judy said in court, "but Janice said to me, 'Judy, we caint have no more of this,' and I went downstairs and got the new broom and we pushed it up his"—Judy blushed with embarrassment—"his bottom," she finally said. "And then we tied a string around his"—Judy paused again. "Prepuce," the district attorney prompted, and Judy went on: "Peep ruse? My daddy called it his"—she told the district attorney in a stage whisper—"*his Pope's hat.* Anyway, I wasn't having that man pee-pee in the bed again."

On the third day, the force of Daddy's bowels expelled the broom handle. His prepuce had ruptured with the pressure of urine. Because he called Judy and Janice very bad names—they never revealed what those names were—Judy stuck two fingers into Daddy's mouth, grasped his tongue and pulled it out beyond his lips. Janice thrust a knife blade through his tongue perpendicularly, and left it there—Daddy's pierced tongue protruding, and the blade and handle of the knife pressed against his face.

The fourth day was Mardi Gras, Fat Tuesday. On their return from work, Janice and Judy discovered that Daddy had managed to free his tongue of the knife—by the simple expedient of pulling his tongue into his mouth, allowing the knife to sever it. He had spat blood over his chest and abdomen for hours. Judy sprayed Daddy's face with D-Con bug killer until he was blinded. Then she cut five notches in his right ear with her cuticle scissors.

On the fifth day, Janice and Judy discovered that Daddy had once again soiled the bed linen. This may well have been surprising to them, considering that Daddy had had nothing to eat in those five days and that the only thing he'd drunk was the blood that flowed from his severed tongue and the urine Judy squeezed into his mouth from the wet sheets.

"This is the last straw," Janice told Judy.

"I caint hardly blame you for being mad at him," Judy commiserated.

They untied Daddy from the bed and put him on the floor. Judy put a pillow over Daddy's face. Janice climbed on top of him and pressed the pillow into his face to stop his breathing. Her three hundred and ninety-seven pounds on his torso crushed all his internal organs before he could even struggle for breath.

And that is how my daddy, Joe Cane Dakin, died, on Ash Wednesday of 1958, in New Orleans, Louisiana.

My seventh birthday.

Ten

THE kidnapping became public knowledge shortly after the FBI entered the case. Publicity is one thing that the FBI has always done well.

We were all more or less marooned in Penthouse B. Lawyer Weems hovered like an old bluebottle; his faded marble eyes stared at me often enough to give me the shivers. Sometimes a few tiny bubbles of spittle pearled at the left corner of his mouth, like he was hungry for me.

Mamadee had taken Ford's bed, forcing him to sleep on a cot and endure the indignity of sharing a room with his grandmama. He was as touchy as a trapped wasp, blaming me for Mamadee's choice of his room over mine.

I would have slept—if I could have slept—under the piano or on the balcony rather than in the same room with Mamadee. The feeling was more than mutual; Mamadee resented sharing the same air with me so much that her skin seemed to acquire a blue cast, as if she were holding her breath.

Most every day, a migraine knocked Mama flat on her back in her darkened bedroom. When she could get to her feet, she subsisted on Kools and bourbon.

Uncle Billy Cane and Aunt Jude, the only ones who could actually go out unmolested by the press, brought us newspapers and magazines and any other necessaries that the hotel could not provide.

Shrove Tuesday night, when I was supposed to be in bed, I listened at an open window to the cacophony in the streets. It was a lovely noise. I remember it still, and with more clarity than I do most of that bizarre passage in my life. Among the threads, I heard at one point someone drunkenly singing "You Are My Sunshine."

"You Are My Sunshine" is the state song of Louisiana. Daddy told me.

Sunshine.

I saw more rain than sunshine in New Orleans. The newspapers and radio reported that snow had fallen in Alabama the day we left for Louisiana, and I was not there to see it. I told myself a story: Daddy had gone back home to take snapshots of the snow and would soon bring them to us, to prove the miracle to us. For my birthday. Maybe snow tasted like vanilla ice cream.

Uncle Billy and Aunt Jude brought a birthday cake and a Mile-High Pie to the Penthouse for me. The sight of the cake brought me nothing of the excitement and pleasure that I recalled from previous birthdays. I didn't want cake, let alone Mile-High Pie. I made my wish and blew out the seven yellow candles in one shaky blow, but Daddy did not return.

My uncle and aunt also provided a few presents wrapped in clown paper—a flat book shape that was probably a paper doll, a flat square that was probably one or two 45s, a small box that likely contained a charm bracelet or a bracelet of polished pebbles—but I just looked at them, and then I went to the door to wait for Daddy.

"Ain't you gone open your gifts?" Uncle Billy Cane asked me.

I shook my head no. "I'm waiting for Daddy."

Ford sniggered.

Mamadee was disgusted with me. "Roberta Ann, you are indulging that child."

Mamadee grabbed me by the shoulders to give me one of her patented shakes. I let out a wail that must have been heard back in Alabama. Uncle Billy Cane wrenched me from Mamadee's claws. Mamadee was diverted to abusing him as an interfering redneck white-trash no-account, which he ignored as if she were a mosquito.

Aunt Jude picked me up bodily to carry me away into my room. Mama followed her, and stood in the door hesitantly.

Aunt Jude felt my forehead as she sat on the bed and I sat in her lap.

"This child is clammy. She is shivering and shaking." With a glance at Mama, Aunt Jude added, "Roberta, do something useful. Fetch a jigger of bourbon."

Mama cocked an eyebrow at Aunt Jude's temerity but followed the instruction anyway.

Aunt Jude poured the jigger of bourbon into me.

"If that makes her sick," Mama said, "you can clean it up."

"The child has made herself ill, fretting after her daddy." Aunt Jude spoke without acrimony, almost as if Mama had not said anything. "You might have a doctor for her. She is not right, Roberta, not right at all."

Mama must have been worried that her fitness as a mother might be questioned, because she did summon the hotel doctor.

He examined me, had a low-voiced exchange with Mama and Aunt Jude, and gave me something, a sedative of some kind.

I didn't care that he had questioned Mama and Aunt Jude about my mental status. "Miz Dakin, I do not misunderstand, do I, this child is weak-minded? Highly suggestible? I see more of it with every passing day. Parents are mystified. Fortunately the cause is easily identified. Don't let her watch the television or listen to the radio, and never permit her to have comic books. Dear lady, you have more burdens than anyone ought to have to bear, but I must be frank with you. A child of her hysteric tendencies will become more difficult as she approaches puberty. You may have to consider special arrangements. If I can be any help."

I just wanted him to go away and for Daddy to come back.

That doctor did me a kindness, though, as the sedative he gave me, with the bourbon, brought me a long, velvety oblivion.

The shift of the bed under Mama's weight when she came in to sleep woke me enough so that I could rub her feet, but I did it in a daze. Only after she was unconscious and I was lying next to her did anything like real mental clarity return. All at once I was fully awake, fully aware of Mama, of my every breath, of the reality in which I was cocooned. The scream that had yanked me to consciousness ached inside my skull. A lightbulb blowing out feels like this, I thought, and, of course, the lightbulb hurt when it died. There was no fear in me anymore, only an expanding unfamiliar silence, a sense that there was nothing more.

On Thursday, the sixth day, the second ransom note arrived.

Judy DeLucca delivered it herself when she brought up Mama's coffee and brioche that morning.

"I found this outside the door," Judy told Mama and handed over a pink envelope.

Mamadee and Ford were still slugabed, so we had the new note to ourselves. Mama had a darkness around her eyes like a terrible illness was inside her. The nasty perfume on the note made me sick to my stomach again. Mama grimaced as if the smell hit her that way too. She opened the note.

Joe Cane Dakin is a Dead Man if You Don't Listen to Our Instructions
Janice + Judy

"Well, *what* instructions?" Mama said. "What *damned* instructions?" She looked right at Judy as if she were asking her. "And who is Janice and who the hell is Judy?"

"Well, I'm Judy," Judy said.

"Oh, not you," said Mama impatiently.

Mama wadded up the note and threw it at me. "As soon as I finish my breakfast, Calley, I am calling the FBI."

Judy was backing out of the room but Mama stopped her.

"You brought me three brioche yesterday, and this morning there are only two," Mama said.

"Janice is having trouble with the oven heat," Judy said. "It's uneven. She had five dozen brioche too tough to leave the kitchen."

"Tell Janice I am not interested in her difficulties with the oven. Tell Janice I am worried to death about my kidnapped husband and I need three brioche in the morning, and not just two, to keep up my strength."

When Judy left, I said to Mama, "Maybe they did it."

Mama was buttering one of her brioche. "Maybe who did what?"

"That Judy, and the Janice that bakes your brioche. Maybe they're the ones that took Daddy."

Mama snapped at me. "Calley, I am living in hell. I do not need this idiocy of yours."

A moment later she asked, "Do you suppose that Judy the nitwit and this Janice the cook wrote these notes as a joke?"

"But where's Daddy?"

Her face clouded. She lit a cigarette while she brooded and then she went to put on her makeup.

As soon as Mamadee and Ford appeared for breakfast, she showed them the note. Then Lawyer Weems had to see it. He observed, as we all had, that it was very like the first one, and advised that the FBI be informed. Eventually he billed Mama for that advice, and got what he deserved: no payment at all.

An FBI agent came, took the note into custody, and asked Mama, "What instructions?"

"I asked the very same question. I asked the girl who brought me my breakfast this morning. I asked my seven-year-old child. They could not tell me. I have no idea what instructions I am supposed to follow."

"Then we wait for the instructions."

"I hope they come soon," Mama said. "Because I'd like to see the FBI pay for what this hotel is costing."

No instructions came that night or the next morning. Judy came though, bringing only one brioche.

Mama was almost too furious to speak. I thought for a minute that she might put her cigarette out between Judy's eyes.

Judy saw Mama was mad and said quickly, "Something happened to the oven. Janice said it about nearly exploded in her face when she tried to light the pilot."

"There is no excuse for bringing me teensy, tough brioche and undrinkable coffee, not at this hotel's prices!" Mama snarled.

But after Judy left, Mama called the FBI and said, "There is a Judy Somebody-or-other who is a chambermaid in this hotel, and there is a Janice Something-else who works in the kitchen, and I don't know why I have to do your business for you, but if I were J. Edgar Hoover, I would ask them what they would do with a million dollars if it fell down on them out of the sky."

When she heard of all this, Mamadee was first incredulous and then appalled. She had not known, as Mama and I had, that the hotel chambermaid and the pastry cook bore the same first names as the signers of the notes. Nor had Ford. He was shocked, and even angrier than Mamadee that no one had made the connection.

"I tried to tell Mama," I tried to tell him.

He paid no more attention to me than she had.

"How could you not realize?" Mamadee hissed at Mama, while Lawyer Weems frowned his disapproval.

"Maybe because I've had everybody in the world telling me what to do for the last seven days!" Mama shouted. "That girl is a moron, I caint see how she could manage to kidnap an ashtray!"

By this time, Judy DeLucca and Janice Hicks had broken all Daddy's bones, beating his corpse for more than forty minutes with the bottom of a Black Maria cast-iron frying pan stolen from the hotel kitchen and wielded in turn by each. By pressing hard, and cutting off his head, both feet, then his legs, and his hands and arms, with a cleaver also stolen from the hotel kitchen, they succeeded in squeezing most of Daddy into the footlocker. When she was arrested, Janice had Daddy's left foot in her imitation alligator-skin purse. His head, left forearm and right foot would remain missing.

Judy and Janice confessed immediately to the kidnapping, torture, murder and dismemberment of Joe Cane Dakin.

Judy told the police that someone had broken into the apartment and stolen the missing parts. Janice's baby brother, Jerome, wrote a letter to the *Times-Picayune* complaining that the police had done nothing at all to investigate the robbery next door.

Not surprisingly, the details were kept from me at the time. I am not sure that even Mama knew them all. I have patched the story together from a crazy quilt of the contemporary newspapers and periodicals, from court records and the reports of private investigators. In the yellowed old newsprint, the pictures of Daddy, of Mama being taken into the police station for questioning, and of Judy DeLucca and Janice Hicks at the trial, they all look as if they are playing parts in a black-and-white James M. Cain film.

In 1958, the world was still largely black-and-white, and

not just racially. People still read newspapers and magazines and listened to the radio. Only a minority of people owned a television set, and those sets were mostly black-and-white. Since the triumph of living color, it is the past that is rendered in black-and-white, and olden times in sepia. Even if still living, a person photographed in black-and-white is now dead to the eye, as if film and print mirrored the ghost to be.

I hardly know Mama. She is so young, too young to have been my mama, or Ford's. In these photographs, she is a tabloid starlet. She brings to mind those early photographs of Marilyn, hardly out of her teens.

Mamadee looks at Mama and sees herself thirty years younger. Hair in glassy waves, a fur tippet flashing a diamante fur clip around her shoulders, Mamadee is the ghost of Mama Future, if Mama lives so long, and allowing for changes in fashion. Mamadee's upper lip is furrowed with bitterness, her spine stiff with resentment. There is a glint of something like panic in Mamadee's eyes, as if she feels a heel wobbling under her. Perhaps it is only an accident of the photograph.

Lawyer Weems, with his slicked-back hair and in his three-piece suit, seemingly made for a larger man, could be some congressman interrogating suspected Communists before the House Un-American Activities Committee.

Most boys on the cusp of puberty are anything but beautiful. Ford was. I was too young to see it. And now I see the acute awareness of a feral creature, ready to bolt at the snap of a twig. The photographs cannot quite catch him; some part of him seems always surging into motion. The film is too slow, the flash too weak, the aperture too small to fix him, physically, as he was escaping the Ford of then, evolving into the new model Ford.

I look into Daddy's faded eyes in the formal headshots taken for business purposes, the snapshots from the convention or retrieved from Alabama newspaper archives. I see now that they are like my own. They are the eyes of a ghost, interrupted and restless. His dead lips tell me nothing.

What the articles, the accounts, the chapters in the books, and the testimony at the trial did not reveal was the motive for the kidnapping.

The million dollars would have been a motive, it's true, but only if Janice and Judy had attempted to collect it. They knew Mama had it. Everybody in the hotel, and everybody in New Orleans, knew Mama had the money, in small bills, in a footlocker brought by Lawyer Weems on the Dixie Hummingbird from Montgomery.

It is strange to me that no one then pointed out the coincidence that the footlocker that held the ransom money was identical to the footlocker into which Janice and Judy had worked so hard, so bloodily, so ineffectively, to cram Daddy's remains. Same size, same color, same manufacturer. The war was only over a few years, and given the number of troops under arms, I suppose there must have been hundreds of thousands of the things floating around the country.

When asked why they had singled out Daddy for abduction, Janice said, "Because he was staying on the twelfth floor."

When asked the significance of the twelfth floor, Judy could provide no answer at all.

When asked why they had not made any attempt to collect the ransom, Judy said, "We were waiting for the right time."

When asked what the right time would have been, Janice could only shrug.

Why had they tortured Daddy?

Why, when he was dead, had they mutilated and dismembered his corpse?

Why, having gone to the trouble of hiding his torso in a footlocker too small to hold him, all of him, did they leave the footlocker at the foot of the bloodied bed? For lack of a colored man who needed fifteen cents to carry it down the stairs?

In other states, in later years, Judy and Janice might have been judged insane. In Louisiana, in 1958, Judy and Janice were found guilty of kidnapping and first-degree murder. Janice and Judy admitted all the details of Daddy's torture. If they had left anything out, nobody could imagine what it might be. But the two women died without anyone ever discovering *why* they had done what they'd done.

What was the prompting? That was the great mystery, why the case is written about even now.

But here is the truth of it: Janice and Judy had no idea why they had done what they had done. There had been a motive all right, but the motive was not *theirs*. It was someone else's.

In 1958, when I was only a seven-year-old, I was quite certain I knew why Daddy had died.

He died because Mama and I went shopping.

He died because we had gone into the shop that ticked.

He died because Mama's brown Hermès Kelly pocketbook had disappeared, to turn up later inside a locked filing cabinet.

The very day we found the first note, I tried to explain all this to Mama, but she grabbed me by the shoulders and shook me hard, and cried, "What shop, Calley? What are you talking about pocketbooks for? Who in God's Green Glory is Mr. Rideaux, and caint you see that your Mama has other things to think about?"

Eleven

TWO days after the recovery of The Remains, we returned to Montgomery on the Dixie Hummingbird. It was my first train ride. There were still a lot of firsts in my life at age seven.

The three of us sat by ourselves in the back of a coach, away from the few other passengers. They gawked at us and whispered to one another but left us alone once the train began to move:

gotongotongoton

The footlocker of ransom money was in our coach. Mama made me sit with my feet up on it all the way back from New Orleans. Perhaps she thought no one would suspect that a stupid-looking little girl with overly large ears and clutching a Betsy McCall doll in one fist could possibly have a footlocker full of money under her Mary Janes, or the key to it on a red silk string around her neck. And I was indeed stupid, thanks to the hotel doctor's tranquilizers still lingering in my small child's body. Mama's well-developed facility for believing what she wanted to believe allowed her to pretend that despite the weeklong coverage in newsprint and on the airwaves, the passengers sharing the car were totally unaware of the kidnapping and murder of Joe Cane Dakin. Murder was even then no rarity in New Orleans but the murder of a rich white man is always news anywhere.

Mama had no appropriate widow's weeds with her but while waiting for the coroner's release of The Remains and the departure of the next available train, she had obtained an off-the-rack black suit, black pumps and a veiled hat. She had to lift the veil from time to time to have a cigarette. Her makeup only seemed to make her complexion more pale, and her eyes more bruised and swollen with tears. When she spoke, her voice was thick and shaky and distant.

Ford kept his face turned to the window. He wore a new black tie with his navy gabardine Sunday church suit. He had not cried when we were given the bad news but his fingernails were chewed to the quick. Every chance he had he punched, tripped or gooched me. At one point, he backed me into a corner away from the adults and told me that Daddy had been slaughtered like a hog and butchered. That the two women who did it had intended to cook and eat Daddy. That they had collected his blood to make blood sausage. The excessive detail only convinced me that he was lying, as usual. I wriggled free and escaped to the safety of Aunt Jude's skirts. I almost knocked her over, hugging her.

All the black in my entire wardrobe was on me, in the form of my black Mary Janes and black patent leather belt. Some mothers dress up their little girls like dolls. If Mama ever had done it, she had given up on it by the time I was able to dress myself.

All my dresses, skirts and blouses had the cookie-cutter, ageless, sturdy look of a school uniform. For this return trip, I wore the grey dress with the white Peter Pan collar under my navy wool coat. The red silk string was long enough to hang unseen beneath the dress. The dress and coat were the clothes I had worn on our shopping trip in the rain. Mamadee had sent them out to be pressed on the Monday after Daddy disappeared. I have wondered since if Judy DeLucca had pressed my coat and dress. Certainly they had been returned to the closet with Hotel Pontchartrain paper capes over their shoulders.

As we rode into Alabama, I stared out the window too, but no snow remained to be seen. Try as I might, I could not grasp the magnitude of the calamity that had befallen us. I hardly comprehended what death was. Whatever it was, it happened mostly to old people. I had seen them. Mama and Mamadee shared the conviction that a child was never too young to drag to a funeral parlor or a funeral. I could not recall the specific occasions, only the old people asleep on their satin pillows in their ponderous beds. I do remember that I had felt no fear, no revulsion, and certainly no grief.

But my daddy had not grown grey and wrinkled and shrunken. He had simply gone out and not come back. Everyone insisted that he was not going to come back. I knew that it was childish, so I hid it, but I still clung to the fantasy that he would. I was exhausted with the ceaseless tension of listening constantly for his step.

A porter came with a hand truck to take the footlocker off the train for us. He was a balding middle-aged man with black-framed glasses, arms powerful with the burden of his work, and a uniform worn with pride. He winked at me and gave me a hand up to sit on the footlocker as he trundled it

takatakataka

after Mama and Ford. Mama didn't notice. To be fair, she did have a lot on her mind at the time, but it was also simple fact that she usually looked right through colored people. Ford was pretending that he was alone in the universe or else waiting for everyone to fall down on their knees and beg his pardon for existing.

"Did you know my daddy?" I asked the porter.

He blinked and tilted his head at me questioningly. I guess he saw in my face some answer to his unspoken question because then he smiled and nodded.

"Not personal, Miss. I am sorry for your loss, though. I hear tell Mr. Dakin was an honest man in his dealings." He spoke so softly that Mama could not hear.

"Thank you," I said and repeated the formula that I had heard at wakes and funerals: "I am gone miss him."

I might have asked him if he knew Ida Mae Oakes but Mamadee was in sight, waiting for us near the exit from the lobby. As soon as we were informed that Daddy was deceased, she hastened back to Alabama before us. It was almost as if she were squeamish in the face of the worst. It had fallen to

Uncle Billy Cane Dakin to accompany Mama to identify The
Remains. Mr. Weems had lingered another day to help make
arrangements and then hightailed it after Mamadee.

"Calley Dakin, get down off that thing right this minute,"
Mamadee cried. "What are you, a little heathen? Roberta Ann
Carroll Dakin, you might have had the decency to buy the man
a coffin!"

Mamadee thought anything that I was doing was bad so I
wasn't surprised to be found in the wrong yet again. I didn't
understand the rest of it because I was still ignorant of Judy
and Janice's footlocker.

Mama's black veil hid her face but did not muffle or disguise the fury in her voice. "Mama, I am ashamed of you. You
might have had the decency to spare me your ridiculous remarks. You know perfectly well that Joseph is in a mahogany
coffin in the baggage car."

Mamadee did. She just wanted to be sure that no one in the
station was unaware of the notorious Widow Dakin and her
children.

"You might try to act like a grieving widow, Roberta Ann,"
Mamadee scolded.

"What would you know about that, Mama?"

Mamadee seemed to grow taller, like clouds rushing to
build up to a tornado. I thought for an instant that she might
change into something else, like the archangel driving Adam
and Eve from Eden that I had seen once in a picture in a Bible.
But she allowed herself to be distracted, pretending that it was
necessary for her to oversee the stowing of our luggage in her
Cadillac at the curb outside the train station.

A man in a black suit and white gloves, the mortician, was
at the curb too, with a hearse backed up and open. He was
someone I had seen before, amid the flowers and polish and
the whispering of his funeral parlor.

The mortician hurried to Mama's side, to press her hand
between his and murmur consolations. We waited on the sidewalk while solemn porters wheeled out Daddy's coffin on a
metal flatbed rack. The metal device was all hinges and could
be raised and lowered, so the coffin could be slid smoothly
into the back of the hearse. Observing it,

creaketycrumpetythumpety

as it was moved, helped me avoid thinking about what was left
of Daddy being jostled and disturbed inside the coffin. I didn't
really believe there was anything in it at all. The porters removed their hats to Mama and the mortician.

The mortician again pressed Mama's hand and bowed his
head to Mamadee before he replaced his hat and hurried to
take his place in the front seat of the hearse. A uniformed
chauffeur, an elderly colored man who had been hauling
white people to their white morgue and then to their white
graveyard since Moses was bawling in the rushes, drove the
hearse. He was a fixture, like so many of the colored people in
our lives, indiscernible from his function.

Mamadee would drive only a white Cadillac, replacing it
every three years. Mama had never said anything to her nor
had Daddy ever remarked upon Mamadee's automotive dis-
loyalty but we were all aware of it. Her Cadillac always had
standard shift because it was gospel that a standard saved gas.
Driving a standard was just one of the ways Mamadee informed the rest of the world that she knew what was what. The
only problem was that she had never really mastered it.

Once we were all in the Cadillac, Mama in the passenger
seat and Ford and I in the backseat with the footlocker between us, Mamadee

grrrrreech

turned the key and

unk

jerked at the shift and stamped her feet on both the gas and
brake pedals. The gears shrieked and the car jumped where it
stood. Continued assault on the gearshift finally produced forward motion,

screepped

up over the curb and

unnka

down again

bunk

and onto the street.

"I have found this whole dreadful business humiliating in the extreme," Mamadee said. "Nothing like this has ever happened to the Carrolls. How could you let it happen?"

We were already well versed in the indelible stain upon the Carroll reputation as Mamadee had expressed the same feelings repeatedly while she was in New Orleans with us. This time, Mama did not take it lying down. She had been waiting and scheming the whole time to get her own back someplace where nobody who mattered might be listening. Mama and Mamadee were in most ways just alike. Like magnets with the same polarities pointed at each other, they forced each other away.

"I did *not* let anything happen," said Mama, each word slow and distinct. "Nobody asked me if they could kidnap Joseph, torture him, murder him, and then try to fit him in a footlocker that wasn't big enough to hold him."

This was the first mention of the other footlocker in my presence. Immediately I glanced at Ford. He was rigid, his face white—all the proof I needed that whatever she meant by torture and fitting Daddy into the footlocker was true. Ford had claimed earlier that Daddy had been butchered. Just the thought of the two women cutting off Daddy's head and his limbs stunned me.

Before that moment, for me, torture meant talking when someone had a headache. Whenever Mama had a headache and I said two words within range of her hearing, she would cry out, "Calliope Carroll Dakin, you are torturing your mama!"

Because I had not known Daddy's torso had been fitted somehow into a footlocker, I had no idea until then that it was identical to the one that contained the ransom. My imagination, however, was entirely adequate to the image of Daddy's torso being crammed into the ransom footlocker. I could see myself crammed into a commensurately small space, immobilized, without light or air. An instant's terror struck me breathless: Mama had made me sit with my feet up on that footlocker, with the key on the silk string around my neck, all the way back from New Orleans. But there was the unclaimed ransom, the coffin and the hearse, and Mama's explicit statement to Mamadee that Daddy was in the coffin. And, of course, I was used to the outrageous assertions that were Mamadee's stock in trade.

Mamadee barged right on. "If I had known this was going to happen, I would never have allowed you to marry that man. People are laughing, Roberta Ann, they are laughing, and it is hard for me not to laugh right along with them. To think that Joe Cane Dakin was murdered by the Fat Lady in the Circus."

Mama was silent for a moment. She must have had thoughts along this line even before Mamadee brought it up. Forever after, for Mama, the dreadfulness of the business seemed to condense in that one peculiarity.

Calley, she'd say in that despairing tone that made you want to kill yourself and take a few close friends along with you, *you know what the worst thing was? The worst thing was that woman weighed three hundred and ninety-seven pounds.*

"You did not *let* me marry Joseph," Mama said.

"I did my best to stop you."

"I clearly remember you saying, 'Roberta Ann, if you do not hog-tie Joe Cane Dakin, I will.' "

"Roberta Ann! That is a falsehood! I would never be so vulgar!"

"You always thought he was a country fool."

"I never!"

"You kept right on buying Cadillacs. It was a deliberate insult to my late husband and I! Do you think either one of us mistook it for anything else?"

"You are distraught, Roberta Ann." Mamadee spoke then in the reasonable tone she always took when she had driven someone to shrieking. "I am gone ignore every silly thing you have said." Having arrived at a position of virtue, she changed the subject. "You have made plans for the funeral of course?"

"I thought I might be able to get out of these shoes first," snapped Mama.

"Really, Roberta Ann, how coarse of you. Your son is listening. You ought to have the funeral somewhere near Joe Cane Dakin's people."

"Why?" Mama's tone made it clear that she did not give a candle stub what the answer was.

"Because there won't be as many people coming to gawk!" cried Mamadee. "Because you know what will happen if you have it here in Montgomery or in Tallassee? You might as well rent a circus tent! And all those Dakins will turn up and remind the whole world how low you married!"

"Mama," Mama said in a suffering voice, "Joseph's funeral will be at St. John's. The governor and his wife and a director of the Ford Motor Company will be in attendance. And so will a whole gaggle of Dakins and the only thing to do is pretend that they are as good as anybody else. Did you ever hear that some mothers actually try to comfort their children in their times of need?"

"I've heard some children speak with respect and gratitude to their mother," Mamadee retorted.

Mama tossed back her veil, opened her pocketbook—the brown Hermès Kelly bag—poked around in it, fished out her cigarettes and lighter and lit up. The smoke exited her tremulous nostrils in a furious stream.

From time to time I glanced across the footlocker at Ford. He stuck his tongue out at me once. Another time he put his hands up to the sides of his head as if they were ears, to flap at me. Then he turned his face to stare blindly out the window. When I saw his reflection in the window, I realized he was looking at himself.

Mamadee ground the Cadillac up the driveway of our home and clashed to a halt in the turnaround. A silence settled on us as we looked at the house. It was a fine Big House, one of the best in Montgomery, Mama always said. I remember enormous trees, tall pillars, deep porches and inside, rooms with high ceilings and sun-struck chandeliers.

A sawhorse stood at the bottom of the front steps, with a sign on it.

NO ENTRY

The words at the bottom said something about by order of somebody or someone.

An orange garland of tape hung around the pillars and there was another sign on the front door. I could make out the letters of **POLICE LINE** repeated on the tape, just like decorations I had seen repeating **HAPPY BIRTHDAY** or **MERRY CHRISTMAS**.

"Why did you bring me here?" Mama asked in a choked voice. "You should have told me!"

"You think I knew?" Mamadee said. "I would hardly drive out of my way, would I?"

None of us believed her. Nothing was more characteristic of Mamadee than driving out of her way to kick someone near and dear in the gut.

"I caint believe the police have searched my home. Or was it the FBI?"

"Both. You caint stay here." The note of triumph in Mamadee's voice was barely repressed. "You will have to come stay with me at Ramparts."

Mama sank back in the seat and lowered the veil over her face.

"Yes, Mama. Yes, Mama. Yes, Mama. Yes, Mama. Are you satisfied?"

Mamadee turned to her. "Why, Roberta Ann Carroll Dakin, whatever do you mean? How could I possibly derive satisfaction from the plight of my widowed child and her orphaned children?"

Mama made no answer. I could see that she had decided she was not gone talk to Mamadee any more, at least for a while.

"What about Portia and Minnie and Clint?" I asked.

Portia was our cook, Minnie cleaned the house, and Clint did the chores.

"Be quiet, Calley Dakin," Mamadee snapped. "The help is none of your business. I am certain sure, however, that given the way colored people gossip, they knew before you did that Joe Cane Dakin was dead. I fired the lot of them as soon as I got back from New Orleans!"

Mama's cigarette smoke spurted even more violently at Mamadee's high-handedness.

I knew, of course, that the colored servants had nothing

more important to do than gossip about their white employers—it was a very popular topic with Mamadee, Mama, and all their female friends. The ladies were all still seething about the bus strike when the colored help all walked to work rather than take the bus on account of Miss Rosa Parks. Miss Parks refused to ride in the back, for which she was arrested and all the colored people threw a hissy fit. Most of the maids and cooks and chauffeurs and yardmen were late to work every day for months and talked back something terrible whenever they were chastised. Now they could all ride in the front of the bus, but everybody was still riled and hardly speaking.

I remembered what Daddy said to Mama's lamentations when it started: "Well, darling, that egg's cracked, and the chick's not gone get back into it."

I remembered what Daddy said because Mama fired Ida Mae Oakes the very next day.

Twelve

RAMPARTS loomed over the small town of Tallassee from nearly its highest point. The house was surrounded by several acres of big old live oaks festooned with Spanish moss. For all intents and purposes, Ramparts was the Carroll Museum, dedicated to the eternal glorification of the Carrolls. There was hardly a wall without a portrait of some Carroll or other, or Carrolls in multiples: Judges Carroll, State Senators Carroll, State Representatives Carroll, a U.S. Congressman Carroll, a Lieutenant Governor Carroll, a State Attorney General Carroll, a General Carroll and three Captains Carroll.

I expect all those old Carrolls were like other people, each a mix of good and bad, of strength and weakness. For a fact, most of them had owned slaves and all of them had been good segregationists—the sort of moneyed white who secretly supported or ignored the Klan and its terrorism. They were hypocrites, I mean, like most of us.

I never knew my granddaddy, Robert Carroll Senior, because he died before my birth. Captain was his commissioned rank during WWI and Mamadee always referred to him that way, as Captain Carroll. Mama used to say that the town was too small and everybody knew each other too well for Mamadee to call him General Carroll, but that she would have if she could. Robert Carroll Senior had been the sole inheritor of the Carroll Trust Bank and some other Carroll properties— once upon a time, there were plantations and a couple of mills of one kind or another. In fact, there was even a Carrollton in western Alabama, but if there were any Carrolls living in it, Mamadee was not on speaking terms with them.

Though the Carroll Trust Bank never went bust in the Depression, the Carroll fortune suffered, or so Mamadee claimed in her most penurious moments. Captain Senior managed to hold on to the bank and Ramparts, and to provide Mamadee with Cadillacs and an estate sufficient to keep her from the poorhouse. Mamadee made miserly economies over the pettiest items, while justifying other, larger expenses on the grounds of value. I doubt that she was ever truly hard up, as I have observed this behavior in many wealthy people. Perhaps it is only a tingle of shame that causes rich people to chintz and chisel over pennies while indulging themselves in great luxury without hesitation, but that may be giving credit where none is due.

In its salon, Ramparts sported a Chickering baby grand. It had been locked up for all the years of my short life, except for the day every year when the tuner came to tune it. Mamadee did not play but she was not about to let anyone else play either. Nor did Mama play, and I had not been able to discover if anyone else in the family ever had. I already knew that it was hardly the only piano in the world that was less an instrument than a very large elaborate pedestal for candelabra, a vase of flowers, or a wedding portrait in a silver frame.

My personal favorite room in Ramparts was Captain Senior's old library. Mamadee almost never came into it, for one. It was called a library because it had a bookcase in it, though hardly anybody ever cracked any of the books on its shelves. The old books were falling apart, the edges of their pages crumbling and the leather bindings cracking and flaking. Every time I picked one up, I sneezed. The books were mostly about explorers, and illustrated with many old maps in pastel colors: sky blue, mint green, rose, butter yellow. All my life since I have enjoyed looking at maps, those glorious illusions that we can know where we are.

On the wall behind his desk, there were several pictures of Captain Senior, all of them with men and guns and dogs, and none with Mamadee. The wedding photograph of the two of them was in the foyer, and the big one of Mamadee in her wedding dress was on the Chickering.

A 1913 Victrola with a plaque inside declaring that it was a Victor Talking Machine stood next to Captain Senior's favorite leather chair—still, after all these years, imprinted with the shape of his buttocks. As a smaller child, I had busted my lip several times trying to turn the crank to make the turntable of the Victrola turn. Like Daddy's coffin, the Victrola—or rather its cabinet—was mahogany, which I knew because Mamadee and her maid, Tansy, had warned me more than once not to scratch it.

In the cupboard part of it, there were big old heavy records. Nobody seemed to mind if I scratched *them*. I had been playing with them since I was no more than a baby. They were heavy and sharp-edged. When I was too small to carry them, I had picked one up and dropped it on my toes. I still remember how entirely purple all my small toes became.

The 78s sounded as if they had been recorded at the bottom of the sea, and were wonderfully punctuated.

Poppetyshushshushpopshush

Though later I realized that Captain Senior's musical taste was pedestrian, at the time, the 78s provided lovely noise to me. "Alabama Jubilee," "Hard Hearted Hannah," "Red River Valley," "Down Yonder," "The Tennessee Waltz" and "Goodnight, Irene" are some that I recall.

On one side of the fireplace was Captain Senior's Westinghouse Superheterodyne radio. It still worked just fine. There was no television set in the room or anywhere in Ramparts. Mamadee thought television was a passing fad, like 3-D movies. From the way she used to skirt the console at our house in Montgomery, I suspected that she was afraid of it.

I got as far as the library and had the cupboard open to take out some records when Mamadee stuck her head in the door and said, "Calley, you are bound and determined to scratch that cabinet. Go on upstairs and unpack."

We visited often enough to have our own regular rooms. Mama's room went back to her girlhood. Daddy used to make little jokes to Mama about the bed whenever we came to visit. Mamadee altered nothing in the room after Mama married Daddy, requiring my parents to sleep in Mama's old bed. Fortunately it was at least a full bed. Crowded, Daddy used to say, but cozy.

To me, the most interesting thing in Mama's room was the curling color snapshot of her that was stuck in the frame of the vanity mirror. In it, she wore a sleeveless blouse and the wide knee-length shorts of the forties. She sat on the verandah railing back against a pilaster, hugging her knees.

Her hair was parted in the middle and curled back and away in that forties' hairstyle that I have never figured out. Not that I could have done it with my hair. I knew that this was how Mama looked when she met Daddy.

Ford's room had been Mama's younger brother's—the junior Robert Carroll. Balsa wood airplanes hung from the ceiling and a framed copy of "Invictus" hung over the desk. A small bookcase was crowded with boys' adventure stories full of Toms and Joes and Franks and Dicks and goshes and gollies and gee willikers. I vaguely recall banners on the walls and a diploma of some kind hung with a gilded tassel.

Another bedroom, furnished with twin beds, had belonged to Mama's older sisters, Faith and Hope. I only knew it because Mama said so, just once. I had an idea that they were either in jail, which was the worst place I knew of short of hell itself, or they were dead. Portraits, photographs and snapshots of Junior were here, there, and everywhere at Ramparts, but I cannot remember so much as a curling snapshot of Faith or Hope. I might have slept in that room, except the beds were never made up, the rugs were rolled up against the walls, and dustcovers shrouded every object. The woodwork of the door frame in the hallway was curiously pitted with nail holes. I concluded that at some time the room had actually been boarded up. It would not have surprised me if it had been, and Faith and Hope left to starve to death within, as punishment for some perceived defiance of Mamadee. Possibly a scratch on the mahogany of the Victrola.

The room I was accustomed to using was up a short flight of stairs from the others, under the eaves. Once a servant's room, the narrow meager space had been taken over at some time by Junior, who may never have actually slept in it. The greater height in the house of that room must have offered better reception for his radios. The room accommodated a single bed of brown-enameled iron, a dresser with a Bakelite radio on it, and a wooden chair and desk that had seen some hard days. On the desk was a shortwave radio, a spill of pamphlets and old books about ham radio, and a suitcase record player. From the rod in the small closet hung a net bag of mothballs. On the bottom of the closet floor was a wooden orange crate of records, the cardboard sleeves all marked with the name Bob Carroll Jr.

The crate of records was better than pirate gold to me. The records were all far more recently pressed than Captain Senior's; many of the songs could still be heard on the radio. The box contained recordings by Charlie Parker, Count Basie, Duke Ellington and Dizzy Gillespie, and more, *hits* (as they were called on the radio shows) like "Don't Sit Under the Apple Tree," "Swinging on a Star," "Rum and Coca-Cola," "Sentimental Journey."

Among the records, I kept a rusty chisel, stolen from a toolbox in the barn, in case Mamadee boarded up the room while I was in it. I was big enough now to get out the window, so I probably wouldn't ever need it, but I left it as a courtesy to any other kid Mamadee might board up in the room in future.

Under the iron bed was an old stained china pot with a cracked lid. Over the bed, a few dusty books, with *Robert Carroll Jr.* inscribed in them, held each other up on a homemade wooden shelf. One was Peterson's *A Field Guide to the Birds of Eastern and Central North America*. It was a first edition, published in 1934, not that first edition meant doodly to me then. Another was *Birds of North America*, also dated 1934, with 106 full-color plates of Louis Agassiz Fuertes's paintings. It was a Bible-heavy old book, which for me added to its authority. Hall's *North American Trees: Guide* was easier to take off the shelf without braining myself. The third bird book was the most recent, a 1946 *Audubon Bird Guide: Eastern Land Birds*, by Richard Pough. It had green binding and a comfortable fit to the hand. There were three or four others, all pertaining to the natural world, and in their margins, someone had written notes in a script faded to illegibility. I had been looking at those books since I was old enough to reach the shelf and before I could read. Fortunately, Mamadee never came near this room, so I did not have to worry about her catching me with the books and taking them away, which she surely would have for fear that I might enjoy them.

Once I had overheard Mamadee remarking to one of the women with whom she played Bridge, that when her Bobby died, it killed Captain Carroll too, sure as God Made Little Green Apples. I reckoned that meant Captain Senior grieved himself to death, a common fate of the bereaved in Alabama. I had to wonder now that Daddy was dead—if he really was—if *I* could grieve myself to death.

Almost outside the window, one of the old oaks whispered and creaked, and in it, the birds and the squirrels and chipmunks carried on their daily lives.

Mamadee's yardman, Leonard, had placed my suitcase on the bed, my record player on the floor and my Betsy Cane McCall doll and box of paper dolls on the bed. He had opened the window a few inches to air out the room; now it was chilly. I flung my coat on the bed, opened my suitcase and one of the dresser drawers, threw the contents of the first into the second, and slammed them both shut. I slid the suitcase under the bed next to the pot. That left the doll and my paper dolls. I lifted the box top and looked down into it. Betsy McCall Was Still In Pieces. At Ramparts.

My stomach grumbled. I ran downstairs and banged through the doors into the kitchen. Tansy paused with her chopping knife over the carrots she was dicing.

"Gone tear tha hinges right out the wall," Tansy said. "You git, gal. I don't need no chile unfoot in my kitchen. Somebody could be done a harm."

"I'm hungry!" I cried. "Desperate hungry!"

"So's a million Chinamen. Git."

Tansy did the cooking and the light housekeeping and found professional fault with the succession of hard-up women who came in to do the heavy work. Mamadee had fired every servant she had ever had, or had them quit. Tansy had been fired or quit everywhere else and the only job she could get was at Ramparts. They were stuck with each other. Tansy gave Mamadee somebody to rag everyday, and Mamadee gave Tansy somebody to resent everyday.

I banged back through the doors out of the kitchen and headed down the hall for the library.

Ford lunged out of nowhere and grabbed my wrist. He spun me off course and pushed my face against a wall, holding my arm behind me. I opened my mouth to scream and he kneed me in the small of the back, so I couldn't get any air down my lungs.

"Ssshhh," he whispered in my ear, strong-arming me into the powder room. His breath smelled of bourbon, which meant that he had penetrated the defenses of Mamadee's liquor cabinet once again. He shoved me inside and shut and locked the door behind us. I finally got a look at him. His hair was raked up and down and he had been crying. His nose was leaking. He wiped it with the back of his hand.

"I am gone crazy," he said in a croak. "I caint take this no more. Mama got Daddy murdered and chopped up by those women. I do not know how but she did. You know it. You don't miss the sound of a mouse fart." He threatened me with a curled fist. "You tell me how she did it and you tell me why she did it right now, or I swear I will kill you, Dumbo, I will cut your stupid ears off your stupid head and shove them down your throat!"

"She did not!" Then I lowered my voice to a whisper. "Mama did not do what you just said. You are a liar, Ford Carroll Dakin, a liar and a bully."

We stared each other down for a long moment.

Then Ford said, "She's gone kill me next. You would like that. You would help her."

I shook my head no. "Course I would help her, but Mama ain't gone kill you. Why would she? Why would she kill Daddy?"

"Money," he whispered. "Get rid of me, she gets all the money."

I knew money was important. Mamadee and Mama talked about it enough. I just could not see how any amount of money explained what had happened to Daddy, especially since I was not entirely sure exactly *what had happened* to Daddy beyond two crazy women having killed him and cut him up and stuffed most of him into a footlocker. Mama had not killed

Daddy; those women had. And those crazy women had never collected the ransom.

And while Mama had threatened to kill me so many times that I could hardly take it seriously, I knew that she had never threatened to kill Ford, not in my hearing. She doted on him; he could do no wrong in her eyes.

"Money? You can have mine. You can have that silver dollar I got hid in my bedroom at home." I reconsidered. Daddy gave me that silver dollar for my fifth birthday. "If you really want it." Now it seemed like we were dickering. "You could let me have that Fred Hatfield card you got."

"I can take that old silver dollar anytime I want. You are never getting that Fred Hatfield, you might as well forget it."

I was relieved; if he took it from me, then I was absolved of the guilt that a trade would have carried.

I heard Mamadee's step in the hall.

"Mamadee!" I whispered.

Ford held his finger to his lips. We both froze. Mamadee paused at the powder room door.

"Calley? Ford? Ford, baby, you in there? I heard you. You sick, baby boy?" The doorknob rattled violently. "You unlock this door right now."

The solitary window was too high and small for escape. There was no way out. Ford never did have sense enough to make sure he had a way out. He shot me a look of warning and flicked the lock.

Mamadee stood in the open doorway with her hands on her hips. "Just what is going on?"

"Nothing, ma'am," Ford said. "We just had to do some crying, so we come in here so as not to bother anyone."

My stomach gurgled loudly.

"Calley," Mamadee said. "How many times have you been told not to swallow air?"

She engulfed Ford in an embrace that he could not gracefully escape. I lingered only long enough to enjoy his discomfort.

"My poor, poor orphan boy," Mamadee murmured. "Don't you worry now, I'll keep you safe."

Slipping past them and out the door, I heard Ford hiss, sadly, like a tire with a nail in it.

I stopped with my hand on the doorknob of the library. Mama was inside, talking on the telephone.

"—never informed that the police were gone to search my home. I never saw a search warrant—" There was a pause for an answer, and then Mama continued, "I beg your pardon? You had no business 'sparing me,' Mr. Weems. You had no business authorizing an invasion of my home. You do not have my power of attorney"—her voice went high and shaky—"that was only to get the ransom money! You had better explain this right now. I will expect you within the hour."

The telephone receiver crashed down onto its cradle.

Mama blew her nose. "Jesus God," she muttered.

I opened the door and peeked in. She was sitting at Senior's desk.

"You heard everything, I suppose," Mama said. "You never mind those words I just used. I am having a crisis. I do not know what is gone on but I do not care for it one bit."

"Mama, would you like me to rub your feet?"

She chortled incredulously. "Yes, I would, Calley. Yes, I would."

Mama yanked up her skirt and unhooked her garters. I pulled up a hassock and sat on it to roll down her silk stockings and rub her feet.

"The only useful thing that silly old man had to tell me was that your late beloved daddy owned a plot in some backside-of-the-moon boneyard. Isn't that just the cherry on the whipped cream!"

I guessed that boneyard meant cemetery but the significance of owning a plot, a single plot, in one, escaped me. All I knew was that Mama did not like it.

All the good of the foot rubbing I did went to waste, like the meal that Tansy had prepared for us. An hour later, two hours later, Mr. Weems had not answered Mama's summons to Ramparts, nor was anyone answering her phone calls to the Weems house. The Edsel was still on its way back from New Orleans, by arrangement with Uncle Billy Cane Dakin, and Mamadee wouldn't let Mama have the keys to the Cadillac. Mama threatened to walk to Mr. Weems's house. Tallassee was and is a very small town, so that no place, not even Ramparts, was very far from anywhere else. Mamadee's response was to lock Mama in the salon. While Mama was hurling ashtrays and candlesticks, breaking lamps and punching out windows with a chair, Mamadee called Dr. Evarts.

Thirteen

DR. Evarts had been born and raised in Chicago, gone to
college in New York City and studied medicine in Boston. He
had settled in Tallassee, Alabama, for the simple reason that
there he would have no competition at all. Before he came, the
nearest doctor was in Notasulga, twenty-two miles distant.
With a near-monopoly in Tallassee, Dr. Evarts made upwards
of fifty thousand dollars a year in 1958 dollars. The town provided an office for him. He secured the staffing of his office
by marrying a competent, efficient and reasonably attractive
registered nurse. It was a sensible, practical marriage—even a
love match, if love of money on his part and of social status
on hers was love enough. He also owned the small hospital
where a few of the old and terribly sick hung on past the time
that their nearest and dearest could care for them and where a
few of the babies having trouble getting born either made it or
didn't. Dr. Evarts got kickbacks from drugstores and the drug
salesmen and the morticians and from the bigger hospitals in
Montgomery when he sent patients to them, usually for complicated operations. He was received in the finest homes as a
near equal. No more than a near equal; after all, no one was
ever going to confuse him with a Southerner.

Except for his twice-annual vacations, he was on call
twenty-four hours a day every day of the year. He paid a retired doctor from Montgomery to come out and tend his practice during his vacations, not because he cared that much
about his patients but he did not want to encourage any

poaching of his practice by hungrier physicians in reach of Tallassee.

Of course, he had to deal with Mamadee and the other grandees—*grandees* was one of Daddy's words for them, confusing me (when I was just a knee-baby) into a belief that all the superior folk of Tallassee were somehow related to me through Mamadee. Daddy also called them pooh-bahs. The grandees and pooh-bahs expected immediate attention, immediate relief, and then argued about the bill.

Dr. Evarts also treated the multitudinous diseases of the abjectly poor whites of the Alabama countryside when they could find a dollar or two. Pale and malformed and destitute, these unfortunates led lives hidden to all but the social worker, the sheriff, and the physician. They were deviled with diseases that Dr. Evarts's professors had declared eradicated. The dollar that he demanded from them for an office visit barely covered his costs, and for that reason alone, he slept the sleep of the just and righteous. His conscience was not so advanced for Dr. Evarts to treat coloreds. The nearest medical care for them was in Tuskegee, and how they got there or found the money to pay for their care, was of no interest to him. I learned later that when a colored male made the mistake of entering his office, Mrs. Evarts would determine if the man's complaint was likely to be syphilis, and if so, Dr. Evarts would direct the man to Tuskegee, to participate in the eventually notorious study in which syphilis was *not* treated. He was not the first or the only white physician to follow this practice; all the white physicians in the county had agreed to do it, as part of the study. I have read that colored physicians did also.

He was a good-looking man with a fine head of silvering hair—all the ladies said so. He must have been in his midforties at the time I knew him. Before his marriage, he had admired Mama, or so Mamadee claimed. Mama always smiled secretively when the subject came up. It strikes me as doubtful, given Mama would have been all of ten or eleven when Dr. Evarts arrived in Tallassee. Much of what I know about him, I learned as a child, overhearing Mama and Mamadee and their friends discussing him. The rest I discovered years later, in researching Daddy's murder.

Mamadee had ordered Ford and me to our rooms. Ford

lurked behind the balustrade of the grand staircase in Mamadee's foyer, peeking and listening. I went out a side door and up the nearest live oak with a view into the salon—hand over hand and in my socks. I could see Mama clearly. She paused to light a cigarette. Then she went on breaking

Krikkrik

the remaining bits of glass out of their muntings in the French doors. With the cigarette between her lips, she wielded a silver candlestick. It broke the muntings with a sound like a wishbone snapping.

Around the corner of the house, Dr. Evarts's two-year-old black Lincoln rolled on the gravel of the drive. Mamadee personally opened the door to him before he could ring the bell.

Mamadee rattled the key in the lock and flung open the door.

Mama had already slipped the candlestick behind the nearest sofa cushion. She flicked her cigarette out into the debris beyond the threshold of the broken doors.

Mamadee stopped short in feigned shock at the destruction.

Setting down his bag by the sofa, Dr. Evarts spoke in a soothing voice, "Now, Roberta Ann."

Disheveled, barefoot and bare-legged, she took a step toward Dr. Evarts and swooned into his arms.

"Oh, Lewis." She sobbed. And then, raising her face to the ceiling, she went on, "Sweet Jesus, thank you, thank you, for sending a friend in my time of need!"

Mama knew, of course, that Dr. Evarts had been called. She went all limp and weak in his arms and he carried her to the sofa.

"Roberta Ann," Dr. Evarts said gravely, "your mama is your best friend, you know. You have had a terrible time, haven't you? Forgive me, my dear, I am remiss. Please accept my deepest condolences."

Mamadee passed Mama her handkerchief and Mama wiped her eyes, allowing Dr. Evarts to slip a syringe from his bag.

"I'll bet you haven't slept since this horrible tragedy started, have you?" he said as he pumped the syringe, squirting a little fluid out the needle.

Seeing it now, Mama recoiled. "I do not need whatever that

is, Lewis. I just need for that damned lawyer to answer my questions."

With the syringe in one hand, Dr. Evarts swabbed at her near arm with a little pad. "This will get you to sleep, my dear." He paused to look at her bare legs appreciatively.

She yanked her arm away. "Who the hell do you think you are, Lewis Evarts? Mama wants you to knock me out and haul me off to the mental hospital, doesn't she? She wants everybody to think I am crazy. Well, I am not. I am as sane as you are, Lewis."

Dr. Evarts sighed and put down the syringe. "Roberta Ann, nobody is going to put you in the mental hospital. Now, you let me help you get to sleep. You'll feel a lot better in the morning."

"No! You can take that needle and stick it in Mama if you want. Then I will go over to Winston Weems's house and he *will* talk to me or I will know the reason why."

Dr. Evarts glanced quickly at Mamadee, who stood with her arms crossed, glaring at Mama.

"Win's had a gallbladder attack," Dr. Evarts told Mama. "I was there not an hour ago. He's no spring chick, Roberta Ann. It's all been a terrible shock to him too."

Mama was amazed, at least outwardly.

Out on my tree branch, I heard the lie in the doctor's voice. Mama could not, of course, though she assumed it. She never could hear the lie in her own voice. However could she hear it in anyone else's? How could she hear the truth and know it to be so? I have wondered if she did not spend her whole life assuming everyone was lying about everything all the time, all because she had a tin ear for truth.

"I knew it," Mamadee said. "Roberta Ann Carroll, you've thrown a big tantrum over an old man being too sick to come running at your beck and call. What would your daddy think of you, carrying on like you did not know any better?"

Dr. Evarts picked up the syringe again. He reached for Mama's arm.

"Lewis," Mama said. "Put that thing back in your bag and get me a glass of bourbon. That and a cigarette will put me right and I will sleep like a baby."

Dr. Evarts nodded and put the syringe away.

"Lewis," Mamadee protested.

"Mrs. Carroll," the doctor said, rising to his feet, "I think a little bourbon would do us all good."

Mamadee shot him a poisonous glare. One of the things—such as having the unplayed piano tuned—that Mamadee continued to do after Captain Senior's death, because she had always done it, was to keep the house stocked with the finest bourbons. Everyone knew it. Her circle relished the challenge of forcing her to part with a glass. Ford raided it whenever we visited, just to prove that he could.

Mamadee went to the salon breakfront, where behind glass doors dozens of crystal glasses stood holding their few ounces of empty air. In daytime, when the draperies were drawn open, the glasses broke the light into rainbows, just as prisms did in the antique shops Mama and I used to visit. Below the glass doors were mahogany doors, and behind those were cut-glass decanters, very like the ones in Penthouse B of the Hotel Pontchartrain in New Orleans.

On the side of the tree that was hidden from the house, Ford came scrambling up to look into the salon with me.

Mama tucked her legs underneath her on the sofa and lit a cigarette. Mamadee took out three glasses and a decanter. As she poured, Dr. Evarts admired the spill of bourbon into the glasses.

I touched the key on the string around my neck. I was hungry enough to eat the key and have the string for dessert. It was cold outside and I was shivering. Abandoning the tree to Ford, I went down it and retrieved my shoes.

I found Tansy at the table in the kitchen, eating a piece of the hot fruit casserole that was supposed to be dessert. Without invitation, I scrambled onto the other chair at the table. Tansy lumbered out of her chair to fetch a chipped dish and a cloudy glass from the cupboard where she kept dishes for her use and Leonard's. She poured milk for me and then spooned fruit casserole into the dish. She topped it with a scoop of vanilla ice cream and put it down in front of me, with a spoon.

Sitting down again with a grunt, she watched me while I wolfed the fruit casserole and drained the glass.

"You got any space for chicken pie?" Her tone was sarcastic.

I nodded violently.

Getting up again, she brought me a piece of the pie that been sitting on the top of her stove and was still warm. She refilled my glass. "Onliest one that wants my food is you. The Lord be's humblin' me. I'm thinking *'whatsomever you does for the least a mine, you does for me.'*"

"Thank you, Tansy. Did you see the snow?"

"Snow? Snow in Alabama! Lying be's a sin, Miss Calley Dakin!"

I changed the subject. "You got any Scotch tape?"

"What if I does?"

"I need some."

She studied me awhile, trying to decide if I was responsible enough to be entrusted with tape. When I had cleaned my plate and drained my glass again and said thank you yet again, she produced a roll of tape. It was yellowed with age.

"Don't you be gittin' up to no good with none of my Scotched tape," she said.

I held up my right hand and made the two-fingers-up, thumb-across-palm Girl Scout pledge gesture that I had learned from the older girls in the schoolyard.

"What's that hoodoo?"

"I promise," I said.

"Git. Yo face make me tired."

I left her muttering in the kitchen about spoiled white children, and what her mama would have done to her, had she wasted food, never mind the luxury of Scotch tape.

I bounded up the two flights of stairs to my room. The sticky on the tape was mostly dried up and I came to the end of the roll very quickly. The tape made an ugly as well as useless bandage. It would not hold paper doll Betsy McCall's neck and head stuck to her shoulders.

The room was as cold as it was outside. My stomach was too full. I just had time to yank the old pot from under the bed before Tansy's chicken pie, her hot fruit casserole and ice cream and a pint of milk, slightly used, made their reappearance in it.

Shortly after Dr. Evarts's car left, I heard Mama's bare feet on the stairs and then the door of Mama's bedroom slammed below me.

"Roberta Ann!" Mamadee called up the stairs but Mama made no answer.

I crept downstairs, pot in hand, and tapped on Mama's door. In a moment, Mama unlocked and opened it. She looked down at me, registered the pot in my hands, and made a face.

I slipped past her and took it into her bathroom to dispose of it.

Mama stood in the open bathroom door. "I suppose Tansy let you make a pig of yourself?"

I rinsed out the pot in the basin and then helped myself to Mama's Listerine. "You want me to rub your feet, Mama?"

"I am gone have a bath, Calley. You can wait in my bed. Go get your pajamas on while I draw my bath."

That was more than I could hope.

My pajamas were four days past their last wash at the Hotel Pontchartrain. I dropped them on the floor with my grey dress and underpants and socks. I did have clean underpants. I put them on and padded back to Mama's room.

"My pajamas are dirty," I told her when she let me in.

She sighed a long-suffering sigh and poked around in a drawer and found an old undershirt of Daddy's. It was cotton, softened by many wearings and washings. On me, it made an oversized nightdress, but at least I was decent. I was more than decent. I felt all at once as if Daddy's arms were around me.

"Don't wear those underpants to bed," Mama said, as if I didn't know that wearing underpants at night is nasty.

I dropped my underpants, picked them up and folded them the way I found them in my drawer at home: crotch up, sides over, like an envelope.

Between Mama's sheets, I hugged a pillow. As Daddy's undershirt warmed me, I realized I had been shivering and no longer was. My stomach was calmer. Perhaps because I felt better, I thought of Ida Mae Oakes. I let myself hope that she might come to see me, to offer her condolences. She might come straight to Ramparts, knock at the kitchen door, and be offered refreshment by Tansy, but insist on first seeing me. Or she might come to the funeral and the reception.

Mama had to wake me up when she came to bed. And we began a new ritual.

Mama had had Leonard place the footlocker with the ransom locked inside it in an even bigger old cedar chest at the foot of her bed. She strung the key to the cedar chest onto the red silk string around my neck. That first night at Mamadee's, when she had waked me again, she unlocked the cedar chest and checked the locker. Mama did not allow me to take the silk string off my neck and so I had to kneel down in front of the chests so she could fit the keys into the locks. It was so much like kneeling by the bed, I felt as if I ought to say the bedtime prayer.

That night I dreamt for the first time of finding such a footlocker and lifting the lid. Sometimes in my dreams—to this day—I find the ransom. Sometimes I find Daddy, alive, neatly folded like a jack-in-the-box, ready to pop up and surprise me. And sometimes I find what you would expect me to dream of finding: the nightmare, the bloody broken, profoundly *unpleasant,* nightmare.

Fourteen

WHEN I collected all my dirty clothes to give to Tansy, I kept Daddy's undershirt, hiding it away under the pillow on the cot upstairs.

It was Sunday. Mama told me to put on my overalls. That meant that we were not going to church. We had not been to church since leaving for New Orleans. Perhaps we were never going to go again. We were just going to kneel every night and every morning next to a footlocker full of money instead. Mama did not explain.

Mama teased Ford awake and made him come down to breakfast. He slumped in his chair, staring blearily at the bowl of cornflakes that Tansy put down in front of him. Mama put a spoon in his hand. Ford stirred it through the cereal listlessly.

"You are pining," Mama said. "That's all I need, two sick children."

Ford gave me a quick surprised glance. I made to puke over his bowl to show him how I was sick too.

Tansy turned away from us hurriedly, making an odd noise. She pretended it was a sneeze, snatching a handkerchief from her voluminous pinafore and blowing her nose but I believe that she was trying not to laugh.

"Of course," said Mama, "Calley did it to herself. Tansy, how could you let Calley eat herself sick? Don't give her a lick of dessert at dinner! You hear?"

"Yes, ma'am," Tansy agreed, as she filled Mama's coffee cup.

Ford let go of his spoon. It slid into the bowl of cornflakes.

Tansy picked it out with a small pair of sterling silver ice tongs. When she presented him with a clean spoon, Ford let it *thunk* dully onto the tablecloth.

"Ford, darling," Mama begged, "if you don't eat, you'll fade away to a shadow."

"When we goin' home?"

Mama turned to Tansy. "Tansy, I believe your brioche are much superior to the brioche at the Hotel Pontchartrain."

Tansy's smile went by so fast, it was hardly ever there.

Maybe the mention of the Hotel Pontchartrain reminded her that the brioche baker there had proved to be a homicidal maniac. When I saw Tansy's face go blank, it crossed my mind that Mama might have been a little more delicate in her compliment.

Ford gave Mama a minute or so and then asked, "You gone bust some more windows today?"

"Maybe I will. You want to help?"

"'Less I get a better offer."

Mamadee always had her first coffee in bed. Mama was still buttering brioche when Mamadee came down.

Ford immediately begged Mamadee to be excused and was, with a kiss.

"Excuse me, Mamadee," I piped up.

"Are you still here, Calley?" asked Mamadee, watching Ford's exit with the addled ecstasy of a dog tracking a raw steak.

"Yes, ma'am."

Her gaze moved glacially in my direction until she was staring at me. Then she made a noise of disgust—a *tzzt*.

"I'll be glad when the Good Lord closes my eyes and I don't have to look at your sullen pout until Judgment Day."

"Me too," I retorted airily.

"What?"

"I'll be glad when you're dead."

She slapped me across the face and then across the back of the head.

"Shame!" Then she clutched at her chest and sank back in her chair. "Vipers in my bosom!"

Having heard from more than one preacher that the Good Lord never sends us trials we cannot bear, I wanted to hang around to see if she died, but keeping in mind that she might still have strength for more slapping and calling on the Good Lord, I went as far as the door and stood outside it.

The heart attack passed instantly.

"I swear that child is not human at all. Some troll stole your real baby and left Calley in her place," Mamadee told Mama in a perfectly normal voice. "Winston Weems will be here at eleven-thirty, after church."

"Really." Mama lit a cigarette. "Gallbladder crisis all over?"

"It would seem so. I remember how I suffered with mine. Why, I begged Lewis Evarts to take it out and end my misery over and over, and he would not, because the operation is so dangerous. I was in bed from the day after Thanksgiving 1954, to Easter 1955, and thought sure I would faint and fall down right there in church, Easter Sunday."

Mamadee's medical and surgical reminiscences might very well continue; the list included, besides the gallbladder, four lying-ins, an appendectomy, kidney gravel, a hysterectomy and chronic migraine, all a lot tougher on Mamadee than on other individuals so afflicted.

From up in the old oak, I occupied myself watching Leonard remove the bits and pieces of the broken French doors and sweep up all the glass inside and out. He measured every which way and scratched the numbers in a greasy old notebook.

He went off for an hour and came back with his old daddy. Daddy Cook was at least as old and deaf as God but he still helped Leonard out when it was a two-man job. It wasn't the work he enjoyed so much as bossing Leonard. Leonard backed his old homemade pickup truck as close as he could and the two of them unloaded several sheets of plywood. Leonard told Daddy Cook what to do and then Daddy Cook, who hadn't heard a syllable of it, told Leonard what to do. Their method seemed to work just fine.

It looked like the salon was going to be too dark for Mama's meeting with Mr. Weems.

Old Weems drove up the driveway on the mark of eleven-thirty. He had his big lawyering briefcase with him. On the verandah, he stopped to mop his brow with his handkerchief.

By then I was on the roof outside the window of my room, in the shadow of the eaves, watching for him. Ford was inside on the iron-framed cot, leafing through an old *National Geographic* and snapping a brass cigarette lighter that he had found behind the paperback books on the shelf over the bed. The lighter did not work as it had no fuel in it but the clicking was sufficiently irritating to amuse Ford.

"He's here," I said.

Tansy admitted Mr. Weems into the house.

"He look sick to you?" Ford asked me.

"No more than usual. He's still all grey."

From the top of the short flight of stairs, I could hear Tansy showing Mr. Weems into my granddaddy's library. Then Mamadee came to make Mr. Weems welcome.

I hissed at Ford. He dropped the *National Geographic* and the two of us crept to the corner of the short flight, waiting for Mama to leave her bedroom.

Tansy stumped upstairs and softly knuckled Mama's door. Mama came out wearing one of her Lauren Bacall getups: her navy silk trousers with the sailor waist and a striped jersey, with high-heeled sandals. Her hair was up, revealing her slender neck and the sapphires set in gold flashing from her ears. She did not look like a widow. Of course, besides the store-bought weeds, she had only the clothes with her that she had packed for New Orleans.

When Mama and Tansy were safely down the stairs, Ford and I crept into Mama's bedroom and gently eased the door shut. Her room was over the library. Since the library hearth shared the chimney with the one in hers, all we had to do was stretch out on the hearth and put our ears to the cool ceramic tiles.

"Mr. Weems," I heard Mama say on entering Senior's library.

"Miz Dakin." Mr. Weems sounded cold and dry as a dug-up old bone. I wondered if he smelled that way too.

There was a settle in the library, with two chairs to either side. Mama took the chair on the side nearest me. Mamadee dithered a moment and then punished the settle. I do not mean that Mamadee was heavy. She had a biggish bottom but the rest of her was no more than well upholstered. What I mean is that the settle was on the delicate side. Mr. Weems lowered his skinny buttocks into the other chair.

"I trust you are recovered," Mama said.

"Thank you, my dear, I am." Mr. Weems coughed then, as if to threaten a relapse. "May I ask when the visitation hours will be?"

"Never. I am not having every fool in Alabama gawking at my husband's coffin and trying to imagine what's inside and what it looks like. The funeral will be the day after tomorrow at ten."

Mr. Weems drummed his fingertips nervously on the arms of his chair.

"I have spoken to the police," he said, "and also an agent from the Birmingham office of the Federal Bureau of Investigation. The FBI would like to interview you again at your earliest convenience. The search of the house has been completed. There is no objection to your returning there from either the police or the FBI. However, the lien-holder does object."

"The lien-holder?" Mama's voice faltered and then recovered to assert, "There are no liens on that property. Joseph bought it outright. We owned it free and clear."

"I am sorry to have to tell you, dear lady, that it is *not* free and clear. Your late husband, God rest his soul, mortgaged the property to the hilt. It has been in the process of foreclosure for some time. Had not the tragedy intervened, the foreclosure would have occurred on Ash Wednesday. The lien-holder has been patient because of the circumstances."

Mama jumped up. "I don't believe you! It's a lie! He would have told me. He never kept his business secret from me. You know perfectly well that he always wanted me to know everything! You've heard him say it yourself, that he would be dammed if he left me a widow without a clue, the way so many men leave their wives! I have my own checking account and not only did he keep it full, he never once told me that I spent too much or unwisely!"

Tansy's knock interrupted Mama's tirade. Tansy came in, bearing coffee things tinkling and liquids sloshing on a tray. Nobody said anything while she served. Mama lit a cigarette and moved around below me, hunting up an ashtray.

Once the catch of the door clicked closed again behind Tansy, Mama burst out again. "Winston Weems, this is bizarre, this is crazy!"

"It is *true*," Mr. Weems said stiffly. "The lien-holder is the Atlanta Bank and Trust of Atlanta, Georgia. Evidently your late husband did not want anyone in Alabama to know of his financial difficulties. Indeed, it was canny of him."

Mamadee sipped coffee. Remarkably, she had remained silent.

"I want to see the mortgage. And Joseph's will," Mama said, "right this minute."

Mr. Weems sighed. A creaking of hinges and old leather followed, as he opened the briefcase to extract a file.

"Mortgages," he corrected Mama. "The dealerships are mortgaged as well. Your late husband has been robbing Peter to pay Paul. Indeed, I fear there may be a question of fraud on his part." Mr. Weems sounded inordinately pleased. "See for yourself."

A weight of paper thumped onto the coffee table, followed by a scuffle of paper from the top.

"Here is the will. It is little more than boilerplate. As required by law, you as his widow receive one-third of the estate."

Mama blew smoke harshly. "What kind of game are you playing? I saw Joseph's last will when he updated it. It was hardly boilerplate. There are trust funds for the children and I am his residual legatee."

Mr. Weems went on, "This latest will was executed on February seventeen of this year. It was not executed in my office. I never saw it until it was discovered in your late husband's safety-deposit box here in the Carroll Trust. In this testament, Ford Carroll Dakin is the residual legatee, receiving the other two-thirds."

Mama's breathing was hardly louder than the whisper of the coal of her cigarette.

"Unfortunately," Mr. Weems continued, "there is no estate. There are no assets, only debts."

"That is not possible," Mama said.

There was a chink of china and a slop of coffee, the sounds of her pouring herself a cup with a less than steady hand.

"Lies, lies and libels. How dare you slander Joseph."

"You may not believe me, Roberta Ann," Mr. Weems replied, "but I am genuinely sorry for your loss, and genuinely appalled to discover the state of your late husband's affairs. The fact remains that he has left you with one-third of less than zero, and he has left young Ford with two-thirds of less than zero."

He stood. The briefcase latch snapped. "The lien-holder advises me that you may remove some personal effects from the house, under my supervision. The list is in the folder, along with my resignation. Good day, madam."

Mama took a single step forward and made a sudden movement. Liquid sloshed through the air and spattered something. From the immediate gasp, it was clear that the something was Mr. Weems's face. Mamadee gasped at nearly the same instant.

For a moment there was only sniffing and shuffling and the snap of Mr. Weems's handkerchief being whipped from his breast pocket. He cleared his throat and mopped his face, and then his tie and shirtfront.

Mama blew prideful smoke. Then she calmly poured herself another cup of coffee.

The lawyer picked up his briefcase and made for the door.

Mamadee followed him at his elbow, murmuring to him: *She was horribly embarrassed, horribly shocked, she would never be able to look him in the face again, poor Roberta Ann was unhinged with grief and shock, not that that was any excuse,* and more of the same.

Mama snorted contemptuously. Her nails scratched a little on the coffee table and the paper as she picked up the files. She took a few steps to the desk and the weight of paper whumped again onto it. The wheels of the desk chair creaked as she pulled it under herself and sat down.

She heaved a big disgusted sigh. "Joe Cane Dakin," she said, "I would like to dig you up and put you through a meat grinder! Hell will feel good to you when I get finished!"

Tansy opened the door without knocking.

Covering our mouths to stop ourselves giggling, we listened to Tansy's indignant heavy breathing and muttering as she mopped and wiped and scrubbed at upholstery and rug.

Ford and I did not speak until we were back in Junior's radio room. He flopped back onto the bed and stared at the ceiling.

"This is some fancy caper," he said. "Some scheme afoot. We need a detective."

I sat down at the end of the bed, next to Betsy Cane McCall. "This ain't TV or a movie or a story."

He crooked his arm to put his wrist under his head. "You know where this is headed, Dumbo?"

I shook my head. "No."

"The Chair. The Hot Seat. Your daddy got himself murdered and your mama hired it done."

I picked up Betsy Cane McCall and threw her at him. "Liar!"

He swatted Betsy Cane McCall away.

"*Your* daddy," I said. "*Your* mama. You will go to hell for lying about your own mama for the worst crime there is."

"Think so? There's worse. You ain't old enough to know what they are. One of them is havin' ears like yours though."

"The better to hear your lies," I said.

"You ain't special. You are a freak. A throwback Dakin. You know what a throwback is, don't you?" He came to his knees and pretended to be a monkey. *"Huhhuhhuh,"* he gibbered. Then he stopped being a monkey and put his feet on the floor. "You are a degenerate."

I waggled my ears at him.

He took a quick step toward me, grabbed me by the shoulder and tried to shove me off the end of the bed. My glasses nearly fell off my face. I shoved back and kicked him in one knee. His pretty Carroll eyes went all watery.

He staggered out of the room. He never could take it as hard as I could give it out.

The odd thing was that he never mentioned the ransom money, or the even odder fact that Lawyer Weems, Mamadee, and Mama had said nothing about it. It was as if it had evaporated.

I rearranged my glasses on my face and Betsy Cane McCall on the pillow.

In the early afternoon I went to see Mama.

"Go away," Mama said to my knock. Her eyes were full of dark worry. She looked melted with unhappiness.

I went to Mama and hugged her.

"Do you have giant plugs of wax in your *ears,* Calley Dakin? Did I say *go away?*"

She touched the keys hanging on my neck and checked the knot on the silk string. The string had come from one of her shoe bags.

"Calley, I have read those papers until I am half blind. Joe Cane Dakin is damned to hellfire for what he has done to me. That string around your neck with the keys on it is all we have got in this world for sure, so you better not lose it."

I might have asked about the ransom money but just then I heard the Edsel. She would have lied about it anyway. I raced out to meet Uncle Billy Cane Dakin.

Fifteen

"PLEASE, please, please, Mama," I begged.

I could tell that she was not listening. She was freshening her lipstick, and all her attention was on her lips in the mirror.

She and Ford were going to take the Edsel to our house in Montgomery to pack up those personal things that Mr. Weems had informed her that she could have. With Mama and Mr. Weems not on speaking terms, Mamadee was going also, in her Cadillac, to oversee Mama and make sure that she did not take anything not on Mr. Weems's list. We were allowed to have our own clothes and something called personal effects, which I construed to mean my paper dolls already cut out of their books. I reckoned that our clothes were the wrong sizes for anybody at the bank in Georgia that had foreclosed.

Mamadee insisted that Mama's jewelry was part of the estate. All the pieces that had been in the safe-deposit box in Montgomery had been seized when it was opened under Mama's power of attorney by Mr. Weems. But the jewelry Mama had taken to New Orleans was either on Mama or in Mama's pocketbook, and it was going to take Mamadee and Winston Weems and a whole army to get it away from her.

She barely glanced at me. "Calley, if you do not stop nagging at me, I'm gone slap you."

"It is a *silver* dollar."

She looked right at me as she capped her lipstick. "'It's a *silver* dollar,'" she mocked me. "Would you kindly strive to remember that I have a few other *concerns* on my mind?"

I was certain then that she would try to get to it before Ford did. The trick for me would be to steal it back. I did not want to go with her to get it myself. A shivery scared feeling choked me like a peach pit. If the house were empty of Daddy, it would prove that he was gone forever. And if Daddy *were* there, would he still be Daddy? He might be a haunt, or worse, if there was such a thing.

While they were gone, I climbed the oak to watch Leonard and Daddy Cook install the new French doors, replacing the ones that Mama had broken. They knew I was up here, so I did not have to try to be invisible. They did not mind if I sang a little, so I did, and sometimes they would sing with me, and then laugh, like it made them happy.

Tansy was in a good mood too; she brought out coffee and sandwiches and lemon cake for us all. Leonard brought her a lawn chair and she sat herself down and picnicked with us. Actually, I sat in the tree and she put my sandwich and a milk bottle of iced tea in a basket and I dropped a rope and hauled it up. It was more fun that way, and, for once, Tansy didn't seem to mind me having fun.

After we were all replete and patted our stomachs and observed that if we ate one more crumb, our bellies would burst, I climbed down and helped her take the dishes back to the kitchen.

Tansy tipped up her chin a little to signify upstairs, and told me that she was not being paid to mind children and to get out from under her feet before I broke something.

All that lunch made me sleepy. I went upstairs and flung myself on the iron cot. I did not wake until, from the depths of dreaming, I heard the Edsel and the Cadillac return. The afternoon had worn on, the light in the narrow room under the eaves begun to dim. I wiped the wet corners of my mouth on the pillowcase. Though the room was cool, I was sweaty. I had been having a daytime nightmare. Daddy's arms around me would not let go. Daddy's head tumbled from his shoulders. Judy DeLucca in her maid's uniform and a huge fat woman whom I did not know picked it up and tried to tape it back on with a huge strip of Scotch tape. I wanted to cry out for Ida Mae but my throat was cut and taped too, my voice stuck like lint on the sticky side.

Suddenly everyone except me was going in and out of the

house, up and down stairs, in and out of bedrooms. Leonard and Tansy and Mamadee and Mama and Ford trucked in boxes and suitcases. It was boring to hear. I waited for Leonard to bring me up a suitcase or a box of my clothes, maybe even some toys. What could a bank want with my doll-house? But he did not, because they had not brought any of my clothes or things from the house in Montgomery. What I had was what I would have.

Not until I could look them in the eyes, or hear the lies, either in their voices or in their silences, would I know whether Mama or Ford had gotten to my silver dollar first. I was relieved. I would outgrow the clothes anyway and the toys too. If Mama and Ford had brought me nothing from our house that was no longer our home, they had left behind whatever might have clung to those things as well. The very dust of our old house might bear some dreadful unknown bad luck or curse or haunt. That house was a closet of memories that I needed to lock away until I was old enough to examine them safely.

Sixteen

ON one side of the church sat the governor and his wife, the mayors of Montgomery, Birmingham, and Mobile, a delegation from the Ford Motor Company in Detroit, most of the successful businessmen of Alabama, most of the grandees and pooh-bahs of Montgomery and Tallassee and points in between and thereabout, Dr. and Mrs. Evarts, the two FBI agents from Birmingham, and Mamadee, Ford, Mama and me.

The most interesting to me of the group of dignitaries was the director from the Ford Motor Company. His hair looked painted on. When the light struck his rimless glasses just right, he seemed to be as empty-eyed as Little Orphan Annie. He had no discernible lips either, and his teeth looked older than he did. He looked like he might be cold to the touch, like a croaker. I thought he must be Mr. Henry Ford, the younger one, but I found out next day from the newspaper that his name was Mr. Robert S. McNamara. The *S* stood for Strange, which in itself was impossible to forget.

On the other side were about four hundred Dakins, or so Mama said, but Ford told me later that small-business people and a passel of country folk actually filled most of those pews.

"About a hundred of them were Dakins," Ford said. "Hundred and one, counting you, and a hundred and one and maybe half, counting you and what's left of Daddy."

He didn't count himself. It was fine by me if Ford didn't want to be counted a Dakin.

Mama had always emphasized the unregenerate wickedness of the Dakins—by which she meant that they did not have any money. So instead of paying attention to the minister or to the woman at the organ whose amazingly orange hair was marcelled like Mamadee's, or thinking about Daddy lying dead and chopped up in the coffin, I stared across the aisle at my uncles and their families, and all the kin that I barely knew. My Uncles Dakin—Jimmy Cane, Lonny Cane, Dickie Cane, Billy Cane—uncomfortable in their cheap and rarely worn suits, sat solemn as a row of old men in rocking chairs on the verandahs downtown on a Saturday night. Like the surface of the moon, their complexions were deeply scarred and thickened. Their wives, the Aunts Dakin—Jude, Doris, Gerry, Adelina—were uniformly slack at the bosom, as though mother's milk and comfort had been sucked right out of them. Though not all were bone-thin, the fat they carried looked dense and hard. The flowers in their hats were faded, their dresses to a woman, the plastic-belted, collared rayon shirt-waist in every size and any color, so long as it was dark, that hung on the racks at Sears. My cousins, the Sons Dakin, were numerous and fidgety. They did not take well to the hard oaken pews and the hand-me-down jackets that pinched in the shoulders or were too short in the sleeve. There were too many of them for me to remember all their names or to whom they belonged. They did a good deal of sniggering and staring at Ford and me. There were no Daughters Dakin.

At least on that side of the church. On our side of the church, there was me. I had new white gloves and a new hat, a white straw boater with a black ribbon band and streamers, which Mama had had to go out and buy when she realized that I didn't have a thing to put on my head or hands for the funeral. As usual she bought the hat too big, so it would fit down over my twinned ponytails and ears. Wisps of straw tickled my ears unmercifully. When I tried to look around more, Mamadee dug her fingernails into the nape of my neck.

Mama had, of course, expected the worst of the Dakins but none of them wept audibly, though their bandanna hankies got used to mop up the occasional tear and they blew their noses loudly. At least there were no outbreaks of "Praise Jesus." When they looked at Mama at all, it was sidelong.

Outside the church, before we got into the cars for the

graveyard, my uncles held their hats in their hands and yanked at the hard, tight knots of their ties.

Aunt Jude hugged me and cried, "You poor baby! I know you are desolate."

The other aunts murmured their agreement and patted my head.

Mama hastened to say, "This little girl is not a particle as desolate as I am. Not a particle."

But the aunts did not touch Mama and they did not speak to her directly. Mama mistook this as a signal of respect for her person and her station. The Dakins did not bother with Ford either, or Mamadee, and Mamadee and Ford did not bother with the Dakins.

On the off chance that they were voters, the governor came over and shook the hands of the Uncles Dakin. He paid no attention to the Aunts Dakin. Likely as not, they voted the way their husbands did, or not at all.

We got into the Edsel that had been washed clean of road dust first thing in the morning by Leonard. Mama had driven us to St. John's in Montgomery in it. Mama was not about to ride in Mamadee's Cadillac. She and Mamadee were only speaking to say pass-the-salt-please and thank-you and whatever cuttingly courteous spitefulness they could invent.

The drive to the graveyard was so long that I dozed off. When the Edsel came to a stop and I woke up, we were out in the country. Mama crammed my hat back onto my head and I straightened my glasses on my face. I had been expecting one of the cool shady green cemeteries in Montgomery or Tallassee. Mamadee had said that Daddy's burial would be a circus unless it was out in the backside-of-the-moon. Evidently she had won over Mama on that count.

But there was no grass, just prickly weeds in patches. The weeds were rooted in coarse sand, amid pebbles with edges so sharp I could feel them biting the soles of my Mary Janes. Crumbling concrete marked out the sunken rectangles of the graves and all the tombstones tilted forward as if they wanted a better look at the man or woman or child or stillborn infant they commemorated. On nearly every grave a cracked clay pot or old milk bottle held dried-up old flowers. The few trees thereabout were all bent and scraggly and seemingly half dead. They looked like the paper trees we cut out in kindergarten for Halloween decorations, so the bats and ghosts would have some background beside the moon. On one raggedy pine perched a crow. Its beak prospected busily underneath one wing.

"Where are we?" I whispered dry-mouthed to Ford.

"Hell," Ford said. Adding, "This is where they bury Dakins."

He snatched off my glasses and smeared them with his thumbs, before flipping them back to me. While I was trying to get them back on my face, he pushed me toward Mama.

Blinking through the blur on my lenses, I caught up with Mama and grabbed at her gloved hand. "Where is this, Mama?"

"The Promised Land. Where your daddy bought himself a plot. That's what they call it. The Promised Land."

I wasn't old enough to wonder why Daddy had bought this plot, or when, or why just one plot instead of a family one. It was more significant to me that when I looked around, Mamadee's Cadillac was nowhere to be seen, nor was she, nor any of the other grandees or notables or pooh-bahs.

The two FBI agents had come though; I saw them getting out of their black Buick sedan, and taking off their fedoras. One of them had a bald spot. I had known they were FBI agents as soon as I had seen them drive up to Ramparts on Monday. They looked like the other ones, the ones in New Orleans. Mr. J. Edgar Hoover must have figured if they all looked the same, nobody would notice them. Maybe *men* wouldn't notice them. Any half-wit woman would notice right off, two men looking like they dressed out of the same closet.

The pair of agents had spent most of Monday afternoon with Mama. They had been very interested in the papers that Mr. Weems had turned over to her. She had to develop a sick headache to get them to leave.

Ford and Mama and I were on one side and the tribe of Dakins were on the other, just like at the church, except that now it wasn't the church aisle between us, it was Daddy's coffin, being lowered into Daddy's grave.

That graveyard is still my image of the life—of the

death—that comes after dying. Blurred. Recognizable but barren of any comfort whatever.

The woman with the marcelled orange hair who had played the organ during the funeral service came around with limp sheets of mimeographed paper that smelled of pears. The green plastic frames of her cat's-eye–shaped glasses were studded with glittering rhinestones. She was wearing Tangee lipstick, I could tell.

"Calley and I will share," Mama said.

"No," the woman said pleasantly, "the little girl gets one of her own."

She held out the limp pages and I took one. Not from the top and not from the bottom, but from somewhere in the middle of the limp stack. Typical of the mimeograph process, the words were smeary, and the greasy state of my lenses did not help me in making out the words. The gloves on my hands made holding the sheet difficult as well.

These were hymn sheets. As they were passed out to all the Dakins, a preacher—not the one from St. John's but a rotund lay preacher with mail-order dentures and a shiny-seated suit—recited the verses about *To Everything There Is a Season*. It is very popular at funerals, presumably comforting to the mourners, but in this instance, I realized when I was some years older, it was grotesquely inappropriate.

When the preacher was through, the woman with the marcelled orange hair raised up her hand as if everyone had been talking and she wanted silence, though no one was doing anything at that point but clearing throats, blowing noses, and shuffling from one foot to another.

She shut her lips tight and hummed a note.

Then all the Dakins began to sing.

> *There's a land that is fairer than day,*
> *And by faith we can see it afar;*
> *For the Father waits over the way*
> *To prepare us a dwelling place there.*

I sang the way Daddy did. Mama sang very loudly, to drown me out. Ford stepped on the side of my foot, which only made me sing louder. None of the Dakins seemed the least surprised that I could sing like Daddy. We all sang the word *there* to rhyme with *afar,* which made Mama cast her eyes heavenward very briefly. No archangel of proper pronunciation saw fit to punish us with a lightning strike, however.

> *In the sweet by and by,*
> *We shall meet on that beautiful shore;*
> *In the sweet by and by,*
> *We shall meet on that beautiful shore.*
> *We shall sing on that beautiful shore*
> *The melodious songs of the blest,*
> *And our spirits shall sorrow no more,*
> *Not a sigh for the blessing of rest.*

It was on the chorus after this second verse that I got into trouble. The words on my mimeographed sheet were different from everybody else's.

Everybody else had the chorus just as it was before. But the words I sang were just for me:

> *By the dark of the moon*
> *Thou wilt rise on that beautiful shore*
> *In the ashes and ruin*
> *And Thy bones will be washed of all gore.*

Uuuuhk shrieked the crow in the raggedy pine.

As soon as we had finished the chorus and all the Dakins were starting on the fourth verse, Mama grabbed the mimeographed page out of my hand and hissed at me, "Calley, what in the hell are you doing?"

> *To our bountiful Father above,*
> *We will offer the tribute of praise*
> *For the glorious gift of His love,*
> *And the blessings that hallow our days.*

I tried to get the page back from her—the mimeographed page that I had chosen from out of the limp stack that the woman with the orange marcelled hair had offered to me. The page I had chosen the way a volunteer from the audience chooses a card from the magician's proffered deck. The page that had a message on it meant just for me.

But Mama threw it into the hole under Daddy's coffin in the ground. It fluttered down like Betsy McCall's head when I sliced it off. Then the Uncles Dakin lowered Daddy's coffin into the crumbling pebbly earth on top of it. It seemed to me less that they were interring Daddy than that they were making certain I could not retrieve the ripe-pear-smelling mimeograph.

I threw myself onto the coffin, only to be snatched out by the long arms of an uncle. I struggled wildly in the tightening enclosure of those strong arms.

" *'You are my sunshine,'* " I sang out, " *'you make me happy when skies are grey.'* "

Hushing and shushing me, Uncle Billy Cane Dakin carried me away.

Seventeen

THE funeral reception for Daddy was at Uncle Jimmy Cane Dakin's house—a big old place in the backside-of-the-moon country outside of Montgomery. When I saw the place, I realized that Mamadee must have won this battle too.

Uncle Jimmy Cane's house was sided in wide weather-beaten unpainted boards. It had narrow doors, narrow short windows with only a couple of panes each, and three or four dormers indicating a warren of half-story rooms that were surely as frigid in the brief Alabama winter as they were sweltering the other ten months of the year. A wide, dusty porch undulated three-quarters of the way around the house. The whole thing stood raised up on stacks of brick five feet high, with cool dark sand beneath where snakes made swirled patterns and raised miniature dunes. A dusty field that in another season would be scabby with a failing crop of some unpalatable vegetable planted by Uncle Jimmy Cane Dakin, his wife, Gerry, and their pack of boy Dakins surrounded the house.

Mama had no intentions of going inside. She parked the Edsel a few yards from the house. Uncle Jimmy Cane Dakin brung an old twig chair down from the porch and arranged it next to the car for Mama. There she smiled a sad smile and spoke a few soft words from behind her veil to various Dakins when they approached her with their halting condolences.

Ford took off his tie and stuffed it into his jacket pocket. He refused even to look around but slumped into the backseat with his hat yanked down to cover most of his face.

Mama said, "Calley, go inside and see if you can find me

something to drink with ice in it. And wash the dead bugs out of the glass before you pour anything into it, you hear me?"

Mama said this last just loudly enough to be overheard by a Dakin or two, and just softly enough that they might think she had not so intended.

The Uncles and Aunts and Cousins Dakin parted before me, creating a winding path that led up to the creaking wooden steps. They murmured and cooed at me soothingly.

The screened door opened before I touched the handle. The woman with the marcelled orange hair, the very one who had played the organ at St. John's and passed out the hymn sheets at the Promised Land graveyard, beckoned me inside.

I had visited Uncle Jimmy Cane Dakin's house half a dozen times with Daddy but this visit—final, though I did not know it—is what I remember of it. In the Edsel, I had made a surreptitious effort to clear the lenses of my glasses with the hem of my dress without significantly improving their clarity, so I continued to see everything in a haze. The rooms were square and high-ceilinged. The sun had bleached the chintz curtains in the windows almost colorless. Long dried-out wallpaper with patterns faded past comprehension blistered and peeled on the plastered wall. The linoleum on the floor buckled like the coverlet on a slatternly made bed. The kitchen sink wore a homemade skirt made of a worn-out checkered tablecloth, while there were no proper kitchen cupboards, only open shelves on iron brackets. Aunt Gerry cooked on a wood-fired black-iron range, ironed with the flatiron on the shelf above the burners, and stored perishables in an icebox. The kitchen smelled strongly of the beagles that slept behind the stove.

I kept looking through the open doorways for a glimpse of Uncle Jimmy Cane Dakin or Aunt Gerry, or Aunt Jude or Uncle Billy Cane—anyone at all would do, so long as it was not this woman I did not know, who had given me that mimeographed sheet of pear-smelling paper in the graveyard. My stomach roiled with uneasiness.

"I am not *really* a Dakin," the woman confided in me, as she drew me deeper into the house. "My half-sister's niece by marriage married one of Jimmy Cane Dakin's grown-up boys, but he was killed when his pickup ran into a five-point deer on the Montgomery highway, and later she died giving birth to triplet sons. Only one of the boys survived but he was never right in the haid. So I am not a Dakin, like you are, but I am connected to the family, so I guess I am connected to you."

I nodded in mute agreement.

"How is Roberta Ann Carroll Dakin taking it? The death of your daddy, I mean?"

It seemed odd how she called Mama *Roberta Ann Carroll Dakin* instead of *your mama*. The oddity made me cautious how I answered.

"Everybody says it is hard on her."

"That's right," said the woman with the orange marcelled hair—as if her question had been *What is the capital of North Dakota?* and my answer had been *Bismarck*.

"And by the way," she said, as if this were my reward for having given the right answer, "my name is Fennie."

"Fennie what?"

"Fennie Verlow. I have already prepared a glass of sweet tea for Roberta Ann Carroll Dakin, who must be exhausted with holding up in the face of her desolation and grief. Just let me add some ice and you can take it out to her."

Fennie came up with a handful of ice cubes from a cooler on the kitchen table, and dropped them one by one into the tall glass of sugared tea.

"Take it to Roberta Ann Carroll Dakin, honey." As I took the glass from her hand, she added, "And you can tell her that I washed all the bugs out the glass before I poured the tea."

When I repeated Miz Verlow's message, Mama's eyes widened behind her veil as if she had seen a ghost. Her fingers failed to grip the glass and the iced tea spilled out onto the crumbling track the front tire had made in the bright sandy earth. Mama swooned, seeming to melt right there in the twig chair. Aunt Jude and Aunt Doris and Aunt Gerry hurried over. One of them lifted her veil back over her hat so they could pat Mama's cheeks, daub her temples with dampened hankies, and coo comfort at her.

Mama came around long enough to whisper weakly, "Today had more hours in it than I expected."

Then Mama's eyes rolled up in her head. She would have slipped right out the chair if Miz Verlow had not suddenly been there to help the aunts. The four of them gently lifted her into the front passenger seat of the Edsel.

Miz Verlow whispered in Mama's ear. Nobody was close enough to hear but me and Ford, who had dropped his hat and leaned forward in the backseat.

"You caint drive this car, Miz Dakin. You are a desolate widow with two orphan children and no man to guide you or provide for you or side with you against the world. So ride soft and ride safe and let me take you home. You sleep cool and cushioned and dream of Joe Cane Dakin like he was still alive. I will drive you safe home."

At first, I took it that Mama was unconscious again and did not hear any of Miz Verlow's soothing instructions. But I was wrong.

Mama heard enough to murmur, "You drive. I just want to close my eyes. Don't let Calley talk."

The Aunts Dakin finished loading up the trunk of the Edsel with the funeral baked meats, jars of soup, covered casseroles, foil-covered tins containing things that were baked in layers, wrapped-up cakes, pies with crusts that floated like scum over chunks of unknown fruit in dark syrup, and Nehi drink bottles filled with dense, sugary liquids and stoppered with saturated corks. And all these foods smelled of burned dyes, warping linoleum, unwashed bodies, and the spattered residue of rendered fat.

Ford and I sat silently in the backseat, both of us tensely aware of Mama's condition. Mama breathed slowly, unmoving as Miz Verlow adjusted the visor against the sun.

As we passed a Tallassee town line sign, Mama's eyes fluttered. A moment later, she stretched and yawned and began to grope for her Kools in her brown Hermès Kelly bag.

"Calley," she said, "show this nice lady—whoever she is, and it does not seem to me that she could possibly be a Dakin—show this nice lady the way to Rosetta's. We are going to leave all that food at her house. It was very nice of the Dakins to go to all that trouble. But I will not—and you will not—we will never—eat anything that was cooked by a white woman who cannot write her own name."

"Aunt Jude can write her own name," I volunteered. "Daddy says she gone all the way to the tenth grade."

Ford said, "Shut up."

"Amen," said Mama.

"I already know the way to Rosetta's," said Miz Verlow. "And by the way, my name is Fennie Verlow."

Mama spoke around lighting the cigarette between her lips. "Pleased to make your acquaintance."

I said, "And she is not a Dakin either."

Ford whipped his tie out of his jacket pocket and snapped it at me.

"You think I would have said what I said if she had been?" asked Mama.

Mama and Fennie Verlow laughed together.

Rosetta's girls unpacked all the food and carried it inside her house. Before the trunk had been even half emptied, children and neighborhood mothers were clustering at the back door. When all that was done, Miz Verlow drove us to Ramparts.

"Calley, Ford, help Roberta Ann Carroll Dakin inside the house," Miz Verlow instructed us. "She is still far from completely herself."

Ford and I helped Mama up the steps—she was indeed still somewhat shaky—and we beat on the front door until Mamadee came herself to open it.

The instant Mamadee saw me, she said, "Somebody *else* better be dead, Calley Dakin, because there is no other excuse for you making a racket like that!"

Mama swayed just then, and it looked to me like it might be Mama who was the somebody else dead. But Mamadee did not want to believe that Mama wasn't carrying on.

"Roberta Ann Carroll," she scolded. "Get your head up and stand up straight and breathe."

Tansy arrived, still wiping her hands on her apron, and took Mama's arm. With Ford on her other side, they set out to help Mama upstairs. Mamadee followed them, ragging at Mama the whole way, accusing her of carrying on to get sympathy.

"You would think you were the first woman ever widowed! Other women bury their husbands *every day*," Mamadee declared.

I chortled at the image that came instantly to mind: mobs of black-clad women wielding shovels, the coffins of their husbands sitting handy to the holes the widows were digging.

Maybe each woman had more than one husband to bury. Maybe the husbands didn't stay buried, but dug their way out every night, and the widows went through the burying all over again the next day.

Then I remembered Miz Verlow was just outside, waiting for someone to ask her inside. People who did favors for the Carrolls were asked inside and served a glass of sweet tea. If white, the helpful soul was served sweet tea in the second parlor, and if colored, in the kitchen.

When I opened the front door, Miz Verlow was not waiting on anybody or anything. The key to the Edsel was on its hood.

Eighteen

MAMA really had been overcome. I knew how poorly she slept at night and how little she ate. My own sleeplessness kept pace with hers, so I was perpetually wore out. When I ate, I ate ravenously, causing my meals and snacks to come right back up. After this happened several times, Mamadee declared me unfit to sit at the table and banished me to the kitchen. Tansy must have felt some pity for me, for she fed me plain boiled rice and canned peaches, which I usually could retain. To make sure everybody knew that advantage was being taken of her, she grumbled the whole time about having to cook separate meals.

Mama spent the days immediately following the funeral first writing notes back to all the people who sent flowers to the funeral, and their condolences, and, in a cloud of cigarette smoke, going over and over Daddy's papers. The FBI agents visited again, sometimes for short conversations, sometimes for lengthy ones. Mama flirted with both of the agents, and from their responses, it was clear that they were charmed. Or taken in.

Not surprisingly, Mama's migraines plagued her so much that she used up all the BC and Goody's Headache Powder in the house.

One night while I was giving her a foot rub, Mama said, "I ran into your friend at the drugstore."

"What friend?"

"You know. What's-her-face. Orange hair. Fannie."

"Fennie, I think. Miz Verlow. How could Miz Verlow be my friend, Mama? She's a grown-up lady. What did she say?"

"Oh, she just ran on like she thought I was somebody who cared. Told me her sister had a house on the beach near Pensacola—as if I cared whether her sister was alive or staring at the wrong side of a coffin lid—and said we could go down there and stay for a while."

"Where's Pensacola?"

She ignored the question. "I would *never*—and when I say *never* I am talking about the eternity of the angels—I would *never* throw myself on the mercy of a Dakin."

Mama expected me to remind her that Fennie was not really a Dakin. I stayed silent. My mind was jumping ahead to looking up Pensacola and finding out where it was, as soon as I could do it without Mama knowing.

"Or anyone else for that matter," Mama concluded.

She could not help a quick glance at the cedar chest that held the footlocker.

Everybody knew *everything,* as they always do.

Everybody knew that Mama had arranged for Daddy to be buried like a dead dog in a ditch in the middle of nowhere.

Everybody knew that if Mama had had the nerve to hold a proper reception after the funeral, all the rich and powerful and respected people who had known Daddy would not have attended, for fear of association with a suspected murderess.

Everybody knew that Daddy had somehow embezzled his own assets and Mama had had him murdered, no doubt in hope, at the very least, of getting the insurance.

Everybody also knew that Mama had embezzled his assets and then arranged to have him murdered.

Everybody knew that Mama must have done something truly terrible to my daddy to get him to revoke a generous will and leave Mama the legal minimum.

Even Mama was frightened—though she never said so aloud—that he had done it to punish her for something that either she hadn't remembered doing, or had failed to realize at the time was so horrible as to justify such a revenge. And Mama was frightened that the FBI kept rummaging through Daddy's papers, and asking her questions. Mama had a lot of fears, many of them entirely justified.

Only once did anyone wonder aloud why Daddy had omitted me entirely from the will. Rosetta, the colored woman who sewed Mama's clothes, to whom we had taken the funeral meats, was pinning Mama, to take in a waist, up in Mama's room. Rosetta had been Mama's seamstress since Mama was a girl, and even after Mama married Daddy and moved to Montgomery. Sometime long ago, Rosetta had been Mamadee's seamstress, but they had had a falling-out. It was to spite Mamadee that Rosetta went on sewing for Mama, and Mama went on hiring her. Rosetta had not forgotten the specifics of her own quarrel with Mamadee, but she had long since settled into taking Mama's side.

Rosetta asked Mama, "But why dint Mr. Dakin Are-Eye-Pee, leave something to—?" with a jerk of her head in my direction.

I was cross-legged on the floor, pinning scraps Rosetta had given me on Betsy Cane McCall.

The look Mama gave me, the question was brand-new to her.

"Probably he thought Calley was not his child," Mama said. "Course I do not think she's mine either."

I pretended not to hear Mama's answer. I stuck Betsy Cane McCall with one straight pin, right in her head.

Of course I was Daddy's child. Had not Mama and Mamadee informed me all my life at every opportunity that I was pure-D, backside-of-the-moon Dakin?

The fact is, *I* was excluded from the will—though the estate be nothing at all—but Mama had not been. If Mama saw everything that had happened as a plot against her, it was natural for me to feel the same way, only more so. It meant little to me in terms of wealth. A seven-year-old with a sweaty dime in hand is wealthy. My silver dollar meant more to me than a million-dollar ransom. But now that it was pointed out to me, I could not help wonder if Daddy had forgotten me. Or worse. The only comfort was in clinging to the belief that the will was fake.

Being at Ramparts had begun to seem less like a visit and more like an exile. I missed going to school. I surely did not want to go home to our old house in Montgomery. I did not know where I wanted to be, other than not at Ramparts. I daydreamed about Pensacola, in Florida, on the coast of the Gulf of Mexico, where Fennie Verlow's sister lived.

Ford grew more tiresome, indeed loathsome, with every passing day. When not trying to trip me up on the stairs or trap me in a corner to gooch me or pull my hair, he tormented Mama. He would come into whatever room she might be in, sit down and stare at her wordlessly. If she spoke to him, he would not answer. If she tried to give him a hug or a kiss, he would flinch away from her or even push her away.

At first Mama was puzzled. Then his coldness and rejection began to frighten and distress her. I might have doubts that she loved me but there was no doubt about her feelings for Ford.

Her already troubled sleep frayed to near-nothing, I knew—despite having a bed of my own up that short flight of stairs to Junior's radio room, I managed to go sleep in her bed after rubbing her feet every night. Several times a night, she would get up and go into the bathroom to smoke. She lost weight that she did not have to lose. When she put on her makeup in the morning, she often paused for long moments, staring at herself. Sometimes she seemed to be looking at herself critically. Other times, she seemed to be looking through the mirror into some other time and place. The darkness around her eyes scared me.

One day Ford would not get out of bed. After he wet the bed, Mamadee called Dr. Evarts, who came and talked to Ford. Then he talked to Mama and Mamadee. He told them that Ford was deeply affected by Daddy's death and the family situation. Ford was high-strung, Dr. Evarts explained, and the shock had been terrible for him. Without question Ford was *scarred for life* and must be *handled with kid gloves*.

What *handled with kid gloves* meant was soon evident. Mamadee went out and bought a color television set for Ford and had it installed in his bedroom. Just getting it up the stairs required both Leonard and the man from the appliance store. Ford settled in to spend most of his time on his bed, watching television. Tansy brought him meals on a tray.

Sometimes Ford pretended to sleepwalk. In that state, he might pee directly out the window. Or he might go into the kitchen and eat whatever he wanted, drinking milk right out of the bottle, or juice from the pitcher, or spoon sugar directly from the bowl to his mouth. He might let a glass or dish drop from his hand on the floor and stand there amid the shattered bits with a look of confusion on his face as if he did not know where he was or how the dish or glass had come to be broken.

I came out of the house early one morning, so as not to wake anyone else up, and found a note under a windshield wiper of the Edsel. It was on pink paper and written in green ink. It read

Murderess

The pink paper was damp, not with dew but scent, Mama's scent. Shocking. I ran back into the house and got Mama up to come out to see it. She was not happy to be waked from the few morning hours of sleep that she was getting.

"This better be important," she threatened, pocketing her cigarettes and lighter in her dressing gown.

The note woke her up in the wrong way. She snatched the paper out from under the wiper and tore it to bits.

Then she slapped me. "If you didn't do this, just count it as a warning not to copycat."

But it was not the last note. They turned up in her handbag, on her pillow, in the frame of the vanity mirror in her bedroom, even in her pockets. They were all on pink paper, all written in green ink, and all said the same thing. After she tore them to bits and flushed them, she did not acknowledge them. She locked up her scent in the cedar chest. When she thought no one would notice, she looked all over the house for the pink paper and for a green ballpoint pen. She never found either item. She seemed not to understand that even if she did, she still would have no proof of the identity of her tormentor.

If Ramparts was no refuge, she could not show her face anywhere in Tallassee—in the drugstore, the church on Sunday—without being followed by whispers that were just barely whispers. If the words were too soft for her to make out, the tone was audible always, and always it was accusatory. Mama kept her spine straight and her head up but in the privacy of Ramparts, she was jumpy. Every passing day was like the Chinese water torture (a practice Ford read about in one of his boys' yarns and threatened me with whenever he remembered it), wearing her down a little more and a little bit more.

We stayed at Ramparts through the warming days and nights, through dogwood and magnolia blossoms, the leafing out of the trees, the return of the hum of bees and the racket of the birds courting and nesting—a period of about two months. For most of that time, I was able to be out of doors. Mama was preoccupied and nobody else seemed to notice whether I was there or not either. I didn't care whether they did or not; I just wanted to be out of sight and hearing of Mamadee and Ford— my enemies, my tormentors. Away from them, I could remember Daddy. Out of their hearing, I could speak and sing to myself in his voice, so as not to forget it.

My childhood memory of Tallassee was that it was an up-and-down sort of place, in the middle of which a great wall of water fell over a dam and raised a mist. The ups-and-downs were much greater, the houses and stores and trees much larger, the streets much longer, of course, to a child of seven. I wandered all over. In the margins of the old bird and tree books on Junior's bookshelf, I marked the ones that I already knew and the ones that I encountered in my meanderings. Grackles and catbirds, hickory and catalpa. The names in my mouth were satisfying. It felt a little like being in school again.

Frequently I tramped to the Birmingham & Southeastern train depot. Bump & Slide Easy, Daddy used to call it. No regular passenger trains stopped there anymore—though the mail still did—and the depot was next door to abandoned. The windows of the old depot were tall, with low sills that allowed me to peer through the glass that was as dusty as an old blind woman's eyes. In Sunday school and in church, I had heard many times that we see through a glass darkly. As I peered into those windows into the depot I realized all at once that a *darkly* was not an object like a pair of sunglasses or binoculars but an adverb, describing a manner of seeing. Because right then, I was seeing through a glass darkly.

Nineteen

GETTING an even dozen blown clean without cracks took me nineteen eggs. Tansy had herself a satisfying rag about it but the only real consequences of my combined profligacy and clumsiness would be a head of meringue to shame the Pope on the lemon pie. After girdling the eggshells with strips of lace ribbon, I dyed them in water and vinegar and food coloring. While they dried, I wove a paper basket and collected hanks of Spanish moss to make a nest in it for the eggs. Slipping the ribbons off the eggshells, I found the results exquisite. I placed them in the basket with a care that was not less than a jeweler might give to a Fabergé egg, and centered the basket on the dining table.

It was the first time we went to church after Daddy's funeral, and because it was Easter, Mama had a new outfit. Since Ford was scarred for life, he stayed home. Otherwise he would have had a new suit, which he probably would need, for despite his terrible bereavement, he was growing like Japanese knotweed. Mamadee had a new outfit. Rosetta the seamstress clucked a little when she found out that I did not have all new clothes, as everyone knew that new clothes on Easter brought good luck, and old ones, bad. Even at seven, I thought the custom was silly, since it should be obvious that anyone with new clothes had enough good fortune to afford them, and old clothes were surely sign of poverty or perhaps meanness.

I wore my grey dress and my black Mary Janes, which were good enough for Daddy's funeral, and was told by Mamadee to be grateful to have a straw boater and gloves I had only worn once. I fidgeted through Sunday School before the service, and then, during Easter service, I fought the scent of lilies so thick that it was smothering. I actually fell asleep for a few seconds at a time, only to jerk awake again. A strange thought intruded: If I were Jesus, I wasn't having any success moving the rock aside.

On our return from church, having taken off my boater and gloves, I went directly to the table that was now set for dinner to admire my basket of eggs. Mamadee followed me but she did that all the time and I thought nothing of it. I assumed that she wanted to make sure that I didn't break any of her crystal.

"Exquisite," I murmured to myself.

From behind me, Mamadee said, "Pride goeth before a fall."

Then she jabbed me in one shoulder blade with the hatpin she had drawn from her hat.

In shock, I shrieked, "Jesus God!"

Mamadee slapped the back of my head.

"The Lord's name! On Easter!"

"You stuck me with that hatpin!" I shouted.

"I did not!"

I could have spat. I lifted my chin and declared, "I hate you."

Mama heard it all. Saw it all. She was right there in the doorway of the dining room, with her hat in her hand.

"Go to your room, Calley," Mama said.

As I passed her, she slapped the back of my head. Maybe she thought Mamadee hadn't done it hard enough.

"She's a monstrous little heathen," Mamadee said. "How you can doubt for two seconds that Calley is writing those terrible notes to you, I don't know."

"I am not," I shouted from the stairway. "I never did! You lie!"

I took the rest of the stairs two at a time. I was confident of enough of a head start that Mamadee would not be able to catch up with me. I slammed the door of Junior's radio room behind me hard enough to crack the glass in the window. The whole house echoed with that slam. It echoed longer for the silence that followed it.

Opening the door again, I stomped back to the landing and

shouted into the now churchy stillness: "I'm gone wet the bed now! Somebody call for my color television set!"

My provocation produced no response.

Back in Junior's radio room again, I poked out the glass from the windowpane and climbed out onto the roof. There I sat cross-legged and made plans. I would run away. Find one of my Dakin uncles. One of them would take me in—Billy Cane and Aunt Jude for sure. If Mama did not want me, she should have left me with them anyway. The thought of Ida Mae Oakes came to me, but, of course, even if I had known where to find her, I could not go to her. Should I take three steps into the colored part of town, some grown-up would take me by the hand and walk me right back out, and find some white grown-up who would return me to Mama. Ramparts might as well be on the backside-of-the-moon from there.

A crow was eyeing me from the nearest live oak but one. I made eye contact with it. It shouted a great ugly *cawwwww!* I shouted it back. The crow took off as if the devil were after it. A few minutes later, it settled on the same branch. It went side-to-side, claw-to-claw, deciding where on the branch to clutch. It kept its cold eyes fixed on me the whole time. By way of experiment, I moved suddenly. The bird jumped. But when I froze again, it stayed.

Crows have a great deal to say to one another, and some of it is fairly obvious, just as it is with people. Certain sure that one crow will let all the others in the neighborhood know when a dog or cat makes an appearance.

After a few moments to reassure the crow that I meant it no harm, I did some cawing.

The bird listened carefully. Then it flew away and I saw it drop a white bomb smack on the windshield of Mamadee's Cadillac.

When I crawled back inside, I stripped the case off the pillow, to stow a clean pair of underpants, socks, Daddy's undershirt, and Betsy Cane McCall and my paper dolls. I shucked my dress and threw it on the floor. Kicked my Mary Janes into a corner. I considered cutting the silk string from around my neck and flushing it down a toilet or throwing it out the window, keys after it. My shoulder blade hurt. I checked the inside of my dress and found a blood spot inside it from the pinprick.

I carried the dress out to the front stair landing and threw it down into the foyer.

"Liar!" I shrieked.

Again, nobody responded. It was as if I were alone in the house.

I went back to my room and flung myself face down on the bed. The close air thickened with the scent of lilies.

A beam of sunshine fell upon my face like a gentle warm hand. I floated, weightless and elegant, upon a current. One toe held me to the earth, my only mooring a slender ribbon of green. I was all ear, white and fleshy ear, and the current that rocked me whispered a ceaseless song in a familiar voice.

The sounds of the silver and china in use downstairs in the dining room woke me, along with pangs of hunger. The odor of the clove-studded ham wafted up the stairwells. Mamadee and Mama were the only diners. The only conversation at the table consisted of polite murmurs of please-pass-the-something and thank-you and you're-welcome.

Nobody came up to bring me anything to eat or to tell me I could come downstairs.

I played all the swing and bebop records from the crate in the closet as loudly as I could crank the volume on the record player. All at once the turntable began to slow and the needle screeched in the groove. The turntable stopped. I unplugged the record player and plugged a lamp into the socket to see if the socket was live. It was not. I checked the other sockets in the room and all were just as dead. Someone had shut off the power to the room.

They must have forgotten that I did not need a record player. I sang all the songs that I could remember at the top of my lungs.

I peed in the pot and threw it out the window, twice.

The records were strewn all over the floor. When I collected them up to re-sleeve them in their cardboard jackets and line up in their crate, I saw something glint under the bed. Flat on my stomach, I squiggled under far enough to retrieve it.

I flung myself onto the bed and studied on the thing from under the bed. It was made of braided silk threads, like a fancy tie-back on a drapery, but very fine and light. It was not a tie-back, though. One loop of the braid sported a tiny gold buckle. Another separate Y-shaped loop went around the first in three places. It looked a little like a pair of suspenders on a belt, only for someone very small.

The Y loop fit over Betsy Cane McCall's head with ease, to hang upon her very small shoulders, but the belt part of it was far too big for her. I was able to wind the little belt part around her a couple of times. Then I pulled one of her little sweaters over it and it was safely hidden away. Somewhere, I concluded, was a doll it fitted. Something to look for in the vastness of Ramparts.

By twilight of the long spring day, I was very hungry indeed. Sprawled on the bed in the gathering dark, I heard the sounds of Mama and Mamadee and Ford having their suppers from trays in their rooms. At first it made me furious again, until I realized that it might be a good time to sneak downstairs to the kitchen.

So I did. Never having bothered to dress again, I was barefoot in my underpants. I padded into the empty kitchen. The aluminum-foil-shrouded Easter ham was the first thing that I saw when I opened the refrigerator door. Beneath the foil, it was carved into perfect slices. The smell of it spurred my already intense hunger. I snatched a slice and bit into it, even as I was suddenly overwhelmed with the sensation that it was meat, dead meat, between my teeth. Cold dead meat, cold as clay. The thick desiccating salt, the cloying sugar-syrup taste, with a bit of tough tooth-resistant skin on it, billowed in my mouth. My stomach revolted. I like to swoon and puke and choke all at the same time. I spat out the bite into my free hand and thrust both pieces of meat back under the foil. My mouth felt gritty, as if I had been eating dirt.

The remnants of the lemon meringue pie rested on a lower shelf of the icebox. Scooping up a handful of meringue and lemon filling, I filled my mouth. The sharpness of the lemon, the cleaner bland sweetness of the meringue, overcame the ham tastes, and its cool sliminess slid past the constriction in my throat easily. The remains of the pie disappeared, as I ate with my fingers until I was full. I followed the pie with sweet tea from the pitcher. It was not a neat meal. Gobbets and orts of piecrust, lemon filling and meringue ringed the floor where I stood in front of the open icebox. I burped loudly. Some of the pie was crusted around my mouth. I ran my tongue out as far as it would go and around my mouth by way of cleaning my face.

Then I wandered into the dining room to look at my eggs in their basket. It was all the Easter basket I was getting. The year before, the Easter Bunny had left a huge basketful of candy with a stuffed bunny in it. Ford had called me stupid and told me the secret; that's how I found out that Daddy was the Easter Bunny. Remembering it made me feel aggrieved all over again—at Ford for telling, at Mama for failing to provide a basket this year, for Daddy, and not just because he was no longer able to be my Easter Bunny.

Tansy had cleared the table, so my homemade basket was all there was on it again. When I was close enough, I saw that every egg in the basket was smashed flat. For a fraction of a second, I could hardly breathe. Then I saw that under the mound of fragments, there was another egg, a whole one, the only whole one left. Brushing away the bits and pieces of shell, I picked out that one whole egg and held it in one palm. It was blown out and dyed, but not by me. I knew my own. It was pink as an azalea blossom, and patterned in a contrasting web of green.

Mama left her room upstairs. I turned toward the dining room door and waited.

She paused in the doorway to ask, "Calley, what are you doing?"

I held out the egg in my palm. "Somebody smashed my eggs. I found this one. It's not mine."

Mama came closer to take it from me. She barely glanced at it. "Looks like the other ones to me."

"Well it isn't."

Mama made a face at the basket of smashed eggshells. "After all the time Tansy spent helping you with those eggs, you smashed them all to bits."

"I did not!"

Her fingers closed around the one whole egg and crushed it. For an instant, she blinked rapidly and then opened her palm and looked down. In the tangle of fragments was a small roll of paper. She dumped the mess on the table and picked out the note. Unrolling it, she gave it a hasty look, as if looking at it too long might blind her. Green ink, pink paper. Then she handed it to me.

"You're so hungry," she said. "Eat it."

I shoved it into my mouth, chewed frantically and then spat the cud of paper at her. And turned and ran again. She didn't bother to come after me.

Twenty

ONE night in early May, Mama and Mamadee sat out on the verandah. They smoked cigarettes and rocked side by side in tall green-painted rockers. The crescent moon peeked through the leaves of the nearby live oak in front of the house.

I see the moon
And the moon sees me

I was up the tree, passing for a mockingbird.

"Mama," Mama said, "I'm out of cash. With everything tied up in this horrible mess, I need something to survive on. Maybe you could lend me a little now and then until it's all sorted out."

Mamadee's silence went on too long. "I will have to see what I have on hand, Roberta Ann."

Mama laughed. "You know to the penny what you have in your purse, Mama. I have to find another lawyer, a real one. You know it's going to cost me one-third of everything to break this will."

Mamadee flicked a spatter of angry ash away into the night. "Why can you not get it through your head that there is nothing to break the will for? I would advise you, Roberta Ann, to keep your trap shut from now on about the will."

Mama fumed for a moment before she spat out, "I was a widow first, Mama, but now someone has made me a victim."

"Of course you would see it that way," Mamadee said, "but I am not sure that it shines in exactly that light for everybody."

"What are you talking about?"

The longer the introduction to something unpleasant, the more unpleasant it always turns out to be.

So Mama urged Mamadee on. "Just tell me what everybody in the whole damn town is saying, Mama. It can hardly be worse than the things I've said about them, except I am always telling the truth."

"You went to New Orleans," Mamadee said in a condescending tone, "with the intention of murdering your husband. You hired a fat woman and her friend to do it. He found out about the plot and rewrote his will, only you did not know about it, and had him killed anyway, and now it just serves you right to be left high and dry."

"Is that what people are saying?"

"Except most people add a few details. And the only good that people have to say about you is that at least you hired white women to torture and murder him and cut him up afterward."

The two women rocked in furious silence for a while, inhaling and exhaling like a pair of dragons threatening each other with smoke signals.

Mama ground the fag end of her Kool into the lid of a Ball jar that she was using for an ashtray. "People probably do say that. But other people say something else."

"What something else do other people say?" Mamadee's tone of voice plainly expressed her belief that Mama was about to fabricate.

"Other people say Joseph's death had nothing to do with me, that Winston Weems and Deirdre Carroll just found a way to get their hands on Joe Cane Dakin's money. They typed out a will, paid the witnesses to swear that Joseph really signed it, and they're trying to make everyone believe it was me who is guilty. So I will get run out of town, and you can hire another fat woman and her friend to kill Winston Weems's idiot wife and you and Mr. Weems will live high on the hog till you both rot."

"People are saying nothing of the kind," said Mamadee. "I suppose you have sold that fabrication to those silly FBI agents."

"It makes more sense than the other."

"What makes the most sense, darling, is the part about you getting out of town."

Mama's rocker ceased to rock. "I caint believe my ears. No, I lie. I can believe my ears. You gave my sisters away as if they were old clothes. You never wanted any of us, except Robert."

"Careful, careful, Roberta Ann. Stir the mud, raise a stink." Mamadee took her usual tack: Any resistance to her plans evidenced wanton lack of virtue. "If you are too selfish to consider me, have a thought for Ford. Those two women are going on trial in a few days. The scandal will be revived to sell newspapers. You might be wise to find someplace where you can lie low. And not just until the sensation of the trial is over. For ten or twelve years. You and Calley. Ford is in far too fragile a state to be left to your care. In fact, I am quite sure that any reasonable judge would find that it is your fault that the boy is in such a terrible way and that you are an unfit mother."

Mama caught her breath audibly.

Mamadee knew every judge in Alabama. Many of them owed their black robes to her contributions to their campaigns and her influence. Mamadee could make her threats come true.

Mama shook out a new cigarette and fired it up.

"My own mother." Mama's first draw on her cigarette was shaky. "Have you ever loved me, Mama?"

Mamadee disdained any question. "I am ashamed to have to remind my own daughter that out of the goodness of my heart, I have paid a very expensive hotel bill in New Orleans, as well as the burial expenses of her bankrupt husband, and that she and her daughter have been eating at my table and sleeping under my roof for these past months, and charging to my accounts all over Tallassee. And more importantly, Roberta Ann, I have not forgotten that you have *a million dollars* in a footlocker that rightly belongs to the creditors of Joe Cane Dakin's estate. And you dare ask me for loans."

Mama jumped up. With her left hand on the other forearm and her cigarette in her shaking right hand, she stalked away stiffly into the darkness under the live oaks.

In the solitary quiet that remained, Mamadee rocked complacently. She coughed lightly, and then chuckled.

My sisters, Mama said. Like old clothes. To whom had Mamadee given Mama's sisters? And why? Perhaps the answers could be found at Ramparts, in the back of a closet, the bottom of an old trunk, an attic, a cellar, a barn. Ramparts was suddenly interesting again.

I should have known that meant there was no chance in hell that I was going to get a chance to find out.

Twenty-one

MAMA shook me before sunup with her finger to her lips to shush me. I was already awake, just keeping my eyes closed. She had been up awhile, putting on her face, fixing her hair, and dressing. She wore a tailored suit and a smart hat. Without a word, she pulled her suitcases out from under the bed.

I dressed hastily and helped her pack. Once I glanced in her vanity mirror and saw her slipping in a jewelry case behind my back. It wasn't one of hers.

A sheet of paper on the dresser caught my eye. It read: *Deirdre Carroll is hereby authorized to act in loco parentis for me, Roberta Ann Carroll Dakin, in relation to my minor son, Ford Carroll Dakin, until his majority.* It was typed, except for Mama's signature at the bottom, so I knew it was something Old Weems had conjured up.

Then we opened the cedar chest, lifted out the footlocker, and crept down the stairs with it. The thing was horribly heavy. I had no idea that money could weigh that much. Moving Mamadee's petticoat table could hardly be more difficult.

Mama tore up her nails and stockings. Somehow she managed not to say any bad words.

By the time we stowed it in the trunk of the Edsel, I was staggering. Mama saw I needed a break. I sat down on the curb for a few minutes and examined the scrapes and bruises and nicks and cuts on my legs and feet. My overalls had given me some degree of protection but because I had been barefoot, my feet had suffered most. They were bleeding from multiple cuts and not only bruised all over, but several of the nails were bruised black.

Mama brought another one of her big suitcases down. Then I went upstairs again with her. We made several more trips down with the rest. The Edsel settled on its springs with the weight of it all. We did it all with hardly a word between us.

In a low voice, she told me to go get my suitcase and be quick about it.

I was up the stairs and down again in all of four minutes. The books in the suitcase shifted heavily with every step, so that I staggered against the uneven and unreliable burdens of it and my record player. Mama was just coming out of the downstairs powder room. She was barelegged.

She stopped me with a look.

Setting down my suitcase and then my record player nearly tipped me over. I dashed into the powder room. Mama's torn stockings were in the wastebasket.

Mama darted in and out of the house with light steps. When I came out, my suitcase and record player were sitting where I had left them. Anxious that Mama might leave without me, I stumbled out with them. The suitcase banged against my legs, seconding the black-and-blue I was already sporting on them.

She was standing by the open trunk, a pair of Mamadee's silver candlesticks wrapped in linen napkins in her hands. She tucked them neatly between the suitcases. Other napkin-wrapped objects were visible that had not been there previously.

My tennies were in the pockets of my overalls, along with Betsy Cane McCall. I wore Daddy's shirt under my overalls. The toothbrush and comb I had taken to New Orleans with me were still in Mama's bathroom. My coat still hung in Junior's closet. I would have liked to have all those things and the crate of records too. That Mama would leave me if I tried to go back for any of them, I was sick-to-my-stomach certain.

There was no room for my things in the trunk. Mama even had luggage filling the backseat. I tried to fit my record player in.

Mama hissed. She reached past me, yanked out the record

player and dropped it on the driveway. The impact popped open the lid, spilling the records inside onto the gravel. Mama snatched up my suitcase, gasped at its unexpected and unbalanced weight and dumped it onto the floor of the shotgun seat. She picked me up bodily, slung me into the Edsel and slammed the door.

Frantic to recover my record player, I scrabbled at the handle. Mama dove into the driver's seat to reach over me and lock me in. Then she slapped me hard, making full contact with my left ear. My head rang with the pain.

As Mama turned the key in the ignition, Mamadee appeared on the verandah. Mamadee was still in her nightgown, silk kimono, and kidskin mules, with her silvery hair up in pink rollers. Greasy white cream covered her face. The flush from the powder room or the slam of the car door must have wakened her, or else some instinct that Mama was stealing her blind. Clutching her kimono over her bosom with one hand, Mamadee hurried to the driver's side of the Edsel to rap sharply at the window.

Mama yanked out the cigarette lighter, jammed her cigarette onto its red ring, and put the gears in reverse. Then she rolled her window slowly down. Her cigarette smoke rushed out into Mamadee's face.

Mamadee coughed as she tried to speak. "I caint believe you are leaving without saying a word! Not a word about where! Those FBI men are gone want an address and the papers for Ford's custody have to be—"

Mamadee never got another word in.

Mama glanced quickly over her shoulder and punched the accelerator. Mamadee almost fell down. I was thrown forward into the dash, bumped my face, and bounced back into the edge of the seat. My record player crunched like the glorified cardboard box that it was under the Edsel's wheels. Mama wheeled the car into a turn that took it off the gravel, over the grass, and then back onto the driveway. My scramble to gain some purchase left me hugging the back of the seat. The tires of the Edsel spewed gravel against the parlor windows as Mama floored it in drive.

Behind us, Mamadee ducked, holding up her hands against

the pebbles and dust that peppered her. In the filtered light of the sun on the horizon, she was whitened from head to toe like a ghost. I never saw her again, in life, but we heard from her, Mama and me, and by then she was a ghost for real.

Twenty-two

ROBBED of breath to speak, let alone to cry out in protest, I wanted to snatch the wheel and send the Edsel smack into the nearest tree. An equally violent fear possessed me that she would dump me out on the side of the road and drive away. Or, as now seemed entirely possible, she might back over me deliberately as she had my record player.

My ear still stung and ached. Huddled in the seat, I wanted my daddy back with a greater desperation than ever before.

On a red dirt country road out of Tallassee, Mama put on her sunglasses against the sun rising into a clean blue sky. If the maps in Captain Senior's library were still correct, east would take us to Georgia. Pensacola was nearly due south. Mama must not know where we were going. Why else would we be driving east?

The road passed through already dusty fields and stands of scrub oak and by abandoned houses overrun with kudzu. Mama lowered the windows, so the smell of the unwashed, uncombed countryside swept through the Edsel. Dogs chained to trees slept in farmyards, where raggedy chickens pecked the dirt apathetically. Mosquitoes were already swarming blindly out of the sharp gullies on either side of the road. My daddy once told me that water moccasins nursed their young in those gullies.

The familiarity of sitting in the shotgun seat as I had when I had traveled with Daddy comforted me. That was what he called it: the shotgun seat. Every passing mile took us farther from Mamadee. My record player was as busted as Humpty

Dumpty. I would not give Mama the satisfaction of grieving openly for it. My fists uncurled, my jaw relaxed, as the Edsel rolled onward. Mamadee was behind us. A blessing worth the loss of my record player.

We arrived at a crossroads where there was no sign or marker, and no view of house, store, man or cur. Not so much as a red cloud of dirt to show a vehicle had passed there recently. Not a blackbird in the sky, not a grackle, not a starling, nor rusty blackbird, nor crow of any kind, fish or common—and in Alabama, there are always blackbirds in the sky.

Mama stopped the Edsel in the middle of the intersection. She turned off the ignition.

"What am I going to do? My place in the world, my darling son, my husband, have all been taken from me."

Her voice shook. She actually did feel victimized. Her conviction of it was enough to make me believe that somehow she had been.

"You still have me," I reminded her.

The cynical look she gave me was about what I expected for my sycophancy.

"I promised your daddy," she said impatiently, and looked one way and then the other. "We could turn right, or we could turn left. Or we could go straight ahead and see where this red dirt road takes us."

I wanted to know what she promised my daddy. I looked every which way, as she had, and then upward. Still no blackbird in the sky, nor anything else.

"Let's go ri—" I began, then instantly amended. "No, I mean, let's go left, Mama. I want to go left."

Suddenly a flock of blackbirds came wheeling overhead.

"Count the crows," Mama said.

"One for sorrow," I chanted, "two for go, three go left, four turn right, five stop now and stay the night—"

"Oh shut up," exclaimed Mama. "I didn't mean literally. Calliope Carroll Dakin, I swear you are retarded. You've got it all wrong anyway. You're always getting things wrong. I thought I was going to die of embarrassment when you sang the wrong words at that god-awful cemetery."

Mama looked to the left. She sighed as if she saw the Emerald Towers of Oz there. Then she looked at me, smiled crookedly, and shook her head, as if to advise me that the Emerald Towers of Oz were a mirage and a betrayal. She gave a quick glance to the right and rejected that way too.

"I want to try straight ahead."

I pretended to think about it for a bit. "We caint go left?"

"Not today." Mama turned on the ignition.

The Edsel leapt forward, raising red dust on both sides of the car.

I opened the glove compartment and took out the road maps. Mama immediately held out her right hand. In my road trips with Daddy, I had studied his maps all I wanted. Mama snapped her fingers impatiently. I gave up the maps. She transferred them to her left hand and tossed them out the window one by one. I turned around in my seat to watch them flying away behind us, map-birds in the wake of the Edsel, flapping paper wings all barred with roads.

The glove compartment still held a manual and a pencil stub. I took them out and wrote on the back of the manual the road signs as we passed them:

Carrville, Milstead Goodwins, LaPlace, Hardaway, Thompson, Hector, High Ridge, Postoak, Omega, Sand-field, Catalpa, Banks.

It would be years before I would see them again, except in an atlas of the states.

Outside of Banks, Mama pulled over to the side of the road. We made water in a little pinewood. On such empty roads, our modesty was at little risk. We had tissues for blotting but I thought it wiser not to remark upon the absence of a place to wash our hands.

Then Mama sat behind the wheel and stared down the road toward Banks. She touched up her lipstick in the mirror. She yanked out the ashtray and emptied it out the window onto the side of the road. She lit a new cigarette. When she started the Edsel again, she made a U-turn away from Banks. We passed through Troy and into Elba.

We had driven over one hundred and twenty miles. I longed to have the maps back. I was almost certain that the route we had taken to Elba was easily twice as long as it needed to be, in part because of the detour in the direction of Banks. I had no idea why Banks was of any interest to Mama.

Mama seemed uncertain where to go next. She seized upon the fact that it was past time for dinner—the midday meal in Alabama—and declared that if she did not eat soon, she would faint. In fact, she was more than hungry; she was exhausted.

Elba is a small place in Coffee County. The best thing about it, Mama said, was that we knew nobody there and nobody knew us. She was wrong about that. The best thing about Elba to me was that it was south of Montgomery, the worst was that it was nowhere near far enough south.

No doubt things have changed since those days, and Elba sports a Holiday Inn or a Motel 6, or even something as grand as a Marriott Courtyard, but then, the choice was between the Hotel Osceola, Slattery's—which was locally called Sluttery's for its fleas, Mama told me—or a boardinghouse. Mama would sleep in the Edsel before she would stay at a boardinghouse. She explained that everything and everyone in a boardinghouse was so ashamed of themselves that the blinds were always drawn, that the mattresses had all been died on, by somebody or other, and that everyone used the same bathroom, which with the awful food, created a universal constipation, which was all anyone in a boardinghouse ever talked about: being bound up. Impactions, Mama said.

The Hotel Osceola lacked the grandeur of the Hotel Pontchartrain by a country mile. To my surprise, when we entered it, Mama went straight to the desk and asked for the best room. The best room was on the third floor and it was the only room in the whole hotel that had a bathroom to itself. Mama went back to the Edsel with the fat man behind the desk and had him bring in some of our luggage—a suitcase of hers, my little red one, and the footlocker. Mama left me in the lobby while she accompanied the man with the luggage up to the room she had taken, as if she expected to spend the night there. I was disappointed and worried. What if Mama changed her mind and turned around and took us back to Ramparts?

She came down again and we had dinner—in the dining room downstairs, where we could look out at Elba's Main Street, and speculate on which of the old men sitting, chins on their chests, in the rocking chairs on the verandah of a general store across the street, might actually be dead. At two o'clock, we were the last to be served and all by ourselves. Mama guzzled glass after glass of unsweetened iced coffee and kept complaining to me of the heat, though it was not hot, not at all.

I remember thinking even then, it is a good thing Mama doesn't worry about me. Because if she thought she was responsible for me too, she would be even worse off in her mind.

"It's a good thing we have that footlocker upstairs, isn't it, Calley? Maybe it failed to save your daddy's life, but it sure as hell is gone save ours."

That's how upset Mama was—she said "hell" in a public place. She said "ours" too, reassuring me a little.

Upstairs in the best room, she got way more upset. For the first time since she had tied it on me, she undid from around my neck the silk string with its pair of keys. The one key, of course, was to her cedar chest back in Ramparts; she tossed it onto the counterpane of the bed. Then she knelt by the footlocker to unlock it.

It was empty.

Except for the dark stains of Daddy's blood.

All color drained from her face. She rocked on her heels and staggered to her feet.

"Oh Jesus God! Jesus God!" she cried, and bolted to the bathroom.

Of course I followed and saw her kneeling at the commode, vomiting the iced coffee-black contents of her stomach.

When she pushed herself back onto her haunches, I dampened a washrag at the basin and gave it to her to wipe her mouth. Then I dampened another and bathed her face as she raised it to me. Her shivering and shuddering and shaking alarmed me. I wanted to run to the telephone and call the desk for a doctor.

She grabbed my wrist and pleaded with me. "It was there this morning, Calley! You saw it! It was there when we got up this morning and it weighed so much, we could hardly move it. The only key was on the string you had around your neck and you never took it off, did you?"

"No, ma'am."

"Did you?"

I had not. But I believed at once that the money had not been stolen from the trunk, not at all.

After we had gotten it out of Ramparts and into the Edsel, and Mama and I had gone back into the house, someone had simply taken the trunk with the money in it and in its place had left the identical trunk, which had once contained Daddy's dismembered torso. At seven, I had yet to watch enough television or see enough movies to understand that the bloody footlocker should have been in an evidence room in New Orleans. In the end, I picked up that information from police procedural paperback novels, sometime in my early teens. If I had known, I probably would have figured that if Mamadee could fix judges in Alabama, she could fix cops in New Orleans, Louisiana. I still believe it.

Mama began to recover herself, allowing me to help her to her feet and to the bed. She flinched away from the footlocker and closed her eyes so that she would not see it. Once she was off her feet, I went back to the bathroom to wet one of the washrags again with cool water. I folded it over her closed eyes and sat down next to her to take one hand in mine.

"Get that *thing* out of my sight!" Mama's words came from between her gritted teeth, behind the mask of the washrag on her eyes.

I was able to shove and drag the footlocker into a closet and close the door. It smelled. It reeked of old blood, like the butcher's shop. The odor was so foul, I could not understand why we had not smelled it instantly upon entering the room, or how Mama and the man who brought it up could not have noticed.

"What are we gone do?" Mama asked me in a despairing voice.

"What about Fennie?" It was the question Mama expected to hear from me, I think.

"What could Fennie do? We don't even know her name."

But Mama got Fennie's name right this time. By saying *we don't know her name,* Mama implied it would be all right if I could provide Fennie's surname, and furthermore some way of getting a signal of distress to her.

"It's Verrill," I said. Mama didn't care for me to read her too closely. "Verrill. No, that's not right. Verlow. It's Verlow."

"Does that do us any good?"

I shook my head.

"For some reason," Mama said, "I have the feeling that Fennie Verlow doesn't live in Tallassee."

"Me neither."

"Me either, Calley," Mama corrected me. "Wherever that woman does make her humble abode, she might have a phone, but we don't have the number, do we?"

"No ma'am."

"Well then, I suppose if you want to be any good to me at all, you had better go downstairs and find your mama aspirin for her throbbing head."

"I need some money."

"Go downstairs and beg for it, darling."

I just stood there, hornswoggled.

"Might as well get in practice, because from now on, we'll be begging something from somebody every day of our lives. Today is just begging two dimes for a tin of aspirin from the first kind-looking gentleman you run across in the lobby. Don't ask a lady, darling, because she'll give you twenty cents, but afterward she will dig till she finds out exactly whose little girl you are."

Mama lied. O my did Mama lie. We were not yet paupers. She had not mentioned her jewelry or any of the valuable items she had taken from Ramparts, nor her secret store of cash, very possibly including my silver dollar. And we had the Edsel. She could sell it. I knew what it sold for—an amount that was a fortune indistinguishable from the missing million-dollar ransom to a seven-year-old.

As I closed the door, the telephone rang in our room. That *brrrring* of the telephone in a hotel room in Elba, Alabama, where no one knew we were, let me breathe again.

It was Fennie, of course: no need to linger to be sure of it.

Mama said, "Hello," in her sweetest voice—always reserved for strangers.

I ran down the corridor so that I would not hear any more.

Downstairs, I did not beg for twenty cents for Mama's BC. I went up to the lady at the tiny counter just inside the front door of the hotel. She sold Chiclets, Tiparillos, and the *Dothan Eagle*.

Wrinkling my brow, making sure my glasses were a little crooked, I said, "My mama has a throbbing headache and she sent me down for some BC but she did not give me any money. She said I could charge it to our room like we did in New Orleans one time—"

The counter lady was a young woman, hardly more than a girl. She might have cooed over an infant but ambulatory children were of little interest to her. Presented with a lump of a girl child of questionable intelligence, she wanted to get rid of me more than she wanted to confirm that I was, in fact, the child of a registered guest. She slipped the BC across her counter as she smiled artificially at someplace over my head.

Mama never asked me where I got the money for the BC. She had other things on her mind. She had to figure out how to leave the Hotel Osceola with the grandeur befitting her station at the same time she skipped on the bill.

"We are going to meet your friend Fennie's sister in Pensacola Beach," Mama said. "When I mentioned that you had never seen the Gulf of Mexico or played in white sand, your friend Fennie would not hear the end of it. So, because of you, I suppose we have to leave *this* place and go to *that* place."

Mama was appropriating what Fennie Verlow must have asked, I knew.

"Oh, we can stay here, Mama."

"No we can't. If we stay here we will run up a bill. We go to your friend Fennie's sister's in Pensacola Beach or else you go back downstairs and start begging a good deal more than twenty cents for a pack of BC tablets."

"How did Fennie know we were here?"

"She has relatives here in Elba"—so much for no one in Elba knowing us—"or that's what she said. Maybe one of them works in the hotel kitchen. Or is a chambermaid. Or runs the telephone exchange."

"Maybe," I said. "So maybe we could just get in the car and drive off like we were gone to visit somebody and leave everything here and that way nobody knows we have left and Fennie's relatives can take care of everything when the people downstairs are not looking."

Mama looked at me with thoughtful amusement.

"I know what happened. I must have been walking alongside the gutter one day and a little baby reached up and grabbed the hem of my skirt and that little baby was you. Because no real daughter of mine would counsel theft and deception."

"I am sorry, Mama."

"And you are deeply ashamed too, I hope, as befits a proper young girl."

"Yes ma'am."

That's exactly what we did.

No one stopped us when we drove away from the hotel without baggage or receipt. And the luggage was waiting for us when we arrived at Fennie's sister's house.

Twenty-three

THE drive south from Elba to Pensacola is a little less than two hundred miles, though it does not look nearly that far on a map. I had time to wonder why Mama's first thought had been of Fennie. I watched Mama closely. I listened to everything she said. It was the gas gauge that convinced me that Mama had no idea what was going on, after all.

We left the hotel by the front entrance—to go in any other fashion would have been tantamount (to Mama, at least) to be branded with a *P* for pauper. On our grand parade through the dinky lobby of the hotel and out to the Edsel, parked in one of the spaces in front of the dining room, Mama indulged in a running verbal debate with herself about whether we really wanted to visit our (imaginary) aunt Tallulah out on the Opp Road. I wished that I had an aunt Tallulah, just to have an aunt of that name. For a wild instant, I wondered if my real aunts, Faith and Hope, lived on the Opp Road, under the name of Tallulah. Faith and Hope Tallulah, secondhand clothes.

No one paid any attention to Mama's performance.

I knew no one would stop us and that we would get to Pensacola Beach. I expected Fennie's sister to be like Fennie. I even expected that Fennie herself would be there to greet us.

Mama was still sighing with the effort of the earth-shaking decision when she settled behind the wheel and fiddled the key into the ignition. She looked in the rearview mirror as she backed out and kept checking it. From long experience, she managed to pop in the cigarette lighter and light a cigarette, using both hands, as the ungrand Hotel Osceola shrank in the

mirror and fell away behind us. She held the cigarette between
two fingers as she blew smoke.

"Look out the back for the sheriff and bend your ear for the
cock of a rifle, baby. Because you have to tell your mama
when to duck," she said.

Hanging over the backseat, I pretended to watch for the
sheriff. Oddly enough, a sheriff's car appeared just as we were
leaving Elba. I did not draw Mama's attention to it. The sheriff was not after us. I had seen enough television to know that
sheriffs do not shoot just anybody for minor things like speeding or skipping a hotel bill. And if we did get stopped, no
mere deputy, let alone a sheriff, would have a chance against
Mama. What she had done to those FBI agents, she could do
to any mere man. And to the best of my observation at that
time, any man was mere.

"We have crossed the border into Florida," Mama said
about an hour later. "You can sit down and rest your eyes,
Calley."

As I sat down, I happened to glance at the gas gauge. I took
a second look. It read empty.

I might have mentioned it to Mama. Likely she would say,
*Well, it's a good deed of you to point out that little fact to me,
and I suppose we should stop at the nearest filling station, but
who do you suppose is gone pay for the gas when I ask the nice
man to fill up the tank of this gas-hog Edsel your daddy
wished on me?*

Somehow it would be my fault that the tank was empty.
She could pretend that we had no money to refill it.

And that was why I said nothing. When the Edsel finally
stopped running on fumes, she would have to cough up some
of her secret stash of cash to buy some. I might even get a
glimpse of my silver dollar.

I wrote Florida on the manual and then under it, the first
town name I saw: *Prosperity.* My daddy had told me "prosperity" meant livin' high off the hog. Funny if we were to run out
of gas in Prosperity. And then *Prosperity* was behind us, in
every sense. We came to *Ponce de Leon*, and turned west
toward the sun.

That sinking sun seemed to set fire to the tall pines on the
west side of the highway. Except for that little bit of time out-

side of Banks and a little bit more in Elba, in that one day we had driven from sunrise to sunset. And now the gas gauge read one-quarter full. Something must be wrong with it.

"What's Ponce de Leon?" I asked Mama.

She flicked a cigarette butt out the open window. "Some historical Spanish fairy. What do I look like, the *Encyclopaedia Britannica*?"

I tried to imagine how a Spanish fairy might be different from an American fairy. It had never crossed my mind that fairies might have nationalities.

Argyle. Defuniak Springs.

Argyle I knew: It was a pattern for a sweater or socks.

"What's 'Defuniak' mean?" I asked Mama.

"Throwing a kid out the car window for asking too many questions," she answered.

The gauge crept down toward empty again. As close as I watched it, Mama never looked down at it. The sun disappeared behind the jaggedy pines and then it set beyond the horizon that Mama and I could not see.

Mama turned on the headlights. The gas gauge tank showed just a little more than half full.

Crestview, Milligan, Galliver, Holt. Harold, Milton, Pace, Gull Pt.

I didn't have any questions about those places. Crestview and Gull Pt. were names about the places themselves, where you could stand on a crest of land and see some kind of view, or someplace pointy where there were a lot of gulls. The others were places named after people and I did not know a one of them, though there was a kid at school named Jerry White, and I knew of a man called Milt who once worked for my daddy at the Montgomery dealership. He didn't work out. By Gull Pt., the needle on the gauge had again dropped almost to E.

"Mama."

She didn't answer.

"Mama, do you know who Mamadee gave your sisters to?"

Mama shot a furious glare at me. Her jaw worked.

"I wish I did," Mama lied. "I'd put you on the next train, plane or automobile, right to 'em. Mail you COD if I had an address."

Having driven more than a hundred miles from Elba, we

reached Pensacola a little past nine o'clock. I ached to pee again. Mama drove around downtown Pensacola, up and down its streets—***Zaragoza, Palafox, Jefferson, Tarragona, Garden, Spring, Barrancas, Alcaniz***—and back again. Some blocks looked a lot like the French Quarter. All the stores were closed and even at the hotels most of the lights were out. A clock outside a bank read nearly ten o'clock. Eventually we found our way to the waterfront.

Mama stopped.

"It's a snipe hunt. To humiliate me, because I am your mother and your *friend* Fennie Verlow is jealous of the hold I have over you."

I felt then what I could hardly have articulated at seven— that, if true, it would be the first time she would ever care enough to want a hold on me. I sat up and looked around, making a show of how far I turned my head and how long I hung out the window.

"You said Fennie said her sister's place was at Pensacola Beach. This is all docks. I don't see a beach nowhere."

"Anywhere," said Mama. She gunned the engine. "I'd forgotten—she did say Pensacola Beach."

She made a U-turn right in front of a Pensacola police car.

"That damned beach better be close because we are almost out of gas," she said.

The police car burped at us.

Mama moaned but pulled over immediately.

The police car parked in front of us, a policeman climbed out, and presently looked in the open window at Mama and me. He had a broad face, and when he removed his hat, he exposed a receding hairline. He beamed at Mama with a full-moon jolliness.

"Good evening, ladies," he said. "I believe that you must be lost."

Mama smiled the way she did at a man when she wanted something from him.

"We are," I piped up. "We're supposed to go to Pensacola Beach."

"Hush," Mama told me with none of her usual irritation. "My baby is so tired, Officer, she has forgotten her manners. She is correct, however. We seek Pensacola Beach."

The policeman gave me an indulgent look. "I see she is a tired lil gal. You want to take the next right and then two lefts. That will take you back to the Scenic Highway—you've noticed the signs?"

Mama nodded.

"You turn right onto the Scenic Highway and it'll take you straight across the Causeway to Gulf Breeze, and there's no place else to go but straight ahead over one more itty-bitty bridge, and there you'll be, Pensacola Beach."

"Oh my," Mama said. "It's a different place than Pensacola. No wonder we couldn't find it."

"Yes, ma'am," the policeman agreed. "Now you best go along and put that tired lil gal to bed. My sister Jolene's got one like her. They sweet lil things, no trouble to nobody."

Mama fluttered her eyelashes. The policeman grinned even wider as he stepped back.

"Good night, ladies," he said, with a nod of his head.

He put his hat back on and stood by the side of the road and watched as we drove away.

"I thought he was gone give me a ticket for sure," Mama said, as she glanced up at the rearview. "The end to a perfect day."

We turned again onto the road—the *Scenic Highway*—that had brought us into Pensacola. We could see black water with a shiver of moonlight on it. The road brought us to a long bridge arcing over the water to another shoreline. The Causeway.

"Thank you, Mr. Policeman," Mama said, and laughed.

As we crossed that Causeway bridge, the cipher of the moon hung over us, in the night sky.

> *I see the moon*
> *And the moon sees me*

If the moon was seeing me, it was by sneaky-peek, for the leak of its light was no more than that from a twitched drapery.

On the other side was a sign that said *Gulf Breeze*, and then quickly the second itty-bitty bridge the policeman had mentioned, on the far side of which huddled a few dark buildings of indiscernible purpose. This was Pensacola Beach. Straight ahead was black water. The fragile horns of the moon pointed right.

"Right!" I blurted to Mama. "This is where we turn right."

This time Mama offered no argument. She made the turn and drove on. The pavement came to a quick end. The road became steadily narrower, the gravel looser, till on either side, there was black water that smelled of brine and bad shrimp. The unpaved road snaked between moon-pale sand and coarse, black high grass. The rind of moon was directly above. I could see it only when I pushed my whole body out the window and looked straight up into the sky. There was no sign of where we were, or of what was ahead.

And at last the Edsel chuffed and shuddered. Mama jerked me back inside. The Edsel gave another shudder, and then stood motionless in its tracks. Its lights quivered like a guttering candle flame.

"Out of gas on a dirt road in the middle of the night," Mama said. "And who has brought us here except you and your friend Fennie?"

"Sorry, Mama."

"You should be. She might have had the courtesy to tell us that Pensacola Beach isn't the same as Pensacola, and it's on an *island,* across two damned bridges, one long and one itty-bitty. If I'd known that, I might have stopped for gas."

"I see a light."

"Where?"

I pointed.

"I don't see it."

Mama turned the key in the ignition. The weak light from the headlights wavered and winked out. She pushed the button to turn them off with a sigh. "There goes the damned battery."

We were in near-total darkness.

"I still don't see it," she said.

"I do."

I pushed the car door open and—quite unintentionally— fell out into the pallid sand.

"Don't hurt yourself," said Mama. "I do not need an injured child to add to my troubles."

I pushed the car door closed. "It's a house, Mama."

In fact I had seen neither house nor light.

"Knock loud because they might be asleep."

I trudged off through the sand. It sank in over my tennies and over the tops of my socks. My feet itched. They were tender and painful from the morning's battering with the footlocker.

Amid the shadowy tall grass, I squatted to relieve myself. Then I climbed to the crest of the dune, where I saw the light that I had lied that I had already seen. The light in the window of the house that I knew belonged to Fennie's sister.

The scene was one-dimensional, no more substantial than a childish collage of pieces of dark construction paper. Sparse vegetation, dune and sand, sickly moonlight on panes of glass, verandahs up and down, were all mere raggedy fragments overlaid on the rough dark. The cloud passing over the moon made it wink slyly.

The light in the window went out. The sudden loss stunned me in place, but then, on a lower floor, a new light in the shape of a warped door opened. A core of darkness split the light instantly, like an iris opening; a crooked silhouette waved to me.

A voice called, "I see you, Calley Dakin! Bring your mama to me now, child!"

Twenty-four

"YOU are moonstruck and delirious," Mama said.

Dismiss the message she might, but she slipped off her driving shoes all the same. She collected her pumps but did not put them on. Barefoot, clutching her Hermès bag to her bosom with one hand, she paused to lock the car before she took my hand and let me lead her. A cloud eclipsed our pitiful slice of moon and we flailed onward, every step potentially off the edge of the earth.

"Scorpions hide in the sand," said Mama. "This grass is a mecca for fleas. I'm gone break a leg, stumbling around in the dark on these dunes. If I don't die of a scorpion sting infecting a broken leg, it will be a miracle. You'll be an orphan then, a pitiful orphan. You'll be in an orphanage until you're old enough to fend for yourself because you won't stand a chigger's chance in a hurricane of getting adopted. Jesus God, what was that? A buzzard? That looked big enough to carry off a grown man."

I took it for her way of whistling past the graveyard.

But when we reached the top of the dune, Mama ceased her ranting.

The moon reappeared in the sky to spill its narrow measure of light upon the breakers and silver the beautiful shore.

SssssssssSSSSSSsssssssssSSSSSSsssssssss

I was struck silent as Mama was.

Before I had seen only the dunes and the house on the

dunes, the light in the window and then the door, and the silhouette of the woman who had called to me. Not the Gulf of Mexico directly behind it, not the water

ssssssssSSSSSSSSsssssssSSSSSSssssss

on the sand. I had not *heard* the Gulf of Mexico—I mean the greatest part of its noise, that of the water reaching the sand, the sand releasing the water. Before, I realized, the only sounds had been my own, and the natural twitching and sighing of the vegetation. *This is not childhood memory refocused and refined.* I had not *heard* the Gulf. It *must* have been silent. There could have been no waves at work upon the beach, for at the distance from the house I would never have been able to hear Fennie's sister calling to me.

Mama was struck silent for a different reason.

"Oh, Calley," she whispered.

She was all atremble. I squeezed her hand hard but it still shook.

"Mama, what's wrong?"

"Nothing, nothing's wrong, baby. But that's not Fennie's sister's house."

"Yes it is, Mama. She called to me."

"It's my house, Calley. It's my grandmama's house. I lived there all the time that Mama and I were not getting along. That's where I was happy, Calley, the only place I was ever really happy. I loved my grandmama. I loved her so much, Calley. I loved her more than you love me."

Mama had never before mentioned her grandmama. Nor had I known that Mama and Mamadee had lived apart before Mama married Daddy, except for the semester Mama had spent at college. The information was so startling that it smothered any resentment over Mama's claim that she could have loved her grandmama more than I loved her.

"You lived here before?"

Mama laughed. "Of course not. Grandmama's house was in Banks. Grandmama died when that house burned down."

Mama started down the dune. I had to run and skid down the declivity to keep up with her. I had never seen her move so fast when not going from one expensive shop to another.

"Oh look, Calley!" Mama pointed at the yellow light that suddenly glowed in the same upstairs window as before. "Fennie's sister is going to put me back in my old room!"

The front door stood ajar across the weathered planks of the deep verandah. A white-haired woman peered out at us from the doorway. It was she who had called to me from the open doorway of the house on the very edge of the Gulf of Mexico.

Where the waves had been silent so I would be able to hear her voice.

"Stamp your feet," the woman instructed.

Mama pounded up and down on the floor mat, shaking the sand loose from her bare feet.

I had never seen Mama obey so short and sharp a command—and one from a stranger too—with such immediacy and willingness. I stamped my feet like a little echo.

"I'm Roberta Carroll Dakin," Mama said, trying to peer over the woman's shoulder into the interior of the house. "You must be Calley's friend Fennie's sister."

"I am Merry Verlow." The woman placed a gentle emphasis on the *am*.

"You call her Miz Verlow." Mama swatted the back of my head lightly.

As if I didn't know that "Miz" was how you addressed all women, single or married.

"Welcome to Merrymeeting."

Mama started. "Merrymeeting?"

Miz Verlow gestured inclusively. "My home."

Mama was in a kind of distracted daze as she looked all around, but she shook it off, to say archly, "I am very happy that you are not a Dakin."

"I confess I have only heard of the Dakins, through Fennie, of course," Miz Verlow said, "who is related to them somehow. You are the first one I have actually met and I must say I am pleasantly surprised."

The derogation of Daddy's relatives, especially by someone who had never met any of them, went over very well with Mama. "Well, you would not be so pleasantly surprised if you met any of the others, because I am not a bit like the rest of them. I am by birth a Carroll, after all."

"Oh?" Miz Verlow said. "Do come inside. I expect your feet are just about to take leave of your ankles, walk off this verandah, and dig a grave for themselves in the sand." She stopped as I started past her. "Calley, just shuck those tennis shoes right here."

In the reflection of a mirror above a deal table in the hallway, I saw the glisten of a tear on Mama's face. What caused that tear was something that Mama had expected but had no right to expect—that in Merry Verlow's house, she would find the same furniture, the same runners, the same faded lithographs, the same crack in the newel post that Mama remembered in her grandmama's house. But she was far too exhausted to try to reconcile the existence of a duplication here, almost one hundred and fifty miles away on the Gulf of Mexico, of her grandmama's house, long since reduced to ashes in Banks, Alabama.

But all she said was, "What is that noise?"

"The waves on the shore." Miz Verlow was amused. "It is high tide."

Mama moved almost blindly toward the stairway. I was embarrassed, for we were guests of Miz Verlow and Miz Verlow hadn't invited us to go upstairs. Mama had not spoken one word of thanks for Miz Verlow's hospitality.

I must have looked stricken, for Miz Verlow playfully flicked one of my ponytails.

"Miz Dakin," she said to Mama, "I'll trouble you to leave me the keys to your vehicle. It has to be moved first thing in the morning, to open the road."

Mama stopped, fumbled in her bag, and then dropped the keys into Miz Verlow's outstretched palm.

"Are the candles all snuffed?" Mama asked vaguely.

"I see to it myself every night," Miz Verlow answered.

Mama reached for the banister and began to ascend the stairs, as slowly and ceremonially as a bride processing down the aisle. As if there were a bridegroom waiting for her.

Miz Verlow nodded toward Mama. "Go help your mama undress, child."

"But—"

"She knows which room is hers. Tonight and for the time being, you will sleep with her."

"Thank you, but—"

"Your bags from Elba are in the room. I have put everything away. Your mama will know where to find things. The two of you will be sharing the bathroom at the end of the hall with two other guests. I always leave a light on."

I blurted, "I like the sound of the waves."

Miz Verlow smiled. "Sometimes it seems as if that's all you can hear, and sometimes you can hardly hear them at all."

She turned off the light in the foyer.

"Mama says this house was her grandmama's, in Banks, Alabama. Then she said it burned down."

"You are just seven, child. Have you ever heard that we see through a glass darkly?"

"Yes, I have." I remembered the windows at the train depot. "Mama said that she was happy in her grandmama's house."

"Roberta Carroll Dakin happy? That's a sight you and I and the angels in Heaven would like to live to see."

Maybe Miz Verlow knew everything.

Or maybe Miz Verlow was just giving back nonsense for nonsense to a little girl who was up past her bedtime, disoriented by a long ride and her mother's bizarre declarations.

We reached the landing, where a diamond-shaped window with a border of squares of stained glass looked out toward the endless moon-colored highway of beach. Beyond it, the Gulf of Mexico rolled as black and depthless as the sky in which the waxing moon still rode.

" 'I see the moon,' " Miz Verlow whispered next to me, " 'and the moon sees me.' "

Mama called my name softly from somewhere above.

"I have her, Miz Dakin," Miz Verlow called back just as softly. "She will be up in a few minutes. I want to give her something for your feet."

"Oh, that would be so nice." A door closed softly.

I still watched the view from the landing. "Is Miz Fennie Verlow coming?"

"What do you think?"

I shook my head in the negative.

"Where do little girls get it into their heads that they are supposed to be happy? There are other things that are so much more important for little girls."

How she got from her sister Fennie's absence to my expectations of happiness, I had no idea. I did not realize what an odd thing she had said until years later. But I knew that she did not mean all little girls. She meant Calliope Dakin and no one else.

"Like saying the right things," I ventured.

"That's right."

"And taking care of Mama."

"So is that."

"And not asking so many questions."

Miz Verlow flicked my ponytail again. "Roberta Carroll Dakin has got one smart little girl."

I shook my head no. "Mama doesn't think I'm smart."

"The opinion of Roberta Carroll Dakin doesn't mean one hoot in hell to me or to my sister, Fennie."

She showed me the bathroom and put out a toothbrush, toothpaste, a bar of soap, a washrag and a hand towel. She gave me a jar of scented cream for Mama's feet and left me with a casual good night.

I brushed my teeth earnestly, more earnestly than usual, and washed my face and neck and ears with care. Miz Verlow must see that I was a proper child, fastidious and obedient, lest I be the cause of her sending us away. I thought of Ford, stuck back there, in Alabama with Mamadee. Later I understood that it was less his choice than it appeared. But just then, he was as gone as Daddy was. I wondered if I would miss him as I missed Daddy. Probably not, I concluded.

At the foot of Mama's bed, I sat rubbing the cream into her feet by candlelight. Gently I daubed away the grains of sand that had lodged in her toenails. The sand had scratched the red polish, so it looked as if she had tiptoed in blood. I tried to make out the shapes of the room's furnishings, wondering what colors would show by day in the draperies, the carpet, the upholstery, the paper on the walls, the pictures hanging there.

The ocean outside never stopped its sighing. I listened to a voice that sounded—or seemed to sound—beneath the waves. It might have been singing, or it might have been asking questions. My eyes began to close and I shook my head, to keep from falling asleep.

From within the house, I heard other sounds: Merry Verlow's step in the hall, an interior door being opened and closed—Miz Verlow going to bed. But we were not alone with Merry Verlow in this house. I detected the even breathing of sleepers, a faint cough, snores, the creak of bedsprings as someone shifted, a whisper of sheeting, a plumping of a feather pillow. I did not recognize any of them as characteristic of the people I knew.

Ida Mae Oakes bent over me and murmured in my ears, both at the same time, a magic she could do; her slow-sung lullaby was the rolling *shush* and *slosh* of the surf upon the sands. I was oh so very tired.

"You can stop," Mama finally whispered. She pinched the flame on the candle. "Come up here and put your head on my shoulder."

I set aside the jar of cream and crept up beside Mama in the bed. The hard lump of Betsy McCall in my overall pocket pinched me. I slipped her out and under the pillow.

I tuned my ears to Ida Mae's

Hushabyesleepyheadhushabyeneverstophushabyesleepyhead

coming from the Gulf. Another note intruded.

"I hear somebody in the next room, Mama," I whispered. "I hear someone moving around and talking to someone. I hear wings."

"Of course you do, silly girl. It's your great-grandmama. She can never get to sleep before two o'clock in the morning, and she keeps everybody else in the house awake doing it."

Twenty-five

HAVING slept in my clothes, my overalls and Daddy's shirt, I woke up feeling grubby, piratical, and oddly naked. Light and unbound. No keys pricked the base of my throat with their small, sharp teeth, no silk string hung on my neck.

Breakfast noises and smells evoked an instant, almost painful explosion of hunger. We had not eaten since lunch in Elba the previous day.

Going to the nearest window, I slipped between the draperies and the windowpane. The mysteries of the previous night were resolved neatly into an ordinary pale early morning, lightly shadowed by the low angle of the rising sun. By daylight, I could see the dune between the wide bleached swathe of beach and the house. The beautiful shore. The sound of the Gulf had not ceased in the night.

I went to Mama to nudge her gently.

"Mama, smell the breakfast!"

She opened one eye reluctantly, wrinkled her nose, and then sat up for a languorous stretch and yawn.

"Lord what a fine smell that is. Coffee. Bacon." She breathed deeper. "And I smell the saltwater too." She sounded almost happy.

She cast off the bedclothes, took her robe and bathroom things and hurried down the hall.

Though I had washed my face and brushed my teeth before bed, I had forgotten the rubber bands in my hair. Consequently, the bands and my hair were interwoven into a witch's nest.

When Mama came back from the bathroom and saw me

gingerly tugging one strand at a time, she grabbed me and about scalped me tearing the bands out. I gritted my teeth. Wincing and wailing would only make it worse. She dragged a comb through my hair. It felt as if she were yanking out what was left of it. But there was enough left to tie up again, with the old rubber bands cleared of strays.

Then she put on some clothes—a simple white blouse, dark trousers, and sandals. She did the pageboy with the barrettes and lipstick, and was all ready for a Loretta Young entrance.

We followed our noses down the stairs into the foyer through which we had entered the previous night. It too was revealed in daylight to be an everyday room. My tennies were still there, just inside the door, all shaken out and ready to wear. I slipped into them and caught up with Mama.

Mama did not seem disoriented. She might have been following her nose, or perhaps the house was as familiar to her as she had said. She made straight for a wide doorway that had not been there the previous night. Among the sounds I had heard earlier had been the slide of pocket doors back into the walls. It must have been those.

Mama halted in the doorway. "Who are these *people*?"

I peeked past her. Several strangers were breakfasting at the long mahogany table, where a colored woman in a maid's uniform waited upon them. The breakfasters all paused in their fast breaking and their conversations to smile at us welcomingly.

From behind us, Fennie's sister emerged at Mama's shoulder.

"Miz Verlow, these people aren't *Dakins,* are they?"

"They're my guests."

"Your guests . . ." Mama's voice faltered. She took a deep breath and murmured through gritted teeth, "Your *paying* guests, you mean . . ."

"Of course."

The idea that a relative, even one connected to us as distantly and obscurely as Merry Verlow, might rent out the rooms of her home to strangers was humiliating to Mama— much worse than being suspected of conspiring to commit the brutal murder of one's husband. Letting rooms was the first wretched public admission of financial need. Of all the delusions that furnished Mama's world, the belief that the entire world was awaiting eagerly—nay, plotting—her downfall from the decayed social structure she was born to rule was the most ridiculous. But I was only seven and as much as I had come to distrust Mama, and to feel unloved by her, I had too little knowledge of the world not to feel as she did— threatened by forces just beyond my grasp.

We had nowhere else to go. Despite her horror and dismay, Mama was waiting for Merry Verlow to come up with some reason we should remain. I despaired. What could Miz Verlow possibly say that would relieve Mama of the humiliation and disgrace that she thought it her duty to feel and display?

"They're all Yankees," Miz Verlow whispered to Mama.

It was the only perfect, the only right, the only sufficient thing for Merry Verlow to have said.

Merry Verlow's clientele were none of them wealthy but they were comfortable. Their reasons for spending weeks or months on this beach were various and of no import to Mama or, at that point in my young life, to me. I was far more interested in the beach than I was in Miz Verlow's guests. They were merely a collection of grown-ups I did not know. What would make them bearable to her was they could not bring back tales to anyone we knew, or so Mama came quickly to believe.

With as charming a smile as I ever saw on her face, Mama took the seat at the head of the table. She settled instantaneously upon the role of hostess, with all its subtle implication of ownership.

Mama addressed the table in general. "I am so pleased to be able to join you all for breakfast."

The breakfasters murmured a polite chorus of welcome.

One of them asked Miz Verlow whether the newspapers had arrived yet.

Miz Verlow threw her hands up in mock dismay. "Not yet! I expect the printer doesn't know we're waiting on him!"

The guests chuckled amiably.

Having claimed the chair at the head of the dining room table, Mama directed the conversation at that first breakfast and every subsequent meal that she took with the guests.

I had not an inkling where I was supposed to sit. I looked to Miz Verlow for direction. She prodded me toward the maid who in turn shooed me ahead of her through a swinging door into a butler's panty and onward into the kitchen.

Another colored woman, floured to her elbow dimples, was kneading dough. The two women exchanged a glance. A white-floured forefinger pointed me to a small table in a corner. I took it for granted that it was where the maids ate their own meals.

My experience had been that nearly all colored people, except the very old, tended to be terse in the presence of whites. Small white children often seemed to be exempted from that caution, and so I knew that colored people were more talkative among themselves. After a few exchanges, I had heard enough from both of the women who worked for Miz Verlow to realize that their speech was as terse and even more opaque than that of the colored people in Alabama and Louisiana. The syntax, accent, diction, cadence and even timbre—words that I did not know at the time, though I grasped their sense— those aspects of their speech were different to my ear, in significant as well as subtle ways. I do not wish to depict a well-developed subdialect as ignorance or stupidity—that is, I loathe the thought of portraying them as characters from *Amos and Andy*. My seven-year-old sense of their speech is an unsatisfactory compromise.

"Sit," said the cook, as she indicated the table. But she reached out as I passed her and pinched my upper arm. "Scrawny," she murmured to the maid. "Not a decent broth in it."

The maid smothered a laugh in her palms. Then she put a breakfast down in front of me: grapefruit juice, a hobo egg—a hard-fried egg—broken bits of bacon and a sausage patty on the plate. I wondered how they knew that a hard-fried hobo is my favorite kind of egg. The egg in its frame of toast was right out of the iron spider; the breakfast meat had come off of plates returned to the kitchen, too cooled or unwanted for the guests. I was a little bit too young and too hungry to be insulted. I didn't look up again until it was all inside me.

The maid came back from the dining room, carrying a tray heaped with dishes cleared from the table. Once she put it down, she took a mug from a cupboard, spooned in an eye-opening quantity of sugar, poured in coffee and then topped the mug with a thick layer of cream. And to my astonishment, she set it down in front of me. While in the past I had stolen sips of coffee from the abandoned cups of adults, never before had I been given any coffee just for myself, let alone a rich feast of a cup.

From the backstairs, Miz Verlow came into the kitchen with another tray, from a single breakfast. Somebody had had breakfast in his or her room, if not in bed. Perhaps Merry Verlow herself. The sounds of the house were too new to me to be sure of the numbers of residents in the house.

"Calley, this is Perdita," Miz Verlow told me with a nod to the cook.

Perdita's mouth twitched in the briefest of smiles.

Miz Verlow nodded toward the maid, "Calley, this is Cleonie."

"Clee-owny," I repeated.

Cleonie gave me a nod as she lowered the tray to a counter next to a sink.

"Calley's gone help you wash up the dishes, Cleonie. You teach her the proper way."

Silently, Cleonie drew a step stool up to the sink. I climbed onto it.

"Her crystals fuss," Cleonie instructed me. "Then her silver. Drain out, fill up. Nex her plates, bowls, cups, sarvin' dish. Drain out, fill up. Her mixin' dish, cook pot, pan. Dry ever piece so it dowen spot nor rust none."

Cleonie shook Ivory flakes into the freshet of hot water from the faucet into the sink. She looked around. Miz Verlow was gone.

"Chile, them hears make a harring green. You fly wit 'em?"

"Clone-nee June Huggins's blaveration make ma hears hurt," Perdita scolded. "You talks too much. Mo' you talk, less you git done. Leave her chile be."

Cleonie carefully lowered a glass into the soapy water. "Better not break a one these glasses. They be her real crystals." She turned to Perdita. "Who payn for what she break? Or is it come out a ma pay?"

Perdita sniffed and flung the dough to the board as if it were Cleonie's question. "Howse I to known? Ax Miz Verlow."

Cleonie looked at me critically. "You a glass buster ever I seed one." She handed me a clean rag. "Lemme see you do."

Cautiously I fished the glass from the sink. The heat of the water turned my hand bright red but I bore it wordlessly.

"Hot water be's the onliest thing to wash proper."

I swabbed the glass and rinsed it. She took it from me and wiped it dry with a sacking towel. She held it up to the light. Then she lowered it and looked at me solemnly through the bottom of the glass.

I was able to look out the window over the sink. To my surprise and pleasure, the Edsel was parked there, with some other vehicles. One of them was a '56 Ford Country Squire. A silver coupe of a make unknown to me and with a Maryland plate sat idling within sight. Miz Verlow stood next to it, bent to the open driver's side window. The driver was a woman, or at least wearing a woman's hat, a high-style fedora, at an angle that shaded her face.

"Good-bye," Miz Verlow said, stepping back.

The woman behind the wheel lifted a gloved hand in a small wave and then the sedan drew away.

Miz Verlow watched it go and then turned and went into the house through some door that I could not see from where I stood.

A few minutes later, Miz Verlow emerged into the same area outside the kitchen window from another part of the house. She had wound a handkerchief around her head and changed from skirt and blouse to coveralls rather like the ones mechanics wear. As I washed the glasses, she began to unload the Edsel onto a handcart. The ease with which she lifted the heavier cases and bags revealed an unexpected physical strength.

There were a lot of dishes to wash and dry and a lot of luggage to unload. Miz Verlow disappeared from time to time with the loaded handcart. I could hear its wheels rumbling up a ramp beyond my vision, but which had to be fairly near at hand. A door would open, the reverberation of the wheels changed, and the handcart's burden would be unloaded inside the house. Somewhere nearby there was another staircase, a backstairs for Cleonie and Perdita and Miz Verlow.

My hands became redder and then wrinkly, as if the skin were too sodden to stay stuck on. I was frankly tired by the time I finished and did not much care if Miz Verlow magically folded up the Edsel, loaded it onto the handcart, and made *it* disappear into the house.

When Cleonie left the kitchen, I heard her on the backstairs. Then, behind her step, the sound of bundles of linen came thumping down from above through a chute to an unseen bin.

Miz Verlow returned, restored to ordinary dress of skirt and blouse. The handkerchief was gone. I noticed then, for the first time, that her hair was not white, as had been my earliest impression, but white-blonde, like Jean Harlow's. It was not marcelled, like Fennie's. Rather she wore it coiled in braids around her head. Fine wisps escaped the braids to make a barely perceptible halo. Miz Verlow's skin, though, was not that of an old woman, nor was her bearing. I had little interest in her age at the time, but if asked, I would have reckoned her casually as neither as young as my mother nor as old as Mamadee.

Though she wore lipstick, she was otherwise barefaced. Mama having made me aware of jewelry, I noticed that Miz Verlow wore a gold band and solitaire on the third finger of her right hand. She never spoke of a husband, dead, departed or divorced, and I never saw any photographs of her with any man who might pass for a spouse. Now, of course, I can imagine many reasons why an unmarried woman might wear the signifiers of marriage. Back then I merely expected that sometime or other, a Mr. Verlow would make an appearance. Too young to have fully grasped the conventions, I did not yet understand that Merry Verlow was far more likely to share a last name, a maiden name, with her sister, Fennie, than that they had somehow married men with the same last name.

Miz Verlow came through the butler's pantry, making a brief inspection of the crystal and china now returned to their cupboards.

"Did Miss Calliope Dakin do a proper job?" she asked Perdita.

Perdita looked at me impassively. "She done."

"Good." Miz Verlow's hand went to a pocket at the seam of

her skirt and when she opened her palm, there was a nickel in it. "You best save it, Calley. Anything you break, you have to pay for."

I looked at the nickel. Then I shook my head.

"You best save it for me."

Miz Verlow studied my face. Then she pocketed the nickel. "We will have an account between us. Let's go find your mama."

Miz Verlow stopped in the foyer to pick up a bundle of copies of the local newspaper from just inside the door. They were tied into a fat roll with a piece of string. Miz Verlow slipped the knot and shook them out. Black ink stained half the front page. It was an extraordinarily ugly black, that ink, and I had an immediate revulsion to it. None of the guests wanted to touch them either, so those papers would remain unread.

Mama had taken coffee on the verandah with some of the other guests, and then, with fewer of them, begun a social cigarette break. It was a fair day, warming gently from the cool of the early morning, and there was much admiring of the view of sand and sea going on among them.

Miz Verlow placed the newspapers on a convenient wicker table and apologized to the guests, with the observation that something disastrous must have occurred at the newspaper's printer.

Ordinarily, not all her guests were interested in seeing a newspaper, particularly a local one. Most of Miz Verlow's clientele wanted to get away from the rest of the world for at least a time.

The same inkblot problem with the newspaper occurred several days running. Then the printer apparently cured it. Some weeks later it occurred again but only on one day.

When I was rummaging through all the ephemera having to do with Daddy's murder, I finally saw those papers without blotches. What the ink obscured, of course, were the accounts of the trial in New Orleans of the two murderesses and their subsequent sentencing.

The very first paper also reported that no evidence had been found to link the widow Dakin to the crime. She was not in attendance at the trial and could not be reached for comment. The paper also reported a strange coincidence. But we were to learn of that event through quite another channel and at another time. The last blotched paper reported the strange deaths of Judy DeLucca and Janice Hicks.

At the time, I paid next to no attention. Mama never was a newspaper reader—not of respectable ones anyway, and not even the tabloids, at the time—and I was too young to care about any part of a newspaper aside from the funny pages. And for all I knew then, the local newspaper was often late and ink-blotched into an unreadable condition.

"Miz Dakin," Merry Verlow said softly. "May I have a word?"

Smiling graciously, Mama butted her cigarette in an ashtray and followed Miz Verlow back inside, where I was waiting.

"Did Calley break something? You just go right ahead and hit her."

"I have not found that hitting children improves them," Miz Verlow said, "and I know that it does not improve me."

That brought Mama up short. She had taken Miz Verlow, who had given her back her own bedroom and put a light in it for her, for an acolyte. Now Miz Verlow was making declarations.

Miz Verlow went on. "I have put some gasoline in your vehicle and brought it to the back of the house. As a matter of convenience, it is my practice to ask guests to leave their car keys with me, as our parking space is so limited and vehicles may have to be moved. I have taken the liberty of unpacking your vehicle and sending your luggage to your room. You may store anything you wish in the attic, which is locked, of course. You need only ask for the key should you desire to retrieve anything that you choose to store at anytime. If you would like to go up now and see to its disposition—"

Mama's mouth was set in a straight line that meant nobody was putting anything over on her. "I believe I'll do just that."

She started upstairs.

"Go out and play, Calley," Miz Verlow said, without looking at me.

She followed Mama up the stairs.

Twenty-six

TO give the two women time to reach Mama's room, I sat on the floor and worked at nonexistent knots in my laces. Then, leaving my tennies at the door, I went barefoot up the stairs.

They were above me, barely inside Mama's room. To my dismay, they gave no sign of moving. I was expecting them to go in and close the door. But they just stood there, not even talking. When I reached the top of the stairs, Mama and Miz Verlow were in Mama's bedroom's open doorway, staring at me. Somehow they must have heard my creeping progress up the stairs.

I bolted for the bathroom. When the doorknob would not turn for me and I realized that it was occupied, I turned back to Mama and Miz Verlow, the panic on my face more genuine than it might otherwise have been.

Miz Verlow pointed down the stairwell. "Under the stairs."

I whirled and raced down the stairs.

Behind me, Mama said, "I caint tell you how many times I've told that child not to wait until the last minute, Miz Verlow."

I had little choice but to follow through with my feint and hie for the WC under the stairs. It was an unavoidably dark little room with a steeply rising ceiling and at that moment, unoccupied. I spent a few minutes closeted there. I decided I might as well, so I did. It was worth noting just how much I would be able to hear from that location. On exiting, I was careful to give the door a little more force than it needed to close, so that it would be heard upstairs. Going through the foyer to the screened door onto the porch, I opened it and then let it slap shut, as if a kid had run outside.

I crept up the stairs again. Mama's bedroom door was closed.

I studied on my options. Ear to the keyhole was a ridiculously exposed position. There were doors up and down the hallway and on either side of Mama's bedroom. Most of them opened on other bedrooms, or even small suites, as I would discover soon enough. I sidled along the wall, testing doorknobs as silently as I could, and preparing myself to explain to some adult that I was lost and could not remember which room was Mama's. One after another doorknob proved unmovable.

Reaching Mama's door, I held my breath past it. I turned the hall corner. The hall ended on the landing of the backstairs that went down to the kitchen. Only one full-height door broke the blankness of the wall. A small metal door was set in the wall at waist height. It had to be the laundry chute, the source of the *whumps* I had heard. When I tried the knob of the full-height door, I discovered a walk-in linen closet. Quick as a single beat of my heart, I was inside it, with the door closed behind me. Mama's voice in relentless low complaint helped me locate the best listening post, the wall that the closet shared with our bedroom.

The closet walls were lined with cupboards below and open shelves above. On the open shelves were ribbon-tied stacks of towels. I used the cupboard counter to heist myself onto a shelf about six feet from the floor. A layer of towels softened the hard wood of the shelf, and stacks of them gathered around myself masked me from inadvertent discovery—so I hoped. In my pocket Betsy Cane McCall made an uncomfortable lump, so I extracted her and tucked her among the layered towels. Then I could open my ears completely.

"I know what was in my vehicle," Mama said, her voice all sharp cutting edges. "Explain, if you please, why everything is not here."

"But everything is, Miz Dakin." Miz Verlow did not sound at all threatened.

Mama stamped her foot. "I will not be robbed again!"

Miz Verlow paused briefly and said, "I have heard it said that a thief cannot be robbed."

"Just what's that supposed to mean?"

"It means that I have given you refuge in my home as a favor to my sister, Fennie. This favor is not without its costs to me, Miz Dakin, as you can easily understand. You have very little means, and I am aware of no prospect of future income. You have a choice. You can accept my terms or you can go elsewhere."

Mama tore a match across a matchbook with savage intensity, a flame popped and sizzled, and she drew on a cigarette. "Even if everything you just said was true, I don't even know what your terms are!"

Miz Verlow told her.

Cleonie padded softly down the hall.

I held my breath again in the hope that she would pass by. The door open; she entered. She began to take linen from a cupboard. Then she turned to the towels. All at once she paused. She lifted the towels behind which I was hiding with Betsy Cane McCall. Cleonie hooked up an eyebrow at the sight of me.

I held my finger to my lips pleadingly.

Like a bird, she cocked her head and caught Miz Verlow's deadly calm murmuring. Cleonie's lips pursed in disapproval. She dropped the towels down in front of me again and picked up another stack. The door closed behind her.

Even a dunce could see that my luck was clinging to a cliff edge by its fingernails. I crept out of the linen closet half a minute after Cleonie left it. Before the second half of that minute had passed, I had hustled myself and Betsy Cane McCall right out of that house.

Beyond the first great dune and the raggedy parade of tall grasses, the water of the Gulf of Mexico worked quietly upon the sand. Morning light and low tide cast the beach as wide as a desert; there was no end to it in either direction. Breathless from my escape, I paused at the top of the dune to look all around.

Behind me, Merrymeeting stood high and alone. Nowhere could I see any other houses, only swales of sand and the strange greenery.

I wasn't particularly interested in the house. Big as it was, I was no stranger to big houses. Unlike other houses though, this one stood on what seemed to seven-year-old me to be tip-toes. In this, it was more like Uncle Jimmy Cane Dakin's house on its brick piers than Ramparts or our house in Montgomery, which had actual stone-wall foundations and underground cellars. Piecrust lattice skirted the verandahs, hiding a considerable space beneath the house. Scribbles of evergreen shrubs sprawled low along the bottom edge of the latticework. Whatever color the structure had once been, the weather had beaten every bit of it out of the wood, shingles and brick, so the house seemed oddly insubstantial. An insistently real television antenna poked above one of the roofs. It made me think of the stave on which music is written. The antenna meant that Miz Verlow did not think that television was a passing fad. I had not heard a television yet but that only meant that it was off.

In the near-enough future, I would learn Miz Verlow's rules about use of the radio-hi-fi-phonograph console and the black-and-white Zenith television that squatted in the small parlor. Guests might listen to radio, either the Stromberg Carlson in the library or one brought with them, but must mind the volume in deference to their fellow guests. The television set was available for a very limited time each evening, with majority rule in choice of programming.

A drapery twitched. Miz Verlow looked out at me from Mama's window.

Spinning about, I raced down the dune toward the beach. Some of the allegedly Yankee guests had also come out to play. A few were already settled on wooden and canvas chairs brought from the verandah to the beach. Another few tramped along the beach.

Scurries of little birds rushed the negligible waves in retreat and were immediately routed in peeping frantic flutters by the incoming wave. I hunkered down at the edge of the water to watch and listen to them. Their names as yet unknown to me, their voices were enthralling. I became aware too of the squeak of the clams under the sand. The water dampened my tennies but I wouldn't melt.

After some time, I straightened up and used my toes against the opposite heel to kick off my tennies. If Mamadee had seen me do it, I'd have gotten a hiding for sure. *Lazy and careless of expensive footwear, two evidences of degeneracy at once.* I picked my tennies out of the water and flung them toward the dunes.

The shore seemed to go on forever. I started to run through the water where it sloshed upon the sand. I had no destination nor any desire to ever stop. I just ran. It was a glorious feeling to be moving barefoot through the shallow of the water at the greatest speed I could summon from myself. The long day's travel in the car must have wound me up like a spring. Of course I was nearly always wound up like a spring. Nothing more or less than the violent energy of childhood, as uncomplicated and irrational as the very elements themselves, propelled me.

When my side finally stitched and I slowed, I was out of sight of the house and of a single soul. On one side of me sparkled the restless water of the Gulf. On the other, a wilderness of dunes dozed in the sun. Behind me and before me, the sand stretched down the middle. As I turned back in the direction from which I had come and moved higher on the beach, out of the shallows and onto the wet sand, I left behind me the only footprints on the beach. I jumped high, twitching myself into a half-turn, and came down facing the other way, so that I could walk backward for a while, amusing myself with my false trail.

Distantly, a pickup truck or small van worked along the dirt road beyond the dunes. From its open windows came a faint but steadily strengthening female voice, with an accent like Desi Arnaz:

> *I'm Chiquita Banana*
> *And I've come to say*
> *bananas have to ripen in a certain way.*

I went back to the top of the dune, where I could see the road. A small, shabby van rolled at no great pace toward the house, its windows down. On its side were the words:

ATOMIC LAUNDRY

The driver of the **ATOMIC LAUNDRY** van wore his black hair in a crew cut. As I ran closer, I saw that he was Chinese. Or Japanese. I was ignorant of the fact that there were any other varieties of Asians. Ford had once informed me that Japanese could be distinguished from Chinese by the direction, up or down, of the slant of their eyes, but I could not remember whether it was up for Japanese, down for Chinese, or topsy-turvy. In any case, I assumed that Ford was lying, as usual, so it didn't matter.

The **ATOMIC LAUNDRY** van driver waved at me as he rounded the side of the house toward the kitchen. I raced down the dune and after him, arriving in time to see Cleonie lean out an open window on the second floor.

Chiquita's song had given way to a Bosco ad:

> *Chocolate flavored Bosco*
> *Is mighty good for me*

The van's driver killed his radio.

Leaning out the window of his van, he called out, "Yoo-hoo, Missus Cleonie Huggins!"

Cleonie waved and disappeared into the house.

The van man began unloading wicker baskets of ironed and folded bed linen, and of towels. He was a small, neat man, in white trousers and a white jacket of a uniform kind. His shoes were brown and very polished. He looked young to me—by which I mean that his skin was unwrinkled and that he had no white hair—but otherwise he was one more adult in a world full of them.

By way of the door with the ramp, Cleonie emerged carrying a wicker basket of unlaundered linen and exchanged it for one of the clean ones. The van man remarked that it was a nice day; Cleonie agreed. Going in and out of the house, she made the exchange of baskets several times. I tried to help but the basket was too heavy for me.

"You too small," the van man told me, as if it were news to me.

The discovery that Cleonie might change the beds and clean the bathrooms but that she did not launder the linen was momentarily interesting. Investigation (I asked Miz Verlow) revealed that the water from the well was too precious to use for laundry, so all the linen and clothing went off to the **ATOMIC LAUNDRY** in Pensacola.

Over the next few days, I discovered that Merrymeeting depended upon the services of many tradespeople. A milk truck delivered milk, cream, ice cream, butter and eggs and, most of the time, the newspaper. If the newspapers missed the milk truck, they might arrive with the mail lady, who in those golden days came twice a day and once on Saturday—or with one of the other deliveries. Local fishermen—one of them Perdita's husband—brought fish and shellfish to the back door for Perdita's perusal. Miz Verlow ordered what Perdita wanted by way of meat from a superior butcher in Pensacola, who subsequently delivered it. Groceries were also delivered. Local people often knocked at the back door with some seasonal delicacy. And while all this busyness was going on, Miz Verlow's house ran smoothly, by and large, so her guests hardly knew how much went into it.

I stumbled after Cleonie up the ramp and into the house.

"Cleonie, where's the laundry chute?"

"Rat 'ere." She tipped her chin straight ahead of us.

We were in the back hall behind the kitchen, at the bottom of the back stairway that rose to the landing where the linen closet was. The backstairs allowed Cleonie and Perdita and Miz Verlow to move about the house without being underfoot of the guests. A small high door like the one that I had seen up the backstairs was set into the wall we faced. The bottom edge of it was at my eye-level. The wooden knob was an easy reach and immediately I pulled it open. Inside was an empty tin-lined cylinder of space. On tiptoe, I stuck my head in and looked up the tube rising to the higher floors. That inspection completed, I bounded up the stairway. Cleonie came hurrying after me.

The door to the laundry chute on the landing was closed. Just beyond Cleonie's grasp, I yanked it open and, letting out a rebel yell, dove into it headfirst.

My stomach felt like it was falling faster than the rest of me but I barely had time to notice it before I was spilling out the open laundry chute door on the first floor. My face met the floor and the rest of me was right behind, on top of it. The impact was briefly stunning, as if I had run into a wall, before the blood started to spurt from my nose. My glasses fell off my face as I curled like a possum.

Cleonie and Perdita arrived from different directions.

"Hit jez jump," Cleonie told Perdita. "Whump!"

My eyes were blurry but I could still see the disbelief on Perdita's face.

"An natchell," she muttered. And then said clearly, "You be's *an natchell,*" to me.

"Azz," she told Cleonie, who rushed away

When Cleonie clamped a dish towel packed with ice on my face, I realized that Perdita had, in fact, said, "Ice."

Miz Verlow came down the backstairs and took in the situation with a quick glance. Seizing my hand and pulling me to my feet, she plucked my glasses from the floor with her free hand. She nudged me toward the stairs.

"That was very noisy," she told me as she followed me upstairs. "If anyone had been trying to sleep, the poor soul would thought the roof had blown off."

"Yes'm," I agreed, from behind the muffle of ice pack and swelling face.

"Thoughtless of you," Miz Verlow continued. "I would have expected it from a boy."

"I wisht I was a boy," I mumbled.

"Well, you're not and a good thing too. I cannot abide boys. Let's get this straight, Calliope Dakin." Miz Verlow spoke without any apparent anger. "You are not going to become the house hellion. You will not behave as if you are a satanic familiar or some motherless child or any of the other roles that you may have adopted in the past. In this house, you are going to become the Calliope Dakin you will be for the rest of your born days, and that Calliope Dakin"—she paused on the second-floor landing and closed the laundry chute door—"that Calliope Dakin is going to know how to behave."

I snuffled. "I should have waited until there was laundry at the bottom of the chute."

She looked down at me. "Exactly." Then she gave me my glasses. The plastic frame was broken across the nose. The glass parts were all smeary.

"Miz Verlow, what's '*an natchell*'?"

" '*An natchell*'?"

"Perdita called me '*an natchell*.'"

Miz Verlow smiled thinly. "A natural. Some poor soul who is feebleminded."

I was severely let down. I had been hoping that *an natchell* meant pirate or daredevil, or *something* wild and brave.

We arrived at Mama's bedroom door. Miz Verlow knocked lightly with her knuckles.

On opening the door, Mama's unnaturally sweet smile vanished at the sight of me, to be replaced with a look of triumph.

"I take it," she said to Miz Verlow, "that Calley has succeeded in changing your mind on the subject of corporal punishment."

"Not really." Miz Verlow pushed me toward Mama. "I fear that I overestimated the ability of a child of her age to go without maternal supervision."

With that swift turn of the knife, Miz Verlow left me to Mama's mercies.

Mama closed the door after her.

"Well," said Mama, "it certainly is remarkable how the childless always know everything there is to know about child rearing."

She looked around. "Where's your suitcase? Get yourself some clean clothes and go sit in the tub, Calley, so you don't bleed on anything but that towel and your clothes. When you've stopped, take a bath."

I crouched over my suitcase, cast into a shadowy corner of the room. I had two clean pairs of underpants and a clean pair of overalls cushioning the books from Junior's shelf, and a bunch of Betsy Cane McCall's clothes—more of hers than mine.

Mama looked down over my shoulder for a few seconds and then smacked me on the back of the head.

"That's what you packed?" She slapped my face. "Do I

look like a department store to you?" She snapped her fingers. "I can just replace your clothes like that? Clothes cost money, Calley, a lot of money and we are dirt poor now. Dirt. Poor."

I pulled at the lobe of my left ear and stared at her defiantly.

"We," I said. "Are. Not. Dirt. Poor."

She slapped me again. "I should buy you a red jacket and a fez and let you pass for an organ grinder's monkey. At least you might come home with a few pennies in your hat. Get out of my sight."

Twenty-seven

WHILE I bathed, I contemplated Miz Verlow's terms and Mama's reactions, which had been almost more interesting than the terms.

You reside here at my pleasure.

You will obey my rules.

Your room and board I will take in barter from those goods that came with you. Or you can choose to work, but only here on this island and with my consent or approval.

You will attempt no communications with anyone without my foreknowledge and consent.

You will make no contracts nor incur any debt without my foreknowledge and consent.

You will not leave the island without intent to return, nor travel more than fifty miles away without my foreknowledge and consent.

You will not abandon the child here. Understand that she is all that stands between you and a fate worse than the one that befell your late husband.

The child will go to school.

The reach of your enemies is long and their enmity persistent. If you cannot agree to this, you will imperil your life and freedom.

There is no negotiation of these terms.

The choice is entirely your own.

Mama had begun disdainful, she had sniffed and snorted, but at the end, she had been trembling with anger and fear.

Nothing that I could imagine was more appealing to me

than staying where we were. Since I had feared all along that Mama would abandon me, it was no shock to find out that Miz Verlow suspected it of Mama as well. The talk of peril and enemies and enmity was uniquely satisfying. Not only did it confirm my own sense of precariousness, it did so in the guise of a fairy-tale stricture: Break a rule as simple as speaking to a stranger, and be punished with a hundred years of naptime. The relief to me of having Mama firmly tethered to me, and to this place, was immense. The nature of the perils, of the enemies and their grudges, did not need to be elaborated. *My daddy was in bloody pieces.* Somebody, something, had done us a terrible turn. It was only wise to reckon they might not be done with us. A seven-year-old does not normally or naturally think very far beyond the moment, but raw fear forced it on me.

Having bathed and washed my hair, I swished the two pieces of my glasses through the soapy water. I dried them and put them, with Betsy Cane McCall, in the pocket of my clean overalls.

Miz Verlow caught me on the backstairs landing again, putting my bloodied towels and clothing in the laundry chute.

"Child, I've seen bramble bushes with birds caught in them that were still neater than your hair," she said. "Get your mama to comb it and tie it up for you."

Mama's door was closed and locked. I had tried it already. My face hurt. My head hurt. I realized that the throbbing in my head was what Mama meant by a headache. I could not think what to do next.

Miz Verlow's voice softened. "You need an aspirin, Calley."

She drew me along with her, through a door and into an ell of the house and down a hallway and into a bedroom. I was surprised to see her open a door into another bathroom. This bedroom—hers, it came to me—had its own private bath. She came out of the bath with a damp washrag, a glass of water and a small orange pill.

The little orange pill may have been the first aspirin I ever had. Certainly I have no memory of such a thing even existing in the house in Montgomery. This aspirin was not only orange in color; it had a tang of orange and grittiness on my tongue that raised goose bumps on my arms.

She picked up a small bottle from the dresser and poured a few pearly drops into one palm. After rubbing her palms together, she very gently worked the stuff from the bottle through my hair. She massaged my scalp the way I did Mama's feet at night. The pain in my head began to fade. Then she combed my hair and tied up my ponytails. It didn't hurt a bit.

"How about some ribbons?"

One second, one long piece of yellow ribbon draped her fingers and the next, there were two, flickering away from the blades of the shears with a cool faint whisper. The shears were very sharp, sharp enough to take off a finger or a foot, and well oiled too, for the pivot of the blades moved with only the slightest of sounds. The whole ribbon fell hypnotically into two perfectly equal parts between the flash of the two blades.

"Who was the lady who left this morning?"

"I thought you would never ask. Why do you think that she was wearing her hat to obscure her face?"

"So I would ask who she was."

Miz Verlow laughed softly. "You are sharp as the blades of my shears, Calley Dakin."

My tongue was suddenly thick in my heavy head, my eyelids impossible to lift.

*

THE sound of the dinner bell woke me. I had no memory of falling asleep. My neck was stiff and damp and I was hungry. It seemed to me that the dinner bell *was* my hunger, ringing right inside my head and in my stomach.

Now warmed by my body heat, the damp washrag sat like a deflated old toad on my forehead: I flung it off. The pillow was damp from my wet hair. So heavy had my sleep been that I had drooled a little. My earlobes and behind my ears and my neck were crusty with the tracks of it.

I slipped off the bed and went into the bathroom to pee and wash my face. A small high window was propped open to the salt air and the intricate conversation of birds and sea and wind. The room itself was imbued with a complex aroma, something like a spice cupboard all mixed up with a medicine cabinet.

The yellow ribbons around my ponytails shone back at me

in the mirror over the basin. My swollen face was muddy with bruises. The yellow of the ribbon was exactly the wrong color; it made my hair more colorless, my skin hectic, the discoloration of the bruises violent. My head hurt again just looking at myself. When I felt in my pocket for my broken glasses and Betsy Cane McCall, I found nothing.

But I was so hungry, I was hollow clean through.

I found my way back to the foyer and the dining room and would have gone onto the kitchen but Miz Verlow was there at the table, with Mama and the guests who wanted dinner, and she stopped me with a commanding look.

"Miss Calley Dakin," she said, "you are late. Beg pardon, please, and take your seat."

She indicated a chair with the slightest of gestures of her head.

"Beg pardon," I tried to say but it came out all thick and clogged as if I had a cold.

Mama snickered.

No one else did.

I fell on my dinner as the wolves on the Assyrians—at least that's the way I remember it, wolves on Assyrians—ate everything on the plate Cleonie put down in front of me: ham steak and red-eyed gravy and cornbread, and creamed corn and scallop potatoes and green beans cooked with side meat, and bread-and-rice pudding with whipped cream. I drank three whole glasses of sweetened lemonade. To the consternation of the guests, to Mama's horror and humiliation, to Cleonie's wrinkled nose, and to Miz Verlow's apparent indifference, I finally slid woozily off that chair and vomited on the turkey rug.

"Concussion," said Miz Verlow shortly. "Put the child to bed."

Twenty-eight

WHEN the first morning birds woke me, I was tangled in a coverlet on the floor. Mama was asleep in the bed. Horrid dreams had fevered my night. I did not want to recall any detail. When I finally did, I wished heartily that I had not.

My first concern was thirst. At that very early hour, I had the use without challenge of the bathroom we shared with other guests. I gulped from the tap like the barely domesticated little animal that I was. And then I did the opposite and relieved myself.

I became aware of feeling a little less substantial, a little lighter on my feet. After splashing my face and head, I brushed the sick taste of my nightmares from my mouth. A few strands of my hair fell into the basin, into the foam of toothpaste spat.

My hair was loose, the ribbons and rubber bands left on Mama's dresser, along with the gap-toothed comb that she had assigned me since I had lost mine. My scalp felt lighter than usual. I was a fright, of course: my eyes half-closed with swelling, my nose like a moldy potato. I made a face in the mirror and stuck out my tongue at myself.

When I crept back into the bedroom, intent on getting my clothes and scooting out again, Mama was just stirring. She opened one eye, saw me, moaned, and turned over, yanking a pillow over her head.

I dressed as swiftly and quietly as I could. The rubber bands, the yellow ribbons, the comb, all waited on the dresser. It felt as if they were watching me: the rubber bands gasping, the comb gnashing its uneven teeth, the ribbons flickering like snakes' tongues that would burn when they bit. I slipped out without touching them and with an intense sense of having escaped.

Cleonie and Perdita were in the kitchen already, Miz Verlow in conversation with them, so I was able to creep out of doors unseen and unheard.

The light edging over the eastern horizon brightened the foam on the breakers in the west to a dazzling pure white. A fleet of pelicans flying parallel to the shore passed almost silently over my head, throwing their huge shadows over me and onto the white sand. They seemed very close and very large. My relative small size enlarged them to enormity.

Up and down the beach, at watch in the swash, stood solitary herons—*harrings*. Suddenly I understood Cleonie's pronunciation. As I approached the nearest, it seemed entirely indifferent to me and yet was aware of me; I saw it in its eyes and heard its heartbeat surge. It too was a large bird, taller than I was, but its legs were stilts, its long neck as thin as my wrist, its head no bigger than my fist. A long, thin inky slash of droopy feathers atop its skull, and the long feathers on its chest, ruffled in the breeze.

A law firm of birds waded in the swash or near it: sanderling, dunlin, dowitcher, sandpiper, willet, stilt and avocet. Pelicans, skimmers, terns and gulls hunted just offshore.

As I squatted barefoot on the beach, a breeze ruffled my hair, and took away a strand. And then another.

A fish crow screeched a loud *awk* and hurtled toward me. It passed over my head with its claws outreached, snagged lightly, and was gone. I did not need to see the strands in its claws to know that it had taken some of my hair. The interesting sensation was the absence of resistance from the hair. It was painless. The hair went quite willingly where it was tugged. It no longer felt rooted or connected to me in any way.

I made an *uhhk* at the fish crow. In a black vortex, a dozen or more fish crows hovered over me, diving toward me, skimming away a few strands of hair at a time, rising away again. My scalp felt more and more naked. The sea breeze passed as a cool ruffling through thinner and thinner locks. The birds played around my head acrobatically, teasingly, and their wings fanned me from every direction until I heard nothing else. Some of their cries sounded like questions—*uhuh-uhuh?* Others like answers—*brruhk.* My throat grew dry from conversing with them, and then they were gone.

I could hear other things again: the other birds, the tall, swaying grass on the dunes, the slosh and splosh and sigh of the water, the swift scuttle of ghost crabs emerging from their holes in the sand, the wet breathing of the clams under the sand. And then the raucous mirth of a laughing gull.

The beach and the birds enthralled me to the extent that if awakening hunger had not brought me back to the house, I might have stayed there all day. I had yet to understand how much sustenance was all around me.

Mama was again at the table in the dining room, with the guests and Miz Verlow.

Mama's eyes widened at the sight of me. She gasped as if she were choking on a fishbone. Miz Verlow handed her a glass of water. Mama got her tubes cleared, patted her mouth with her napkin, and recovered her poise. The guests, after initial murmurs of alarm, maintained an uneasy attentiveness to their breakfasts.

I took my place at the table and thanked Cleonie when she put a plate down in front of me.

"What is the meaning of this, Calliope Carroll Dakin?" Mama's voice was half-strangled and very low.

"The meaning of what?" My mouth was full of warm fresh-baked buttery biscuit.

Mama took a deep breath. She wore only lipstick at this hour of the morning, so the reddening of her face was undisguised. Everyone else concentrated on his or her meals. The table could have easily been a refectory in some monastery under vow of silence—not that I knew at the time that there were such things as refectories, or monasteries, or vows of silence.

"Leave the table," Mama said.

I placed my fork neatly on my scrambled eggs, slid from my chair, took my plate and made for the kitchen. I helped wash up the dishes.

No one said a word about the fact that my scalp was hairless. As I was drying my hands, Perdita summoned me with the crook of a finger. She whipped a linen napkin around my head in complicated folds and secured it with a small tight knot high on one side. She left my ears exposed. Then she twitched the cloth on either side and the folds bloused out and covered my ears.

On the wall next to the door to the butler's pantry was a small mirror that Miz Verlow, Perdita and Cleonie checked nearly every time they left the kitchen. From the way she invariably rolled back her lips to check her teeth, Miz Verlow had a horror of having spinach or lipstick on them. Cleonie and Perdita were just vain—vain as peacocks. They always smiled at what they saw. Their pleasure in their own looks made me think of them with awe as about the most beautiful people in the world. Perdita placed the step stool under the mirror so I could climb up and see myself. The napkin was snowy white, and with my blacked eyes and swollen face, I looked like an odd sort of white-capped owlet.

Mama was madder than a nest of paper wasps busted open with a hickory stick. I know because I did that once, when I was too young to know better, and got stung so many times, I wet my pants. But I was fearless. What could she do to me? Make me wet my pants? Black my eyes? Scalp me bald? Tear me limb from limb?

Miz Verlow was in the upstairs hall when Mama marched me toward our room.

"Miz Dakin, I beg your pardon," said Miz Verlow. "I forgot to mention that I do not allow corporal punishment in this house."

"I beg your pardon, Miz Verlow." Mama's every word cutting as Miz Verlow's own shears. "Calley is mine and I shall raise her as I see fit."

Miz Verlow shook her head. "I remind you, Miz Dakin, of our agreement."

Mama paled. Her hand fluttered to her throat. "You cannot be serious. You must be mad."

"Loretta Young again? Please don't waste your acting talent on me, my dear. You will not use any form of corporal punish on Calley under my roof. Is that understood?"

Mama went all Mamadee-rigid. Her fingers twitched, yearning for something to throw, eyes to scratch out.

Miz Verlow seemed hardly to notice. Wishing Mama good morning, she turned away.

Mama stalked past me into our room and slammed the door.

Miz Verlow paused, her hand hovering suddenly over the folds of the scarf around my head as if to pet me, but she did not actually touch me.

I let myself into the room, still dark against the sun. Mama was sitting at the vanity, tucking up loose strands of hair. In the mirror, Mama narrowed her eyes spitefully at me.

"Want me to rub your feet, Mama?"

She kicked off her shoes and flung herself onto the bed. "Don't think your Merry Verlow is putting anything over on me, Calley Dakin. Don't think you are either. I know a game when I see one."

I hesitated.

"Rub my feet, Calley," Mama said impatiently. "The least you can do is make yourself useful."

That, at least, was a well-established principle.

After a while Mama was calm enough to talk again normally and reverted to her favorite subject, herself. "I have been so distraught that I forgot that you were skipping school." As if I were deliberately doing it. She went on, "When it starts up again, you are going to school. You may not learn anything but at least you won't be under my feet all the time."

I liked school—the learning part of it anyway, and the being out from under Mama's feet. In the meantime, I was caught up in exploring the island.

As soon as I was out again, I ventured across the road and all the way to the other side of Santa Rosa Island. Miz Verlow's house stood at a narrow waist of the narrow island, but that side of the road was nonetheless different in striking ways from the Gulf side. On the bay side, the sand mounded up chaotically, as if the dunes had been tied in knots. Sand pines and shrubs crowned the high places and other kinds of trees and shrubs grew in the low places. Some of the low places were wet, at least some of the time, and had their own kinds of plants and critters. The old deranged dunes nestled areas of salt marsh. What beach there was, was narrower and less cool, as the body of the island and the vegetation gave it some protection from the winds off the Gulf. Between the island and the mainland was the quieter water of Pensacola Bay, with more boat traffic. On the nether shore Pensacola was laid out before me like a toy town.

The sight of Pensacola reminded me of our journey from Tallassee and of Mamadee and Ford. I did not want to be reminded. Nor did I want to remember losing Daddy in New Orleans or our life before that loss. More than anything else, I wanted to hold on to Daddy alive. I spoke to myself in his voice, repeating things that he had said to me. He was still with me; I still heard his voice, even if I had to make it myself. I hardly needed the obvious reasons for protecting myself from the loss and the trauma and the grief. As any child does, I lived far more in the moment than most adults do.

My trek across the road had inspired me to inquire of Miz Verlow if she had a map of the island. Indeed she did. In her tiny office just inside the foyer—it looked as if it had once been a coat closet—she had her desk and chair and file cabinet. The file cabinet stored numerous folders to answer the questions of her guests: local maps, restaurants, events, churches, and so on.

The map she gave me was a simple one, but could not be otherwise: Santa Rosa Island is a strip of sand, miles long and, at that time, with one main road more or less down the middle. The west end of the road is called Fort Pickens Road, and the other, the Avenue de la Luna. At the west end were the abandoned Civil War fortifications of Fort Pickens, and facilities for camping; the eastern end of Santa Rosa Island was part of Eglin Air Force Base. Of course I had heard airplanes, jets and props both, but had given them no particular thought: Pensacola presumably had an airport. There were bridges at three points on the island, with clusters of small businesses, hotels and motels, and residences at the island end of them. The short westernmost bridge connected a small intervening island, where a village had named itself Gulf Breeze. From it, the long Causeway reached to Pensacola.

The physical divide of the island from the mainland was one kind of safety. I would have erased that Causeway from the map if I could, but at least the bay it crossed constituted something of a moat. Mamadee did not know we were here. The crazy maid and the crazy cook from the Hotel Pontchartrain would never be able to find us here. Miz Verlow was another kind of safety, less obvious and of untested reliability, but a fallback position to Mama without a question.

Still, when I asked Miz Verlow if she had seen my broken glasses or my Betsy Cane McCall, she surprised me.

"I am not responsible for your belongings, Miss Calliope Dakin," she said, very severely. "They are entirely your own responsibility."

Of course she was correct. It seemed to me that I saw well enough without my glasses, and Betsy Cane McCall, well—I hardly missed her. I forgot the paper dolls and Rosetta's shears in their shoebox. Santa Rosa Island was a better toy than I had ever had. Or would.

A day or so later, when I wanted clean clothes, I noticed that the bloodied clothes and towels that I had thrown down the laundry chute had not been returned to me. When I inquired of Cleonie if she knew where they were, she frowned and said that she had never seen them at all. She would have remembered them because of the blood, she said, which she would have soaked in cold water before sending them out to be laundered. I looked frantically but was unable to avoid Mama's wrath that I had managed to lose one of the few changes of clothing that I owned, to say nothing of Miz Verlow's towels. Mama made me sleep on the floor for a month.

Twenty-nine

THOUGH the very young heal quickly by nature, the salve Miz Verlow gave me for it hastened the process. What it was, I do not know. Like all her nostrums, it came unmarked in a little glass jar or bottle. They all smelled of some flower or herb.

Rarely was there any more in the jar or bottle than was needed, the most immediate exception being Mama's pale green foot balm, which Miz Verlow provided in cylindrical milk glass containers like short fat candles. The contents would last a week. The fragrance was a new one to me, but not to Mama.

Mama declared that she had been looking for just that balm for years. It was the one that her beloved grandmama had used. It must be an old recipe, she advised me, for her grandmama's foot balm had been made up at the local pharmacy. Either Miz Verlow had had the recipe herself or a source in some pharmacy that still had the recipe; the important thing was that Miz Verlow deserved as little credit for the superior foot balm as Mama could give her. On occasion though, when it suited Mama, she would praise Miz Verlow's foot balm extravagantly, and speculate that it would make a fortune if it were made commercially available.

Merrymeeting had two parlors. The small parlor— relatively smaller—was, as I have said, home to the television set and the radio-phonograph console. Miz Verlow's collection of LPs included commonplace classical music, musicals and film soundtracks. She allowed me to use the turntable in the late afternoon, before supper. The Zenith television in the opposite corner remained of only minor interest to me. Pensacola only had one television station, WEAR, and the offerings were limited. I knew how to operate the Zenith and how to adjust the rabbit ears, and did so for the guests who on occasion wanted to watch some particular program in the early evening.

The large parlor boasted the biggest bookcase in the house. On leaving, guests often abandoned books. The left-behind volumes found a new home in the big bookcase in the large parlor, or in other smaller bookcases around the house. Miz Verlow had been shelving or reshelving the books when I arrived, but before I went back to school, I took over the job. In those first few days, I thumbed through the slew of books on birds and shells and native plants.

Miz Verlow happened on me studying on one of them, on the floor behind a big wing-backed chair, so as not to be underfoot or bother anyone. She told me that I could keep the ones that I was studying in Mama's room, unless a guest asked for it. I added them to the books that I had stolen from my dead uncle. In the room that Mama and I shared, I had a bottom drawer in a dresser for my clothes. My books fitted under my clothes well enough, at least for a while.

Later, Miz Verlow took me with her on long walks to gather herbs and bark used in her medicinals. One of these plants was the shrub that grew up against the skirts of the house. As soon as I smelled it, I recognized it as one of the ingredients in Mama's foot balm. Miz Verlow said its common name was Candle Bush, after its yellow flower spikes. Perdita and Cleonie called it Burnin' Candles.

For a week, Miz Verlow sent a nightcap up to Mama every evening. Mama slept late in the mornings and arose in a cheerful mood. I was able to slip out each day without disturbing her.

When I was rubbing her feet at bedtime, Mama would bemoan her woes and then swear that she would get Ford back and the money and see her mama in hell. Those goals required a lawyer, of course; she complained bitterly to me that she had no money for a lawyer. She could not hire a Florida lawyer anyway, because Florida lawyers couldn't practice law in Alabama. She knew that for a fact because she had called a firm of lawyers in Pensacola, right out of the phone book. She consoled herself with the conviction that the lawyers in Pensacola were likely all drunks anyway, or profoundly incompetent in the protection of widows and orphans.

Mama was so gracious and sweet to Miz Verlow that no guest would ever suspect that Mama hated her. Mama had spent her life at war with Mamadee. What could be easier or more convenient than to replace Mamadee with Miz Verlow. Mama could never admit to herself that she did not, in fact, signify all that much to Miz Verlow.

Mama played Southern lady of the house to the guests when they were around. She did not speak of what had happened to Daddy nor did she hasten to reveal that I was her child. Miz Verlow introduced me merely as "Little Calley." Some of the guests concluded that I was some foundling benefiting from Miz Verlow's conscientious charity. Others hardly noticed that I existed, which was fine with me.

I never minded the chores that structured the day. They made me feel as if I belonged. After I washed up after each meal, Miz Verlow showed me the page of a notebook on which she kept the record of each nickel that I earned. Until my bruises healed—only a few days—I ate in the kitchen.

Miz Verlow's guests most commonly departed on Saturday, new ones arriving on Sunday evening. Taxis summoned from town took away the guests who had not come in their own vehicles, and the parking lot emptied of everything but Miz Verlow's Country Squire and the Edsel.

By one-thirty in the afternoon, Cleonie and I had the customary Saturday dinner buffet cleared away and the table reset for the supper that Perdita was preparing. Miz Verlow would serve it, allowing Perdita and Cleonie to take their leave. By three, the beds were stripped and remade, the bathrooms cleaned and restocked with the necessities. Thereupon, the colored taxi came to drive Cleonie and Perdita to the lives they lived in Pensacola. They would return Sunday evening by nine P.M. The other six nights of the week, they slept in a room behind the kitchen. It had its own little closet with a basin and a toilet.

On the shabby old dresser that the two women shared were

family photographs that I had not yet had sufficient opportunity to study. Perdita and Cleonie were respectable AME church ladies and worshipped as conscientiously as they worked for Miz Verlow.

Their AME church was not included, of course, in the listing of local churches and their schedules that Miz Verlow provided for her guests. The most exotic church on that list was St. Michael's Roman Catholic in Pensacola. Jews, Baha'is, Mormons and Muslims never did get any listings, nor did any snake-handlers or Holy Rollers. Pensacola certainly had some of each and no doubt they all had their places of worship. Pensacola had then and has now as many churches as any other town, so about anyone not a total heathen could and can find their own brand. Heathens, of course, have nothing to complain about.

In her defense, Miz Verlow expressed absolutely no interest in the religious affiliations or practices of her guests. If she knew that some of them were Catholics or Jews or Buddhists who practiced their religions anonymously, it did not stop her letting them her rooms. I am confident that she would have found a means of turning away a suspected snake-handler, not because she had any particular feelings about snake-handling but to spare her other guests being proselytized. She had a great feeling for the privacy of her guests that she observed by her own idiosyncratic set of rules. And she was quite willing to drive them back and forth to the place of worship of their choosing.

That very first Sunday we did not attend church at all.

Mama said, "I cannot take you out in public looking such a fright. I don't suppose the inconvenience to me entered your calculations, did it?"

"I ain't got a dress anyway," I said, "or a hat or coat or gloves."

Reminded that I had arrived at Merrymeeting with little more than a couple of changes of clothes in my suitcase and had lost one change, Mama glared at me.

"I was nearly growed out of the grey dress anyway," I pointed out.

She pursed her lips. "I suppose you think good clothes

grow on trees? Stop saying 'ain't' and 'growed.' You've been raised to know better. I swear the Dakin in you has destroyed all the Carroll."

Mama slept in until noon that Sunday and then spent the afternoon on the beach. It was scarcely warm enough yet for sunbathing but Mama had decided that she was sickly pale, due to pining away in widowhood and having lost a child and all the other terrible shocks of recent months, and so she shivered on a chaise in her sunsuit. I was in charge of fetching her coffee or another magazine from the house. Sadly for her, I was also her only audience.

Mama explained to Miz Verlow the necessity to go into Pensacola to buy me a dress. On Tuesday, with her guests all settled, Miz Verlow drove us to town in her Country Squire. Miz Verlow knew where the best store was, she assured us, which happened to be having a sale on children's clothing. Between flattery and pointing out all the bargains to be had, Miz Verlow baited Mama into buying me not only these new dresses, but a new coat, new Mary Janes, new socks and a hat, another straw boater that fit over the napkin on my head, new underpants, new pajamas, and new overalls and shirts. Each piece of clothing fit me, but it was all in colors that made me look half dead. I was indifferent. I never had had any pretty clothing and didn't expect any. The whole collection really came surprisingly cheap, which pleased Mama intensely. Of course, after all that shopping, I had to massage her feet for an extra-long time that night.

Mama was forced to give me a few inches of closet space to hang my three dresses, but she made me unload the books from my clothes drawer to accommodate the rest of my new clothing. She threatened to throw the books out. My wails brought Miz Verlow, who saved my books by granting me the lowest, least used shelf in the linen closet.

The following Sunday, the first in May, Miz Verlow very kindly chauffeured Mama and me to Christ Episcopal. A blind fog obscured our passage on and off the island as thoroughly as the dark of night had on our arrival, yet Miz Verlow always seemed to know where she was.

My appearance with the napkin around my head under my new boater caused a little flutter in the church. Mama wore black, including her veil. When we left the church, the pastor took Mama's hand in his at the door. I thrust myself between them and stepped on the toes of the pastor's well-shined shoes, producing a satisfactory wince and the release of Mama's hand.

On our return, the mist so blurred Miz Verlow's house, it appeared to be abandoned. The lights were all out; the power, off. Inside, the house felt empty as an old barn. The diffuse, feeble light of the dark day did not penetrate the darker corners of the house, while the cold damp pierced us all to our marrow.

Miz Verlow sent me to the kitchen to fetch the cold plates Perdita had left for us. We ate in the dining room, by the light of a single yellow candle in a silver candlestick that had come from Mamadee's house. I was not so foolish as to mention that I recognized it. What interested me more was that the candle was obviously homemade—not crudely either, but with skill. As it burned, it gave off a tarry but not offensive odor that made me think of Mama's foot balm.

Little as I wanted to think about Miz Verlow's terms, I was not enough Mama's child to be able to exclude from my thoughts that which was—unpleasant. On the contrary, the more I wish not to think of something, the more I do. I have learned to think what I have to think when I have to think it. Naturally, unwelcome thoughts return but they do so less annoyingly.

Once dinner was out of the way, Miz Verlow suggested cards.

Though Mama's first reaction to the suggestion of Sunday card playing was a scandalized hitch of one eyebrow, she realized immediately that her outrage was wasted without an audience. She sat down to the card table with a coy lack of enthusiasm. Mama always loved cards. She played the worst and had the worst luck of anyone I ever knew. In Mama's world though, she was a sharp, a player without equal. Presented with an opportunity to exercise her skills, she seized upon it. Quite aside from anything else, cards might very well provide her with leverage over Merry Verlow.

Mama and Miz Verlow and I sat down in the large parlor to play Hearts. My card playing skills at that time were very basic but I already knew enough to let Mama win. Rather than open new, we played with an old deck of cards, a red one with the initials CCD on the back. My initials—though the cards were at least twenty years old, and truly unfit for anything but cheating at Solitaire. The parlor was as quiet as it could be with the three of us in it, speaking as little as possible, concentrating on the cards. Our only light was the candle that Miz Verlow brought with her from the dining room. Its light was magnified by the parlor's enormous mirror, hanging opposite me and the fireplace behind me. The small flame burned intently, the burnt wick collapsing sadly into the pooled melted beeswax. In the mirror, it appeared as a tongue of fire, kindled out of the depthless shadows in the reflected fireplace. The scent of the burning candle reminded me of the church service we had attended, and of my daddy's funeral.

It won't make any difference.

"What won't?" Mama responded tersely, glaring at her exposed cards in hope of defying Miz Verlow's unexpected gibe.

"Pardon me?" said Miz Verlow.

Miz Verlow and Mama then looked at me, though the voice that had spoken possessed neither the scale nor timbre of a seven-year-old girl child.

Miz Verlow passed the question on to me. "What won't make any difference, Calley?"

It won't make any difference to me simply because I am dead.

We were at that moment all looking at one another. None of us had spoken.

So who had?

We were alone, the three of us, in that isolated house.

Mama was stricken pale. Even Miz Verlow looked distressed. It fell to my lot to deal with the matter. And to me, Calliope Carroll Dakin, whose initials were on the deck of playing cards on the little triangular table before us, it was perfectly obvious whose voice had sounded in the stifling front parlor. I looked in the mirror. Her face looked out, not at us, but as if through a window. Her eyes were wide and teary with terror.

"Mamadee, is that you?" I asked.

It is, and it isn't.

"Shut up!" Mama snapped at me.

I kept my eyes fixed on the mirror but before I could tell Mama to look into it, Mamadee's voice spoke again:

You don't have to be rude, Roberta Ann.

Mama jumped up and strode toward the door, preparing to fling it open—even though she knew as well as I that the voice was not coming from the hallway or from any other part of the house.

I am not out there, Roberta Ann.

Mama stopped with her hands reaching for the door. Then she took a step backward as if the door itself had spoken.

Miz Verlow rose. "Are you in here?"

She was like a miner, digging deep to rescue a child tumbled down a disused shaft. Breaking open a crumbling wall, she softly questions the dead, soft darkness, *Are you in there?*

I understood then that neither Miz Verlow nor Mama saw Mamadee in the mirror.

I don't know. I don't know where I am. But I know I see who killed me—

"She's lying. Mama's not dead." Mama looked at me hard. "If my mama were dead, we would know about it."

"Are you dead?" I asked aloud.

Mama grabbed my shoulders and shook me hard. "Stop pretending to be Mama!"

Then she looked around her, as if something were hiding behind her back. Eyes wide as ever I had seen them, she was visibly shaking.

"Mama!" she wailed. "You caint be dead!"

Suddenly the room was colder, as if someone had opened a window. The candle flickered and went out. Thin threads of white smoke rose from its wick.

The voice exclaimed in outrage: *Roberta Ann Carroll, that is my candlestick on that table!*

Mama was not to be diverted by mere issues of ownership.

"You want to make me feel bad!" she cried. "Well you caint make me feel bad because number one I did not kill you, and number two I never even knew you were dead, and number three, I don't believe you are my mama because we don't have ghosts in our family! There are no Carroll ghosts!"

The ghost—or whatever it was—had no response to

Mama's barrage of illogic. Mama dug her fingers out of my shoulders. Miz Verlow started to move toward the door. She was going to try to get us out of there before anything else— and anything worse—happened.

Then, abruptly, Mamadee spoke again, asking a confused, tentative question: *Roberta Ann, where on earth are you?*

"What does she mean?" Mama whispered to me.

I replied in the voice that seven-year-old girls use when reciting an Easter verse at the front of the church: "We are in Pensacola, Florida, Mamadee. In Miz Verlow's house. She is distant kin to the Dakins but not related to them by blood."

Again the voice came, soft and fumbling, addressing Mama and ignoring my reply and me.

I am looking at a chair, Roberta Ann, that chair right behind you—my mama did the bargello on that chair. So where on earth did you get it? Because I know that chair burned up. It burned up in 1942. Are you in Mama's house again, Roberta Ann?

"No!" Mama cried, "It's 1958 and this is Pensacola Beach!"

It's Banks, said Mamadee's voice, *and this is a house that burned down, due to your carelessness with candles, before Calley was born. So if you are here, then you are dead—both of you—and I'm glad. . . .*

"She doesn't mean that," Mama whispered hotly in my ear. "She doesn't wish we were dead."

"Why are you glad we're dead?" I asked Mamadee.

Because then, Calley, you wicked wicked little witch— Mamadee laughed, the same laugh she used to laugh when she read in the morning paper that someone she did not like had died before she had—*because then, Calley, I will not have to warn you about what's going to happen to you. So now maybe they will let me go back. So maybe—*

I guess "they" did let Mamadee go "back," because she left right then in the middle of her thought, and we never heard her voice again.

Thirty

MAMA'S mind fastened not on what had happened but on what it might mean to her. If it had truly been Mamadee's ghost who had spoken, then Mamadee was dead. The idea of Mamadee dead and gone threw Mama into unbearable panic; it meant that the rope she had been hauling on all her life was all at once loose at the other end. The reality of Mamadee's death could hardly be countenanced; it stuck in her craw like a mouse in a snake's belly. Before she could digest it, she had to figure out why she had been informed of the fact—if it were a fact—by such extraordinary means.

If that were not enough, Mamadee's cryptic remark, *I won't have to warn you about what's going to happen to you,* was guaranteed to unsettle us. Mama had to find an interpretation of that sibylline pronouncement that was not a portent of evil.

I was willing to say it had been Mamadee's voice, simply because, if it were, Mamadee might very well be dead. I certainly hoped so, with all my heathen heart, and was only disappointed that she had not complained of the singe and stink of hellfire. I could think of no reason that Mamadee should tell the truth just because she happened to be deceased. To this day I have found no reason to believe that the human soul, duplicitous to its core, suddenly becomes truthful just because it comes to be divorced from a corporeal form. I knew that I had held a conversation with Mamadee. I held my tongue, awaiting further developments. Waiting for Mama to realize the obvious.

Miz Verlow quietly collected our scattered cards and dropped them into a wastebasket. She picked up the candlestick.

"Lordy, I *am* cold," she said. "I believe I will indulge myself in some hot tea. If you should like to join me, I am sure the kitchen will be more comfortable than this ever-so-depressing dark room."

With this very reasonable excuse to escape the parlor, we repaired to the kitchen. It might have been the one time in her life that Mama went into a kitchen eagerly. The sudden conviction seized me that Mamadee had spoken not to inform us of her death and not to give Mama or me a warning but because *I* was in the room with Mama and Miz Verlow. From beyond the grave, she was pointing one of her knotty, meticulously manicured fingers at me. She wanted Mama and perhaps Miz Verlow to believe that I was either the source of a deception—or else her killer. Or both.

Miz Verlow settled the candlestick on the table. "Do sit down, Miz Dakin. I am going to fetch a shawl against the chill while the kettle boils. Would you like me to bring you a shawl or a sweater? One for Calley?"

Mama nodded.

Miz Verlow filled the kettle and lit the gas under it, then left us alone for a few minutes.

I busied myself fetching cups and saucers, teaspoons, a teapot, sugar and a cream jug from the butler's pantry, as I had been so recently trained.

The kettle shrieked as if to herald Miz Verlow's return. She smiled at me when she saw how busy I had been. Around her shoulders she had drawn a very fine soft wool shawl of a slate color.

For Mama she had brought Mama's own black cashmere sweater, and for me, a sweater of coarser wool. It was not my sweater. I did not own one anymore. The sweater Miz Verlow fetched for me was pilled and clearly hard-worn, with red blobs on a yellow background that were both busy and ugly. The sweater smelled too, of long storage in mothballs, and of something else, a rank mucky smell that reminded me distinctly of an outhouse. Mama shrugged quickly into her sweater without remarking upon the fact that Miz Verlow must have entered Mama's room and opened Mama's closet to obtain it.

I stuffed my hands through the sleeves of the yellow sweater with its peculiar red motif, and with considerable effort, forced the sharp-edged buttons through the too-tight buttonholes. The sweater did not make me warmer. If anything, I felt colder. The wool prickled my skin. It was badly knitted too, lumpy in some places, loose to the point of gaping in others, and so tight around my armpits that it cut into my skin. Once it was on me, I was instantly convinced that it had belonged to a child now dead. I could hear that child choking in the waves, and the water drawing it relentlessly down. When I tried to unbutton it to get out of it, my fingers were too cold to manipulate the buttons through the buttonholes again.

Miz Verlow hummed while she made the tea and poured it. I recognized the tune.

"You are my sunshine," I sang in my own voice, *"my only sunshine."*

"Stop it, Calley!" Mama cried. "My head's killing me."

Miz Verlow leaned over Mama. She took one of Mama's unresisting hands and then the other and wrapped them around a teacup.

"Hold the warmth, Roberta Ann. Drink it up. It will help your poor head."

Mama wanted to believe Miz Verlow; I saw it in her face.

Miz Verlow sat on one side of Mama while I wriggled into the chair on the other side.

The candle flame reflected darkly in my tea; it looked as if it were burning inside the liquid. The tea burned my mouth, and all the way down my throat. It was Lapsang souchong, its normal flavor adulterated by the taste of wax and charred wick. The surface of the tea in the cup settled and I stared again at the candle flame in it; my head felt heavy, my eyes strained. My scalp felt as if it were bleeding from thousands of pinpricks; I could feel the stubble poking through the follicles.

Mama put down her empty cup and Miz Verlow refilled it. Mama looked at me.

"Calley," she said, in a flat, ugly voice, "you were making that voice, I know you were. Mocking me! Mocking my poor darling mama!"

With a slow shake of my head, I denied it silently.

A mild, amused speculation danced in Miz Verlow's eyes as she looked from one to the other of us.

"Do it," Mama said, "Say 'It won't make any difference,' in Mamadee's voice."

I looked at Miz Verlow and shrugged.

Miz Verlow seemed unsurprised and very interested.

"Don't you call me a liar," Mama said. "Don't you make me look crazy, Calley!"

Miz Verlow reached out and touched my wrist but she spoke to Mama. "Miz Dakin, we have had a shock. I take it from what you say that the voice we heard was that of your mama. Why ever do you think that Calley was somehow speaking in that voice? We were both looking right at her. I did not see her lips move except when she asked The Voice a question."

Mama ignored her. Mama said my name angrily. "Calley!"

"Uh-uh, Mama, I caint make Mamadee's voice without moving my lips."

Miz Verlow's fingers around my wrist tightened. "But you can mimic your grandmama's voice."

" 'Roberta,' " I said in Mamadee's voice, " 'where on earth are you?' "

Mama shuddered.

"Is that your mama's voice?" Miz Verlow asked her.

"Yes," Mama whispered. "To the life."

"I have to move my lips though," I pointed out. "And I ain't makin' mock."

"Say something in my voice," Miz Verlow told me.

So I did. " 'Say something in my voice.' "

In the silence that followed, I took a big gulp of the tea in my cup. Speaking in someone else's voice made me dry. The tea scorched my throat without relieving my thirst.

"I should have taken Ford and left her," said Mama. "I believe she is possessed."

I ignored the gibe about my being possessed. I had heard it before; it meant nothing much to me.

"Ford did not want to go," I reminded her. "He wanted to stay with his color TV. And Mamadee."

"Ford." Mama's voice rose with excitement as she finally realized what the first consequence of Mamadee's passing was. "I'm going to get back my baby boy!"

Just then the lights flickered on and off, and then steadied in the fullness of the electrical power restored. The flame of the candle seemed to shrink.

Miz Verlow reached across the table to pinch it out.

Black smoke like fleeing souls writhed from the wick. The odor of the burnt wax hung in the air; the taste of it in my mouth, charred and greasy. The odor and the taste and the tea leaves in my cup seemed to be all that remained of the visitation. It struck me that the leaves at the bottom of my cup made a pattern like the ugly red blobs on the sweater Miz Verlow had fetched me. Never before had I seen such a strange design. Polka dots most often keep their distance from one another but these not only stood alone but made short lines and angles and yet there was no symmetry to them. Some of them looked like spots of dried blood.

Mama reached into a skirt pocket for her pack of Kools. Crumpled and wrapped around its meager bouquet of three butts, it was no wider than the packet of matches tucked between its cellophane and foil. She was rationing her cigarettes against the chance of bumming some from one or more of the newly arriving guests, and tomorrow morning's walk to the gas station at Pensacola Beach for more. She began poking around the kitchen, hunting an ashtray.

Miz Verlow took the teapot back to the stove to add hot water.

The candle had subsided into a new shape and the melted wax was slightly translucent. I touched the candle to confirm its warmth. It took the imprint of my fingers as if it were ink. Under the crash of waves and a rising wind, I heard a distant motor, one I recognized.

"You might as well have that candle, if you want it, Calley, it's just a stub." Miz Verlow turned to face us again, with the teapot in both hands. "And we can spare a stub."

She had not seen me touch the candle, nor had Mama.

Mama snorted smoke.

"Don't let her have any matches," Mama advised, dropping her lit match hastily into the ashtray in her other hand as its flame nipped her fingertips. "Not if you don't want her burning down this house!"

Miz Verlow poured herself another cup of tea. She didn't sit down again but stayed on her feet, looking down at me.

"Do you do that often, Calley?" she asked. "Burn down houses?"

I shook my head no. I wondered if I should tell Miz Verlow the lady with the fedora was returning.

"Too bad," Miz Verlow said. "Some days, I would insure this one to the roof beams and buy the matches for you."

Mama near choked.

When she recovered from her coughing, she said, "Name the devil! Are you trying to give Calley ideas?"

Miz Verlow never answered the question. She put a hand to one ear, listening.

"I do believe I hear a guest arriving."

Thirty-one

OUTSIDE the world was still submerged in fog. I raced from the front door to the drive, leaving Mama and Miz Verlow to follow in a more dignified fashion. There was nothing to see, not yet, though the motor *thrum* continued its approach. As I stood hugging myself against the cold, the wind twitched the fragile veils of mist. My teeth chattered; my skin goose bumped.

"Calley," shouted Mama.

I turned toward her voice.

A ghostly giant stood right in front of me. My breath stopped in my throat. As the fog shivered and rippled, the giant shivered and rippled over me, as if to engulf me.

The oncoming vehicle was behind me, the noise of its approach increasing, the sweep of its lights intensifying even as the giant ghost loomed closer over me. An automobile horn blatted violently.

A sudden gust dissolved the giant ghost. The fog-colored coupe, smoothly losing momentum, sailed by along the milky way of its own headlights.

I scampered back to the verandah steps to find Miz Verlow smiling at the coupe while Mama, at her side, peered at it anxiously. When I slipped behind Mama, grabbing at her skirt, she yanked the cloth from my fingers briskly.

"Stop being such a baby," Mama said, but her attention was riveted on the arriving guest.

Like the servants in a BBC period-costume film, Mama and I stood to one side as Miz Verlow opened the door of the silver coupe with the Maryland plate. A woman emerged from behind the wheel.

Everything about the lady was grey, yet she seemed neither old nor faded at all. She appeared older than Mama and Miz Verlow, younger than Mamadee, and there was nothing stupid or weak about her. She was no ghost out of the fog but a woman of dense human substance. Her presence calmed me. The giant ghost figure that I had seen seemed at once to have been nothing more than a flighty delusion.

When she drew off her driving gloves, her hands were exquisitely manicured, and the skin younger than that of her neck. Obviously she protected and cared for her hands, even though they were not in themselves beautiful or elegant. They were entirely unremarkable hands, square and short-fingered. Soft of course. This woman never did a lick of work for herself, or even stooped to playing tennis or gardening. She wore no rings or bracelets.

As I was sorting out these memories, I realized that she looked like someone whose face was familiar to me. Years would go by before I was able to put a name to the face.

Miz Verlow introduced her to us that night as Mrs. Mank.

Mrs. Mank's hair was grey, shot with strands of black, and fashioned in short, tight, rather harsh waves. Her eyes were grey too, a lighter grey than the pearls around her neck. Her cheeks, pale with powder, were full and round, her nose sharp and long and cold like grey marble. The pink of her lipstick was like Mama's palest lipstick with a coating of grey ash. The dress she wore was of two shades of nearly indistinguishable grey, the piping pearl grey, the basic fabric a little more silvery. A double strand of pearls glistened around her neck and her earlobes held fat pearl studs.

Her shoes were softly burnished pewter in color; Mama told me later that they were handmade. She also said that they were about her size, a size five; they may have been size fives but Mama's shoe size was a six. That never stopped her cramming her foot into a five or a five-and-a-half. Mrs. Mank's stockings were silk, the color of cobwebs.

Mrs. Mank smiled warmly. "Roberta Ann Carroll Dakin, at last."

Her accent was not the familiar accent of Alabama or

Florida or Louisiana, nor was it anything that I recognized as
obviously foreign—the ones like the Chiquita Banana lady's,
or the hoity-toity English accent that I knew primarily from
television and radio. If her plates were Maryland plates, I
speculated, she might be from Maryland; her accent might be
that of Maryland.

Already disconcerted by the most recent events, Mama
must have been more than a little dazzled by the silver coupe
that Mrs. Mank drove—a foreign make at a time when few
Americans drove foreign cars—and then by Mrs. Mank's
pearls and by Mrs. Mank's sheer presence.

Mrs. Mank looked at me briefly, the way most people did,
expecting very little and apparently finding somewhat less.

Intent on making Mrs. Mank welcome, Miz Verlow accompanied her to her rooms. Mrs. Mank had a private bath
and a sitting room as well as a bedroom, a suite created by un-
locking doors between connecting rooms. Miz Verlow surprised me by asking me to bring up Mrs. Mank's luggage. She
must have known that it consisted only of a train case and a
Gladstone bag (a term I had picked up in the short time since
our arrival at Miz Verlow's house). At first they seemed heavy,
but before I had taken two steps from the open trunk of Mrs.
Mank's foreign automobile, they seemed as light as if they
were empty.

Once I had delivered the two pieces to Mrs. Mank's suite, I
returned to close the coupe's trunk. The automobile fascinated
me: a low, long-nosed, short-tailed two-seater with wire hub-
caps, so unlike the American makes that I knew by sight. The
Edsel looked gaudy next to it. Where the Edsel sported a
blinding weight of chrome and a squared-off roofline, fins,
scallops and deep-set owlish headlights above its massive split
bumper, this vehicle was—tidy, elegant, secretive. While the
Edsel thrust itself forward, as if to plow through the air, Mrs.
Mank's car occupied its own space wholly. The Edsel was
boxy; the whole body of Mrs. Mank's coupe curved. It was
chromed, to be sure, but unconventionally and elegantly. The
headlights sat *on* the very hood, in their own chrome-edged
caverns. On the hood and the trunk a medallion depicted a
leaping horse, and another medallion, a horse with wings,
head-on. And on the trunk, in script, was the word

Pegaso

Like Pegasus, the winged horse. *Pegaso* must be foreign for Pegasus but what brand of foreign, I could not begin to guess. I tried it out to myself in Mrs. Mank's voice and accent: *Pegaso*. Evidently it was not a magic word, for no magical event occurred—no sudden flash, no piano trill, no winged horse pawing the sand.

The glove box was locked, preventing me from educating myself from any manuals or registration forms that might have been inside it.

The wind had risen and become urgent, shredding the fog and blowing it away. It snatched at my clothing, trying to drag me toward the beach. But it was not great enough to muffle the sound of two more vehicles on the road from the Pensacola Beach.

The yellow sweater provided no warmth. It felt as if it were shrinking in tight bands around my chest and neck and wrists.

I ran to the kitchen for a pair of shears and began cutting the buttons off the sweater. I started at the bottom, as it was easiest. The edges of the buttons had not dulled in the time since I had forced them through the holes, and they were hard to grasp. But I succeeded, at the cost of a few cuts and a little blood, in getting the blades of the scissors behind the shanks of the buttons and through the thread holding them to the wool. Despite the relaxation of the wool as the buttons fell away onto the floor, the one at the top was the most difficult, with my chin tucked to the point of the scissors blade. The threads gave way very suddenly to the gnawing of the blades and the button popped the highest and widest of them all— popped directly onto Mrs. Mank's forefinger and thumb, as if it were on an elastic string. *I never heard her enter the kitchen.* An instant's terror snapped through me; it was like touching an electrical socket.

She stood there in the middle of the kitchen, looking down at me. Her face was as straight as her back.

The button flickered between her fingers and was gone.

"Waste not, want not," she remarked. "Or so I have been told."

And then she passed regally out of the kitchen by way of the swinging door to the butler's pantry. As she walked through the dining room and the foyer and out the door onto the verandah, I listened to her step. It was as audible as anyone else's would have been.

I collected the three other buttons from the corners where they had rolled. The sweater still bound me at the armpits. I struggled out of it, bundled the buttons and the candle stub on the kitchen table into it and looked around for a place to hide it for a while. The kitchen was about to be busy; no place in it was safe from disturbance. Opening the door to Cleonie's and Perdita's room, I dropped my bundle just inside.

The new arrivals were climbing out of their vehicles outside.

The previous Sunday, I had helped Miz Verlow put out the refreshments. I meant to do it all by myself today but the weird visitation from Mamadee's voice, and the ghost giant in the fog gave me greater impetus; the long list of responsibilities put off both the immediate shock and the consideration thereof. I raced into the parlor, where the coffee urn stood ready to go, and plugged it in. Then I hurried back to the kitchen. By the time the guests had been shown their rooms and had time to relieve and refresh themselves, I was supposed to have everything needed in the reading room, arranged around the coffee urn on the big piecrust table: cups in their saucers, coffee spoons, little plates and napkins. There was tea to make, the hot water jug to fill, cream and sugar cubes, lemon slices, and plates of sweets and savories and little crustless sandwiches left by Perdita in the refrigerator, for me to array. Nothing was larger than a bite or two, so as not to spoil anybody's supper.

Mama drifted in first. She made a sad job of pouring herself coffee. She too was still trying to absorb the voice and its utterances. Her cigarette shortage added to her restlessness. I was not surprised to have her frown at me over her cup as she raised it to her lips.

"I'll pour for the guests, Calley. Go somewhere else. Children should be seen and not heard."

I had not said a word. I hoped that her hand steadied before she actually had to pour for someone other than herself. Turning to leave, I nearly ran into Mrs. Mank.

"Oh Lord," Mama said. "Calley, apologize for stepping on Miz Mank's toes!"

Mrs. Mank smiled coldly at me and even more coldly at Mama. "No harm done, Mrs. Dakin." She clearly articulated the "Mrs." "This little girl is a busy little creature, isn't she?" Mrs. Mank continued. "I expect that she has more to do."

"Yes, she does," agreed Mama, with open pleasure at the thought.

Though I was very curious to see how Mama and Mrs. Mank would get along, I was also aware that Miz Verlow needed me. I could almost hear her in my head, calling my name.

Outside, around the back, Miz Verlow was stacking her trolley with luggage. I ran up to her and helped her push it up the ramp into the back hall.

"I hope you grow fast," she said. "I caint wait for you to be able to sling some of these bags for me."

I stood straighter and tried to look bigger. The implication that I was going to live in Miz Verlow's house long enough to do any growing thrilled me.

She stepped back from the trolley to take a breather.

"Miz Verlow," I asked, "did you ever see a ghost?"

The question did not seem to surprise her.

"I might have."

That was as good as an admission to me. "What size was it? Can ghosts be different sizes?"

She shook her head at me. "Slow down, little girl. I said that I might have. That doesn't make me an expert."

Which meant she didn't want to tell me. And also that likely ghosts did have different sizes.

I veered into yet another question. "Do Florida newspapers print bitcharies about dead people in Alabama?"

Miz Verlow chuckled. "Obituaries, you mean?"

I agreed that that was what I meant.

"Only if the dead person in Alabama were very important or died in a very unusual way."

What if Mamadee was not as important as she had seemed, or pretended to be? Of course, we had no idea how she died, if she had.

I tried another tack. "Is there another way to find out if a person is dead?"

"A phone call to that person's address might suffice. Or to a friend or acquaintance." She changed the subject. "You are very good at making voices."

I shrugged.

"I thought you might be. Fennie mentioned something—" Miz Verlow didn't finish. "Your mama says you were the fussiest baby ever."

Everything that ever happened to Mama was the mostest, we both knew, so I made no response. I was distracted with the speculation that Miz Verlow had just hinted that I might call Mamadee's number and use somebody else's voice to inquire as to whether Mamadee was still in the land of living or had gone to her eternal reward in Satan's fiery embrace. I thought of calling one of my Dakin uncles. One of the uncles, one of the aunts, would know for certain sure if Mamadee was dead yet. I would have to ask an operator for a number.

Miz Verlow continued, "You hear extraordinarily well, don't you?"

"Yes, ma'am." I agreed as softly and humbly as I could.

Ida Mae Oakes always told me bragging on a gift was crass.

"Must be hard to concentrate," Miz Verlow said, as if we were talking about finding the right size of shoe.

It had taken me most of my seven years to get as far as I had, learning how to shut out enough of the world so I could think. Of course I knew, by the time that I was three or so, that I heard quite a lot more than other people, and that other people didn't seem to know how to imitate sounds the way I did, more or less naturally. Ida Mae Oakes stuffed my ears with cotton balls to help block out some of the relentless noise, and then I did it for myself. Later still, I figured out that I could sleep by accepting the noise, attending it closely until I floated away on it. When I told Ida Mae, she said that she was some relieved, what with the price of cotton balls always rising, and the boll weevils, and had I noticed how rough and red her hands had gotten from picking cotton and all? She made me laugh until the grits shot right out my nose.

I still thought, maybe sometime I would meet somebody who heard as much and as well as I did, and they would be good at making the sounds they heard as a matter of course. The closest I have ever gotten to a person like me have been the autistic savants I have encountered: I know of half a dozen who are blind and on first hearing can play any music on the piano, and adapt any music to any style, all without a moment's instruction or practice. I think now maybe it was an accident that I can see. That said, *I* could—and can—hear the imperfection of my own mimicry. I am not a musician nor a chanteuse, but something much more like a record player. And as for acuity of hearing: The noise of the world is not only distracting; it can be outright painful; it can be deathly exhausting.

But I just nodded to Miz Verlow.

She said my name, "Calley?" Her voice dropped to a near whisper. "Calley, can you hear the dead?"

I blinked at her. Her question explained far more than I could answer.

"Yes, ma'am," I told her, "but it ain't worth hearing."

She looked shocked. "You mean that you don't understand it?"

I pressed my lips together. I felt like I had blurted out a secret. I was not about to tell her that I had *seen* Mamadee in the mirror as well.

Miz Verlow looked at me appraisingly for a moment.

When I didn't say anything more, she turned back to the trolley. "I think you can take this little one."

It was a small suitcase, an overnighter, and not heavy, at least until I was several steps from the top of the backstairs. But I managed. By then, I was wishing I would hurry up and grow bigger faster too.

Bobbing around inside the parlor again, clearing the used crockery to a tray, I heard Mama's step on the verandah and caught a glimpse of Mama, pacing there. Mrs. Mank was with her. The two of them smoking—Mrs. Mank's cigarettes, I had no doubt, as Mama would not have shared her last cigarettes with a dying soul. I listened closely but they were not speaking to one another. They seemed merely to be having a peripatetic and companionable smoke—a younger woman in black, an older woman in shades of grey. A couple of other guests were also so occupied but those individuals were strolling to the beach, trailing their wisps and puffs behind them.

It troubled me—it made me fearful—to think of Mama and Mrs. Mank conversing, but I could not have said why.

The guests had scattered their cups and saucers and teaspoons and napkins wherever they might, around the parlor and the other rooms of the ground floor. In great haste I collected them all and returned them to the kitchen, where I had already drawn the dishwater. Miz Verlow had instructed me to count all the cutlery and dishes, so I knew that everything that I had taken out was recovered. But Mama and Mrs. Mank did not know what I knew.

I slipped out as noiselessly as I could and idled along the verandah, my face fixed to convey the concentration of a small girl hunting forgotten cups or spoons.

The verandah went almost entirely around the house, from the kitchen at the back to the seaward front and on around the nether side. Disappointingly, Mama and Mrs. Mank had taken chairs next to each other and sat there silently gazing out at the guests who were wandering to the beach to see where they had come, or just to shake out the stiffness of their various journeys.

"There is no china or silver on the verandah," Mrs. Mank said, without looking at me. "Take your very large ears, Calley Dakin, and find Merry Verlow, who undoubtedly has means to occupy your small hands, if not your nose."

Mama snickered. It sounded just like one of Ford's noises.

Angry at being caught out, I blurted, "It's not fair that everybody can tell me what to do."

Mrs. Mank laughed rudely. "Next you'll want the vote."

The heat rose in my face. My transparent skin unfailingly betrays me.

"My daddy told me that people that step on other people," I said slowly, "are liable to get their ankles bit."

Mama sat up straight. "He never! You are a wicked little liar, Calley Dakin!"

I curtsied mockingly and sailed away. Behind me, Mama could not apologize sufficiently for my outrageous behavior. Fine by me.

In the kitchen I climbed my step stool and washed the dishes. I was very thorough and dried everything carefully, and set it all out again in the pantry to do double-duty after supper. As tired as I was already, the supper dishes, in their settings on the dining table, were yet to be dirtied.

I went upstairs to the linen closet. There I made myself a nest, within reach of my half dozen books. No one would know where I was; no one could command my services, such as they were. Why I was so convinced that a windowless cupboard deep in a big house must be safe from ghostly voices and apparitions, I could not have explained. It just seemed logical. As if I were tuning a radio, I tuned my ears to the sounds of the Gulf. The sloshing susurrations, so like a heartbeat, let me down gently into sleep.

Thirty-two

NO more than a couple of hours after the Edsel spat gravel at her, Mamadee drove her Cadillac the three and a half blocks to downtown Tallassee. She parked in front of Mrs. Weaver's dress shop. There, she went inside and announced that she was going to buy every umbrella on the premises. When Mrs. Weaver reacted with understandable surprise, Mamadee only replied imperiously that she had her reasons for the purchase. Mrs. Weaver then apologized that she had only five umbrellas for sale, but added that she would be happy to relinquish her own umbrella at an appropriate discount.

"Why in the *hell* would I want *your* old umbrella?" Mamadee replied.

Mrs. Weaver sniffed discreetly, sure that Deirdre Carroll had been drinking and before the noon hour, but she was disappointed. Only momentarily however, for in a quarter of an hour, she had convinced herself that she had indeed smelled bourbon on Deirdre Carroll's breath.

Mamadee deposited the five umbrellas in the trunk of her Cadillac and then went to Chapman's Department Store, where she bought every umbrella for sale in the ladies' department, every umbrella for sale in the men's department, and the one undersized frilled parasol that was for sale in the children's department. She gave her car keys to a salesman and told him to just put all her purchases—the umbrellas—in the trunk of her Cadillac, and that she would be back in a while to retrieve the keys. While the salesman was stowing the umbrellas in the trunk of the Cadillac, Mrs. Weaver came to the door of her shop and shared her belief with him that Deirdre Carroll had been drinking before noon. The salesman observed that he wouldn't be the least surprised.

Half an hour later, Mamadee returned to the department store with a little colored boy in tow. The child was burdened with five brown paper parcels, each with one or more umbrella handles sticking out of it. Mamadee had gone to every store and every shop and demanded to purchase every umbrella in current inventory. At the Ben Franklin Five and Dime, she had procured seven, two at the Harvester's Seed and Feed, three at Bartlett's Hardware, two at Durlie's Dollar Store, and one at the Piggly Wiggly—the tail end of a Morton Salt promotion. She had found none for sale at Dooling's Barber Shop, the Tastee Freez, the Alabama Power Company, Ranston Insurance, Smart's Jewelry, or at Quantrill's Lighting, Plumbing and Gas Fixture Supply Company, but she certainly had inquired.

Retrieving her car keys, Mamadee led the little colored boy with the fifteen umbrellas to the Cadillac. When he had shut the trunk, Mamadee carefully counted out not the promised twenty-five cents, but thirty-three dollars and thirty-two cents. Handing it over, she told the boy to come round to the house later so that she could make up the penny shortfall.

When the little colored boy had wandered off in the stupor of his unanticipated wealth, Mamadee entered Boyer's Drugstore, the only retail establishment in downtown Tallassee she had not yet visited. Here, however, she did not ask for umbrellas but rather marched directly to the pharmacy counter, and impatiently placed herself behind an elderly farmer whose deafness was severely slowing his purchase of a proprietary senna preparation for his even more elderly mother.

The pharmacist, Mr. Boyer, was surprised to see Mamadee at his counter. She always sent a maid if she needed a prescription filled or wanted an illegal refill of her blue paregoric bottle. She almost never came herself.

Having dealt with the deaf old farmer, Mr. Boyer steeled himself, smiled obsequiously and asked, "Miz Carroll, what can I do for you?"

Mamadee lifted her chin high into the air, to show its soft underside.

"Look at this place," she demanded. *Place* was the word

used to refer to a small bruise, blemish, or wound of indeterminate origin.

"I caint see anything from here," puzzled Mr. Boyer. "Maybe I better come around."

The pharmacist came round and closely peered beneath Mamadee's chin. "I still don't see anything, Miz Carroll."

"Well, it's there! I can feel it!"

By this time everybody at the fountain counter in front of the drugstore had turned to watch and listen.

Mr. Boyer started to press his index finger against the underside of Mamadee's chin, but she jerked back in alarm.

"Don't touch it! Just give me something to make it go away."

Mr. Boyer was at a loss. His wife left her station behind the counter and came to the back of the store.

"Is it a blister, Miz Carroll?" Mrs. Boyer asked.

"It is not a blister," Mamadee retorted. "It is a boil. I know it is a boil."

"I caint see anything either," Mrs. Boyer said gingerly, trying not to give offense.

"Do I care a hoot in hell if you can see it or not? It itches and I want to pick at it but you don't pick at a boil. So all I need from you is something to put on it so I don't pick at it and get it infected."

"Give her something," Mrs. Boyer muttered to Mr. Boyer.

Mr. Boyer hardly needed prompting. He mixed up a quantity of cold cream, cod liver oil, diaper-rash cream, and calamine, and filled a squat glass jar with it, typed out a label instructing *Apply As Warranted,* and handed it over to Mamadee. "I'm not supposed to give you this without a doctor's prescription, so I could get in real trouble. It's two seventy-five; I'll just put it on your bill."

By noon, all of Tallassee knew that Roberta Carroll Dakin had fled Ramparts. By four o'clock that afternoon, all of Tallassee knew of Deirdre Carroll's peculiar behavior downtown and in Boyer's Drugstore. Dr. Evarts therefore was not surprised when Mamadee called him up and told him to get over to her house right then.

"I have five people in my waiting room and all five of them have appointments," he told her.

Dr. Evarts intended to judge by her response to this refusal just how dire she felt her case to be.

"If I have to come over there," Mamadee replied, "those people in your waiting room won't be alive long enough to get cured. Do you hear me?"

Dr. Evarts had heard about Roberta Ann Carroll Dakin's departure with her odd little girl but without her son, and about Deirdre Carroll and the umbrellas. Dr. Evarts perceived gossip as an integral part of the life of the town, amusing and informing him, but on which he need not necessarily act. However, once he had arrived at Ramparts, Dr. Evarts realized that the tales he had heard had not been exaggerated. He found the front door open and when he called out for Tansy, there was no answer. The door was open, Dr. Evarts noted, and a sick woman lay within.

He found every door open, and opened umbrellas in every room.

Open umbrellas were propped in chairs, open umbrellas depended from the chandeliers, an open umbrella was planted in the deep pocket of a fox-fur coat in an open closet. An open umbrella filled the horn of the gramophone in Captain Senior's library. A small, open, frilled child's parasol—the kind of thing a six-year-old future beauty queen would brace on her shoulder at an Easter parade—was hooked over the ceiling molding on the staircase landing.

Upstairs, opened umbrellas like enormous black bats squatted on beds, snagged on curtain rods, or kept the rain out of commodes. Dr. Evarts paused to peek into Roberta Ann's bedroom. It appeared Roberta Ann had rummaged her own room like a thief. He peered around; the photograph of Roberta Ann showing off her legs in her shorts was gone. That bothered him more than he would have expected. He had always enjoyed looking at that photograph. Joe Cane Dakin, while he lived, had enjoyed the favors of a very beautiful woman. On the other hand, Joe Cane Dakin's fate was unenviable, to say the least.

Distracted already, he hardly glanced into the next open bedroom door and so passed it before what he saw registered. He took three steps backward and looked again.

The boy, Ford, sat on the edge of the bed. He wore a suit and tie. His hair was damp from a recent combing. A suitcase shared the counterpane with him. He looked bored. Dr. Evarts could not help reflecting what a handsome boy he was, blessed if blessing it was, with his mother's beauty and grace, and with her and Deirdre's willfulness, almost certainly no blessing.

"Took your time." Ford came to his feet. "The old witch has gone batty."

"Thank you for your diagnosis," Dr. Evarts said.

"You're welcome." Ford came to the door. He nodded down the hall toward Deirdre's room. "Well?"

Deirdre's bedroom door was closed. The keyhole was jammed with the ferrule of an umbrella—a small red and yellow affair with a long stem, meant to be raised over the seat of a tractor.

"Deirdre!" Dr. Evarts called at the door.

He tried to pull the umbrella out of the lock, but the point broke off.

He knocked. "It's Dr. Evarts! Are you in there, Deirdre?"

Ford leaned against the wall a yard away, his face impassive.

Though Dr. Evarts heard nothing, he had no doubt that Deirdre Carroll was on the other side of the door. He twisted the doorknob, pressed his shoulder against the panels, tried to twist the broken point out of the keyhole, all in vain. He looked round, stalked down the hall, and snagged the open umbrella that had been hooked over the stem of a gas sconce. It was large and unadorned, with an ebony handle, cold steel ribs, and black silk as thin as crepe. He positioned the steel ferrule against the floor, forcefully pressed his foot against the ribs of the umbrella, warping and then snapping them, straining and then ripping the dyed canvas, until nothing was left but the handle, the stem, a tiny halo of broken ribs, and the ferrule—all that he needed.

Squeezing the ferrule into the keyhole alongside the other, broken spike, Dr. Evarts twisted and pushed and pulled, lifted and jerked down and jerked out and shoved in, until he heard the sound of the entire mechanism of the lock breaking. The knob turned freely in his hand.

The ferrule that had been embedded in the keyhole fell out. It was red, as if it had been heated, and it smoked, singeing the hall carpet.

Ford applauded for a few slow sardonic claps.

Dr. Evarts glanced back at Ford. If Deirdre Carroll were indeed on the other side of the door, someone else must have jammed the umbrella in the keyhole, someone who meant to lock Deirdre in that bedroom.

"Where's Tansy?"

Ford shrugged. "Run off."

As Dr. Evarts had been quite sure, Deirdre Carroll was in the room. Even before he saw her, he heard her breath—soft, labored, stertorous. She lay motionless on her bed, her head turned slightly toward him in the doorway. When the doctor entered the room, Deirdre Carroll didn't speak. Very possibly she couldn't, owing to the boil beneath her chin.

It was nearly round, larger than a softball, and in color a dull black like the soot coating the walls of a fireplace where only the cheapest grade of coal ever burned. Whatever its origin, whatever purulence festered inside it, the black boil was larger and more obscenely bloated than the worst cancerous growth that Dr. Evarts had ever seen. Deirdre Carroll's head tilted back. The glistening black boil was so engorged, it pressed on her lungs below and pressed her jaw shut. It was little wonder she breathed only with difficulty, it was no wonder at all she had not responded to his calls.

Deirdre's eyes rolled in her head as she strained to see him. Avoiding eye contact, Dr. Evarts approached the bed. The surface of the boil was sooty black but it was definitely skin—the charred black skin of burn victims who had to sleep sitting up because it was less painful than lying down. Yet the boil glistened in places—shone with a lick of purple. Realizing his mouth had twisted in disgust, he tried a smile. The attempt failed.

"You should have called me sooner," he said, reaching a finger to touch the black boil. She winced away. He was unable to avoid the panic in her eyes: *Please don't touch it!* The same panic most people had of the needle, of the knife, of the cold steel forceps.

"It's all right, Deirdre, you're just going to feel a little pressure," he said, lightly pressing his index finger against the boil's black burned skin.

It exploded.

Thirty-three

EVEN as I sweated through that nightmare, I realized that I had dreamt and forgotten it several times. But this time, I woke with the conviction that Mamadee was indeed dead.

The napkin around my head had come loose. As soon as the soles of my feet slapped onto the floor, it fell away. I paid no mind. All I wanted to do was get out of the dark closet and wash my face.

When I did, what I saw in the bathroom mirror startled me. The hair growing on my head was not my old dull sandy hair. Its color was very like Miz Verlow's. It was very fine, though, finer than hers, and snarly. Hillbilly tow, I thought: Mama's gone be wild. All I needed was pink eyes. My new hair was still very short, just enough to wind around my forefinger, but that seemed like a remarkable length considering how short a time it been growing. My ears looked very naked. I thought that I looked quite a lot like a blonde monkey.

Downstairs, Mama was charming the guests at supper.

Miz Verlow came up the backstairs. I kept the bathroom door closed until she passed by and then peeked out. She bore a tray. At the door of Mrs. Mank's suite, she stopped, knocked lightly, and was admitted.

I slipped down the backstairs into the kitchen. Cleonie and Perdita had not yet returned. Remembering my little bundle, I hastened to their room to retrieve it. It was gone. The inexplicable absence frightened me more when I was already skittish. I tried to reassure myself that nobody in the house except myself would bother to sneak into Cleonie and Perdita's room.

They had nothing to steal and besides, nobody would want to know what a cramped dingy little space they were accorded.

Miz Verlow was in the kitchen doorway from the back hall when I turned around, having closed the door to Cleonie and Perdita's room with exaggerated caution.

Miz Verlow smiled at me. "Is that Calley Dakin creeping underneath that bird's nest of hair? Or is that some new little girl come to take her place?" She ruffled my hair softly, not so much with admiration as with satisfaction. "My Lord, it makes me think of my hair when I was a child. I believe it's a touch lighter than mine. Someday it will be quite beautiful, even if you never are. Well, Roberta Ann Dakin is not gone care for it one bit. You best take your supper here. Then you shoo back upstairs to your mama's room. My guests get an eyeful of you, they'll think the place must be an orphanage for albino monkeys. Oh, and I left you some shampoo in the bathroom."

She made no remark at all about catching me closing the door to Perdita and Cleonie's room.

For once Mama's door was unlocked, and so while everyone else was still occupied with supper, I was able to wash my hair and bathe and put on my pajamas. I worked a comb through my tangles and managed to stick most of my hair damply to my skull. I could tell it was going to snarl up again the minute it was dry.

I was on my stomach on the bed, studying on a bird guide, when Mama stuck her key in the lock and then yanked it out. She jerked the door open one-handed.

"I left this door locked! How'd you get in?" she demanded, even as she registered my hair. She slammed the door closed behind her without spilling a drop of the drink in her hand. "Jesus God!"

I resisted the impulse to say *He ain't here*. Instead I suggested, "Maybe you didn't turn the key all the way."

Miz Verlow must have unlocked it for me. I was not about to give her away to Mama.

"You didn't creep in under the door?"

Mama put her drink down and patted a pocket in her skirt. With an air of secretive triumph, she drew a nearly full pack of Kools from it. I would not give her the satisfaction of asking her where or how she had obtained them. She was dying to tell but she wasn't going to do it unless I asked. She smoked three of them, one after the other, while I did her feet.

"That woman bleached your hair right out and you never so much as said no please, did you? You caint be expecting me to claim you, can you?"

Falsely meek, I said, "No, ma'am."

"Damn right," declared Mama. "I swear. Nobody with eyes in their head will ever mistake you for anything but a Dakin now."

That was fine with me.

"I believe that woman must have some Dakin blood; her hair's almost that same damn tow color, allowing for a little darkening for age. I wonder how she straightens it. She's trying to make you her little girl, that's what."

Mama seemed very pleased at the thought Miz Verlow wanted something of hers.

"I've never trusted Merry Verlow one sixty-second minute," she said. "I'll see in her in hell before I let her take away my little girl."

Content that possession was nine-tenths of maternity, Mama had done a complete U-turn in about half a minute. She was back where she started, not wanting to claim me, but having to, lest somebody else get me.

What either of those two women had in mind to do with me, other than waiting hand and foot on one or the other of them, was beyond me. All I could hope was that it would not eventually involve Solomon and cutting me in two. Hadn't cutting up Daddy been enough?

I was no more afraid of Miz Verlow than I was of Mama. Miz Verlow might expect me to be her servant, but at least not her unpaid servant. She said please and thank you to me, which was more than Mama ever did. If she was the cause of my losing my hair and it growing back trashy tow, Mama made a point of dressing me in cheap and boyish clothing, and in implying to other people that I was feebleminded. It all washed out about the same to me.

Women went to beauty salons to have their hair cut, curled, permed, bleached, dyed and back-combed; female hair is distinctly mutable in its attributes. To me it was more important that I had lost a sweater that wasn't mine, along with its severed buttons, and a stub of candle, my glasses and Betsy Cane McCall, all since arriving at Miz Verlow's house. Children grasp the idea of *mine*—of property—from infancy. For all of my life, food, clothing, a bed and a roof over it, books and music and toys, had been provided in unexceptional but reliable quantity. What I wore mattered little to me. The toys, the books, the music—all had been introductions, respectively played with, looked at or later read, listened to, and then outgrown, as swiftly as my shoes. But I was not a careless child. I did not make a habit of forgetting or losing things. I possessed enough of the Carroll acquisitiveness—irritated regularly by Ford taking things away from me for the hell of it, or Mama doing it because I seemed to be enjoying something too much—that I could not help feeling the loss of those unimportant things. The Carroll in me declared that I had been robbed, and that what was stolen must be returned.

Being robbed, though, was a mere distraction from hearing Mamadee's ghost, seeing her ghost in the mirror in the parlor, dreaming of her death, and being nearly engulfed by a giant ghost in the fog.

Next morning, I helped Cleonie clear the breakfast table. Only Mama and Miz Verlow still lingered over coffee when Mrs. Mank came down from her suite. In the kitchen, Cleonie handed me a cup, saucer and napkin for Mrs. Mank and nodded me toward the dining room. She came behind me, bearing a freshly brewed pot of coffee and a tray with a full breakfast under silver domes. Once I had placed the cup and saucer for Mrs. Mank, Cleonie poured for her and topped off Mama and Miz Verlow. She removed the covers from the dishes and vanished into the kitchen again. I pulled out a chair and sat down.

Mrs. Mank wore a suit in a peacock-blue polished cotton, with her pewter-colored shoes. Her earrings were silver, set with a stone the color of her clothing; years later I would learn that it was called tanzanite. Mrs. Mank smiled slightly at the sight of me, and her gaze lingered a fraction of a second on my hair.

Mama was too busy noticing everything Mrs. Mank wore, and totting up the likely prices, to spare me so much as a glance. Mama wore toreadors with a white crossover blouse and a little black wrap jacket, not really a bolero but suggestive of one. In her ears she wore the pearl earrings that Daddy had given her for Valentine's. Her feet were pinched into black sandals with Cuban heels.

While Mrs. Mank addressed her breakfast with her total attention, Miz Verlow favored me with a slight smile.

Mama spoke quietly to Miz Verlow, "Maybe I should make a long-distance call."

"Oh no," Mrs. Mank interjected, with her eyes still quite fixed on her plate. "That's a very bad idea."

Mama stiffened in her chair. Who was this woman that she should offer Roberta Carroll Dakin advice on any subject whatever? More significantly, who was Mrs. Mank that she should know what making that long-distance telephone call meant?

Unperturbed, Mrs. Mank chewed, swallowed, dabbed her lips and finally looked at Mama. "Merry told me a little of what happened yesterday."

Mama's glare fell on Miz Verlow, with no more effect than a solitary raindrop sliding down a windowpane.

Miz Verlow turned her smile on Mrs. Mank. "I confide in Mrs. Mank, Miz Dakin. There is no one I trust more."

By the way she drew in her breath, I knew Mama was about to say something vicious.

"Mama, maybe—" I began.

"We do *not* need to hear from you, Calley Dakin, because if any of this is anyone's fault, I firmly believe it is yours. Mamadee would have died and gone straight to Heaven and left us in peace if you had not *insisted* on *chatting* with her as if you were both on a picnic by the waters of *Babylon*."

I was aware of Miz Verlow's watchful gaze on me, and was comforted and calmed by it without knowing why.

Once the first gout of Mama's anger was deflected to me, she was able to address Mrs. Mank in a tone of voice that was marginally civil: "Well, Mrs. Mank, it must sound *very* strange to you. Do *you* believe that we had an unexpected and unwelcome visit from a ghost?"

"Of course not," Mrs. Mank conceded, "but Merry Verlow does not lie, not to me. So when she tells me that she heard a voice and there was no way it might have been anyone in the house trying to trick you, then I believe her."

Mama challenged her as if she herself had not just asserted that Mamadee had spoken to us from the dead. "Then you believe in ghosts."

"Absolutely not," said Mrs. Mank.

"But—"

"But I *do* believe that when someone speaks to you from beyond the grave, you should sit very still and listen."

Mama scrabbled at her Kools while Mrs. Mank again addressed her breakfast.

"*That* I understand." Mama stuck a cigarette between her lips with shaking fingers. "And—" She lit a match, fired the Kool and sucked at it. Around it, she finished, "I am just beginning to think you think like I do." Her voice was full of relief and sincerity. Mama could, with no particular difficulty, believe two entirely contradictory things at the same time. It's not a rare ability but she was a virtuoso. "But if that was my mama speaking to me from the Other Side," she went on, "why shouldn't I just call up and make sure she's dead?"

Mrs. Mank politely daubed her lips again. I was interested to note that her lipstick was unaffected.

"You're certain it was your mama who spoke to you this afternoon."

"Yes," said Mama. "Ask Calley if it wasn't her mamadee."

"Calley, was it your mamadee?"

I hesitated before I answered, "It was her voice."

"You see." Mama took my statement as a reinforcement of her own.

"No," said Mrs. Mank. "Calley is saying something a little different, Mrs. Dakin. She said it was your mama's voice, not that it was your mama."

Thirty-four

I might have told Mrs. Mank and Miz Verlow and Mama then that I had *seen* Mamadee. And I did not. The choice was nothing that I reasoned out, but an instinctive holding back of the information. It was something none of them knew, not about Mamadee, but about me.

"But who else would it be!" said Mama. "She knew me! She recognized the chair that her own mama embroidered! She wanted her candlestick—" Mama stopped abruptly.

"She was wrong about the chair, Roberta Ann," Miz Verlow said. "Because you told me yourself, that house and everything in it burned up years and years ago."

Mama glanced at me as if for help.

"It sounded like Mamadee," I assured her. "But maybe it was somebody else—some other ghost—just pretending to be Mamadee."

"What for?" cried Mama.

"Exactly what I would have said, Mrs. Dakin," said Mrs. Mank. "It might been your mama speaking or it might merely have been the voice of an evil spirit—or entity—or whatever you wish to call it."

"Why on earth would there be some asinine evil spirit after *me*?" Mama demanded.

Mrs. Mank chuckled. "Sometimes I don't even know why *I* do things, so I certainly would never speculate on the motives of evil spirits, or good spirits, or even of this little girl. But with what little I know of this situation, I would urge you not to place a long-distance call to—"

"Tallassee," I volunteered.

"Calley! Will you never hold your tongue?"

I started to slip from my chair. "If y'all will excuse me," I began.

Mrs. Mank interrupted me. "Mrs. Dakin, I think the child should stay."

"I don't," Mama snapped. Then she drew a deep drag and let it out. "But if you say she should, Mrs. Mank, then she will stay. Calley, sit down and stop twitching."

Mrs. Mank went on. "Mrs. Dakin, suppose you put in that long-distance telephone call to—Tallulah? You would, I presume, call your mama's number. If she answers, you'll know she's alive. But what will you say to her? 'Oh, I just wanted to know if you were alive or dead?' You'd look a fool, would you not?"

"I wouldn't have to say that exactly."

"But you haven't spoken to your mama since you left Talla-lulah. If you called her now, and she answered, it would appear to her that you were giving in. Is that what you want?"

"What if I called somebody else in Tall-Tallulah?"

"And ask, 'Could you please tell me if my mama is alive or dead?' " Mrs. Mank gave a little shudder. "Given the circumstances of your leaving your mama's house, the way people talk, your telephone call won't be a secret for longer than it takes for whomever you call to hang up and dial another number."

"But I could be subtle."

"Ask something like, 'Oh, did the florist do a good job on the flowers I told him to put at the foot of Mama's coffin?' "

Mama nodded yes, startled. That was exactly the sort of question she would have worked in.

"But if you ask that question and your mama isn't dead, what will people think? You could take the other route, and say, 'Tell me, as a friend, how does Mama look these days? I'm so worried about her, and she refuses to take my help.' If you asked that and she had been buried a week ago, everyone in town would hear that you didn't even know of your own mama's death."

"Calley could call—"

"They'd know you put her up to it."

Mrs. Mank's advice so far had cut to the white bone of Mama's dilemma. The overriding concern was how Mama would look to others, Mama's well-being, and Mama's ease.

Mrs. Mank speared a last remnant of the sausage on her plate, and consumed it with the same relish she had previously exhibited. At last her napkin flitted at her lips again.

"There is another reason you don't want to place that call, Mrs. Dakin," she said.

"What?"

"Suppose, for a few moments, that your mama is dead."

Mama put on a sad face. "It's perfectly possible. The obituaries are filled with people younger than Mama every day—my beloved Joseph was taken from me in his prime—"

"My condolences," Mrs. Mank said with the tiniest excess of sincerity.

Mama bore up bravely. "Thank you. So what next?"

"Mrs. Dakin, if your mama is dead, why have you not been informed of it? Why didn't *somebody*—your mama's lawyer?—send a telegram or telephone you?"

"Because he doesn't know where we are! Because nobody knows we're here."

"Fennie does," said Miz Verlow. "And if your mama died and anyone were trying to find you, Fennie would tell them you were down here with me."

I started. Why wouldn't Fennie have called and told Merry Verlow, or Mama or myself? Why not call Fennie and ask the question directly?

"So my mama must not be dead," said Mama. Her disappointment was indifferently concealed.

"Not necessarily. What if your friends and relatives were *not* trying to find you?"

Mama pondered a long moment. It sounded like the kind of subterfuge she herself indulged in. "Why wouldn't they?"

Mrs. Mank finished off her eggs before answering. "Something to do with family grievances maybe. Or with money. Your mama's will. Were you on good terms with the family lawyer, for instance?"

Mama's jaw set grimly. "No. He stole me blind. He and Mama. They took my darling boy away from me too."

"Suppose that lawyer is laying a trap. If you make that call, you might be walking right into it."

"But if Winston Weems is going to cheat me *again,* am I supposed to just sit here and do *nothing*?"

"Of course not," said Mrs. Mank. "I only said you ought not make that call yourself."

"So who will?"

"A friend of mine. Another lawyer."

Mama smiled.

"She'll know what to do," Mrs. Mank assured Mama.

Mama stopped smiling. "A woman lawyer."

Mrs. Mank responded without a moment's hesitation. "In deference to your objections to women lawyers, Mrs. Dakin, I will never mention the matter again."

At this moment Cleonie emerged to see if any more coffee was wanted.

Mrs. Mank crossed her fork and knife on her plate and folded her napkin. She smiled up at Cleonie. "I think I'll have this cup on the verandah." Rising with a polite smile and her refilled cup, she started toward the door.

Mama had expected Mrs. Mank to spend the next quarter hour convincing her to *allow* her friend, the woman lawyer, to devote her entire professional career to her cause. Mama simply wasn't used to being taken at her first and always exaggerated word. Panicked, she snatched up her cup and jumped from her chair.

"What a lovely idea!" she cried.

Mrs. Mank stood with one hand on the door, the other holding the coffee cup and saucer. The steam curled up toward her face, and she breathed in the odor. "What idea would that be? Are you reopening the discussion, Mrs. Dakin?"

"Coffee on the verandah," Mama said, "and your woman lawyer friend—both—I was distracted by the thought of losing my mama so quickly after my darling Joseph. . . ." Mama lapsed into Southern-belle helplessness. "I am so flustered! You must think I don't have a brain in my head."

With no more than the faint inclination of her head that expressed a polite agreement with Mama's last assertion, Mrs.

Mank passed onto the verandah. Mama followed, Miz Verlow after her, and I fell in behind.

As Mrs. Mank settled on a chair outside, she smiled at me the way adults smile at children whom they abhor.

Nothing could have reassured Mama more.

Once settled herself, she addressed Mrs. Mank carefully, "You know what it was?"

"What *what* was?"

"Why I reacted the way I did when you talked about your friend the woman lawyer. It was because of Martha Poe. You know who I'm talking about, don't you, Calley?"

Mama wanted me to back up her lie.

"You mean the woman lawyer, Mama?"

"Well, who else? Of course, I know that every woman who gets to be a lawyer just has to be smart, smarter than any man, but Martha Poe I guess is just the exception that proves the rule. The only reason that Martha Poe ever gets a client is that her stepdaddy is a judge on the circuit court and he decides every case in Martha's favor, so I'd probably hire her too. But on her own, Martha Poe wouldn't know how to fix a speeding ticket. She's the only reason I said what I did."

Mrs. Mank's expression softened a little, as if she were accepting Mama's explanation.

I knew that Martha Poe wasn't a lawyer at all—she was a practical nurse in Tallassee, who had once spent two nights at Ramparts when Mamadee was passing a kidney stone.

"I've been thinking," Mama went on, "another good thing about a woman lawyer is that she probably won't charge as much as a good lawyer."

Mrs. Mank stiffened.

Mama corrected herself quickly. "A good *man* lawyer, I mean—a good *woman* lawyer wouldn't charge as much. What is her name anyway?"

"Adele," said Mrs. Mank, with no warmth at all. "Adele Starret."

"Adele is my favorite name," Mama gushed. "If I hadn't named Calley after one of the muses, I would have called her Adele. My best friend in college was named Adele. Mrs. Mank, could I prevail upon your good nature to speak to your friend Adele on my behalf?"

"We'll see," said Mrs. Mank.

"When?" Mama persisted. "Because if it doesn't work with—"

"I'll look into it, Mrs. Dakin. But now, I'm going to enjoy my coffee. Merry, my dear, have the newspapers arrived?"

Mama tried not to press Mrs. Mank about the woman lawyer but when Mrs. Mank finally folded the last section of the third newspaper she had read that morning, Mama was still there, grimly sipping her fifth cup of coffee and barely controlling a very bad case of the fidgets brought on by too much coffee. Mama sighed her martyr's sigh in expectation of Mrs. Mank *finally* saying something, but Mrs. Mank merely gave Mama and me a perfunctory and polite smile.

Mama could contain herself no longer. "Are you going to call her today?"

Mrs. Mank's eyebrows lifted quizzically.

"Are you going to call Adele Starret? Your friend the female lawyer who's going to help me. I mean, your friend Miz Starret who *might* be able to help me. If she wants to. If she thinks it might be worth it."

Mrs. Mank's smile warmed. "Oh yes, Adele."

Miz Verlow came to her feet just a fraction of a second before Mrs. Mank, picking up not only her own coffee cup but Mrs. Mank's as well. Mama rose quickly too but I was faster, and picked up Mama's coffee cup.

"Calley and I will just clear these to the kitchen," Miz Verlow announced.

"Thank you," said Mrs. Mank. "Please tell Perdita how much I enjoyed my breakfast, and especially the sausage. I cannot get sausage as fine as hers anywhere else in the world, and tell her that I have tried."

I believed her assertion that she had tried *all over the world*. To my knowledge, I'd never met anyone who had been *all over the world*. Yet Mrs. Mank was taking the trouble to send Perdita a detailed compliment.

Mama, however, was thinking of neither sausage nor globe-trotting. "You were saying, Mrs. Mank—"

"I was?"

"—about your friend the lawyer."

"Oh yes. Well. I'll speak to Adele today. If she's available."

"Oh thank you so much—"

Mrs. Mank nodded and strolled off along the verandah.

For the next day or so, Mama mostly kept to our room. Pacing up and down, chain-smoking, she cursed Mrs. Mank's infuriating coolness, cursed Mrs. Mank's friend the woman lawyer, cursed Merry Verlow and her sister, Fennie, and all the Dakins and all their relations by blood or marriage, but most vehemently Mama cursed Mamadee, alive or dead, for all the trouble she had caused.

Since it was the place in the house Mama was least likely to go, I spent a great deal of time in the kitchen. There I learned from Cleonie and Perdita that Mrs. Mank was an occasional guest, that she always had the same rooms, took most of her meals in her suite, and that Miz Verlow treated her like the Queen of England.

"Miz Mank onced done Miz Verlow a favor," Cleonie explained.

"And she likes Perdita's sausages," I said, adding sincerely, "probably almost as much as I do."

Perdita didn't say anything to that but that afternoon my iced tea was mysteriously warmed with a dash of bourbon.

Perdita did give me a warning. "You look out, you hear? Miz Mank caint bide churn."

Thirty-five

OVER the next few days, in the rare moments when no one else was within sight, I tried Miz Verlow's office door, in hope of finding Fennie's telephone number. It was always locked. Every time I tried to sneak down that particular hallway to Miz Verlow's room on the same mission, something happened to deter me: She herself appeared, or Cleonie did, or Mama did.

It was Thursday morning when Mama informed me that she and Miz Verlow were driving into Pensacola to shop, to pay the current installments on Cleonie's and Perdita's various layaway plans, and to pick up some important letters that Mrs. Mank was expecting.

I went so far as to ask permission to go with them.

"Calley, no, and that's final. I think you can find something to do here this afternoon."

I sulked. "No, I caint."

"One more word—" Mama threatened, almost absently.

I rocked sullenly in the verandah swing when Mama and Miz Verlow came out the front door.

"What time you coming back?"

"About four," Miz Verlow answered.

"Why are you asking?" Mama wanted to know.

"I was hoping you'd bring me something."

Mama sniffed. "Four-thirty. Maybe even five, depending on how long the lines are. And I don't think we're going anywhere that has presents for children, so don't waste the afternoon *hoping,* because I don't want to see you spend the evening *moping.*" She gave Miz Verlow an arch look, at her own wit.

They got into Miz Verlow's Country Squire and drove off. I stayed in the swing, pretending to study on a bird guide, in case they came back for anything.

Mrs. Mank was in the house—I would have heard or seen her had she gone out. I checked both parlors and the dining room and listened at strategic points all over the first floor.

At Miz Verlow's office door, I looked every which way, listened intently, and then tried the knob. It did not move. Then, before I could take my hand away, the knob moved without any effort from me. I snatched my hand away behind my back, even as I took a step backward and started to turn on my heel to run away. Mrs. Mank reached through the opening door and caught me by one shoulder.

I felt like a handkerchief snatched back from the wind by a huge and powerful hand. The door closed and I was on the inside.

Petrified as I was, I could hardly breathe, let alone speak. *I had not heard Mrs. Mank on the other side of the door*. And now I was her prisoner.

She let go of me and my bare feet found safe contact with the floor.

I still felt frail. She was close enough to force me to tip my head to see her face. As she moved away, she began to resume normal proportions. I was hot and miserable with humiliation, but beginning to feel the instinct for survival. A thousand lies buzzed like wasps in my head.

Mrs. Mank dropped into Miz Verlow's chair behind the small desk. She was wearing little half-moon glasses framed in silver.

"Sit down and hold your tongue."

I did as I was told, sitting directly on the floor with my legs crossed. I had to look up at her again. The tiny windowless room seemed smaller than it ever had before, and I realized that I had never been inside it when the door was closed.

She tapped Miz Verlow's address book on the desk. "You won't find Fennie Verlow's number in this. Merry hardly needs to keep her sister's telephone number in a book, any more than Fennie needs to write down Merry's number."

I felt stupid. Of course two sisters would know each other's telephone numbers by heart. There was no surprise in Mrs.

Mank knowing what I was up to and what I was looking for. I felt her reading me as easily as I could hear a ghost crab skedaddle across the sand.

I tried a feint. "You don't like Mama very much, do you?"

"Your mother?"

"Yes, ma'am."

"Why shouldn't I like your mother?"

"Because you know what she's like. You do, don't you?"

She smiled her chilly smile at me. "Does that mean you know what Roberta Carroll Dakin is like as well?

I nodded.

"But it seems to me that you love her very much, and that you love her despite whatever reservations you may entertain of her character and conduct."

"She's my mama. I'm supposed to love her."

" 'Supposed to'? Whose rule is that?"

"Mama's."

"I don't for one minute believe you do things just because your mother tells you to."

Before I could tell any lies contrary to her assertion, Mrs. Mank continued, "Of course, God also tells you to love your mother—in the Bible, in Sunday school classes, and through the mouths of Christians. Of course, I think it's fair to say that the god of the Jews and the Christ who suffered and died on the cross never had to deal with Roberta Carroll Dakin day in and day out."

Mrs. Mank's observation stunned me, as being both sacrilege and truth.

With bland indifference, Mrs. Mank asked, "Oh, do you believe in God? And the Bible? And Jesus and Heaven and Hell and the Communion of Saints and the Forgiveness of Sins?"

"Yes." I was not lying. It had never occurred to me that any of those things might not be true.

"Yes, of course you do. You're only seven. You should profess belief in the accepted wisdom of your elders. I'm asking, 'Do you believe in all those things—God, the Bible, Jesus, Heaven and Hell, the Forgiveness of Sins, and the Resurrection of the Corrupted Body?' "

"No." The word was out of my mouth without hesitation. If

those things were true, I grasped instantly, Mrs. Mank would not have asked me if I believed them.

"Do you believe in them the way that you believe in yourself—in what you think, and what you feel?"

"No." I thought for a moment, before adding something that was not entirely true. "I believe in you too."

"You have no reason to." Mrs. Mank went on, "Society also tells you that you should love your mother. In general, society is a better voice to listen to than either God or Roberta Carroll Dakin, but society isn't always right. At least not for you."

"But I do love Mama." I was frustrated and confused. I had questions to ask Mrs. Mank but her interrogation of me had put them right out of my mind.

"And you should."

"Why?"

"Why *should* you love Roberta Carroll Dakin? And why *do* you love her?" Before I could answer, Mrs. Mank provided it. "You love her because she is your mama. Because you are a child and you believe as a child. You believe that you need your mama to survive. But think about it—you must know otherwise. Did you ever give a thought to the idea that your father might die before he did? He did die, and you are still alive."

My throat closed and I scrambled across the floor to kneel at Mrs. Mank's small feet in their handmade shoes.

"Please don't kill Mama!" I cried.

Mrs. Mank looked down at me, her small mouth twitching derisively.

"I am not responsible for your mother's life. Neither are you. She is."

My eyes were hot with unshed tears, barely held back out of some instinct that I must not reveal weakness.

"If you ever hurt her," I blurted, and started to blubber and sob.

"You'll do what?" Mrs. Mank said in a bored voice. "Calley Dakin, I don't give a damn whether your mama lives, dies, is raptured up to Heaven or reborn as a gnat."

The words by themselves should not have been reassuring but they were. Mrs. Mank had no plan to harm Mama. The hovering horror of the two mad women who had torn Daddy limb from limb vanished. About this, I did believe Mrs. Mank.

I knuckled the tears into my eye sockets. A handkerchief appeared in front of my face, at the tips of Mrs. Mank's fingers.

"Snot and red-eyed tears are unbecoming, especially with as little as you have for looks. You had better learn to stifle them."

I wiped my face dry and blew my nose. I did not offer to return the handkerchief, which in any case was not monogrammed or of any fine fabric but simply an everyday handkerchief. I did not believe that it was Mrs. Mank's at all.

"However," Mrs. Mank said slowly, "if you wish to keep your mother alive, you must keep her here. Elsewhere, her enemies—your father's enemies—will find her. Shall I tell you a secret, Calliope Carroll Dakin?"

A bolt of terror left me weak. I did not want to know a secret. Already I knew too many.

Frantic to divert the unwelcome knowledge, I choked out, "I know the secret."

"You do?" Mrs. Mank seemed amused. "Well, then, I guess I don't need to tell you."

Was I let down? Worse. It was like diving down the laundry chute: an instant of wild exultation at my own derring-do, wiped away by sheer unmitigated terror of the consequences so foolishly ignored. The certainty that I was mistaken, that I should have listened, seized me as surely as Mrs. Mank had at the door to Miz Verlow's office.

I found myself, still dazed, outside the office door closing on Mrs. Mank. She had put me out as unceremoniously as she had hoisted me into the office.

I was quite certain that Mrs. Mank had wanted me to duck the secret. Manipulation was a second language to me, learned at Mama's knee. It seemed more natural to me than straightforward behavior. Mrs. Mank was another manipulator, the greatest I had yet encountered, and I feared her, without knowing why her string-pulling was so much more dangerous than Mama's or Mamadee's.

It wasn't just physical fear that sent me racing to the beach. I was driven by the instinct that the beach was where I would be able to breathe.

I ran without the joy that normally possessed me in my beach races. Between my bare toes, the sand was almost cold.

The feel of it spritzing away from my toes digging into it made me feel real again. Outside. Outside was itself, and never pretended to be anything else. It didn't care how I took it.

A black gleam in the water caught my eye. When I slowed to a trot to look at the Gulf, the gleam sank into the water but another rose nearby: dolphins at play. I clutched my knees and watched the dolphins. The sight of their permanent grins calmed me; the racket of my heartbeat faded and slowed.

Throwing myself down, I stared up at the sky: it was half of everything, roofless, and even with birds in it, mostly a vast emptiness.

I rolled over to study the sand: pearly grit in uncountable quantity, full of itself as the sky was empty of itself. The sand was marble, Miz Verlow had told me, washed out of Alabama and Georgia over thousands of years before anybody called those places Alabama and Georgia, slow ground to infinite particles in the rivers that carried it. Marble like a rich dead person's headstone. The image of the one my daddy should have came to me: Joe Cane Dakin, RIP. Are-Eye-Pee spelled rip.

I let the din of the restless sand and the rootless sea bear me down. A draft of wind, a sweep of shadow, a crack of vast wings overhead, and I could bear it no longer. I scuttled up the face of the dune into the tall grasses—sea oats and panic grass some of them were—I had found them in my field guides. Panic grass. My head was all apanic, so I must be in the right place, I thought. Sea oats. No oats to see on them. They were the tallest grasses, with raggedy tops where the seeds had been earlier. Other grasses as yet nameless to me. The beach grass did not grow in carpets as lawn grass grows. It sprouted in hanks and billows on the dune face, and clumped along the crest and down the back dune. Thick, tripping vines snaked among the grasses. On the back of the dune sweet-smelling shrubs grew in oases of green and grey-green and blue-green. The sand showed between them like grout between tiles. Despite the natural undulation of the sand in hills and hollows, its grains were not blown about by the wind as the beach sand's were, nor did they roll underfoot as loosely.

At the crest of the dune, in among the grasses, I dropped to my knees and dug with my hands in the hard-edged crystalline grains, hollowing out a place in the shade. The grasses whispered to me, touching me with the most fleeting, creepy caresses. Sand slipped under my nails, and into my mouth and dried my spit. The shade dappled my arms and hands, the sun striped warmth upon my back. I rolled up into the hollow that I had made.

The waves surged upon the shore below and just yards away. I breathed in the salted air. My heart and my lungs found the rhythm of the water. Wet voices surged amid out and in, rollick and curl up, retreat and advance. The voices drowned.

Thirty-six

"CALLEY Dakin! Calley Dakin!"

The echo of my name condensed out of my oblivion: Miz Verlow, calling me. My eyes opened to a darkened day: Twilight had come on, cooler and quieter and more desolate. Yet even in the thickening shade of the tall grasses I saw as well as if it were noon. Better, without the glare.

A mouse crouched very close, right next to my face against the sand. It licked the side of my mouth with its very tiny tongue. Its eyes were brilliant in their blackness, and the beat of its heart a tiny paradiddle.

"Calley Dakin!"

For fear of frightening the mouse, I did not move.

The mouse gave the corner of my mouth a final lick and sat back for a second. It looked almost satisfied.

Miz Verlow advanced upon me from the back of the dune as surely as if she had a map of where I was. The swishing of the tall grasses announced her approach.

The mouse jumped. It seemed to unzip the sand with its tiny paws. The dimple filled at once behind it, and the sand became as seamless as sand can't help but be.

Miz Verlow looked down at me. "I won't ask if you heard me calling."

My mouth was dry. I could manage no more than a mumble. "I was asleep."

"Evidently."

I scrambled to my feet. "I saw a mouse! It was white!"

"Of course it was. That's the color of the beach mice here. You are late for supper."

She spun right around and set off toward the house. I lunged after her, then paused to glance back at where I had been, in my nest in the grass. The sea oats, the panic grass, the grasses whose names I did not yet know, thousands of them, scratched against beach and sky, were all the same, like the grains of sand heaped up to make the dunes and washed down to make the beach, like the drops of water poured together to make the Gulf. My heart sank; I would never find it again. With a catch in my throat, I scrambled after Miz Verlow.

I feared needlessly, as one so often does. Over the years, the moon showed me that self-made hollow anytime I looked. Only on the night of the new moon was it hidden from me. No mouse ever showed itself to me there again, though I saw the beach mice off and on in other locations, but I watched the phases of the moon there. There, I made pets of raccoons, training them to bring me oysters to trade for kitchen leftovers. From there, I spied upon the sea turtles come ashore to lay their eggs and bury them. When sea oats flagged out in seed, I shook out their heads to feed the birds, coaxing them to perch on my fingers. By night, I watched the night-dark waters roil and dash into lacings of spray, or in a quieter mood, rising and falling as smoothly as the breast of a sleeper, under clouds visible even in the dark.

But on that night, after washing and putting on a dress, I was that much later arriving at the table. My plate was cold but not unappetizing, at least to me, as my stomach had woken and was yowling that it had not been fed since breakfast.

Mama spared me an irritated glance that foretold a tongue-lashing later on. Cleonie's arrival at Mama's right shoulder with a plate of lemon meringue pie distracted her. But only for a few seconds, before Mama returned to making quick anxious glances at Mrs. Mank.

Miz Verlow sat at Mrs. Mank's right. To Mrs. Mank's left was a woman whom I had never seen before. Every week so far had brought guests unknown to me, occasionally even at midweek. The only distinction the woman held for me at that

moment was her position so close to Mrs. Mank. No one bothered to introduce me and she paid me no mind.

The unnamed visitor was a big coarse woman, weighing
closer to two hundred pounds than to a hundred-and-fifty. Her
dress, in bright shades of yellow and chartreuse, strained at
the seams. She had chosen a clashing red for her lipstick and
applied it outside the lip line, a strategy I had seen before—
Mama had explained it was an attempt to give fullness to narrow lips. It did not, of course, and was ridiculous, but hardly
uncommon, and if I ever asked a woman directly about her
lipstick again, Mama would slap me silly. Penciled black lines
arced well above the normal position of eyebrows, making the
woman's tiny blue eyes seem perpetually surprised. Her hair,
shellacked in tight waves, was of a color Mama called cow-pie
copper.

Cold mashed potatoes, gelid gravy and warm fried chicken
absorbed my total attention for some time, until people began
to push back their chairs and take their coffee or tea to a parlor
or the verandah.

I caught Mrs. Mank's gesture to Mama, who hurriedly rose
to follow her. The four women carried their coffee to the verandah in polite silence.

Curious as I was, I started from my chair, only to have
Cleonie take a firm grip on my shoulder.

"Not so fast," she said. "Who be's washin' up?"

Then she laughed at my expression and pinched my cheek.
She handed me a tray, with a fresh carafe of coffee and cream
and sugar on it. "Gone, now. Miz Verlow be's wantin' this."

Miz Verlow evidently wanted me to follow. I made haste
and found the ladies settling into chairs circled in a quiet alcove, at a discreet distance from a few other guests also enjoying the spring evening on the verandah.

At this narrow waist of the island, and at an angle to the
house, the alcove provided a view from bayside to Gulf. The
moon, just off the full, was close to rising; its light was already glowing toward the east, at the lumpy horizon of bay
and hummock. That skim-milk luminescence diluted the
darkness of the night and picked out ghostly curds of foam on
the black water of the Gulf.

"Calley," Miz Verlow said as I hove into sight, "come put that down right here."

I placed the tray on the small table at the center of the group.

"Thank you, my dear," Miz Verlow said. "Now scoot. Those dishes in the kitchen won't wash themselves."

Furious with frustration, I raced back through the house, through the dining room and butler's pantry to the kitchen. My step stool was drawn up at the sink that Cleonie had already filled. She and Perdita were seated at their little table, absorbed in their own suppers. I shot past them and out the kitchen door. The startlement in their faces gave me an unexpected kick.

Their chairs scraped as they jumped up but before they could look out the door, or come out onto the kitchen porch, I was under the lattice skirt of the verandah. I scooted along in a crouch toward the alcove but stopped short of it, to catch my breath. Creeping the last few yards, I curled up under the floor of the alcove.

Mama was sitting forward intently in her chair. Alone of the four women, she wore high-heeled pumps, to show off her ankles. To be sure, Miz Verlow, Mrs. Mank and the stranger, not a one of them, could show off their ankles to any advantage. I peered up through the gaps in the wood at Mama's pointy soles.

"Do you know, Miz Starret, if my darling mama is still alive?" Mama said, all solemn and hushed as if she were at a funeral.

"I am sorry to have to tell you that she is deceased," the strange woman who must be Miz Starret said. She didn't sound particularly sorry.

Mama jumped up. "Miz Verlow, I must have the keys to my car. If I leave now, I can lay flowers on my mama's grave at dawn!"

Miz Verlow said nothing. Mrs. Mank sniffed.

"All right," said Miz Starret. "Before you go, would like to hear how your mother died and why you weren't told anything about it?"

Mama had expected someone to try to talk her out of her resolve. Her sails suddenly slack, she paused uncertainly.

"You might also want to know where she's buried," Miz Starret went on, "otherwise you will be running from pillar to post all over Tallassee."

Mama was rocked. "Why? She must be in the family plot. In the Tallassee cemetery. We've always been buried there— the Carrolls I mean. Are you saying Mama *wasn't* buried there?"

Miz Starret shifted in her chair; she was reaching into the pocket of her tight dress.

With some difficulty, Miz Starret withdrew a folded sheaf of tiny lined note pages.

"Your mother," she said, flipping open the notebook as if to consult notes, "was buried in the Last Times Upon Us Church Cemetery."

Mama shrieked in rage. Then she remembered her role, and sank back into her chair in more genteel shock.

"Forgive me, this is such a dreadful surprise."

I had to repress a snicker. Mama was telling the truth for once.

She covered the unfamiliar crisis by groping for her handkerchief.

"My poor mama is surely spinning in her grave. Why was my mama buried in a snake-handlers' cemetery?"

"It's the only place that would have her." Miz Starret's voice was distinctly flavored with the moldy taste of smuggery. "Even at that, Mr. Weems had to pay twice the usual fee to the Last Times Upon Us Church. The elders said the Lord enjoined them as Christians to judge not, so they would provide Mrs. Carroll with a plot, but it would cost them some to conduct special rituals to keep their own hallowed dead safe from any demons that the corpse might yet be hosting."

Mama gave a little moan and shudder at the thought of being lorded over by snake-handlers.

And then Adele Starret told her, in outline, of my very dream of Mamadee's death.

Thirty-seven

THE business of the umbrellas made it nearly impossible to find a place to bury Deirdre Carroll. Her behavior downtown on that Thursday morning, buying up every umbrella that could be bought, taking them home, and opening them all over the house was a much more disturbing phenomenon to Tallassee than the fear of contagion from the strange, rapid, and fatal ailment that had laid her low. Deirdre Carroll, it judged, had gone insane. Practically, it was a mercy that her end came so quickly as it did. That sudden, intense insanity shut the gates of every graveyard within the town limits.

Adele Starret did not tell Mama but I knew what happened next. Never mind that I had dreamed it; any half-wit seven-year-old could have predicted it.

Leonard and Tansy refused ever to set foot in Ramparts again. No other sensible colored person would consider it, never mind the foolish ones. Of the whites, both sensible and idiot, only five could be found willing to enter the house. Dr. Evarts had and would, and no one thought the less of him for it, for his fundamental Yankeeness protected him in some indefinable way from the evil in Ramparts, and he was, after all, a Man of Science. My brother, Ford, would, but of course he thought there might be something in it for him, and, after all, it was his family estate. And Winston Weems would, for the same reason of self-interest, and also to protect his reputation as a hardheaded Man of Bidness. Men like Dr. Evarts and Mr. Weems could not believe in haunts or curses or hoodoos, for such things must necessarily be beyond their purchase or control. Mr. Weems hired two white men who would do anything for a jug, but who were not yet too debilitated by their vices to do the heavy lifting.

Ramparts was emptied in one weekend of almost everything perishable, usable or saleable (out of town, where its provenance was unknown), under the direction of Mr. Weems, Dr. Evarts, and my brother, Ford.

A single piece of furniture was abandoned: Mamadee's bed, its bloody sheets already rotting, still stood in her bedroom.

And the umbrellas. Eccentric currents of air native to the house itself rolled the open umbrellas this way and that in the empty rooms. The tips of the ribs of the umbrellas tapped the floors and walls *tick-tick-tick,* as regularly and syncopated as clocks all set to different times. The rustling, the snicking and clicking, the faint thuds, all echoed through the house, along with its own creaks and groans.

That Ramparts was haunted, there was no doubt. Outside it, the live oaks shuddered, the rags of their Spanish moss twisting and flapping like grave clothes on a revenant mummy. Children dared one another to creep up on to the verandah and stare through the dusty windows. The glass under their palms was so cold that they snatched their hands away. One or more of the opened umbrellas, upside down and right side up, and sideways in every room would move, and the children would run away shrieking. Few returned for a second peek.

Thirty-eight

To Mama, knowing whether Mamadee was alive or not was minor compared to the reassurance that Roberta Ann Carroll Dakin could not be blamed for whatever it was that had happened in Tallassee. The death certificate signed by Dr. Evarts gave the cause of Mamadee's death as exsanguination caused by a tumor of the throat. The usually discreet doctor's hints that Mamadee's sudden dementia had been caused by a brainstorm brought on by hypoxia, from the tumor cutting off her oxygen, were eagerly retailed around Tallassee. Deirdre Carroll had never been beloved of the town, and her gaudy death, entertaining as it was, had shifted the town's sympathies back to Mama. In hindsight, Roberta Ann must have witnessed the first sign of her mother's dementia and sensibly fled, even though it would have been only the second sensible thing that Mama had ever done, the first being marriage to Joe Cane Dakin, and look how that turned out. Even the fact that Roberta Ann and her pathetic child had not returned to attend the brief funeral was not condemned, as no one else had either, aside from Ford and Dr. Evarts and Mr. Weems. Mrs. Weems and Mrs. Evarts had both vehemently refused, on the grounds of declining to be hypocrites. It must have been the only shining moment of nonhypocrisy in either of those two matrons' existence, but was consistent with their parsimonious practice of charity.

"Oh, it's terrible, it's all so terrible I can't even bear to think of it," Mama said.

Of course not.

Adele Starret asked Mama slyly if she was getting up her strength for the drive up to Tallassee.

Mama came right back at her. "I *will* go, but in the morning, when I have had sufficient time to recover myself a little. Since I have already been *deprived* of the comfort of being at my mama's deathbed and holding her hand at the moment she passed over—since I was *not allowed* to weep at her funeral—since I was *prevented* from seeing her casket lowered into the earth of a *snake-handler's cemetery,* there is *nobody* who is going to keep me from at least being there when poor Mama's will is read! *Nobody,* do you hear me?"

"Well, you won't have to make a trip to Tallassee at all," said Adele Starret, "because the will has already been read, probated and executed."

Mama caught her breath in shock.

Adele Starret presented a long narrow envelope to Mama. Quick-fingered, Mama plucked out a single folded page. She went stiff and then thrust it at Adele Starret.

"Please read it for me, Miz Starret," she asked, with a tremor in her voice.

Adele Starret did so.

Everything that Deirdre Carroll, late of Ramparts, City of Tallassee, Elmore County, Alabama, owned, possessed, had control over or interest in, all her possessions, goods and chattels, were bequeathed to her grandson, Ford Carroll Dakin. Until his twenty-first birthday, that inheritance would remain under the control of his guardians, one Winston Weems, attorney, and one Lewis Evarts, physician, of Tallassee, Alabama. The custody of Ford Carroll Dakin had been assigned in separate documents to Dr. Evarts, until such time as Ford Carroll Dakin was twenty-one.

To her daughter, Roberta Ann Carroll Dakin, Deirdre Carroll bequeathed a particular pen, which was contained in the envelope.

Mama still held the envelope, forgotten, on her lap. Slowly she turned it upside down and a cylindrical object rolled out onto her open palm, presumably the aforementioned pen. She dropped the envelope to the floor of the verandah.

Mama sat there stunned.

Adele Starret read on: "To Roberta Ann Carroll Dakin's

daughter, Calliope Carroll Dakin, Deirdre Carroll bequeathed twice what Calliope Carroll Dakin had inherited from her father, the late Joe Cane Dakin."

Mama seemed not to hear that clause as Adele Starret declaimed it. Her fingers had closed around the pen. In the silence that followed Adele Starret's reading of the will, Mama clicked the pen. Its nib emerged and Mama winced and let the pen fall onto the floor. It rolled gently to the nearest gap between the floorboards and fell through onto the sand beneath.

"I caint believe Lew Evarts would do this to me," Mama muttered. Then she said, "Mama must have been as crazy as a mockingbird on a live wire when she wrote that thing. But that's it, Miz Starret!"

"What's it?"

"My mama didn't write the will. Winston Weems wrote it—that snake dipped his forked tongue in ink and signed my dead mother's name to a lie!"

"I photostatted the will at the courthouse," Adele Starret said, "and had a handwriting expert examine it, along with some samples of your mother's handwriting. Your mother very definitely wrote out that will."

I wondered at how quickly Adele Starret must have worked, to have obtained the will (and have it examined by a handwriting expert), samples of Mamadee's writing, the death certificate, and the whole long story of Mamadee's death, since Mrs. Mank had phoned her.

"Then he held a gun to her head while she dictated it!"

"He wasn't there. I interviewed the two witnesses, and your mother was alone but for them."

"Who were the witnesses?" Mama demanded.

Miz Starret rattled her copy of the will. "Mr. Vincent Rider and someone named Martha Poe."

"Rider? I never heard of him. And Martha Poe? What was she doing at the house?"

"Perhaps she was helping your mother with the will."

"Why the hell would she do that? Martha's a nurse!"

"Really?" Mrs. Mank said. She had been so quiet that I had nearly forgotten that she was there. She was smiling in amusement. "I was under the impression Martha Poe was another girl lawyer—like Adele."

Usually Mama remembered and kept track of her lies. That she had forgotten this one was a measure of her distress.

Mama hesitated a moment, then said, vaguely, "I believe Martha studied both medicine and law—at Huntingdon College—but couldn't make up her mind which one to devote herself to—curing people or getting them off the hook." She changed the subject. "And that other one, Rider—some stranger, stranger to me, anyway."

"Mr. Rider is new to Tallassee," Miz Starret said, "so perhaps you never met him. He deals in pianos. Evidently your mama asked him to assess a piano that she had in mind to sell. He is a respectable businessman."

"Mama would never have two strangers, one of them a complete stranger, some piano peddler, witness such an important document."

"Nevertheless, the witnesses both confirm that your mother wrote out the entire will, signed it, enclosed it with the pen in the envelope, and sealed the envelope."

Mama lit a cigarette with quivering fingers. None of it made sense. It was all bad.

What Miz Starret told Mama next was very much worse. "Your son will inherit somewhat over ten million dollars from your mother."

Mama snarled, actually *snarled*. "Mama didn't have ten million dollars! Mama didn't have anything like that! She bought her Cadillacs on time!"

"I tend to estimate low in such matters."

"I am listening to a lie!"

"Then it's not me that's lying," returned Adele Starret. "It's U.S. Steel and AT&T and Coca-Cola that are lying when they tell me how much of their stock your mother owned."

I waited for Mama to speak, to protest, to question, to prompt some mitigating response from Adele Starret. But she was rendered silent for a long moment. Cups clattered, the women sipped their coffee, Mama smoked.

Finally: "I want my baby boy. I'm his sole living parent. I only left him with Mama because he's sickly and she could take care of him. I was always gone go back for him. He'll surely be cheated out of his inheritance by that wicked old shyster Weems. Isn't there something I can do?"

"You did sign him over to your mother, and she made the choice to assign his protection to Mr. Weems and Dr. Evarts. But certainly you can sue to regain custody. You have a good chance. Most courts would be sympathetic to a blood relative, let alone a parent, seeking custody of a minor in your son's situation. Of course if you won, you would still have to work out some arrangement with Mr. Weems and Dr. Evart about access to his inheritance."

"I was cheated once, and now I've been cheated twice," said Mama. "First by the man I married, and then by the woman who gave me birth. It's not up to you and me anymore, Miz Starret, because they both are dead and beyond our reach."

Miz Starret ignored the theatrical declaration to proceed to the practical. "What day did you leave Tallassee?"

"I didn't leave. My own mama hounded me out of town. The day Mama died."

Miz Starret's voice became impatient. "What *day* of the week did your mother hound you out of Tallassee?"

Mama finally got what she meant. "Thursday. I know it was Thursday because there was a brand-new wheel of butter on the table Wednesday night, and the butter-lady comes on Wednesday morning, and there wasn't any left the night before."

"So it was Thursday, the twenty-fourth of the month," said Miz Starret.

"Yes. Thursday the twenty-fourth."

"*Thursday,* the twenty-third," said Miz Starret pointedly, "is how she dated the will. Either your mother got the day of the month wrong, or else she got the day of the week wrong."

"What damn difference does it make? Mama couldn't even remember my birthday and on Thursday she was always thinking it was Friday."

"Here's the damn difference it makes," said Miz Starret, sounding like a real lawyer. "If she made out the will on the twenty-third and just got the day of the week wrong, then she was probably sane, and you are out of luck."

Mama sat up straighter. "But if she got the day of the month wrong, that means she wrote the will on Thursday, the day she lost her mind and went out buying up every umbrella in town. And if she was crazy when she made out the will, then—"

"Then we can contest it," Adele Starret said with great satisfaction.

Thirty-nine

ADELE Starret must have noted the discrepancy in the date when she obtained the will. She might have told Mama at once. But she didn't.

Mama was instantly invigorated. Mamadee might be dead but Mama could still fight her, with no possibility of Mamadee retaliating down the line. Once the money was hers again, Mama would not only be returned to her rightful station in life—rich—but would have Ford back.

Mama was ready to whip Miz Starret off the verandah to her automobile, so urgently did she want the woman lawyer to get started.

Miz Starret was not so easily moved. She had something else on her mind. "We haven't talked about a fee for my services yet."

"I'd give you a million dollars, Miz Starret, just to see justice done, but as you see I have been robbed blind twice already in the past year, and I don't have a penny to my name," Mama said.

"I understand that, and I'm willing to wait until we come to the resolution of the case. Lawyers do it all the time. We call it a contingency fee." Miz Starret continued, "My fee will not be a million dollars. I'll satisfy myself with fifteen percent of whatever may be the total of the estate that eventually comes to you."

After a pause, Mama spoke. "That seems a lot to me."

"I regret to say that I never bargain," said Miz Starret.

She stood. Miz Verlow and Mrs. Mank came to their feet a fraction of a second later.

"Thank you, Merry Verlow," Miz Starret said. "It was a pleasure to see you again."

"Give my love to Fennie," returned Miz Verlow.

"Thank you, my dear," Mrs. Mank told Miz Starret in a grim tone that was just short of an apology.

Mama was too agitated to react coherently.

Adele Starret reached the verandah steps before Mama caught up with her.

"Miz Starret!" Mama lowered her voice but her words tumbled out breathlessly. "I thought you said *fifty* percent. I thought you meant *half*! Of course you get your *fifteen* percent!"

"Fifteen percent!" Mrs. Mank said, from just behind Mama. Mama jumped. She hadn't noticed Mrs. Mank following her. Or Miz Verlow, for that matter.

Clutching the dropped pen, I crept after them, beneath the verandah, until I reached the steps. The skirt there gapped a little, to allow the ascent of the steps, and I was still small enough to slip out, and into the shadows, without being noticed. Quietly I emerged from the shadows to sit on the bottom step, as if I had been there all along.

"Normally," Mrs. Mank said, "my friend Adele wouldn't take a case like this at all. She was considering it only as a favor to me. Even when she takes on such cases, cases with much more likelihood of success, she'd take twenty-five percent at the very least, and her usual rate is a full one-third of the estate."

Miz Starret, Mrs. Mank and Miz Verlow started down the steps, with Mama falling in behind them. They skirted me as if I were a plant pot that had always squatted there at the turn of the railing. I jumped up and grabbed Mama's skirt. She glanced down at me without surprise or any particular interest.

Mrs. Mank and the woman lawyer stood a few yards away, engaged in a seemingly casual murmured exchange. They chuckled. They were recollecting the meal they had eaten at Merrymeeting. Mama couldn't hear them, of course.

"Don't just stand there like a street sign," Mama said, "start praying, because if Mrs. Mank caint get that woman lawyer to contest that will, then you and I are going to starve, and since you are littler, you are going to wither away weeks before I do." Mama hugged herself. "I caint take this anymore," she said finally. "I'm going inside and slit my throat. If they ever finish out there, come in and tell me what they decided."

Mama went past Miz Verlow, watching her friend Mrs. Mank and Mrs. Mank's friend Adele Starret having their tête-à-tête, at the bottom of the steps. The screen door slapped smartly after Mama going into the house.

"The dishes," Miz Verlow said, without looking at me.

I climbed the steps and went to the alcove, where I picked up the envelope, folded it and tucked it into one sock. The pen went into the other. I stacked the cups and saucers the four women had abandoned and carried them to the kitchen. Cleonie and Perdita ignored my entrance. On my step stool, I could see into the parking area, where Mrs. Mank now stood at the open driver's window of a late-model yellow Cadillac, still talking to Miz Starret behind the wheel. Just as I had seen Miz Verlow saying good-bye to Mrs. Mank. At last the woman lawyer turned the key in the ignition and drove away, while Mrs. Mank watched her going.

We retired to our room that night as soon as was decently possible.

Ostensibly in the bathroom to brush my teeth and wash my face, I locked the door and examined the pen and the envelope. On the envelope was written

The Last will and testament of Deirdre Carroll.

The ball of the pen glistened with green ink.

Mama was waiting in our room.

"Give it to me." Mama held out her hand.

One after the other, I removed the pen from one sock and the folded envelope from the other sock and handed them over.

She studied the envelope for a long moment before she looked up at me.

"Do you know what this means?"

I nodded.

Mama threw the envelope down on her vanity and dropped the pen on top of it.

"I caint believe it!" She sat down on the edge of the bed and thrust out one foot.

I tugged off her shoes for her.

"Go take care of your hands," she said.

When I came back from brushing my teeth, washing my face and my hands, she was in her pajamas.

She reached for the ashtray and her cigarettes and settled onto her bed. She watched me open her jar of foot balm.

"I've been a fool," said Mama. "I believed that Mama loved me. Deep down. She loved me. But she never did. She must have hated me."

"Reckon she did," I agreed, sitting at her feet.

Mama waved her cigarette at me. "What do you know about it? You're seven years old. Both your mama and your daddy have loved you every day of your life. You may be a Dakin but you've had every damn thing you ever wanted. Your daddy spoiled you rotten."

Preferring that she rant on, for whatever I could glean from her unguarded speech, I said nothing.

"I don't know why I am the least bit surprised," Mama went on. "I should have seen it. I thought that when I ran away to Grandmama's that I was just trying to get out from under her thumb. I should have thought about my sisters and what she did to them. The only one of us she ever gave a damn about was Bobby. And then Ford. She had to get Ford away from me."

Risking the possibility that she would button up at an interruption, I asked, in a whisper, "What did she do?"

Mama was blowing smoke circles at the ceiling. "Grandmama came and took them away and Mama said good riddance."

I dug my knuckles into the sole of her foot the way she liked and coached her, "Tell me about Great-grandmama."

She closed her eyes. "Keep doing that. Nobody knows how I suffer with my feet. They are just an agony tonight."

A few minutes went by and I figured that she had done talking about anything that I wanted to know.

"My grandmama," she said, her free hand gone to her bosom, "loved me. She really did love me. She *took* Faith and Hope, but *welcomed* me, when I ran away to her. I didn't need to be anything but myself."

"But why did she take them?"

She gave me an irritated look and I wished that I hadn't asked.

"They were special," she said, with a deliberately false lightness. "Very special."

"Why?" I prodded.

Mama narrowed her eyes at me. "We were talking about me."

I applied myself at once to her feet.

"I wasn't as old as you are now when Grandmama took them away. I can hardly remember them."

"What did Grandmama do with them?"

"Raised them," Mama said. "I swear you cannot be my child, you can be so dim."

"Where are they now?"

Mama ground out the butt of her cigarette in the ashtray. "Do I look like a Missing Persons Bureau? Mind what you are about and stop your endless ridiculous questions."

"Yes, ma'am," I agreed.

She settled back and closed her eyes again.

Moments passed and her breathing seemed to even. I capped the jar.

"I was supposed to be Charity," Mama whispered. "Do I look like a Charity to you?"

I gave her no answer.

As quickly and quietly as I could, I shed my clothes and put on my pajamas.

Then she spoke again. "Mama's idea of a joke. Mock Grandmama and make her angry. Ha-ha-ha."

The next sound she made was a ladylike snore.

*

IN the years that followed, Miz Starret's communications were always encouraging and hopeful. A settlement of Mamadee's estate was always just around the corner. The suit to regain custody of Ford was well in hand, according to Miz

Starret, except it never seemed any closer to coming to trial. Though Mama received letters, the occasional telegram, papers to be signed in the presence of witnesses, and sometimes a half-hour long-distance phone call from Miz Starret telling how the case was going, neither Mama nor I ever saw the woman lawyer again.

I began this story by telling about Daddy's death, and the research that I had done gathering the details that had been kept from me. In the course of that research, I came across a photograph of Mrs. Mank's friend Adele Starret.

The photograph showed Miz Starret sitting at a long table. On her left was Janice Hicks and on her right was Judy DeLucca—the two women who kidnapped and murdered Daddy.

The photograph had been taken in the courtroom, at the defense table.

Adele Starret had been their attorney.

Forty

MAMA signed over the Edsel to Miz Verlow almost immediately. The loss did not seem to constrain her. She was spared the expense of upkeep and fuel, thus paring her cost of living to little more than covering her back. In the years to come, she would sell her outdated couturier clothing at a consignment shop and use the money to buy new off-the-rack that was no longer beneath her. Letting her Alabama license lapse, she seemed willfully to forget how to drive. She depended upon Miz Verlow's kindness and that of the occasional guest for transport if she did want to go anywhere.

One morning the Edsel was gone. Miz Verlow offered no explanation. Mama would not lower herself to ask what Miz Verlow had done with it, and its absence actually relieved Mama of the reminder of her losses.

Mama and Mamadee had schooled me from the cradle in dissatisfaction. Mama and I would continue to tug the ends of the rope between us, if only out of habit. But discontent did not come naturally to me. I was in that respect a healthy child; nearly everything under the sun was new to me and very little had yet to stale. I didn't need any promises to be happy to stay right where I was.

Every day after breakfast, a list of chores awaited me. Being useful made me feel needed, and being needed made me feel more secure. The knowledge that I was chalking up nickels in Miz Verlow's account book was a small and secret pleasure—in my opinion, the very best kind.

My hair remained a disgrace. Whenever Mama noticed it

again, she would rant at me about Merry Verlow's high-handedness in bleaching and frizzing my hair without her permission. What with the tangled scrub of déclassé tow on my skull and my outsized ears, I was a goofy-looking kid, which had this minor benefit—goofy-looking is at least disarming.

Miz Verlow did her best to protect my skin from constant sunburn with one of her salves, with imperfect success. She decided that I must wear a hat when out of doors to shade my face. I did, at least when she was around. Perdita made hats for me, a kind of amalgam of a woven-palm Panama and a kerchief that provided corners to tie under my chin when it was windy, and detached for washing. Her hats not only shaded my face, they covered my hair and ears, and slightly muffled my hearing, which was frequently a boon to me.

On account of my skin, I wore long-sleeved shirts under my overalls out of doors, but that was no trial to me. I rolled sleeves and pants-legs and burnt my arms and legs and feet anyway, at least when I was out of sight of Miz Verlow. When she took me with her on her seemingly aimless walks, of course, I did no such thing. I needed the sleeves and pants-legs and socks and tennies too, for some of those walks, as she tramped us through patches of marsh and bog that in summer were just naturally foggy with bugs and the beach that jumped with sand fleas. Miz Verlow had me take home twigs and flowers and seeds and berries and bark and so on, and identify them for myself from the books. As sparsely vegetated as the island seemed at first glance, it supported an unexpected variety of plants on the backsides of the dunes and in the hollows between. A shrub rosemary grew there, and calamintha, conradina, coral root and pinxter.

The most immediate and important lesson was that not everything is in the books. The second was that the curious odiferous shrubs, Candle Bush, that crept round the lattice skirts of Merrymeeting, were from the wild; Miz Verlow had transplanted them from various sites on the island. They were a senna or cassia, unique to the island and naturally dwarfed by the harsh climatic conditions. Cassia alata, var. santarosa, was not in the books at my disposal, or any that I have since examined. Miz Verlow used every part of the plant, from root and branch to the flower spikes that erupted in May to the pods that developed from them, in her preparations.

Before the school summer vacation came to an end, I had begun to know a little of Cleonie's and Perdita's immediate families. Perdita's husband, Joe Mooney, had a snapper smack of his own and fished for a living; as I have mentioned, he was often a source of supply for Merrymeeting's table. Joe had some children from a previous marriage, grown-up boys, who fished with him. He had raised them alone after losing their mama when they were little. He and Perdita had no children of their own.

Cleonie always called her husband Mr. Huggins, leading me to expect that he would be as solemn as a minister. Turned out that he called her Miz Huggins, and the formality of address was a joke between them. His Christian name was Nathan and he worked for a lumber company that imported mahogany logs through Pensacola. He had worked there since a boy, except for his military service. He bossed a crew—a colored crew, of course—that herded logs off the docks. The Hugginses had three girls older than me, and also a boy, Roger, who was about my age. They all lived in one house with Mr. Huggins's mama and Cleonie's mama, daddy, and granddaddy.

When I found out that the Hugginses had a dog and Perdita had two cats at home, I begged Miz Verlow for a pet. I tried to make the request modest: a kitten would do.

"Oh, Calley, I'm sorry that I have to say no. Kittens grow into cats, and cats eat mice and birds."

I had not considered the dietary habits of cats.

"A puppy?"

Miz Verlow smiled sadly.

"Puppies grow up to be dogs," I said. "What do dogs do?"

"Sleep on the furniture," she said. "Leave hair everywhere. Chew things. Smell like dogs when they're dry and wet dogs when they're wet. Grow old and die and make you cry your heart out."

"What's so bad about that?"

She shook her head. "Take my word for it, Calley. You have to be careful what you love because love has to be paid for."

She talked me right away from the subject. I let it go, figuring like any other kid that I could change her mind at some point.

As curious as I was about the Hugginses and the Mooneys, they were only minimally interested in me. They were more than decent to me but they had their own lives. Cleonie and Perdita assumed a degree of authority over me, chiding me as they would have their own, but it wasn't because they *wanted* to have anything to do with raising me. They had standards, and one of them was that any child, colored or white, respected elders.

But I ended up spending a lot of time with Roger, who usually passed his school vacation with his mama at Merrymeeting until we entered our teens. He slept on a cot in Cleonie and Perdita's room during the week and went home for Sundays, just as they did.

I won't say that we were friends but we got along. Because he was a boy, and older than me by seven whole months, he regarded himself as in charge. Naturally we had a few disagreements. The first time that I ever met him, I waggled my ears for him, which impressed him deeply. Roger countered by exhibiting how he could make all his fingers and his thumbs bend backward, and pop his arms in and out of their sockets. I was deeply impressed too, and not just out of politeness.

Miz Verlow had arrangements with the guides who took out deep-sea fishermen who were occasionally guests; she didn't want the trouble of maintaining a deep-sea boat or the larger bayside dock one would require. The Merrymeeting property did run Gulf to bayside, straight across the island, and on the bay was a little beach and dock. Miz Verlow kept some skiffs and a couple of sailboats there. One seven-year-old alone would be hard put to keep that little beach clean, the bitty dock tidy, the watercraft watertight and the sails in good order, but working together, two could. That first summer on Santa Rosa Island, tidying the little beach was among the earliest chores that Roger Huggins and I were assigned as a team by Miz Verlow.

We each had our separate chores indoors, but some we did together simply because four hands made lighter work.

The guest rooms very often could not accommodate all the

guests' luggage, particularly for those who stayed weeks at a time. Roger and I were consequently oft detailed to haul various forms of luggage to the attic for temporary storage. The larger pieces were usually emptied into the closets and dressers of the guests', so the pieces were often more bulky and awkward than heavy.

When first I reached the top of the stairs, my back was to it, and I was facing Roger, over a footlocker. It was a military style footlocker—how could it be otherwise?—but emptied, so we could manage it. We put it down promptly at the top of the stairs.

A long chain, of the kind composed of little metal beads that used to be commonplace for lights and ceiling fans, depended from the darkness overhead. Given a yank, it lit a series of bulbs suspended from the rafters. Though unshaded, the bulbs were of low wattage and dimmed with dirt and dust. By their light that never penetrated to all the nooks and crannies, the attic seemed vast to us then. In memory, it still is to me.

Despite the portholes under the eaves that were meant to relieve the accumulated heat, the attic was stifling in all seasons. As we paused there at the top of the stairs, I heard the coo of pigeons, the ruffling of feathers, a skitter of tiny claws. Crowded as the attic was with inanimate objects, the place was alive with critters: moths, spiders, flies, beetles, wasps, bugs, bats, birds and mice.

We shoved the footlocker into the nearest available space and paused again to look around. Roger and I exchanged a rueful glance; much as we would have liked to explore, we dared not dawdle. Miz Verlow awaited our services.

We would have other opportunities to visit the attic, and eventually, as we grew older, free access to the key that Miz Verlow kept in a certain drawer in her office desk. The attic never got less crowded. We were always finding things in it that we didn't remember having seen previously. Guests not only left pieces of luggage in storage during their visits but for temporary storage while they traveled elsewhere. The temporary storage sometimes became permanent, for reasons beyond our ken. A guest perhaps never returned, or forgot the left luggage, or deliberately abandoned it. The attic housed more than luggage, of course. It held everything that an attic should and then some.

Some of Miz Verlow's guests came and went, and never came back; some visited irregularly, and others were very regular indeed. Some stayed a week while others dallied a month or six weeks. Mrs. Mank proved entirely unpredictable. Her longest absence was five months; the shortest, a weekend. We saw her at least three times a year. Miz Verlow always knew well ahead that Mrs. Mank was coming but she never told me until it was time to arrange Mrs. Mank's suite.

I expected that we would one day see Fennie Verlow. Miz Verlow telephoned Fennie every few days and letters and small packages arrived for Merry Verlow, addressed in Fennie's hand. Mention was made of visiting, but Miz Verlow never did go visit her sister, Fennie. I cannot recall that Miz Verlow ever went so far afield that she could not return to sleep at Merrymeeting.

Miz Verlow never disputed or challenged Mama in her playacting as lady of the manse in front of the guests. In time, even perennial guests who knew otherwise came to behave as if it had always been so. Mama directed the conversation at every meal, permitting no discussion of religion, politics, money or sex. Her rules naturally made for some stultifying conversations—the usual clichés about the weather, and Mama's reminiscences of her days as a Southern belle, just after the war, when sometimes it seemed as if she were talking about the War Between the States instead of World War II— but on many occasions, the guests were more or less compelled to talk about themselves.

Miz Verlow's guests tended to be reasonably well educated—sometimes very well educated—and were nearly always well spoken. Artists and photographers, both amateur and professional, often sat at her table, along with divines, academics, schoolteachers, musicians and many other professionals. A substantial proportion of Merry Verlow's guests were also birders, a group with whom I had an immediate affinity. As the names in the guestbook changed, new subjects were introduced, and old ones continued. While Mama suffered through talk of birds and art and music and many other things irrelevant to the wants and the needs of Roberta Ann

Carroll Dakin, I sponged it all up. The result for me was a level of stimulation that I would never have received in my own home, had not Daddy been murdered and Mama and I cast out.

Forty-one

CAME the first day of school, I walked to the road and climbed up onto the bus, which, except for the driver, proved to be empty. I would be first on and last off, for I lived at the greatest distance from the elementary school.

As soon as I was out of sight of Merrymeeting, I removed my homemade hat. It was one of the few things that I could do to avoid becoming a goat. I could do nothing about my looks, let alone the inevitability that it was known that my father had been murdered and dismembered. The younger they are, the fewer social inhibitions children have. I was immediately asked directly if it was true that my daddy had been suffocated to death and cut to pieces. My first instinct was to act as if I did not understand the question.

A furrowed brow, "Huh?" and the witless announcement that I had seen a mouse on the beach, convinced my questioners that I was twice as stupid as a doorstop. My schoolmates did not persist, thankfully, as the commencement of the school term provided many more excitements than the frisson supplied by gore associated with a newcomer. When I was a little bit older, I realized my instinct had been correct: If ever I had started describing Daddy's murder, I would never have been shut of it.

The learning part was largely effortless and enjoyable; the social part of school, like constant sunburn to me. Science and languages came easily to me, so much so that by the time I was ten, I was being bussed to junior high school classes in those subjects. Social ineptness was expected of those who turned out to be "whizzes" at some subject or other. My schoolmates were in any case as put off by evidence of intellect as they were by overly large ears—waggable ears, after all, constituted true talent, along with being able to touch one's nose with the tip of the tongue, or make armpit farts. My teachers, most of them, were my schoolmates grown up; they suspected any child who gave evidence of being smarter than they were, and nonconformist behavior was swatted as quick as a housefly. Naturally, there were others like me in some way: their physical defects all too evident, or they were intellectually too slow or fast, relative to the norm. Every social group has its castes; I accepted mine with something like relief, as it excused me from the anxiety of being someone and something that I was not. My ability to overhear my classmates whispering and the confidences of the teachers to each other also gave me a useful edge in self-defense.

My formal schooling on the island settled into a dreamy, remorseless repetition of morning and early afternoon hours, five days a week, thirty-eight weeks a year. I rarely thought about it except when I was actually there.

My best school was Santa Rosa Island. Older and younger than its human residents, it was constantly remaking itself over time infinitesimal and infinite, immeasurable by my limited human senses. The great storms that I experienced on that exposed coast—Irene, in October of 1959; in 1964, Hilda, the first real hurricane of my life; the nameless tropical storm that came in June of 1965; and Hurricane Betsy, in the fall of that same year; in June of 1966, Alma would frighten, humble and exhilarate me all at the same time. But no less than the sight of a heron standing in the swash of the storm-wracked shore, one foot on a downed sand pine bole. No less than the peeps playing footsie with the quieted wavelets, the ghost crab peeking out of its tunnel, the hermit crab from a conch shell, the narcissus-pale trumpet of the railroad vine, or the houndstooth pattern of bird's feet on the sand.

How could any ordinary school compare?

For Mama, playacting at Merrymeeting was hardly enough. She discovered that first fall a little theatre troupe in Pensacola and cast herself instantly as a star. The discovery that the troupe had put on *Teahouse of the August Moon* the previous season devastated her. Only the conviction that the show must go on enabled Mama to fight off a massive migraine. She comforted herself with the anticipation of trying out for the new production the troupe was planning: *Anastasia*. For hours, she fussed with her hair, and put on her most regal diamond earrings. Her accent developed a tinge of the foreign, though just what foreign it was impossible to say. Constipated British English was the only element that I could name; the rest had likely never been heard on any known continent or planet.

She returned from her audition with the ever-threatening migraine at full bore, and sore feet, leaving her in misery from the crown of her head to the tips of her toes.

On seeing how white and strained Mama's face was, Miz Verlow sent bourbon and ice for her up to our room.

"So thoughtful of her," Mama said, with her old Alabama accent, and knocked back half a glass at once.

Tears ran down her face as I massaged her feet by candlelight that evening.

"I should have known," she said. "All these little theatre groups are cliques, talentless cliques. Pass me the ashtray, darling. Those people—classless. They wouldn't know talent if somebody came in and knocked them over the head with an Oscar."

Under my fingers, she stretched her toes and flexed her feet and moaned softly.

"Do I look like an understudy to you? I'm supposed to wait in the wings for that mumbling po-faced drip to fall off the stage?" She breathed cigarette smoke at the ceiling. "At least they're going to do *A Streetcar Named Desire* next. I *am* Blanche DuBois. Just look at me."

Depend upon the kindness of strangers though Mama always had, she was not Blanche DuBois, nor did she manage to wish her rival off the stage of *Anastasia*. Each time she went to Pensacola for rehearsals, she came back with a migraine and pain in her feet. The night arrived that she could barely walk.

Miz Verlow summoned Dr. McCaskey, who ordered bed rest for Mama. That was the end of Mama's little theatre career. The migraines let up, and the pain in her feet. When she was on them again, she was summoned by the doctor to have her feet x-rayed. Dr. McCaskey found nothing wrong with Mama's feet that wearing a larger size shoe would not cure. The diagnosis made Mama furious. She made me swear that if she were on her deathbed, I would never ever call that charlatan.

On the twenty-first of November, smoke billowed over Pensacola. Mama and Miz Verlow and I sat on an overturned skiff on the splat of beach and watched the city docks burn. We could taste the soot in the air. The fire stormed on the docks and vomited lurid smoke and ash, the fire trucks and fireboats keened, the hoses and cannons hurled water onto the flames, and the figures of men, shrunk by distance and the enormity of the fire, looked like imps in the midst of hellfire. The cacophony of sound was hellish too; it seemed to me that if one could hear the caterwauling of the damned, it would sound just so. The water of the bay reflected pillars of flames, reveling and dancing, like a sea of drowned candles.

Forty-two

THE spring and fall bird migrations drew many of our guests. Of the regulars, the Llewelyns were actually among the guests when Mama and I first arrived, but I paid them no mind at the time, and in turn, they paid little to me. Dr. Gwilym Llewelyn was a retired dentist who invited everyone to call him Will. Mrs. Gwilym Llewelyn was quite emphatically Mrs. Llewelyn. Her wifely status emphasized by insisting on being "Mrs. Llewelyn" was a feint; her Christian name was Lou Ellen, and that had proved too much poetry for her.

On their return in the fall of 1958, the Llewelyns remarked on my interest in birds. Their enthusiasm was infectious, their pleasure in the birds so intense and immediate, that I was entirely comfortable with them at once. As soon as they discovered that I was unusually good at mimicry of the birds, they all but adopted me. Dr. Llewelyn insisted on examining my teeth and cleaning them with a little dental kit that he carried with him, and gave me free toothpaste with fluoride in it that probably saved my teeth from the high-sugar diet at Merrymeeting. Mrs. Llewelyn took me shopping with her on occasion, with the excuse that she needed me to carry packages. On those expeditions, she bought me shoes and clothing that fit me, and treated me to lunches and teas in Pensacola or in Milton.

Each Christmas, I sent the Llewelyns a homemade Christmas card with an origami crane in it for them to hang on their tree, and they sent me a store-bought card, half a dozen toothbrushes and a supply of toothpaste, and a calendar. My birthday brought not only a card but a gift, which was always what Mrs. Llewelyn called "frivolous." Once it was a poodle skirt, with the requisite petticoat to wear under it, so that navigating the aisles at school was like docking a boat. Another birthday, the Llewelyns sent a girlish diary with a flimsy lock and a set of stationery, with stamps and an address book. Their gifts were the commonplace things that my peers were likely to receive from doting grandparents or aunts or uncles, and I always felt a little less of an orphan when I opened them.

From mid-March to June, the beach offered surcease from the northern winter. From June to September, our near-neighbors in the broiling Southern summer sought relief in the relative cool of the beach. Custom slowed a little in October, and fell off through November, December, January and February, but never quite stopped altogether, as guests found their way to Merrymeeting for reasons that had little to do with climate. Even at Thanksgiving and Christmas, which most folk could be expected to observe at home, a few guests took shelter at Merrymeeting. The Llewelyns always departed in time to spend their holidays with family. Mrs. Mank notably never observed the holidays with us.

Of all of Merrymeeting's guests, the most eccentric assortment were the ones who turned up for Thanksgiving and Christmas.

Every year that I can recall, an elderly couple by the name of Slater arrived in the third week of November and stayed until the first day of January. Mrs. Slater loved Bridge. If she could not make up a table, she knitted. Mr. Slater was always looking for someone with whom to play chess or Pinochle. They were both intense competitors, and I often observed them cheating at games. For old people, their reflexes with cards, pins, and knitting needles were astonishing.

An extraordinarily tall, thin, loose-limbed man, Mr. Quigley, was in the habit of arriving the day before Thanksgiving, staying a week, and then returning for a second week at Yuletide. He played Bridge with Mrs. Slater or chess or Pinochle with Mr. Slater. It was my impression that he was also aware that they cheated and was amused to let them. He painted little watercolors, usually seascapes.

Dr. Jean Keeling, a woman much given to reading, spent

the last two weeks of December and all of January at Merrymeeting. When she wasn't reading science-fiction paperback novels, she listened to opera on the Stromberg Carlson, and wrote a great many cards and letters. She played Bridge and other games with the Slaters and was as quick with her cards as they were, but like Mr. Quigley, seemed not to care whether she won or not. She was kind enough to give me her paperbacks when she finished them, but she was not a particularly gregarious person. She had one close friend among the group and that was Father Valentine.

An old blind priest, Father Valentine settled in the first of November and stayed until February fifteen. He was supposedly Episcopalian and retired, but was not the least bit frail. He paid me to read to him by the hour, which vastly improved my reading skills and vocabulary, to say nothing of my knowledge of the Bible, theology and philosophy. Fortunately for me, Father Valentine also enjoyed mystery stories, and through him, I was educated in the canon of fictional crime. He was voluble, not to say indiscreet, in a perfectly forthright way, not the least bit childishly or maliciously.

These guests' avocations, however, were not what made them our most eccentric guests, nor was it the habit of spending what are normally family holidays at Merrymeeting. It was that they were all adamantly and extremely superstitious, in different ways. They talked and argued about these beliefs as casually as other folks mentioned the weather. It seemed as if someone was always flinging salt over his or her left shoulder or through some other odd little ritual just barely fending off a dire end caused by a seemingly insignificant event.

Father Valentine's bed had to be placed with the head toward the south, to ensure long life.

Each of the others required the head of their bed to face east, for wealth, and regarded Father Valentine's insistence on the south as sheer superstition, and likely to bring bad luck.

They all tied knots in their handkerchiefs for a whole spectrum of reasons unique to each.

Father Valentine informed me that the necklace of amber beads that Dr. Keeling always wore preserved her from ill health.

He also told me that the single blue glass bead on a safety

pin that Mrs. Slater invariably wore on her collar was to ward off witchcraft.

Mr. Quigley and Father Valentine, who both smoked, would never light three cigarettes with the same match.

Mr. Quigley required half an onion under his bed when he had a cold.

Dr. Keeling regarded the same as ridiculous superstition.

Candles were a general fixation.

A candle had to burn in a window from Christmas Eve through Christmas night. It was bad luck for the year if it went out, and good if it didn't.

Seeing oneself in a candlelit mirror would bring down a curse. I was neutral on that one, having seen myself in candlelit mirrors and not felt any particular curse.

Seeing a loved one in a candlelit mirror could be the first notice of their death. That I could believe. I had certainly seen Mamadee in the parlor mirror before the confirmation of her passing.

Then there was the one about seeing a loved one known to be deceased in a candlelit mirror meant one's own death was near at hand. Well, I hadn't been sure about Mamadee, so I guessed that I didn't need to write my will yet.

All the little rituals made for a nervous atmosphere, as if everyone was on tiptoe because someone upstairs was dying.

Mama shushed me a lot. I often escaped outdoors, though the cold wind off the Gulf made my bones ache, my lungs tighten, and my nose run. I hardly ever could remember my handkerchief, so the kerchief ties of my hat were always stiff with snot from wiping my nose on them.

Our first Yuletide at Merrymeeting, Miz Verlow made no preparations until Christmas Eve, when she came back from Pensacola with an artificial Christmas tree.

I was very relieved, as the continued absence of the usual preparations suggested that the holiday was not going to be observed at Merrymeeting. Mama told me to stop being silly; we were bereaved, church-mouse poor, and Christmas had become too commercial anyway. We would observe the true religious meaning of Christmas.

Children were rarely among the guests at Merrymeeting and I have since wondered if Miz Verlow obtained that tree

only for me. It was white, and looked like the roof antenna for
a television set adorned with bottlebrushes. Mama thought it
vulgar. We had always had real Christmas trees.

The fake tree was fine by me. We set it up in the larger parlor. Miz Verlow gave me a spray bottle of some clear fluid that
she had compounded herself—fire retardant, she said—and I
sprayed the tree. The fluid smelled like pine with a hint of
peppermint in it. I wondered why a tin tree had to be fire-
proofed, but it was only one of the many peculiar things that
grown-ups did, like throwing salt over their shoulders, or pretending that they didn't go to the toilet.

The decorations Miz Verlow brought home with the fake
tree consisted of a string of colored lights that were supposed
to look like small candles in Victorian lamps, and bubbled
when they warmed up, and a dozen silver and gold balls the
size of goose eggs. I managed to break eight of the shiny
balls. The tree looked rather naked.

Miz Verlow studied it for a moment, sighed, and went to
the drawer in the desk where the cards were kept. She fished
around it and came up with a greasy old beat-up deck. She
tossed them to me. I recognized them in midair as the ones we
had used when we heard Mamadee's voice.

I gripped them tightly. Did Miz Verlow want to invite Mamadee to speak again?

"Jean," Miz Verlow said to Dr. Keeling, who was en-
sconced in an overstuffed chair in one corner.

Like the other guests and Mama, Dr. Keeling had been observing the assembly and decoration of the tree, but she had
not participated. None of them had.

"Don't you know of something to do with cards?" Miz
Verlow asked her.

Dr. Keeling cocked an eyebrow and then shrugged.

"Calley," she said, "bring me those cards, if you will."

I brought them to her, and she poured them out of their
faded, ragged little box and into her right hand in a single fluid
motion. She let the box fall into her lap. She twitched a single
card from the deck and set the remainder of the deck on the
arm of the chair. Her fingers seemed to flash—I thought I saw
an actual spark—and suddenly there was an odd stiff little
bird sitting in her palm. She held it out to me.

Clever folding had metamorphosed the king of hearts into this angular, unnatural bird.

"Crane," said Dr. Keeling. Her fingers hovered over the remainder of the deck and flickered and flashed and there was another one in her palm. "Origami."

"A bird," Mama told Father Valentine. "Jean's made a bird from a playing card."

Everyone was smiling, including Mama.

"Isn't that the cleverest thing," Mama said.

Dr. Keeling made the next crane in slow motion, so I could see the pattern. Then she guided me one step at a time through the folding of my first crane.

Everybody applauded, and Mr. Quigley whistled through his long bony fingers, and everybody laughed.

Sitting on the floor, I turned the rest of the deck into origami cranes while Dr. Keeling passed a needle and thread through each bird and looped it. Then I hung each of them on the tree, with Mr. Quigley's help on the highest ones.

Everything was so jolly that I let go my fear of provoking ghosts.

When Miz Verlow turned off the lights and turned on the lights on the Christmas tree, everyone again applauded and laughed and agreed it was all quite magical. Then the lights on the Christmas tree wavered, producing a general murmur of alarm.

Forty-three

CALLIOPE, said a woman's voice unlike the voice of any woman in the room. The voice was low and amused and affectionate.

Mama bolted to her feet with a shriek. She looked around the dark room frantically.

Another country heard from, continued the voice, which seemed to be emanating from the fake tree. *Roberta Ann, get a grip on yourself. I should not like to have to ask for someone to slap you out of hysteria. Remember our talk about Shakespeare's indelicacy? There, you see it's only me. Only I would know about it.*

"Grandmama?" whispered Mama, more or less at the tree.

Calliope, said the voice, *I fear that paper folding is not your forte. Still, it is a charmingly eccentric tree.*

"What do you want, Grandmama?" Mama asked. "Why are you here?"

To play the part, the voice replied. A lovely tinkling laugh like a piano glissando shivered the air. *Of the Ghost of Christmas Past, dear child.*

Mama cried out in frustration. "You're talking in riddles!"

You could call it that, agreed the voice. *Let the child stay up tonight to watch that the candle in the window does not go out. I would not care to be responsible for the consequences, should it be extinguished.*

Miz Verlow spoke abruptly from the darkness. "As you wish."

She sounded rather frightened, to me.

Thank you, the voice said. *Calliope, the flap of a wing, a passing breath, a draft from a closing door, could bring down more than darkness. Is there anything drearier than a snuffed candle? A puddle of viscid cooling wax peppered with smuts from a vanished flame? Promise me.*

I hesitated and then whispered, "I promise."

The Christmas tree lights flickered on again. Miz Verlow hastily turned on the other lights. The tree looked utterly fake and trashy.

Miz Verlow looked around the room. "Well," she said calmly, "I think it's time for mulled cider."

"Here, here," said Father Valentine. "Nothing like mulled cider to speed a spirit on its way. I've never seen a more beautiful woman of any age. Who was that extraordinary woman? And when did she die?"

"You saw her?" I asked Father Valentine.

"Of course I did." He chuckled. "No point in being blind except to see what the sighted don't."

Mama flung up her hands and said, "You are all nuts."

Mr. Quigley and Mr. Slater got up to move a chair next to the window in the foyer where the candle burned.

"Calley is not sitting up all night next to that silly candle," Mama said.

"Yes, she is," said Miz Verlow, which produced visible relief in everyone else except Mama.

"I am her mama—"

"Miz Dakin," Miz Verlow said, "I am not feebleminded. Please restrain yourself from saying the obvious."

"I will decide when she goes to bed—"

Miz Verlow said nothing. No one else spoke. Mama looked around nervously. Everyone was studiously solemn and disapproving, except me. I was about to pee myself.

"Excuse me," I cried in a panicky voice, and raced for the powder room under the stairs.

Father Valentine rumbled a laugh behind me and the tension among the grown-ups broke at once.

On my return, none of the guests said a word to me about what had just occurred. They ignored me with an almost religious fervor, as if I were the ghost in the house. Much was made of the mulled cider, and the savouries that Miz Verlow and I put out with it. All their conversation sounded like beans in a rattle to me, a panicky *clickclick-snicksnick*.

When bedtime came, Mama went upstairs without a word, and without me.

Miz Verlow brought me a chamber pot and a thermos of coffee.

"Calley Dakin, if you find yourself becoming sleepy, give yourself a slap across the face. Pinch yourself between your fingers." She slipped a straight pin through the collar of my pajamas. "If all else fails, prick yourself with this pin. Between the fingers, between the toes, anywhere really sensitive."

The double pocket doors into the large parlor stood open, allowing me to see the fake Christmas tree. Miz Verlow had turned off the parlor lights but left on the Christmas tree lights. It was not quite a Christmas card, for the hooks under the fireplace mantel sported socks, real socks. One of Father Valentine's black nylon socks, one of Mama's silk stockings, one of Mr. Quigley's long brown cotton knit socks, one of Mr. Slater's navy-blue socks, one of Mrs. Slater's nylon stockings, one of Dr. Keeling's white ragg wool socks, one of Miz Verlow's knee-highs, and one of my pink cotton socks. The whole business was my doing; I had asked Miz Verlow if we were going to hang stockings. Rarely was Miz Verlow disconcerted but that question unsettled her, though she tried to cover her confusion with a quick *of course*. It made me wonder if Miz Verlow had ever celebrated Christmas or even *believed in Santa Claus*.

Staying awake all night was harder work than I had ever imagined. After everyone had gone to bed, it was boring. I could not read or do anything that would take my eyes away from the candle in the window. I sipped at the heavily sweetened coffee, and listened to the house and the people in it.

Mama coughed, put out her last Kool cigarette of the day, and remarked to no one, "Damn my feet hurt and where's Calley? Watching a stupid candle." Later: "At least I *know* Grandmama is dead."

Father Valentine's murmured prayers were punctuated with flatulence.

Mr. Quigley's snores were audible to anyone with ordinary hearing.

Miz Verlow turned the pages of a book for more than an hour before the click of her lamp and the sigh of her relaxing into her pillow amid the soft whispering settle of her sheets.

Mrs. Slater kissed Mr. Slater and they both turned over, away from each other, and yanked at their coverlet from either side.

Dr. Keeling's toenails snapped between the clippers. The clippings made a dry tick in a small glass dish. When the snapping stopped, she made an emery board grate, and when she was done with the emery board, she spilled the clippings onto a piece of paper on her dresser, folded it carefully, and placed it in her handkerchief drawer, to be burned in the morning. Then she knelt down next to her bed and prayed.

NowIlaymedowntosleepIpraythedogmysoultokeep
ifIshoulddiebeforeIwakeIpraythedogmybonestotake.

Once under her covers, she fell immediately to sleep.

I watched the candle burn and grew sleepier. I pricked myself with the pin. Twisting and shivering, the flame of the candle rose its inch above the melting wax spindle and the faint breath of smoke trailed away from it with my every breath.

Calliope, said my mama's grandmama's voice from the candle, and she sighed. *What a person has to do for a private conversation.*

"Great-grandmama?"

What a mouthful of "grrrs" and "mas" that is. Call me Cosima.

"Yes'm. Cosima."

Child, the first person who knocks upon the door on Christmas morning, you must greet with the lighted candle in your hand.

"Yes'm."

Not everything that you hear is true. Don't say yes'm, please.

"No'm."

Another way to look at it is that truth is a slippery business. Be careful whom you trust. Trust no one wholly.

"You too?"

Facile wisecracks waste my time, little girl.

"Beg pardon," I said.

Oh, that's hardly necessary. You are the vortex, my darling child, the eye of the storm. That is not your doing, but, well, the weather. Forces flowing naturally, so to speak. Do I confuse you?

I nodded affirmatively.

Ah, she said. *Well, you are still a child. How I wish that I could linger long enough to tell you everything.*

"Daddy," I blurted.

Hush, child! she cried. *Call a second ghost and one of us will be obliterated!*

"But—"

Butts belong in ashtrays!

The candle flame flared and whipped violently for a second. I thought it would surely go out then and panic choked me. Then the flame steadied and shrank and was normal again.

"My candle burns at both ends," Cosima said, *"it will not last the night; but, ah my foes, and oh, my love; it gives a lovely light."* She laughed as if very pleased with herself. *Calley, point at the candle.*

A gentle push on my arm thrust my finger into the flame. I snatched it hastily back. The sting of the flame bit it hard, making me wince and shudder and bury my exquisitely painful, singed fingertip in the opposite fist.

Burn bright and fierce, Calley, came the whisper from somewhere over my shoulder.

The shock of the burn wakened me past mere wakening. A wash of energy made me intensely aware not only of the substance of the material world around me, but that I was not sleepy, not the least bit sleepy or tired. I know now that there is nothing supernatural about such a state of mind; I was merely experiencing the clarity and sense of super reality common to those who have stayed awake all night. I suspect that feeling is one of the addictions of the night owl. But then, I took it for the way that Cosima's ghost must feel in this world.

A glance at the mantel in the parlor showed me that each

sock now hung heavy. For an instant, I thought each was filled with a legless foot. I blinked and the socks were merely laden with small mysterious objects. How they had all been filled without my seeing, I could not imagine.

Around the edges of the draperies, I could see that the dark had thinned enough to see through. Christmas Day was at hand.

Forty-four

AT the first mechanical *caw-caw!* of the doorbell, I nearly fell out of the chair. My sudden movement sent the flame of the taper wavering, at which violent anxiety froze me in place. I could not breathe again until the flame stood up straight again. The only time that I had ever heard the doorbell previously was when I was playing with it. It was one of those old brass bells that made a charming metallic *caw-caw!* when its exterior wingish keys were turned. Due to the constant exposure to salt, this particular bell was rather hoarse in its chime. I remember the odd seawater taste of it very well. All one morning I had studied the mechanism, and Mama caught me licking it. She advised me that I was never to touch the doorbell again, on pain of having my hands chopped off, let alone lick it, which would cause my tongue to be cut off. Miz Verlow and Cleonie and Perdita never complained at all; indeed, I thought that they seemed to be amused, at least until Mama threatened to cut off my tongue.

The doorbell ground out its salty *caw-caw!* again. Upstairs, sleepers began to stir in response.

With my finger burnt, finding a way to pick up the candlestick with my dominant hand required considerable caution and effort. The actual gripping of the candlestick intensified the hurt. Fortunately, I was only steps from the door.

I turned the key in its keyhole with the weaker grip of my other hand. The innards of the lock fell over; I tried the knob. It yielded slowly. I thought surely the bell would chime again, angry as the screeching pain at the tip of my finger. The door creaked on its hinges. I peered out at our first caller of the day.

In the cold wind off the Gulf, a woman hunched shivering, her hands shoved into the pockets of a thin Windbreaker. Her face looked frozen—carved of some semitranslucent plastic, like the glow-in-the-dark Virgin Mary on the dashboard of Mr. Quigley's Chevy Bel Air. Through thick glasses rimmed with frost, her unblinking eyes seemed more like eyes frozen in ice cubes than those of a living person. The thickly glossed lipstick around her mouth made a caricature of lips. A fancy gauzy scarf with sequins on it circled her throat. She wore tennis shoes with the rubber toes separating from the dirty canvas fabric.

I let the door fall open and thrust the candlestick at her.

She took her left hand from its sheltering pocket and grasped it. Instantly the candle's flame guttered and died. Her gaze met mine and her head dipped slightly. Her knuckles were reddened and chapped from the cold, her fingernails blue with it. Like her face, her hands might have been made of holy-mother plastic.

"Merry Christmas," I blurted.

In a throaty rasp that I only understood because she spoke slowly, she said *Oh, is it? Is this—Merrymeeting?*

I nodded numbly. She had been heralded by my dead great-grandmama. Like Mamadee, she was uncertain about her location. But I hardly needed to deduce that she was some kind of ghost, as I heard it in her voice. After all, I had been listening to the voices of the dead since birth and it would be peculiar if every passing day did not sharpen my sense of distinction between those voices and the voices of the living.

I am Tallulah Jordan, she said.

I stepped aside; she entered. I closed the door behind her against the wind.

"No one but me is up yet," I told her. "I'm going to make some fresh coffee."

I'd like that, she said.

She was either a coffee-drinking ghost or approved of my making it.

In the kitchen, I gestured toward Cleonie and Perdita's lit-

tle table. Tallulah Jordan placed the candlestick on it. She
scraped a chair away from the table and turned it around and
sat in it backward, watching me as I prepared coffee.

"I can do tea, if you'd rather," I said.

No, no, coffee's the thing for me. She took off her glasses
and polished and dried them on a linen napkin, before putting
them back on again.

I prepared the coffee with one hand tucked into my armpit.
Awkward as it was, I was less likely to drop something if I
didn't use the hand with the burnt finger. While the coffee
brewed, I toasted and buttered some bread. When I put the
plate on the table in front of her, she tucked away the toast as
if she had not eaten for a week. Or years. She licked her lips. I
poured her orange juice to follow her toast. She reached eagerly for the mug of coffee when I offered it.

I took the opportunity to study her while I could. By the
noises above us, I knew that we would be interrupted very soon.

Bony chapped wrists and fingers, bony frozen face, her
chinos belted with worn woven leather, she looked like death
on a bad day. Tallulah Jordan wasn't just underfed, she was
emaciated. Frail. Her hair was stiff and frosted with salt blown
off the Gulf. It was black hair, that solid black that shouts dye.

I poured her a second mug, aware of her studying me as I
had her.

What's your name? she asked. *What's wrong with your
hand?*

"Calliope Carroll Dakin. I'm more Dakin than Carroll." I
didn't answer the second question.

She almost smiled. She held out her hand and I put my own
hand, the one with the burnt finger, in her palm. She kissed my
finger. All at once, the pain was gone. She released my hand
and I stepped back from her slowly, staring at my finger, and
then at her, and again at my finger. The burn was still there but
there was no pain.

When I looked up from it again, the candle on the table
was burning once more.

I heard Miz Verlow's step on the backstairs. My gaze was
drawn toward the door that she would come through and I
tensed like a guy wire.

A cold, bony hand grasped my wrist. I nearly jumped out of my skin. If I had been sitting in that chair by the window again, I *would* have fallen out of it.

Tallulah Jordan stared at me intently as she gripped my wrist.

Listen to the book, she said in her sandpapery voice.

The door to the backstairs opened at the very instant that my hand fell loose from that grip.

Miz Verlow stopped abruptly in the doorway. Her face drained of color, and she sniffed the air as if she smelled smoke.

"I burned the toast," I said.

Miz Verlow frowned disbelievingly at me.

I moved toward her, intending to get away and upstairs as fast as I could. She seized my wrist as I passed her, and let go as if she had burned her hand on me, and looked at her palm as if I had burnt her.

"The doorbell," she said.

There was no question in her voice but I responded as if there were.

"It was me," I confessed. "I'm sorry."

She knew that I was lying. I didn't want to find out what else she knew. Or did not know. She was seething with anger and, more interestingly, fear.

"You let the candle go out," she said.

"No, ma'am."

The "ma'am" did not mollify her. "Who was here, Calley?"

I yawned and fidgeted. "Nobody."

She looked disgusted with me, and I had no doubt that she knew that when I used the word *nobody* that I was only telling the technical, literal truth.

"Get out of my sight, Calley Dakin," Miz Verlow said, "and the next time I see you, I want the truth."

I lunged for the backstairs.

Which book? Which one?

I looked back to make sure that Miz Verlow was not watching me, and slipped into the linen closet, closing the door behind me as silently as I could, in case Miz Verlow was listening.

In a moment my eyes adjusted to the darkness and I could make out the darker dangle of the chain pull with its white ceramic knob at the end that turned on the light inside the closet. I gave it a yank. Both knob and chain felt creepily colder than they should have. I usually enjoyed pulling a light chain, feeling the catch when it was at its full length, and then slowly releasing it, waiting for the instant that the bulb lit, or went dark. In that instant of electric light, I saw where I was and where I wanted to go, and yanked the chain a second time to return the closet to darkness. No line of light would be showing at the bottom edge of the door.

Dropping to my knees, I crept to my shelf of books.

How could I be certain that Tallulah Jordan meant one of these books when she told me to *listen to the book*? Some people called the Bible The Book. She had said *listen,* not *read.*

I ran my fingers across the row of spines. As I touched the *Audubon Bird Guide,* the finger burnt in the candle flame instantly hurt again, hurt as bad as when it was actually in the flame. Reflexively I jerked it back. And it stopped hurting. Stopped burning. I braced myself, and gingerly touched it to the spine of the bird guide again. This time there was no pain.

And a voice said. *This one.*

It was not the voice of Tallulah Jordan, or my great-grandmama or Mamadee. It was the voice of Ida Mae Oakes, the mellifluous, comforting voice of Ida Mae Oakes. My eyes welled and I nearly blubbered. I tugged the book from the shelf and hugged it tight.

I had been up all night. I climbed to my favorite shelf and settled into a comfortable nest of toweling and feather pillows and tucked the book under the pillow for my head. I didn't think of pajamas or brushing teeth or any of the everyday going-to-bed routine. Dr. Keeling's odd prayer came to mind. I heard my great-grandmama Cosima speaking again:

> *Now I wake me to the day*
> *that breaks o'er me with burning ray*
> *If I should live until the noon,*
> *I'll light a candle to the moon.*
> *If I should live the whole day long*
> *I'll sing the sun a heartful song.*

I could hear the water clearly, rushing in and out, and it sighed like great wings

shushabrush, shushabrush shushabrush

all around me.

Forty-five

THE clock seemed to have stopped that Christmas, for when I came downstairs again in the early afternoon, after dinner, the stockings still hung from their hooks and none of the gifts under the fake tree had been opened. It was the first time that I realized that grown-ups did not have to struggle to postpone opening their presents. Such an indifference to the excitement of Christmas morning shocked me, and made me feel sorry for them to have it mean so little to them. It seemed to me in that instant of realization that this was the clear dividing line between being a child and being an adult. Adults were people who had lost the innocent greedy joy of Christmas morning.

Still wearing the previous day's clothing, and looking like an unmade bed, I'm sure, I was fortunately disinclined to mourn my future, thanks to the hunger of a healthy growing child unfed since Christmas Eve's supper. I rummaged myself a bellyful in the kitchen and then wandered to the parlor, where the tree stood forlornly, its odd and gaudy fruit strewn meagerly about it.

Father Valentine sat alone in his favorite chair, wearing his blind-man's dark glasses, and doing nothing. He heard me enter, of course, and grinned.

"Is it Rip Van Calley?" He cackled. "I thought you'd be sitting here with everything all opened when I came down this morning."

"Merry Christmas," I said.

"And to you," he replied. "It had ought to be merrier, really, in *Merry* Verlow's house. I believe I like the smell of the smoke from this wood fire as much as I do the warmth from it. Nostalgic."

"What's that? Nostalgic." I twiddled my sock dangling from its hook under the mantel.

"The way you wish it once was, but of course it wasn't. Bring me my stocking, Calley. I'm tired of waiting for it."

Father Valentine never hesitated to play at being childish, and when he did there was a quaver in his voice that was as good as a wink. It was a relief to have a grown-up at least willing to fake a little Christmas excitement.

Using a hassock as a step stool to reach it, I unhooked his stocking. It was mysteriously lumpy but even though the fabric was stretched thin to near transparency, I could not make out what was in it.

He took it eagerly and ostentatiously felt it all over.

"Grand," he said. "Just what I wanted. So thoughtful."

As if at a signal, the rest of the household began to filter into the parlor, greeting me with Merry Christmases and joshing about Father Valentine and me getting the jump on the presents.

Dr. Keeling paused by her chair to ask, "What do you have there?"

"Mine to know and yours to find out," said Father Valentine. His hands clenched around his stocking. "It's mine and you can't have it."

"Don't want it," Dr. Keeling answered, "but I'd take it if I did."

"No squabbling, you two," Mr. Quigley said. "Not today." He took down my sock and gave it to me.

Miz Verlow and Mama arrived lastly, after the Slaters.

I squatted on the turkey rug with my sock at my feet. There was a rectangular box in it, the corners catching in the fabric, requiring me to work it out a snag at a time. I had it in the grasp of thumb and forefinger when Miz Verlow walked in. She paused to flip a switch and the lights on the aluminum tree bloomed like a dozen candle flames. The cranes on the tree wavered slightly as if on a passing air, but it might have been an illusion caused by the sudden multiple sources of light on the highly reflective tree.

The sock clung to the rectangular box, which was about the

size of a pack of cigarettes. Miz Verlow stooped over me to seize the toe of the sock, and the box slipped out into my hand.

She was smiling at me. If she had been angry or suspicious earlier, there was no sign of it.

"Merry Christmas," she said, and uncurled the fingers of her free hand.

Two AA batteries rested in her palm.

Hastily I ripped the paper from the box and tore it open, to see the transistor radio that the batteries would power.

The guests all laughed and applauded.

"I'm not going to listen to that hurdy-gurdy day in and day out," Mama said. "You hear me, Calley?"

All too clearly, somewhere in my inner ears, as if she were sticking pins in them.

Miz Verlow winked at me.

I remember nothing else that was given me that Christmas, except for the sweater and watch cap that Mrs. Llewellyn had sent. It seems to me that there were no real toys—suitable for my age, I mean. No dolls, no children's books, no records of children's songs, certainly nothing as extravagant as a bicycle. My memories of later Christmases with the same guests, though, assure me that what I received were make-do tokens, like something a parent might pick up at an airport notions kiosk on the way home from a trip, after having forgotten to obtain a real souvenir: a fresh pack of cards from the Slaters, probably one of the several that they always brought with them, a secondhand science-fiction novel from Dr. Keeling, a little cheaply framed watercolor seascape from Mr. Quigley, a chocolate Santa Claus from Father Valentine.

Mama always told me that we couldn't afford Christmas presents. Every year I made something in school for her—a paper ornament, paper angel, a sachet made of a scrap of cloth and filled with the pine needles and rosemary that were commonplace on the island, or a newspaper mâché pot painted with primary colors that began to flake off as soon as the paint dried.

It was always Miz Verlow who gave me something that I wanted, and other gifts that I needed. Sometimes I thought that I loved Miz Verlow more than I did Mama, or even wished that she was my mama, instead of Roberta Ann Carroll Dakin. Of course, I always felt guilty for loving her more than Mama, and wishing such a thing. I feared her more than Mama too, for as I grew, I began to perceive Mama more and more as a paper tiger.

That Christmas, that first Christmas, I unhooked the paper cranes from the fake tree and smuggled them to the linen closet, where in a very high, hard to reach corner, one that I nearly brained myself climbing to, I stashed them in the box that had held the sweater and cap from Mrs. Llewelyn. If I kept those cranes that once had been playing cards, if I had the right candle, I might be able to ask more questions of my great-grandmama Cosima. If I ever felt brave enough. I wished that if she had to speak to me, she would do it without hocus-pocus, like all the other whispering or chittering voices that I heard. Of course I worked mightily to ignore them but now that I knew her voice by name, I would recognize it. Of course. How could I be so stupid? She had spoken to me first by way of introduction. The proof would be when I heard her voice again, and knew it for hers.

And then, oddly, or perhaps not oddly, given what I have learned, the visitation of my great-grandmama, my vigil and my visitor and what she told me that Christmas, went out of my head. I remembered it only in dreams. When I dreamt it, I promised myself to remember when I woke but then, did not. It took a great many dreamings before I did. Before I remembered that I was supposed to *listen to the book*.

Forty-six

MERRYMEETING'S operation and upkeep took an enormous amount of work that Miz Verlow made every effort to keep unseen. Nothing upset guests like unreliable plumbing, while at the same time the finest pipes and fixtures in the world would be tried to their utmost by a succession of paying guests. After she lost a reliable plumber to a freak lightning strike at a church picnic, Miz Verlow cast about, trying several other local plumbers. She was dissatisfied with all until she found Grady Driver.

First, though, she fired his daddy. On his very first call to Merrymeeting, Heck Driver managed to bust a pipe and ruin a wall, not from incompetence but because the Co'Colas he drank one after another, complaining of the heat, were about half cheap rum. The ruination of guest-room wallpaper by the leaking pipe in the bathroom next door was a predictable consequence. Miz Verlow took Heck Driver to task; he cussed her out, and she not only fired him and declined to pay him, she told him she was going to bill him for the repairs.

An hour after Heck Driver stumbled out, leaving his tools where they lay, and drove uncertainly away, his rusted-out van returned with a mere boy at the wheel. I knew him from school: Grady Driver, Heck's son, excruciatingly shy and chronically dirty. He had been sent home repeatedly with nits and been held back a couple times, so even though he was a couple years older than me, he was in the same grade.

Grady knocked at the kitchen door and asked to speak to Miz Verlow.

When she came to the door, he apologized for his father's error, using a formula he had by heart.

"My daddy sent me to beg pardon, Miz Verlow, and not hold it agin him on account of he come out sick to start, from havin' ate bad fried fish last night, but not wantin' to let you down, and maybe I could clean up the mess for you and pick up his tools."

Miz Verlow was in the doorway with her arms crossed under her bosom.

"I will excuse your lie on grounds of your understandable desire to defend your daddy. However, Mr. Driver was drunk. You are too late to clean up, as my maid has already done so, and it requires a competent plumber to repair the broken pipe. But you may retrieve his tools."

"Hit were an accidence, Miz Verlow," insisted Grady.

Miz Verlow had rolled her eyes. "Enunciate, young man. Accident! It-was-an-accident."

Grady swallowed hard and repeated after her. "It-was-an-accident."

"It was not an accident," Miz Verlow said.

Grady looked confused. He was built like Roger, long-limbed and gangly, but poorly nourished for his frame, with a stolid expression on his face that people often took for vacuousness or backwardness of intellect.

"True accidents are surprisingly rare. Most of the events that people call 'accidents' are entirely predictable. Time and again, close examination of the so-called 'accident' reveals incompetence, fraud or drunkenness, or any combination of those faults, as the real cause. The only 'accidental' aspect of the mess your daddy made was the fact he did it here, because I had the random bad luck to have hired him today."

Grady had passed from confused to stunned and back to confused again.

Miz Verlow threw up her hands. "Get your daddy's tools!"

I'd been lurking about the kitchen to see what I could see and hear what I could hear. When Miz Verlow vacated the doorway, and Grady stood hesitant on the threshold, I hauled him inside.

"I'll show you," I told him.

He followed me up the backstairs and down the hall.

292   TABITHA KING AND MICHAEL MCDOWELL

Cleonie and I had mopped up and wiped up and even tidied the tools into Mr. Driver's toolbox but we could not fix the pipe. Miz Verlow had turned off the water to the bathroom and so it was unusable.

To my surprise, Grady made a thorough examination of the scene. Then he took some of his daddy's tools and went to work. Needless to say, I was fascinated, not only by Grady's bold advance upon the problem, but also by what he did. In a quarter of an hour, he had the miscreant pipe repaired and asked me to show him where the water was turned off and on. Once the water was back on, the bathroom was operational.

Then I required Miz Verlow to cover her eyes and let me guide her to the scene, whereupon she opened her eyes on a clean, functional bathroom, and a grinning, though still regrettably unwashed, Grady Driver.

"I kin fixt that wall, Miz Verlow," Grady said, "you got you sum plastern paste."

Miz Verlow shook her head in disbelief.

"Young man, you amaze me. You'll have to come back to fix the wall. I'll have the materials on hand tomorrow."

Grady packed up his daddy's tools again.

Miz Verlow watched him for a moment, sighed, and went away.

I tagged after her all the way to her office. She looked at me inquiringly and I held out my hand.

"He done a good job," I advised her.

She pursed her lips. "You know better grammar than that, Calley Dakin."

I corrected myself, "Yes, ma'am, he did a good job."

She opened a desk drawer, the one where she kept petty cash. I watched her fingers hesitating and then lunging and plucking out a bill. She thrust it at me.

I grabbed it and raced out, catching Grady stowing his daddy's toolbox in the van. Just as Miz Verlow had thrust the bill at me, I thrust it at Grady.

He looked at the five-dollar bill in amazement, scratched his head, and grasped it.

"Much oblige," he said, summoning all his dignity as a substitute adult.

"Hey," I said, "you got nits?"

Immediately he was another kid again and disgusted with me.

"Hey," he said, "you fly with them ears?"

"Hey, that's original, how many times you s'pose I've heard it? My ears come attached to me. You get bugs in your hair from not washin' it."

"I ain't got bugs!" He climbed into the van and slammed the door. "I ain't got bugs!"

By way of underlining my superiority, I crossed my arms and watched him as he drove away. He probably did have bugs again, scratching his head like that.

I went straight inside and washed my hair.

Forty-seven

DRAWN by the growl and beat of the engine, I raced up to the crest of the dune to see it: A black-and-cream Corvette was speeding toward Merrymeeting. Maybe Mrs. Mank had traded her Porsche. I had no burning desire to see Mrs. Mank but the Corvette commanded my attention. When I reached the parking area, its engine was ticking down. The driver was next to it, taking off his sunglasses. He squinted at me and smiled.

He was one of the FBI agents who had interviewed Mama over and over at Ramparts. He had considerably less hair than he had had then, but I knew him nonetheless, and would have known him anyway once he spoke.

"Howdy, Miss Dakin," he said. "Why are you hiding under that big hat?"

I didn't answer his question. I had more important things on my mind.

"I know you."

He laughed. "You are sharp. I believe you were all of seven years old the last time I saw you. You done some growing."

"You ain't wearing your FBI suit."

He shook his head. "Even FBI agents take vacations, sweetheart. Your mama at home?"

I didn't want to tell him. What if he had come to arrest us, and his Hawaiian shirt and chino pants were just a costume to make me think he was on vacation?

"Not saying anything, sweetheart, you might as well be saying yes," he told me.

I got sassy with him. "You're smart for an FBI agent."

He winked at me. "I'm too big to spank. But you're not, not yet."

"I am eleven-gone-on-twelve," I informed him, "and I am way too big to spank too."

He chuckled and then asked, "Miz Verlow at home?"

I saw no harm in promptly answering, "Yes'r."

"Show me the way," he said, with a little bow.

I bowed back, extending my hand toward the front of the house.

He followed me around the corner and along the verandah and up the steps to the front door.

Miz Verlow was in her little office, with the door open. She stood up at the sound of our footsteps on the verandah and emerged into the shadowed foyer.

"Is it Mr. O'Hare?" she asked.

"All day," he said.

Miz Verlow extended her hand and he grasped it.

"Welcome."

"Pleased, ma'am."

"He's an FBI agent," I told her.

Miz Verlow cocked her head quizzically.

"My day job," Mr. O'Hare said. "Miss Dakin and I are old acquaintances."

Merry Verlow's smile disappeared.

"I had understood you to be a guest." Her tone was guarded.

"I am. I am on vacation, ma'am."

"I won't allow any disruption, Mr. O'Hare."

"There won't be any," he said. "I am here for personal reasons only. You must be aware that the investigation into the Dakin case has long been closed."

"Indeed. Nevertheless I must ask your promise that you will not trouble any member of this household on the subject."

"You have it," Mr. O'Hare agreed. "Call me Gus."

"He asked me if Mama was home."

Miz Verlow looked at each of us in turn.

"Yes, I did," he admitted easily. "I won't deny that I wish to see Mrs. Dakin again."

Miz Verlow looked to me again. "Calley, bring your mama here, please."

I shot off to the small parlor. Even if I had not been able to hear the television, I knew that Mama was watching it. It was time for *Queen for a Day*.

Mama was not pleased to be summoned.

"It's important," I told her.

Pouting and muttering, she put out her cigarette and followed me to the foyer.

Miz Verlow and Mr. O'Hare stood as I had left them, and I knew that neither of them had said a word while I was fetching Mama.

"Mrs. Dakin," said Mr. O'Hare.

Mama stopped dead. Her eyes widened in alarm and one hand fluttered toward her throat.

"Gus O'Hare," he said. "We met in unfortunate circumstances."

Mama nodded. She was rigid, fighting the urge to flee.

"Forgive me, Mrs. Dakin, I never thought ill of you and, in fact, you have been in my thoughts in a good way ever since. I happened to learn that you were here. I had vacation time coming and I wanted to see you again. To tell you that I never thought ill of you."

Miz Verlow made an odd noise in her throat.

Mama smiled faintly.

"I did not come here to be a pest," Mr. O'Hare continued. "I would be pleased to spend my few days of leave in this lovely place and have the pleasure of a few words with you, as few words as you might choose, Mrs. Dakin. If you wish me to go away at once, I will."

Mama smiled slowly. "That seems fair."

"All right then," Miz Verlow said briskly. "Let me show you your room, Mr. O'Hare."

Gus O'Hare gave Mama a little bow and a little nod in my direction, and set off after Miz Verlow's wake.

Mama rolled her eyes at me. I covered my mouth. We both tiptoed back into the television room, where Mama turned the television back on and reached for her cigarettes.

"I've made a conquest," she whispered to me, and giggled. I couldn't help giggling too.

"He drives a Corvette," I told her.

"Oh my! Admit it," she went on in a low voice, "he's kind of cute."

It wasn't what Mama said or how she said, so much as I was just old enough to grasp, at last, that Mama might one of these fine days remarry.

Mama had always attracted men. It was entirely expected that many of Miz Verlow's male guests cast an appreciative eye in her direction. However, most of Miz Verlow's guests were couples. The few single men who came to Merrymeeting were rarely what Mama would consider eligible.

To my relief, Mama had previously displayed great tactfulness toward both her married admirers and the occasional single one. It would not do to have anyone's wife alarmed, nor would Miz Verlow tolerate even a flavor of scandal. So Mama never accepted a compliment from a married man without turning it back toward his wife, and her flirtations with single men were as chaste as Doris Day's—at least under Miz Verlow's roof and within sight and sound of Merrymeeting. Miz Verlow was too cynical, I am sure, to expect virtue; she only wanted the conventions observed, and a decent hypocrisy.

I was ignorant, of course, of sexual behavior and sexual tension, and had yet to see the primness of the times for the ludicrous charade that it was. But I was not too young to have seen Mama in action, charming men and women both into doing whatever it was she wanted them to do. I was young enough to feel very little threat and not much more interest in the first two or three single men who showed interest in Mama. Nor had I forgotten that we were bound to the island. Guests must sooner or later depart. In any case, the earliest flirtations were brief.

Mr. O'Hare continued to behave with a distinct courtliness toward Mama. He hastened to hold her chair for her at dinner, and took a chair next to her. He did not force his conversation on her, but with a strict Southern mannerliness, spoke as much to Miz Llewelyn, on his other side, as he did to Mama, and to Mr. Llewelyn, opposite him. His interest in birds seemed unfeigned and informed, without being too expert, which pleased the Llewelyns. He tried to draw Mama into the conversation about birds, describing various ones that he had seen, all of them quite common and recognizable to her, doing things that struck her as remarkable: crows that untied strings and purple martins that outsmarted squirrels at birdfeeders and that sort of thing.

Mama ate up the attention, of course. At the same time, she assessed Mr. O'Hare closely. He was aware of her appraisal, yet remained cool and unflappable. He did not resort to preening, which would have made him ridiculous, nor did he refer in any way to the previous acquaintanceship. Miz Verlow observed approvingly.

Occasionally Mr. O'Hare spoke to me, addressing me as Miss Calley, and with the warmth of an old family friend. He asked after my schooling and activities, and expressed delight at my interest in birds. My wariness softened.

He asked Mama to watch the sunset on the beach. Seeing them rise from their chairs on the verandah, Miz Verlow came to the kitchen, where I was at the sink.

"Calley," she murmured, "Mr. O'Hare is taking your mama to watch the sunset. You had better scoot into the tall grass and eavesdrop. I'll be waiting in my room for you to report back."

Miz Verlow had never asked me to spy on anyone. I did not hesitate, however; Mama was going beyond our sight in the presence of a man authorized to arrest people.

Forty-eight

MIZ Verlow was waiting for me on my return. She put her finger to her lips as I slipped past her, at the door into her room.

"He pointed out stars to Mama," I reported breathlessly, "not that Mama could see them but she pretended to."

Miz Verlow indicated a coffee thermos and a pair of cups on a side table, between her rocking chair and a straight chair. I took the straight chair and she settled into the rocker.

"He thinks Mama is innocent and was done out of Daddy's money."

Miz Verlow sighed.

"She believes him," I said.

"But you don't," Miz Verlow said.

"Mama believes what she wants to believe. I don't believe him, exactly. I believe that she is innocent or she wouldn't need to believe him."

Miz Verlow started and sat back, grasping the arms of the rocker.

"Well, well," she muttered.

"He hasn't got any proof," I continued, scornfully, so Miz Verlow would not think that I was disappointed.

She let go of the arms of the rocker and rocked back very slightly.

"Can't prove a negative," she said vaguely.

It was an interesting way to put it but I would have to wait until later to think about it.

"Mama asked him if he knew anything about Ford. He ducked it. I think he does."

"What does he want, exactly?" Miz Verlow asked.

"He says he wants to restore her good name and get Ford back for her and see her as happy as she should be."

Miz Verlow chuckled. "A perfect gentle knight."

I heard it as "night."

She picked up on my confusion at once. "Knight with a *K*," she clarified for me. "He wants to carry her away on a white horse, like a fairy-tale princess."

I guessed that was a way of saying that Mr. O'Hare had fallen for Mama.

Miz Verlow dismissed him. "He's a fool."

She poured me half a cup of coffee and we sat together in contemplative silence.

Finally she said, "I never want to catch you eavesdropping on me."

I put my cup down. "Sometimes I caint help it, Miz Verlow."

She nodded. "Let me put it this way. I never want to discover that you have overheard me and then repeated it to someone else."

Immediately I wondered why and if I did, what she might do about it.

"Don't try me, Calley," she said, as if she could read my mind. "Go on to bed now."

Mama was not in the room we shared. I found her in the small parlor, with Mr. O'Hare. They each had a glass of bourbon on the rocks, and a glow about them. I pretended that I had come to kiss Mama good night.

I was in my pajamas, ready to do Mama's feet, when she came up to bed. She kicked off her shoes and sat down on her vanity stool to unbutton her garters, freeing her stockings so that I could roll them carefully off her feet.

"Gus O'Hare," she said, as if the name made her feel warm. "What a terribly nice man. Of course, I knew it already—never mind, I don't want to think about that horrible time."

In the morning I was on the beach before the sun rose, along with the Llewelyns and Mr. O'Hare and two other guests who wanted to watch birds.

Mrs. Llewelyn had given me one of her old bird guides, and that morning I carried it in a pocket of my overalls. She knew that I had had an even older Audubon guide, once upon a time, but no longer carried it about. Wrongly deducing that I had lost it, she waited until she thought I was old enough to do a better job holding on to one, and then gave me her hand-me-down. I was glad to have it. I had others, left by other guests, but would not make her feel stupid by telling her so. In fact, I still had that older one, but I had conceived the idea that it was *so* old, that touching it, never mind opening it, would cause it to fall apart.

As we moved slowly and quietly through the tall grass to the crest of the first dune, I fell into step with Mr. O'Hare.

"Mama likes you," I told him, as softly as I could.

He glanced at me, pleasure lighting his face.

"I like her. I like you, Calley."

"You don't know me," I replied. "Maybe you won't like me so much if you get to know me better."

He paused to give me a questioning look.

"Where's my brother, Ford, Mr. O'Hare? What's he doing?"

Mr. O'Hare grasped the binoculars that hung around his neck and looked away at the sky, scanning it.

"He's gone to school. A very good school."

"Doesn't he care anything about Mama?"

Mr. O'Hare looked down at me. His face was grave. "Your brother has come to believe that your mama was responsible not only for your daddy's death but the death of your grandmother, Mrs. Carroll. I am not sure that he will ever forgive your mama."

Then he raised his binoculars to his eyes.

I did not tell Miz Verlow that Mr. O'Hare knew anything about my brother, Ford. I had too many questions of my own that I hoped to have answered.

Why did Ford blame Mama for Mamadee's death? Even if Mama had killed Mamadee, I doubted Ford would have considered it unforgivable. He never had any more love for Mamadee than I did. It was Mamadee who doted on him, and all he ever did for her was yank her strings for what he wanted.

Of course if Mama had something to do with Daddy's murder, that *was* unforgivable, but in order to believe it, Ford must have some knowledge that I did not. I supposed it was possible. On the other hand, Ford was a Carroll and therefore profoundly untrustworthy.

Mr. O'Hare stayed two weeks at Merrymeeting, courting Mama. He took her to dinner at Martine's and the Driftwood, and to the dog-track and to the movies. Mama wasn't particularly enthusiastic about including me, but Mr. O'Hare also took both of us to Goofy Golf and the Famous Diner. That was all it took to make me think Gus O'Hare was Jesus Right Christ on a Popsicle stick. Mama would have slapped me if I'd ever used that expression. Having heard it on the playground at school, I was entranced with it, and anxious to find an application for it. Gus O'Hare fit it fine.

Forty-nine

MAMA sprawled facedown like a limp starfish, on a webbed chaise. Her one-piece green bathing suit, cut low in the back, had the straps undone to expose all of her shoulders to the sun. I finished oiling her back and moved down to the backs of her legs.

I asked her, "Mama, is Mr. O'Hare coming back to see us?"

"Not us, Calley," she answered, her voice bright with a malicious smugness. "Mr. O'Hare is coming back to see *me*. Grown men do not interest themselves in girls your age. When he does come back, I had better not see you hanging all over him the way you do."

"I never," I muttered at Mama's green-clad fanny.

"Don't talk back to me."

"No'm," I agreed. "Mama, do you ever miss Daddy?"

There was long silence, so long that I thought that she had decided not to answer. She reached under the chaise, where she had placed an ashtray, a lighter and her pack of Kools. She fired up a cigarette, poking the butt through the weave of the chaise to suck at it.

Then she said, "Baby, I can hardly recall his face. It all seems like a nightmare that happened to somebody else."

Lines from a movie or a novel or a television show, perhaps one that I had even watched with her. Some Loretta Young thing maybe.

"I remember what Daddy looked like," I said, "and the sound of his voice. Want to hear it?"

"No," Mama snapped. "I don't. I don't know what I did to

deserve you being so mean to me. I haven't had the easiest
life, you know?"

I could argue that point too. I could have said that since
Daddy's death, she had not gone hungry or worked a single
day for wages, let alone volunteered to lift a pinkie, or had the
choice of wearing a pair of hand-me-down ill-fitting shoes or
going barefoot, as Grady Driver did.

"Does Mr. O'Hare ever talk about Daddy—?"

Mama interrupted me. "He does not. Why would he want
to talk about all that old unpleasantness?"

I dropped the suntan oil in the sand next to her.

"I caint imagine," I said, in Mama's voice.

Mama rolled over and sat up, nearly losing her cigarette in
the process.

I stepped back out of her reach.

"If I could, I'd slap your mouth!"

She was too indolent to make the effort. I turned my back
and strolled away, leaving her to burn, one way or another.

Gus O'Hare did return, for the long Labor Day weekend.
Mama made sure that no opportunities occurred for me to be
included in their outings. Then Gus proposed we all go to the
drive-in. Mama resisted awhile, but fearing that she was in
danger of appearing to be intransigent, finally gave in. A
Southern Lady, of course, must never be perceived to be un-
reasonable to a suitor.

Mr. O'Hare borrowed Miz Verlow's black Lincoln. I was
assigned the backseat, and a pillow and a blanket, so that I
could go to sleep when I was sufficiently weary. The first
movie, *Tiger Bay,* could not start before dark, and that didn't
happen until nearly nine. I managed to stay awake for the
whole thing, though I remember very little of it now. I remember Hayley Mills and I remember wishing Hayley were my
name instead of Calley. The next movie was *The Absent-
Minded Professor*. I dozed off.

Their voices drew me to the surface of wakefulness.

Gus: "You must worry about Calley."

Mama made a noncommittal noise.

"Must be tough for her, her ears. I think they're kind of
cute but I bet she gets plagued by the other kids."

"The world's a tough place. She's gone have to be tough to survive in it."

"Ain't that the truth. That's what I like about you, Roberta Ann. You look the world straight in the eye, don't you?"

Mama purred.

"But you're her mama and you love her so much, you want to believe you'll always be able to protect her. She's gone grow up, Roberta Ann. Someday you won't be there for her. She'll have to take care of herself. It would be unkind not to do everything that you can to give her a fighting chance."

"What are you gone on about?"

"Don't take offense, now. I got some money set aside. I'd be really pleased to use it for Calley, to have her ears fixed. Honey, it's just gone be impossible for her to get a decent job with those ears. They make people think she's feebleminded, and she's not, you know she's not. She's got a good little mind."

"Stop right there," said Mama. "I have never taken charity, Gus O'Hare, nor borrowed money, and I never will."

She had, of course, and she would.

It took a lot of back and forth but eventually Gus O'Hare placed a cashier's check for two thousand dollars in her hands. The winning argument, he thought, was his anxiety that in her devotion to me, Mama might reject an opportunity for her own happiness—to which she was more than entitled, after what she had been through. Mama appreciated being portrayed as a victim of her own virtues. Once she had the money, she spun a world of lies about seeing doctors with me.

Mama never missed cadging a magazine, or in a pinch, buying it, that had anything about plastic surgery in it. I had studied them as often as she did, and had a good idea of what was possible and what wasn't. I didn't want my ears fixed. The most any surgeon was likely to do was pin them back, and render me unable to waggle them. They would be just as big as ever. It was wishful thinking on Gus O'Hare's part that some doctor could magically reduce them to normal proportions. Since I was not supposed to know that Mama was accepting money from Gus, I could make no open objection.

All the following winter and spring, Gus O'Hare visited

for a week at every major holiday. He tried to give Mama his late mama's engagement ring on Christmas Eve. Mama tried it on and faked admiring it. Anybody could see that the value of the ring, 12-carat gold set with a tiny garnet, was purely sentimental. Mama never cared for garnets. More importantly, she never cared for anything that anybody could see was more sentimental than valuable.

Overcome with tragic widowhood, Mama was so bereaved that she had never considered opening her heart to another man. It was such a shock—well, she needed more time. When Gus asked her to accept the ring as a friendship ring, she blushed and dabbed at her eyes. In the end she was able to avoid immediate acceptance.

Gus was brave, the poor boob, and admired her fidelity to a dead man as he did her maternal sacrifices for me. He wanted Mama for himself, of course, and was welcome to her, as far as I was concerned, by then.

He returned the Saturday before Easter. I finagled him into a beach walk to see a possible osprey nest, and 'fessed up that the kids at school teased me about my ears. Somehow it came out that I had not seen any doctors about my ears and that, in fact, Mama had done nothing in that direction.

My treachery precipitated the first of several strained conversations between them. Mama was, of course, *devastated* that he no longer trusted her, and insulted and appalled that he should turn out to be mercenary. She got it worked around so that she was the victim, and he wrote a long pathetic letter begging forgiveness. I felt sorry for Gus but I also felt like he was going to find out sooner or later, and I was saving him a few months of delusion.

Mama forgave him, of course, but forgiveness did not include mercy. She sent him away, a brokenhearted man, who blamed himself for having lost a wonderful woman. I was sorrier than I could ever admit. If I were ever to have a stepfather, Gus would have been as good as any. I suppose Mama did show him some mercy; she only relieved him of two thousand dollars. She didn't marry him.

I never asked her what she did with the money.

Fifty

"YOU'VE seen two dogs going at it in the road, haven't you?"

"Yes ma'am."

"Well, now you're ready for that too," Mama said.

She took a tampon out of a box in her dresser and tossed it to me. I had seen them there for years but without any grasp of what they were. If it were not embarrassing enough to be abruptly asking Mama what the blood meant, I wondered how I could have been so dim not to have asked or made any effort to find out what the tampons were.

I was aware that Mama and other grown women were "unwell" occasionally, a more or less regular unwellness. I did not grasp that bleeding was involved, until after a day of stomachache, while in a warm bath, a feather of blood rose from the vicinity of my crotch to the surface of the bathwater. I took it for the output of an unseen scratch.

The blood dissolved into the water. When I dried myself, the towel came away from between my legs with another trace of blood. With that penny drop of blood, I grew worried. No amount of anxious, awkward, indeed ludicrous, self-examination revealed a break in my skin.

Seemingly over the summer, I had developed quivering little cone-shaped bumps on my chest. They were mostly dark nipple. I obscured them by wearing an undershirt under my blouse or work shirt. Some of the other girls came back to school in September with bumps too, but I was too much of a tomboy still to pay any attention to the incessant giggling and whispering among the more advanced of my female school-mates. The older we got, the more the girls at school all seemed to be rendered witless by their very femininity. What had I to say to them?

Like Alice, I was growing taller at a headlong rate. If I were going to get any wear at all out of my clothes, I had to buy them too big, for at the end of six weeks, they would be outgrown. I hardly had time or inclination to notice the pale wisps in my armpits and sparse feathers on the little hummock of my crotch, even if I had known what they signified. I peed from the cleft between my legs, effortlessly and regularly, and had never experienced the slightest difficulty in so doing. I had ears to clean out and nails to groom, hair on my head to wash, and teeth to brush, and sand that I wasn't to track into the house to remove from my person.

When I first told Mama that there was a little blood in my bathwater and showed her the towel, Mama rolled her eyes.

"It's your damned curse," she said in disgust. "How old are you?"

She looked at her fingers as if they would tell her.

"Twelve," I reminded her.

"Damn." She grimaced, taking up her glass of bourbon. "All I need; my life isn't hard enough as it is. I am not old enough to have a daughter on the rag."

Then she said the thing about dogs.

I didn't pay much attention because I was having an epiphany: why the other girls found the word rag so funny, and why they whispered about a curse, and why monthly meant something in particular to grown-up women.

I studied on the tampon.

"You stick it in," Mama told me impatiently. She rummaged the box in her drawer and came up with a leaflet, which she handed to me.

The leaflet proved to be directions. I went back to the bathroom and sat on the closed commode and studied it. The diagrams that indicated the nature and arrangement of my immediate inside female parts were news to me. Aware that I still did not really grasp my own anatomy, I made repeated attempts and eventually did succeed in inserting the tampon. It seemed to make me cramp more, raising doubts that I had done it correctly after all.

Miz Verlow was still in her office downstairs. In pajamas, robe and slippers, I went down and rapped gently at her door.

She said come in, with barely a glance up at me from behind her desk. I remembered Mrs. Mank in the same place.

"My stomach aches," I told her. "I have the curse."

Miz Verlow sat up straight.

"Oh," she said, "oh my. First time? Oh, that's a silly question. And you just twelve." She rose and came round the desk to take my hand. We went to her room. How many times had I gone there, how many times yet to come, to be anointed with her nostrums, given one of the little orange pills, or comforted in her efficient, professional way?

She brought me a glass of water and two tablets. They were vermillion in color; I had never seen their like, but supposed them to be some sort of aspirin. They scraped the sides of my throat going down, so I drank down the whole glass of water.

"A heating pad can help with the cramps," Miz Verlow told me. "Now you go to bed."

I thanked her and left and as I reached the room I still shared with Mama, the ache began to ease. I did Mama's feet and crawled in next to her.

In the morning, Miz Verlow gave me my own room, an awkward little corner thing previously used for storage. I cleaned it out and Roger and I put a cot into it and fixed a shelf to the wall over the bed for my books and that was it. My own room, that I hadn't had since I was six-going-on-seven. Since Daddy was alive. The six-going-on-seven-year-old Calley had longed to sleep with Mama. The twelve-year-old was thrilled to sleep alone. No doubt Mama was too.

Miz Verlow took me to the pharmacy and picked out a smaller size of tampon that she said was meant for young girls. She paid for them.

She also started giving me a vitamin that she compounded herself. It had iron in it, she explained, as the monthly bleeding could make a woman anemic.

Fortunately, my first period was brief and very light, and so my periods remained for many years, never more than a mild nuisance. I was able to stay a tomboy and that was good enough for me. I didn't think of it as "becoming a woman." Though I lived in a woman's body, I was still a child and I thought as a child.

Fifty-one

ROGER Huggins first began to help guests launch the little boats or tie them up, and then to go out with the tentative ones on calm days. There were dolphins to spot, and mullet leaping in the bay. Puddling about made a pleasant low-key outing for those who were nervous of deeper water. Roger grew adept at showing this guest or that one where to fish for mullet, or a secret beach on which to crab.

Miz Verlow made note of his increasing skills as a boat handler and guide, and by the time Roger was thirteen, she had acquired a larger sailboat and a larger, though still modest, motorboat, for him to operate. She didn't pay him much but she did encourage the guests to tip him generously.

If sometimes rocket science is plumbing, plumbing is not rocket science. Grady had mastered the rudiments by the time he was twelve. In the brief periods in which his daddy, Heck, was sober, he managed to teach Grady a little more, and in a pinch, Grady took his questions to the shop teachers. Miz Verlow gave him her custom, provided he never brought his daddy with him. Grady soon knew the plumbing at Merrymeeting better than anyone else.

Being around Merrymeeting brought Grady into contact with Roger. Grady knew something about boats and longed to learn to sail. Soon enough, he was Roger's mate oftener than I was. Often, if a guest was particularly inept in a boat, Grady or I could be a real help to Roger. For one thing, Grady and I spoke nearly comprehensible Southern white American, and while Roger might make an effort in that direction, he really preferred not to speak at all.

This is not to claim that the three of us were Huck and Tom and Jim, drifting on a raft with our poles in the water. What we had in common was working day in and day out and being close in age. We joked around some, argued about work and music, and bitched about our parents. I lie. Roger never bitched about his parents. He knew Mama, of course, but the both of us were shocked by the squalor and misery of Grady's home life. Grady never complained of being poor; he just resented getting beaten up by Heck and his five uncles.

From the time Roger and I first carried a footlocker to the attic, we went there at least weekly. Occasionally, after hauling something to the attic, we had a few moments without another chore, and amused ourselves by rearranging luggage and furniture and bric-a-brac in order to make more room. Nearly weekly, we recovered luggage from the attic to deliver to a departing guest. Familiarity diminished the creepiness of the attic. It became just an enormous closet. Once in a rare while, something would catch my attention, or Roger's, and we would muse upon whatever it was: a postcard found on the floorboards, a crow's feather, the old aluminum Christmas tree, long since replaced with an annual real tree. None of it had any significance and none of it was scary. There never seemed to be any lack of curiosities; we were forever discovering things that we had not previously noticed.

Grady's plumbing chores never took him to the attic but he heard about it from Roger and from me. It was the only part of Merrymeeting that Grady did not know as well as Roger and me. It began to seem unnatural that he had never been in it.

The summer before we were all to start high school, we settled on the day of the annual Five Flags Fiesta, when Cleonie and Perdita had the day off, and all the guests and Miz Verlow were at the Fiesta all day, for Grady's first visit to the attic.

Once the house was quiet, we set off on our mission. So as not to get either of the boys in trouble if we were discovered, I carried the key that I had taken from Miz Verlow's office. The attic, of course, was hideously hot. I wore only a halter and a pair of loose shorts. The boys were stripped down to their shorts. We had a jug of sweetened iced tea that I'd made and laced with pilfered bourbon. We had some cigarettes, lifted singly from one unattended pack or another, and saved up for the occasion. Grady had a lighter. I had a few candle stubs and paper cups for the tea. And Roger had a kitchen timer.

Instantly, muck sweat dampened our bodies and our clothing. We spread out an old canvas tarp and set up near a porthole to share a smoke and drink the syrupy spiked iced tea. Grady lighted three candle stubs. The old used candles seemed to us more sophisticated than the electric bulbs. We dripped melting wax onto the tarp until there was enough to fix the stubs upright.

Grady climbed up on a broken end table and peered all around, getting a sense of the space.

We had a plan. After the first cigarette and the first round of drinks, we were going to explore. We each took a candle stub and moved in a different direction. We set the timer for ten minutes, in which we had to find something to show off to the other two.

I lifted tarps and pulled out balky drawers and rummaged and heard Roger and Grady doing the same. Under one tarp I found what I thought at first was some kind of totem, an object as high as my waist, with seven pairs of frowning owlish eyes one over the other. My first reaction was to start away from its malevolent stares. Bringing the candle closer, I saw that it was a semanier, a narrow chest of shallow drawers. Inlaid dark wood made the brows of the owls, the handles the owlish eyes. I giggled at my childish credulity. Opening each drawer in turn, I was surprised to find each one contained several things. I took a single object. I didn't think about it, just snatched it up, slammed the drawer shut and bounced away as if somebody might catch at it.

My find fit into my closed fist. I was back at our tarp well ahead of the ten minutes. A couple of minutes later, Roger sank onto his haunches next to me. He kept one hand behind his back, and made a motion with the other for a cigarette. I lighted one of our precious stock, took a puff, and passed it to him. Barely under the ten-minute mark, Grady emerged from the darkness, his hands also behind him.

Roger had a spoon. It was a silver spoon, and at the tip of the handle was the thick-lipped, kinky-haired caricatured face of a black boy. Engraved in the bowl was the legend: Souvenir of Pensacola.

Grady had a coconut monkey. I'd made it myself when I was seven or eight, from an immature coconut that washed up onto the beach.

"My old monkey," I said. "Its name is Ford."

The boys laughed.

"Ford?" Grady asked.

"My brother."

"I didn't know," Grady said, and Roger rapped the spoon against the coconut.

"We know you don't know," said Roger.

"It's okay," I said. "I guess I never mentioned him."

Grady was embarrassed at having hit what both he and Roger took for a tender nerve. The only surprise for me was that I felt more for the monkey as an artifact of my childhood than I did for my brother.

I opened my fist, with a triumphant excitement that made me giggle. In my palm a golden egg the size of a quarter glinted from its nest of coiled and braided silk loops.

The boys wowed.

Opening my fingers, I let the egg roll off the tips, spinning out the silk braid behind it. I expected it to depend smoothly from the braid but it hitched almost at once to a stop. At first I thought the braid tangled but then, with the egg in one hand and the braid in the other, I saw that there were two braids. The longer one, on which the egg hung, had a wee gold buckle and looked like a belt. The other was attached to it at three points, like a pair of suspenders. It was not, as I had first taken it, a child's pendant.

"What?" Grady muttered.

I passed it to him.

He pushed it around in his palm. "Looks like a harness. Too big for a mouse, too small for a raccoon."

He passed it to Roger.

"Maybe a rat," Roger suggested. "The 'string to swing it wit'—"

Roger and I sniggered. Grady scratched his head, reminding me of the days when he had nits. Grady never did get past moving his lips when he read.

Roger passed it back to me and they awarded me the first round, and I got to drink twice as much of the iced tea this round. While I drank it, I studied on the egg itself. It was not one piece. A ridged seam went down one side from top to bottom, and a smoother one on the other side. Like a locket, I realized, and pushed down experimentally on the bit at the top, the little gold ring where the braid went through. The egg opened like a book.

"Cowie," exclaimed Grady.

Roger blew a breath out explosively.

They scuttled close to me and we looked at the opened egg together.

On one side, the interior of the egg framed a tiny picture. It was a head-and-shoulders portrait, one of those soft old-timey photographs, and indeed the young woman it depicted wore a hairstyle that I knew was called a Gibson. Her neckline was very low, though, making her neck swanlike under the heavy weight of luxuriant upswept hair.

We were nearly dumbstruck for a long moment.

"She's the spit of your mama," Grady said, "when your mama was younger."

Roger nodded. "Like your mama dressed up with her hair done old-fashun."

Except, I thought, Mama never smiled like that in her life.

I shifted my gaze to the other wing of the egg. Delicately engraved in swooping letters was the name CALLIOPE.

When I showed the boys, they reacted with even more surprise and wonder.

"'At's your name!" Roger said. "All spelt out."

Grady nodded dumbly and then said, "Well, is that her name? Calliope?"

"Dunno." I knocked back the rest of my iced tea and pushed the egg on its silk rope into the pocket of my shorts.

The timer was set for fifteen minutes for the next round. We were supposed to go in different directions each time.

Grady came back with a blue Pepsi bottle. He told us that his uncle Coy had one and claimed it was made before the First World War.

I had a plate. It was a decorative souvenir, with a yellow Florida printed on it. The image of the state was edged with things like pelicans and leaping sports fish and tropical flowers.

In the pocket of somebody's peacoat hanging on an old hat rack, Roger had found a handful of old tickets from the dog-track.

A draw, we concluded.

In the third round, I wandered several moments, with an increasing sense that time was running out. I spun around and plunged into the depths of the attic—and almost put one of my eyes out blundering into Roger's hat rack, the one with the peacoat. I grabbed it by its bole to prevent it falling over and taking me with it. I wound up hugging it. After I caught my breath, I released it from my embrace and stepped back. The peacoat had fallen to the floorboards. Tied around one of the arms of the hat rack was a gauzy and glittery scarf. It seemed so familiar that I thought it must have been Mama's.

I just made the end of the round, with the scarf turbaned around my head.

Roger had a blue-glass candleholder.

Grady had turned up a horsewhip.

The boys admired the scarf teasingly but we all agreed to award Grady the third round. His prize was three paper cups of iced tea to the one that Roger and I each tossed back. We smoked another cigarette before we began round four, for which we allotted seven minutes. Roger and I spun Grady around and pushed him off in one direction. Roger spun me around and pushed me off. He took another direction yet.

I barked my shins on one thing or another and had to brush the loose ends of the gauze scarf out of my eyes. The gauze was as sweat soaked as the rest of me. Even the palms of my hands were damp. I wiped them on my shorts, to no avail, as they were so sweaty that they were sticking to me. I looked around for any sort of absorbent material and spotted a rug covering a trunk. Placing my candle stub carefully on a nearby stack of suitcases, I knelt down next to it to dry my hands on the mangy wool fibers of the scrap of faded Persian rug. With my hands a little drier, I started to rise. A sharp pain exploded in my head. I went back to my knees and then to all fours, bracing myself against the pain that grew duller and more comprehensive. Then I dropped to my stomach, as if by getting lower, I could duck under the head pain. My eyes were tearing steadily but my face was so wet with perspiration it hardly made any difference. Droplets tracked down my face and dripped from my jaw and chin.

I closed my eyes. After a moment or two, the misery seemed to ease. I heard Roger and Grady, already back at the tarp, talking to each other.

I pulled my knees up under me again and pushed upward. A twinge in my head. The scarf around my head felt as if it had tightened. My fingers worked at the knot that held it but the fabric was wet, too slippery to move. Giving up on the knot, I managed to get back on my feet. I could only think to bumble my way back and admit defeat. As I blinked the blur of moisture from my eyes, I saw someone. Not Grady. Not Roger. Someone else. And then I recognized the flicker of shape in my eyes as a reflection, of myself. I saw the frame around it. Propped a few feet away, on top of a cluttered table, was something framed under glass. I snatched it up. It was a large frame but more bulky than heavy. The whole thing seemed to be about the size of the window on the landing, the one with the stained glass in it. The frame was incredibly dusty, and I grimaced at the filth but then I realized the dust was absorbing the moisture from my fingers and palms.

Embracing my find, I lurched breathlessly onto the tarp just as the timer buzzed.

Roger whistled at how close I had come to missing the deadline.

Holding the framed whatever-it-was against my front, I squatted down with them.

Grady produced a box of playing cards folded to look like cranes. Each had a bit of string piercing it that made it obvious that they were meant to be hung up.

Roger had an old black umbrella, like something that an undertaker would have to shelter mourners from rain.

Awkwardly because of its size, I turned my discovery around so that they could see it. I tried to see it myself at the same time but could not, so I propped it against the attic wall and wriggled around in front of it.

"Wow," said Roger.

"Amen," Grady said.

I rubbed at the dusty glass.

It was a framed poster.

HEAR THE STEAM CALLIOPE

DEXTER BROS.

❖

THE GREATEST SHOW
IN THE
SOUTHLAND

❖

THREE RING CIRCUS

❖

THRILLS AND CHILLS
AND ASTOUNDING FEATS

Around the legend that took up the middle of the poster, various circus acts were depicted in gaudy colors.

A parade of elephants, a spangle-clad woman in the how-dah on the first of the great beasts.

Drawn by white horses, a calliope on wheels, with a woman at the organ keys.

A man in a top hat and tails stood beaming in a spotlight.

A mustachioed man in jodhpurs with a whip, surrounded by complacent lions.

A very painted woman with big gold hoop earrings offered a crystal ball to the viewer.

An enormously fat woman sitting on a loading scale.

Clowns, all crammed together in and falling out of a pumpkin-shaped coach drawn by sheep.

Another man in tails, holding a top hat with a bunny peeking out of it.

An orange-haired woman in tights, full-bodied, in a costume like a corset, balanced barefoot on a high wire. Bringing my candle close to the poster, I peered at the high-wire walker. She bore a shocking resemblance to Fennie Verlow. I wondered if I really remembered Fennie Verlow's features that well. The woman could not be Fennie Verlow, for the poster was far too old, the costuming and hairstyles suggesting the nineteen-aughts.

I rubbed more dust away and held my candle stub close and examined every human figure on the poster intently. The fortune-teller's scarves were very like the one around my head. The name Tallulah popped into my mind, but no more useful information than its bald syllables. Did I know the fat woman on the loading scale? The very tall thin man stretching himself like rubber? Could it be Mr. Quigley? The ringmaster in the top hat and tails: Father Valentine? The woman running the calliope was the spit of the current Queen Elizabeth, I thought. No, it was Mrs. Mank she most resembled. I shook my head in amazement, realizing it was Mrs. Mank who looked like Queen Elizabeth—who always had.

The woman in the howdah, sitting cross-legged like a snake charmer, her legs in net stockings. Her face was a rough approximation, I saw with a jolt of my heart, of the woman depicted in the photograph inside the egg. She held a lighted candle in one hand, and on the other perched a scarlet macaw. Lightly sketched upon the bird was the suggestion of a harness. At once I understood the odd nature of the loops of silk in my pocket, the ones on which the egg hung. It was the harness, not of a rat, but of a bird as large as a macaw.

We three huddled close, peering at the poster.

"This is old," Grady said. "Like a hundred years."

"More 'an 'at," said Roger.

"Calley wins all," said Grady.

Roger nodded his head yes.

We sat back on our heels and had another round of iced tea. The ice in it was long melted and the bourbon taste somewhat diluted. Our thirst was greater and we drank eagerly, while we continued to study the poster.

"I'm filthy," I said. "Miz Verlow sees me like this, she'll wan know why."

I had an idea that I was going to go downstairs and clean up. But when I started to get up, I had to sit back down again.

Roger said, "Uh-oh."

"Tight?" asked Grady.

"Am not," I insisted.

"Better stay sat down then," Grady advised.

"I'm gone melt," I said. I leaned forward to blow out my candle.

The boys weren't expecting the sudden darkness around me. They jumped and then snickered to hide their momentary alarm.

I drank the last of the tea. Queasy, dizzy—I closed my eyes.

Grady and Roger got their hands under my elbows and guided me toward the stairs.

They told me where to put my feet. "Down. Now the other."

"Here's the bathroom," said Grady. "Maybe you better stop here and pour some water over your head."

They walked me in and I sank to my knees. Grady pushed my head over the side of the bathtub. Roger turned on the shower tap. Water spurted over my head and down my back. The ends of the gauze scarf dripped down my face and into the bathtub.

The water stopped, one of the boys wrapped a towel over my head, and they sat me down next to the toilet.

"What are we gone do with her?" Grady asked Roger.

"Caint leave her," said Roger.

Between the two of them they half carried me out of the house and out onto the beach and walked me into the Gulf up to my waist. They held me up like bookends. The light outside was a blinding glare. My eyes were running water and everything was blurry.

"One, two, three," the boys counted and they pushed me down under the water. I heard Grady say, "I baptize thee in the name of the Lord." Roger laughed. They hauled me up like a dead fish. I leaned over their arms and vomited into the sea.

"There," said Grady, "reckon you feel better."

They let me down among the tall grasses. Roger squatted next to me, holding one hand, cooing at me.

Grady came back in a few moments with a jug of water, some aspirin and towels.

I was shivering. They wrapped me up and administered the aspirin and water. Grady made a chair of himself for me, holding me between his legs, letting my head rest on his shoulder.

I closed my eyes.

I listened to the Gulf. The nearly ever-present wind. A pulse, a breathing. The more intently I listened, the more I heard "You Are My Sunshine," from the multiple brass throats of a calliope.

Fifty-two

MIZ Verlow was not deluded that I was sunstruck, nor poisoned by a bad oyster.

"I've heard the lie about the bad oyster already," she told Grady.

"Yes'm," he agreed.

I could hear them outside my room, where Grady and Roger had finally deposited me, in all my ludicrous glory.

Some inchoate impulse to help Grady out moved me just then to fall off the bed and crawl under it. Miz Verlow and Grady lunged back through the door that they had just exited.

Just too dumb and too sweet to leave me, Grady had been sitting at my bedside when Miz Verlow and Mama returned from the Fiesta. Mama's feet hurt so it fell to Miz Verlow to find out what Grady Driver was doing sitting in my room, and what I was doing, sprawled like a wino on my sweat-drenched sheets.

Once I was back in bed, Miz Verlow sent Grady on his way. She sat on the edge of the bed and studied the knot in the gauze scarf. Patiently, she picked it out. My head immediately felt less constricted.

From beneath my eyelids, I spied upon Miz Verlow's brief examination of the scarf itself. She made a little face, one of distaste, before she dropped it in the ragged little basket that I used for a trash can. A question struggled to form itself in my head.

"How much bourbon do you owe me for?" she asked.

"A pint."

"You must have gotten most of it." She spoke with real satisfaction. "I caint get you out of doing your mama's feet. Try not to throw up on her."

"Yes'm."

"Take a bath now, and try not to drown. Drink a lot of water though. Grady said that he gave you aspirin."

"Yes'm."

Miz Verlow stood and moved to the door. She looked back at me.

"Was Grady a gentleman?"

I moaned. "What's that mean?"

"You know what that means."

"Are you inquirin' about the purity of Southern womanhood?" I asked in Mama's voice.

"How very amusing," said Miz Verlow, in a tone that made it perfectly clear that she did not find it the least bit so.

"Grady's too dumb to cop a feel, if that's what you mean. Or anything else. Look at me, for crying out loud. I'm ugly."

"So's Grady," said Miz Verlow. "Ugly never stopped sex yet."

"Ha-ha. Roger was there. He chaperoned."

That made Miz Verlow really angry.

"Funny, ha-ha," she said.

If cold were ice cubes, her words could have chilled a nice glass of water for me.

She came back to my bedside and bent over me to say, "I never want to hear of you hanging around with Roger Huggins again, with or without Grady Driver. Do you want to get the boy strung up from the nearest tree? Think of his mama, if you can think of anything but yourself."

She slammed out, leaving me to think about it. I heard her going up the stairs to the attic, and then moving around above my head.

In 1955, a gang of white-sheeted bastards had murdered a fifteen-year-old kid named Emmett Till for whistling at a white woman. It's entirely probable that Emmett Till did not in fact whistle at that woman, or make an outrageous remark, or any thing of the kind.

I might have been only thirteen but I could not claim ignorance of that horror story. Roger had showed me the copy of

Life magazine with the pictures in it, that his daddy had tucked away trying to keep it from him. Nathan Huggins didn't buy that copy at any newsstand. If that issue was sold in any newsstand in Pensacola, it was unlikely that it was sold to any colored man who asked for it. Mr. Huggins's copy came to him by way of a cousin in Chicago. Roger had found it by accident. His daddy found him crying over it, and they had a long talk.

I was chastened. I made myself get up and go to the bathroom to bathe. Lolling in the bathtub, I wanted to sink beneath the water and not come back up.

I made my way to Mama's room and did her feet while she told me all about her day at the Fiesta. Of course it had all been terribly hard on her poor feet. Even as Mama nattered, I found myself longing to crawl into the bed next to her and listen to her heartbeat and the breath going in and out of her lungs, and go to sleep.

Mama stopped talking suddenly. She jammed the butt of her cigarette into her ashtray.

"Calley, baby," she said, "you look like hell. Got your period? You just crawl up here and into this bed."

She slipped between the sheets too, and tucked them up around me. It was too hot for blankets; sheets were only bearable because the punkah fan turned steadily overhead.

Mama began to snore gently. Her pulse fell into a counterpoint with the fan. Seventy beats a minute, I thought. Her lungs were a little cloudy but had been a long time. It didn't seem to be getting worse. She had gotten bonier, I thought. No, her flesh was slacker.

I was overwhelmed with how much I loved her. How much I needed a Mama to love.

Though we no longer slept in the same room, I had gone on, as I had as long as I could remember, massaging Mama's feet.

And frequently Mama would come to my room late at night, shake me awake as roughly as if the house were afire, and demand to know what opinion I had on the subject of Adele Starret and the probability of her contesting Mamadee's last will and testament. She feared that if Adele Starret moved too aggressively against Mamadee's estate, Lawyer

Weems would make it seem to Ford that his mother was trying to defraud him of his rightful inheritance. What then if she lost the suit? She would also be forfeiting her son's love and would end up with exactly nothing, exactly less than nothing. I told myself that I couldn't *know* that she had already lost Ford's love, if she had ever had it, but at my angriest, I was unable to be cruel enough to her to tell her so.

Mama was privately relieved that we heard so infrequently from Adele Starret. Mama convinced herself that the minute my brother, Ford, reached his majority, all the world would be put right again. Once he was out from under the legal authority of that *thief,* that *liar,* that *salt-scum* lawyer Winston Weems, then Ford would take control of whatever was left of the family fortune, and he would raise Mama back to her rightful place in society.

Ford was still alive, I had no doubt. I had not heard his voice among the voices the Gulf waters brought me.

Nightmares wracked my sleep. They were not new ones, which made them all the scarier, for I knew where they were going and still could not escape. On waking in the morning, though, with the *caw-caw* of the old doorbell loud in my ears, the memory was clear in my mind of opening the door to the ghost who called herself Tallulah Jordan, who had worn the scarf that I had found in the attic.

Fifty-three

MERRY Verlow began to keep close track of the key to the attic. When I had something to take up or retrieve, she made sure to be there. She allowed me no loitering time there to find the framed poster again. There was always another and urgent chore to be done. Trying hard to get back into her good graces, I promised myself that I would find it later, and let later become a lot later.

The high school I attended was something of an odd place—newly built, for one, and so lacking both history and cohesion. At least half the students were service brats, which meant the student population was in constant flux. Of the locals, none of us were as well-heeled, as well-traveled or as well-spoken as the children of the military. Our focus was hardly ever really on school, but on our families, on jobs that we had in the mornings before our first classes or that we had to leave for, early in the afternoon.

My courses and classes were arranged so that I could leave each day at two. Grady left at two as well; he did a full day's work plumbing before and after school.

Grady lived with his daddy, next door to his granddaddy and right behind his five uncles. His daddy and uncles shared a couple of chronically broken-down boats from which they derived occasional income. They each had their own chronically malfunctioning pickup trucks, out of which they would sell small quantities of fish or shellfish by the side of the road, to people who didn't know them and wouldn't be able to find them if the fish made them sick. They were all divorced, widowed or abandoned, or some combination thereof.

Having lived so long in a woman-run household, what little I knew about the way men thought, reacted and behaved, I had had to glean from our male guests. Grady and his family were another tribe altogether. They brought to mind my half-forgotten Uncles Dakin. I could not remember any of my uncles being divorced or widowed but they had all been known to drink, get into fights, get arrested, have car wrecks, go bankrupt, do the occasional weekend in the county lockup, and find Jesus during every tent revival that came their way. The power of their wives—short of teeth and hard-worn—had been just as real as Cleonie's power over Nathan Huggins, or Perdita's over her Joe Mooney.

One Saturday night in the summer between sophomore and junior year, Grady and I got high on a six pack of Straight Eight. The beach was the perfect place to hoot and holler and crow. Jokes and teasing and handholding turned to grab-ass and went on from there. Of course we were clumsy and ignorant and made a mess the first time but our randiness sufficed, as it commonly does, to overcome our embarrassment.

We were grateful to each other, oh yes—Grady because of his extreme shyness and me because I was too young to realize that being goofy-looking is no bar to sexual activity. Miz Verlow was right. Our friendship allowed us the candor to admit that *truelove* was not a factor. I wasn't Grady's girlfriend, I just had the basic girlfriend equipment, and he wasn't my boyfriend, just had the basic, etc. We were horny and curious and that was good enough for both of us.

That first time—idiot kids that we were—we took our chances and consequentially did some educational suffering, and got clean away with it. After that, Grady pilfered condoms from his father and uncles, so we didn't worry about that little awkwardness, except for the times when one broke and another one slipped off, and we went through the sweet-jesus-spare-us again, just like everyone who has ever depended upon what, back then, we called safes.

Mama and I were incapable of maintaining a truce for more than a few hours. The only reason we didn't kill each other was because I avoided her as much as I could. At first she didn't realize it and when she did, she got on her very highest horse. After that she tried playing martyr about it. None of it got her anywhere with me. By then, my heart was entombed in Alabama marble.

Mama's pretense that I was not her child occurred more often after I began my periods and intensified when she had become interested in some man. After Gus O'Hare, I recall her dating a wildlife photographer, then a former Navy flyboy come back to revisit his glory days in Pensacola, and then a radio engineer, Ray Pinette. I learned something from each of them, especially Ray. I tried to find something in each of them to like. And I tried to stay out of her limelight.

Mama went to the dog-track, the pictures, out to dinner, off on long romantic rides in her boyfriends' cars. She smoked all she wanted, and drank a lot of expensive booze. She was only unhappy when she wasn't getting her way, and that was going to happen with or without boyfriends. Sooner or later, the real Roberta Ann Carroll Dakin showed up to slap any infatuation across the face, and sink a stiletto heel into its foot.

As I began my junior year of high school, she was making a serious run at a second husband: an officer stationed at Eglin, a colonel no less. Tom Beddoes was twice divorced, due to his efforts to live up to the flyboy standard of infidelity. He had learned his lesson, he told Mama, and wanted only to find a decent Christian woman with a forgiving heart to spend the rest of his life with. Mama took to wearing a gold cross on a chain around her neck.

But she dithered.

Colonel Beddoes's pay grade was excellent, with loads of perks and opportunities for advancement, and even after early retirement, eye-widening opportunities in the military industrial complex. The word "colonel" was a double-dutch fudge sundae on her lips, as "captain" had been on her mama's. But. The armed forces were integrated, none more so than the Air Force, and there were even colored *officers*. As the wife of an officer she would be compelled to socialize with them.

Integration had been creeping into Pensacola, on tiptoe and with its breath held, since Harry Truman desegregated the armed forces. Segregationists rushed to open all-white private schools, of course, most commonly under the aegis of a blue-eyed lily-white Jesus—and not just all over the South but in Northern cities too. Because the Pensacola area happened to be thick with active-duty military, however, the public schools could not resist the expectation of integrated schools by military personnel.

When Mama found out that Roger Huggins was transferring from his old all-black high school to mine, she was horrified. Almost as terrible as the thought of integration was the fact that her dependence on the services of Cleonie and Perdita forced her to mute her indignation.

She was speechless when Nathan Huggins drove up to Merrymeeting one evening in our old Edsel. Its fenders and hood had been replaced at some time, and were different colors—red and blue—from the original, but it was the very one that we had once owned all right. Mr. Huggins had found it being offered for sale at the side of some dirt road in Blackwater. Never having seen it before, he had no idea of its history until I cried out with delight at the sight of it. Mama insisted that we had never even owned an Edsel. Miz Verlow walked all around it and shook her head in distasteful wonder and said nothing.

Mr. Huggins did not dispute Mama's denial or Miz Verlow's obvious disapproval. He picked up Cleonie and Perdita and took them home after work and began to ferry them back and forth. They ceased to live at Merrymeeting during the week anymore: more change.

Mama was pleased to learn that Roger was acutely unhappy at school. He missed his girlfriend, a sweet and very smart girl named Eleanor, who did not make the transfer with him. His old school was closer to home. I only had to look at Roger to know that he felt isolated and vulnerable in the face of the deliberate, stony indifference of the majority and the moronic persecution by a handful of bonehead resisters. Despite the specific warning of Miz Verlow that the best thing that I could do for Roger was to steer clear of him, I made an attempt at offering my support. Roger thanked me and told me that the best thing I could for him was leave him be, to try and settle in on his own.

After ten weeks, he transferred back. I knew that was the

deal that he had made with his mama and his daddy. Rarely have I felt so helpless or so frustrated. I went so far as to accuse Grady, who was entirely innocent of any such thing, of failing to help Roger make a success of integration. After I apologized to him for my hissy at him, Grady sat quietly on the beach with me for a long while.

Then he said, "Roger shouldn't have to be miserable for no cause. You're makin' him feel bad about it. You want to be miserable for a cause, you do it."

I wanted to accuse Grady of being just like the boneheads, but I couldn't.

He put one arm around me and ruffled my snarly hair affectionately.

"Preacher says there's a time for ever purpose," Grady said. "Things'll come round or they won't. One lil ol' Calley caint do it all by her lonesome."

Mama could hardly contain her triumph, though she had done nothing to affect the outcome one way or another.

For the first time in my life, I said, "Oh, shut up, Mama."

That made her jaw drop.

I was too big to hit anymore. I might hit back.

Since the end of my high school education was on the horizon, and I was all too clearly more Dakin than Carroll, the urge to wash her hands of me was getting stronger in Mama.

Ford's twenty-first birthday was only months away.

Mama was incapable of shutting her trap about the fortune coming in her son's hands, so Tom Beddoes knew all about it. It didn't make Mama any less attractive to him. He was interested enough to interrogate her very closely, and to nose about for legal advice that didn't come from Adele Starret.

I didn't care whether Mama stayed anymore, not for my own sake, but I had not forgotten the warning that if she left the island, she would be unprotected. Just because I was out of patience with the woman's whine in my ears, the stink of her tobacco, and her pretentiousness, didn't mean that I wanted her harmed. I heartily wished that she would marry again and go live in Eglin, which was not only on the island, but had armed guards at its gates.

For one, I was very likely to inherit her bedroom, which was much nicer than my hole-in-the-corner. I would paint it a light color and refurnish it with furniture that didn't look like it came from Tara. These thoughts went through my head at the very same time that I knew that I planned to leave the island myself; I wanted to go to college, for one, and I wanted to see the world. Of course I intended to return; there was no thought that Merrymeeting and Santa Rosa Island would not always, ultimately be my home.

On a Saturday morning, I found Merry Verlow in her office, with the door open. I flung myself onto the sole other chair. She glanced up and then down again at her accounts.

"Something, Calley?" she asked abstractedly.

"Yes, ma'am. I want to go to college—"

She looked up and interrupted to me. "Of course you do. You'll be doing your undergraduate work at Wellesley and then go on to Harvard for an MA. You'll live in Mrs. Mank's home in Brookline, which if you check a map of Massachusetts, is a suburb of Boston convenient to both those colleges. Mrs. Mank has a high opinion of your potential."

Rarely had I much to do with Mrs. Mank, other than waiting on her, but occasionally she would announce that she wanted a walk on the beach, just before supper, or just after, and require my presence, so that she might teach me a little astronomy.

And that's exactly what she did. Mrs. Mank would sit on the beach in a rusting old lawn chair, with me at her feet, and she would point out a star, a constellation, a planet, or observe the state of the moon. I learned to find Polaris by the pointers of the little dipper, and from there, Betelgeuse and Rigel, and how to locate Spica by following the Crow's beak. I learned enough to be aware of the night sky, and often, of the day sky, where the cold moon hung pallid and emaciated in the blue sky or Venus burned on the edge of the world.

It took me a minute to catch my breath. Miz Verlow's gaze had returned to her accounts.

"What about leaving the island?"

"What about it?" Her pen scratched some notation on one of her papers.

"Is it safe?"

She snorted. "Of course it's safe. It's all inside the borders of the United States, everybody speaks English or something like it, and you've had all your shots. Stay away from race riots and you'll be fine."

"What about Mama's enemies?"

Miz Verlow's pen described a curlicue in the air. "Oh, she'll always be able to make new ones, wherever she is."

I sat silent for a while, working up the courage to push on in the face of looking utterly foolish.

"My daddy was murdered," I said in a low tone, and despite my best efforts to sound calm and grown-up, my mouth went squiggly on me.

Miz Verlow looked up again and put her pen down. Then she reached into her sweater pocket. Out came a clean handkerchief, which she offered to me silently.

I blew my nose.

"It's a grief that will always be with you, Calley. All I can say is that the passage of time will dull it. Roberta Carroll Dakin's fate is in own her hands, as indeed it always has been. If she is fool enough and he is too, she may marry Colonel Beddoes without objection from me. I would be happy to have the room back. Your brother might have something to say, though."

My brother. I hadn't spared him a thought in ages; he was Mama's obsession.

"How do you know?" I blurted.

Miz Verlow didn't answer the question. She settled her attention on her paperwork.

"Go along, Calley. You have work to do, and as you can see, so do I."

"Why can't you answer the question? There's a lot more that I need to know," I said.

"Too bad," she said. "But it'll give you something to look forward to."

*

A few days later, coming home after classes, I ran upstairs to toss my books into my room and there was Mama, busy rummaging one of my dresser drawers.

"What the hell are you doing?"

The first shock of being surprised flashed into a posture of defiant innocence.

"I need a tampon," she said, in an irritated voice. "I've run out unexpectedly."

She was lying and she knew that I knew. It was a struggle not to throw her bodily out of my room.

"Why don't you get off your backside and walk to the store and buy some?"

"I won't dignify that with a response."

She cringed past me.

"You won't find any money, no matter how hard you look," I said.

In the ceiling of the crookedy triangular closet in my room, a space that I could no longer stand in straight up, I had a hidey-hole. The light fixture in the closet was a bare bulb suspended from the ceiling. All I had to do was loosen the collar of the fixture at the ceiling, pull the light cord down a little, and clear grit and mouse scat around the hole in the closet ceiling. The space accommodated a tin box with my spare cash in it, just bills, acquired mostly as tip money from guests, and so not deposited in my Nickel Account. With the light cord tightened to raise the bulb again, the collar firmly in place, and the bulb kept dirty, the hidey-hole was successfully disguised. Mama would never touch the lightbulb nor would she mess about with a fixture, for fear of electrocuting herself. If Mama were ever faced with changing a lightbulb, she would choose to sit in the dark.

Mama's mouth tightened, the lipstick crinkling into lines at the edges of her upper lip. She wasn't anywhere near an old woman yet but she spent too much time tanning, convinced that it made her flaccid flesh look tighter. She was hardly alone, of course; it was several years before the doctors started warning people about too much sun. Of course any half-wit could look at the skin of people who worked in the sun and see the damage, but no one has ever gone broke underestimating the capacity for self-delusion in the species.

"How dare you call me a thief!"

"You've done it whenever I had a nickel!" I shot back. "How dare you go through my drawers!"

"I have not!" Mama cried, with great crocodile tears standing in her eyes. She rushed away toward her room.

I shut the door and dropped my books on my bed.

Did I want the future that Merry Verlow and Mrs. Mank

between them were conspiring to give me? Wellesley? Harvard? They were names in news magazines. Would they allow me to follow my own interests or had they already determined what I would be become? Those distant places beckoned me, to be sure, and my only other option was one of the state university campuses, or no further education at all. I had no answers about my own future, only a slew of questions.

Where was the moon tonight? In its last quarter? I checked the little lunar calendar in my nightstand drawer where I kept it in a notebook.

The middle drawer of my dresser still stood open. There was nothing in it but a couple of pairs of cotton pajamas from Sears. Most everything in my wardrobe had a Sears label on it. Sometimes I bought clothes at a thrift shop, and those nearly always had a Sears label. Or one from Montgomery Ward—Monkey Ward, Grady called it. Mrs. Llewelyn still sent me an occasional hand-knit sweater, but was far more likely to put cash into a Christmas or birthday card now. She was apologetic, but said that there was no way to know my taste now I was a teenager, and styles had changed so radically. Dr. Llewelyn still sent toothbrushes and toothpaste and floss, though.

My daddy had been murdered. I didn't even have a picture of him. And I was going to go to Wellesley and Harvard and live with Mrs. Mank and Mama was going to marry Colonel Beddoes and my brother might have something to say about it.

I should talk to him, I thought. I wanted to hear what he might have to say, not just about Mama getting married again, but about everything. He was practically grown up now and so was I. Maybe the hole in my life wasn't Daddy's absence so much as it was Ford's. And I didn't even know how to get in touch.

Fifty-four

GRADY found me crouched on the beach, trading pieces of a peanut butter sandwich with my current Rocky Raccoon, for oysters. Grady had two cold Straight Eights by their necks. It was just twilight, so I didn't need my hat.

"Hey," he said.

"Hey back."

I had my oyster knife in my shorts and swiftly shucked the oysters from their shells. I gave some to Grady and swallowed some myself.

We chased the oysters with long draughts from the Straight Eights. I told Grady about catching Mama going through my drawer and how I wanted to get in touch with my brother. I had not told anyone what Miz Verlow had said about me going away, and didn't know how or when I was going to be able to tell Grady.

I asked him, "You see Betelgeuse?"

He was hopeless. He never could see what I saw in the sky.

"Nope. Ain't your mama got an address or a phone number nor nothin'?"

I shook my head.

"So you don't even know where he is?"

"No, sir."

"You sirring me?" Grady mock-cuffed me.

He wanted to go canoodle on the beach. We had our place. It seemed like a reasonable thing to do so I took his hand and we went down the beach and found it again. Grady wasn't so skinny as he used to be; he was starting to fill out to be a man. It felt good to be close to him and have his arms around me.

"You got any ideas?" he asked me. "Ma'am."

I mock-cuffed him back. "Watch it, you!" I leaned back into his arms. "No I ain't got any ideas."

The silence between us lengthened pleasantly and after a while I realized that Grady had dozed off. I poked him in the ribs.

He smacked his lips together. "Damn."

"I need some money," I said.

"Me too. Wanna hold up a bank?"

"You can try it, you want. I'm gone have to bust the Nickel Account, enough for a bus ticket to and from Tallassee. I can find out where Ford is if I go there, I know I can. I'll go right to Dr. Evarts and demand to see my brother."

Grady scratched his head. "I like to go but I got to work."

"Not right now," I said. "But soon, when I get the time off."

I hadn't ever asked for time off and hadn't even considered if I should tell Miz Verlow what I wanted to do with the time or not.

"You won't need a bus ticket," Grady said. "We caint use my wheels, it taint reliable enough, but maybe we could borrow the station wagon, or even Roger's daddy's Edsel that used to be your mama's."

"You're a genius," I told Grady. "Sir."

"Yes, ma'am," he said. "Put your pants on, less go get some more beer."

While Grady collected the rest of the beer in his Dodge, I went into the house and found Miz Verlow in the kitchen making a cup of tea, and begged the use of the station wagon for an errand.

"Beer run?"

"Yes'm."

She tipped her chin at the hook where the keys to the wagon hung. "That boy's vehicle is a deathtrap. You drive. You hold your beer better than he does."

I had an urge to kiss her but when I started to rise up on my bare toes, she gave me an appalled look.

"Put some shoes on, Calley," she said. "You oughtn't drive with bare feet."

I never have figured out what's so bad about driving with bare feet.

"Miz Verlow," I said, as I began to bag some leftovers for snacks, "do you remember Mama's mama talking to us from the dead when I was a little girl?"

She gave me a long steady look. "So you remember."

"Yes'm."

"Do you remember me asking you just afterward if you could hear the dead?"

I nodded.

"You told me that you did. You didn't understand them."

"No'm. I did not. Most of 'em. I mean, I understood what Mamadee said." Another memory surfaced. "Cosima," I said, "Mama's grandmama, she spoke to me twice. On a Christmas Eve. And then." I felt myself jumping off a cliff. "Then Tallulah Jordan came to the door."

Miz Verlow blinked at the name Tallulah Jordan.

"Who the hell is Tallulah Jordan?" she asked, with an edge of mockery in her voice.

"A ghost, like Mamadee was, and like my great-grandmama Cosima."

Miz Verlow blinked again.

"I want to talk to you, in my room," she said. "Tell Grady to go wherever he calls home."

"No, ma'am," I said. "I'm gone with Grady right now."

Miz Verlow's lips tightened with anger. Her eyes livened with an almighty piss-off at me. I noted it with a smug adolescent satisfaction. It didn't occur to me that it was another moment like the one in which Mrs. Mank offered to tell me a secret and I declined. Then I declined out of fear. This time I was exercising my independence.

Miz Verlow took her teacup and stalked out of the kitchen without another word.

I picked up some sandals where I'd left them on the verandah. Grady was already lounging in the wagon's passenger seat. He shoved in the cigarette lighter and lit a Camel that he couldn't afford. Then again, he couldn't afford a cracker or the Cheez Whiz to spurt onto it.

I dropped the paper sack of leftovers in his lap.

"Comestibles," I said.

He poked around in the sack.

"Com-estibles," he said. "I like that word."

We got some more beer in the village and parked down on Pensacola Beach. Grady greased up his fingers on leftover rib roast and then stickied them eating pecan pie out his hand.

He chased the chow with half a longneck and then belched.

I giggled.

He held out his left hand and I licked his fingers clean. Then he twisted around so I could clean the other one.

"Damn," he said. "That's horny."

I took a mouthful of the contents of the longneck I was holding between my legs and sprayed it at him. He just laughed.

Grady and me, we had some good times. I wouldn't ever be surprised to find out that he was related somehow to the Dakins.

Fifty-five

MAMA cooed good night to Colonel Beddoes.

Peeking out the back window of the station wagon, I watched the two of them kiss just before Mama went into the house. I had my hand clapped over Grady's mouth so he wouldn't laugh or make me laugh. The two of us were fair tangled up, where we'd dozed off together, in the back of the station wagon. I lifted my hand from Grady's mouth and sank back down next to him.

Grady gave me a gooch in the ribs. "Mama needs her feet rubbed," he teased.

I gooched him back in his belly and he went for the ticklish place under my chin. The wagon moved with us and I heard the roll of the gravel under Colonel Beddoes's footstep.

It was too late to get away, so I sat up and Tom Beddoes bent his knees a little to look in at us.

He popped open the back end of the wagon.

"I won't ask what you kids are doin'," he said. "I expect Miz Verlow wouldn't appreciate you using the back end of her station wagon for your pettin' party."

I slid out and Grady unfolded himself after me.

"See ya, ma'am," he said, saluted Colonel Beddoes smartly and strolled away toward his old Nash.

I watched him go and tried not to giggle at him adjusting the crotch of his old khakis.

Colonel Beddoes shook his head. "Your mama would be disappointed in you, Calley. That boy's just trash."

"Mama's been disappointed in me since I was born. Any change might be too much of a shock."

Colonel Beddoes frowned. "That's no way to speak of your mama, young woman."

"She's *my* mama. You ain't even my stepdaddy."

He wagged his finger at me and forced a fake smile on his face. "But I may be, I may be."

"Don't get ahead of yourself, Tom Beddoes."

I ran off toward the back door to the kitchen.

Mama was in her bedroom, just kicking off her shoes.

"Let's see the hands," she said, reaching for her earrings.

I showed my hands. She recoiled.

I left to wash them, tidied my nails, lathered up with hand cream, and returned back to Mama's room.

She was in her nightgown, doing her face.

I hung up her dress, put her shoes aside for polishing, and collected her lacies for handwashing.

"You've got beer on your breath," she said.

I didn't respond, just showed her my hands.

She flopped onto her bed. I sat down at the foot of it and spun the top off the jar of foot cream.

"I'm trying to be the best mama I can but you are making it very, very hard."

I crossed my eyes at her.

"You spend way too much time with that boy. I see him out fishing with Roger Huggins. I never see him with other white boys. Any white boy hangs out with coloreds is headed for trouble."

"You're right about that," I agreed. "You ever read *The Adventures of Huckleberry Finn*?"

Mama ignored the question, which was fair enough, since I knew the answer.

"Any girl hangs out with a boy that hangs out with coloreds is headed for trouble," she said. "I've seen many a girl ruin her life for some redneck piece of white trash."

Like my daddy.

"Calley, you are going to have to make do with what life hands you. You need all the edge you can get."

Her right foot was in my hand. Her toenails silvered to match her fingernails. This evening, when she went out to dinner with Colonel Beddoes, she had worn pale pink lipstick. Her hair was in a bouffant that would be a crow's nest in the morning. When a woman wears a hairstyle and lipstick too young for her, it never fails to make her look older than she really is, or so she used to tell me, before she started doing it.

Mama lit a cigarette. "Prepare yourself for a shock, baby. Tom and I are engaged."

"Praise be to Jesus." I gave her foot an extra squeeze before I put it down and picked up the other.

"I don't find blasphemy amusing, Calley. We're going to buy a ring tomorrow."

I made no response.

She smoked awhile.

"Then I'm going to take a little vacation. I'll be gone six weeks."

"Honeymoon?"

She laughed. "No, no. We're not getting married until the fall."

"So?"

"So I need some time to myself. I'll be leaving the first of next week."

School would let out by then.

"Miz Verlow know?"

"She will. You do what she says while I'm gone."

Mama ground out her cigarette.

"Tom wants to be your friend, Calley. He's made me understand that you're nearly grown." She sighed. "You'll always be a baby to me. Anyway, I want you to know that you can ask me anything. *Anything*."

I patted her foot and put it down and screwed the cap on the jar of foot cream.

"Anything." Mama said one more time.

"Mama, you got any pictures of my great-grandmama?"

She sat up in surprise. "My grandmama?"

"Cosima," I said. "That was her name, wasn't it?"

Mama sighed. "No, baby, not a one."

"Tell me what she looked like."

Mama's face softened with pleasure at being asked.

"She was an old lady by the time I knew her, of course," said Mama, "but I saw the pictures of her when she was young. She looked like me, Calley. Mamadee used to say that I was the spit of her mama."

*

"GOOD night, Mama." I closed the door to her bedroom gently.

I wondered who was going to pay for Mama's "vacation," and where she was going. I knew where she hid her cash and her remaining jewelry. She had managed to hold on to most of the jewelry that she had with her when we left Alabama but some of it was gone, sold off, along with all the jewelry she had stolen from Mamadee. Maybe she still had some of Gus O'Hare's money. She must have enough to finance a fairly expensive "vacation." Or a college education for me.

Maybe she was going to see Ford. Maybe we would all run into each other in Tallassee. The thought made me grin. Surprise for everybody.

I glanced out my window at the quarter moon that had crossed the sky most of the way now.

> *I see the moon.*
> *The moon sees me.*
> *And the moon sees the one*
> *that I long to see.*

I hardly ever saw the moon without thinking the first two lines, but the second two, I used only when I sang the whole song.

Did I long to see Ford? I didn't think it was exactly longing. Maybe it was only curiosity.

Mama had been the spit of Cosima. The image in my mind was as distinct as the portrait in the egg locket, the egg locket on the bird's harness that I had found in the attic. The harness and egg locket hidden in my hidey-hole.

Fifty-six

SCHOOL could not let out nor Mama leave soon enough for me.

She no longer wore the wedding ring that Daddy had put on her finger but flaunted a showy diamond ring at table and in one parlor or the other or on the verandah, as if every one of our guests were an unsuccessful beau or an ex-husband to be taunted with it. If that weren't nauseating enough, whenever Tom Beddoes was around, she clutched his arm as if in fear that he might escape. The two of them cooed and cuddled ostentatiously.

In the meantime, the Atlas volume of the encyclopedia was under my bed, for immediate consultation of the map of Alabama, and my lunar notebook was filling up with questions and plans.

1. Alabama Directory Assistance
   a. Billy Cane Dakin (Birmingham? Jefferson Co.)
   b. Ford Agency, Birmingham
   c. Jimmy Cane Dakin (Montgomery? Montgomery Co.)
   d. Ford Agency, Montgomery
   e. Lonny Cane Dakin, Dickie Cane Dakin (Mobile? Mobile Co.)
   f. Ford Agency, Mobile
   g. Dr. L. Evarts, Tallassee (Elmore Co.), Off., Res.
   h. Winston Weems, Tallassee (Elmore Co.), Off., Res.
   i. Adele Starret (Montgomery? Or Tallassee?) (Elmore Co.)
   j. Fennie Verlow (Montgomery? Tallassee?)

I seized any fleeting opportunities when I was alone with a telephone. Eventually Miz Verlow would see the long-distance calls on the bill but I planned to own up unflinchingly and offer to pay her back.

Like a punishment for my petty larceny, any hope of quick contact with one or another uncle, who might know where Ford was, died aborning; not one of them was listed in Birmingham, Montgomery, or Mobile, or in the respective counties of those towns. And in those towns, the Ford agencies—no longer Joe Cane Dakin's Ford-Lincoln-Mercury—had no one working for them named Dakin, and no one able to check any records that might have existed since the agencies changed hands, but somebody "might get back to me when they had the chance."

No Adele Starret or Fennie Verlow was listed in Montgomery or Tallassee. Dr. Evarts was not listed in Tallassee either as regards his office or his residence and there was no office number for Mr. Weems, only a residential one. I supposed Dr. Evarts might have unlisted his home telephone number, and perhaps joined a practice with other doctors, but the directory assistance could not tell me if that was so. Lawyer Weems, old as he was when I last saw him, might very well have retired.

School let out, and a few days later, Colonel Beddoes took Mama to the airport. Within five minutes of seeing the tail end of his MG scoot down the road, I locked myself in Mama's bedroom and went through every last inch of her space and all her hidey-holes. It had been a while since I had bothered with a complete search of her things. I had thought that I knew them so well, they were boring.

The only address book that I found, at the back of a drawer, was one that I had given her for Christmas in 1962: still blank, every page of it, with not even her own name written in the front. In the tin-lined pot chamber of her nightstand were all her papers having to do with Adele Starret's contest of Mamadee's will, including a copy of the document itself. As I read through them all, it was apparent to me that their real purpose had been bamboozling Mama into thinking that something was happening. I copied the return address and office telephone number from one letter with some excitement. When I studied on the will, Mamadee's naming of herself as

Deirdre Carroll stood out as odd in a way that it had not when I was a little girl. She wasn't born a Carroll. She should have had a maiden name in the middle. Unless she was a Carroll cousin of sufficient distance to avoid incest. Or not. Maybe incest didn't apply to Carrolls, the way it didn't to Egyptian pharaohs. More rummage turned up Mama and Daddy's wedding certificate, then my birth certificate. But not Ford's. Had Mama destroyed it in a fit of pique or frustration? Just as likely it was in some file somewhere with the papers that concerned his legal custody.

About Daddy, there was nothing else—no death certificate, copies of his obituary, personal papers or love letters. And of evidence of the existence of any other Dakins, there was none either.

The only photographs were two that Mama had brought from Ramparts: a school photo of Ford at eleven, and of herself, sitting on the railing in her shorts. No wedding photos, no baby photos, no family photos.

Satisfied that there was nothing more to glean from Mama's room, I tidied it up, but with no attempt to make it appear untouched. Mama would think that Cleonie had cleaned it. If she noticed anything out of place, she would blame Cleonie. Any guilt that I felt at Cleonie catching blame, I assuaged with the likelihood that in the chaos of her belongings in which Mama lived, she would not in fact notice at all.

Cleonie was more than able to defend herself. Mama had blamed Cleonie for something nearly every day of our lives at Merrymeeting. Cleonie unhesitatingly met Mama eye to eye and with imperturbable calm, rendering untenable the accusation of the day. The most revenge Cleonie ever took that I could identify as such was in serving me the best portions of whatever was going and of treating me better than Mama did.

Roger told me that his mama looked on my mama as a different species, Mama's insults and idiocies as the natural nastiness of Mama's kind. A cat *will* claw a wicker chair. Beyond a quick squirt of water to drive it temporarily away from its mischief, little could be done but accept cat-clawed wicker. Mama and cats were one of those mysterious ways Cleonie's AME Christian God moved his wonders to perform. I was pleased to think that Cleonie did not allow Mama to be more than the most minor irritant in her life.

One afternoon, Miz Verlow went to the dentist in Pensacola to have a root canal done. I took the key to the attic from her office.

I still hoped to find an old address book, a family Bible, a photo album, a shoebox of photographs, a cardboard box of personal papers. The framed poster. As I groped my way among the litter of objects, many of them shrouded, I thought it unlikely I would ever be able to find anything that Mama had brought with us.

Something fluttered. I paused briefly and the flutter erupted again, out of the dark, an oilier feathered darkness that coalesced into a fish crow, setting gently onto an object nearby. I held still, so as not to frighten the bird, and out of my own animal caution in any new situation.

The crow perched there blinking at me. We studied each other a moment, and then it began to preen itself, darting its sharp beak into its own feathers, looking for whatever itched it. It was a letdown to have bored it so quickly.

Just as abruptly as it had settled, the crow rose suddenly with a loud *uhhhk*. It brushed one of the bulbs in passing, and for half a moment, the light was querulous and confused, showing one thing and then another. I glimpsed a collection of umbrella stands: The handles and shanks rose up from the open tops as if someone had stuffed dozens of flamingos and herons and ibises upside down into the stands.

In another direction, the moving light caught the dusty drops and pendants of a chandelier hanging, lopsided, from a rafter over the coarse-woven shape of a grand piano. The shroud turned the piano into its own ghost. On its back it bore a collection of candlesticks and candelabra and wee-willie-winkies, some of them with the stubs of tapers sagging in them, melted not just by fire but by the heat in the attic.

In yet another pass of the light was a blur of clock faces. All stopped, I knew by their silence, even as I cringed and crouched, to duck the swaying bulb that might hit me. Or light me up for something to see.

The light steadied, still weak and dirty. I put my hand out

to help me rise to my feet again and touched rivets and metal. Starting, I lost my balance and landed on my backside on the dry splintery planks of the attic floor.

The thing that I had touched was a metal footlocker. As my eyes adjusted to the dimness again, I was quite sure that it was green and black. My throat closed with panic. I scrabbled backward, hands and heels to the floor, backside lifted enough to avoid friction with the planks. Out of the darkness came a mocking *uuuhhk!*

If my throat had not been so dry, I might have cried out, but I was spitless.

I came up into a hunker again. I hugged myself and stared at the locker. The dull clasp poked through the tongue of the locker's catch but there was no padlock. I was mesmerized by that loose hanging metal tongue pierced by the clasp; it seemed an emblem of torture, inhuman torture. I felt a little dizzy: torture. Inhuman torture. Not inhumane; how silly would it sound to speak of humane torture. The screams would be of laughter. Inhuman. A cat playing with a bird, a rotten kid sticking a firecracker into a croaker's hind end.

It was another *uhhk* and a rush of wings that broke the trance. I could not make out the crow in the darkness but I knew that it was there, its eyes fixed on me, mockingly. I was not to be allowed to flee the attic until I opened the footlocker.

My approach on my hands and knees bare on the planks was slow and painful, but I wanted to feel that discomfort, to help divert some of the fear, the terror, of what I was about to do. Too quickly, I was kneeling next to the footlocker. I touched the loose hanging tongue in slow motion. It was cool—no, cold—to the touch, under the eaves of that oven of an attic in Florida in May. Hinges creaked as I lifted it, reluctance balled up in an ache in my stomach. The lid rose *screakity screak*.

The locker held only emptiness but it was bottomless. Perhaps it was not a locker at all, but a hatchway to somewhere else. It seemed to me that there were stains on the walls inside and that it gave off an ancient dead-meat smell. Daddy's first coffin, that we had left behind in the Hotel Osceola in Elba,

Alabama—now it was here, and had been all the years that we lived under this roof, under this attic. It had sat there above us, waiting for me to find it.

Carefully I waggled fingers over the top edge and then over the opened locker. Slowly I lowered them, steadily waggling, into the emptiness of the locker. That emptiness was very cold. My fingers seemed to darken and then disappear into the icy darkness inside the locker. I tried to pull my hand out but it did not respond. Again panic rose in my throat and my heartbeat lunged into a violent gallop, but even as I yanked uselessly, I felt my hand again, responding.

Unbalanced again, I fell backward onto my backside once more, my right hand coming after me. For an instant it seemed as if my arm was elongating, and then it was normal and my fingers were closed around something disgusting that I flung back toward the locker. It hit the front of the locker. The impact shivered the locker. The lid dropped down like a mouth full of teeth taking an enormous bite.

Splayed on the planks, I stared through my knees at the thing that I had pulled from the locker. It was doll-sized, not the small kind that my Betsy Cane McCall had been, but baby-doll sized, large enough to fill a little girl's arms for rocking. *Ida Mae, the baby doll I never had.* It was loosely bundled in yellow rags, and its face was wax, droopy pallid yellow dirty wax that looked like a face falling off. Around the misshapen skull was a tangle of colorless hair tied into two ponytails, over knobs of wax like wings that might have been, before the wax softened, overlarge ears. Behind the pink plastic-rimmed glasses, mended across the nose with a cruddy knot of tape, the eyes were sharp metal buttons.

Shaking, I drew myself up and poked the thing with the toe of one sandal. It was soft. Stuffed. A weird rag doll, its body and limbs sewn of cotton scraps. I recognized the scraps; I used to have a pair of overalls and a shirt very like them. I nudged the weird rag doll again and it fell over. The head wobbled as if in a panic and fell off. At its lumpy wax feet, the face, such as it was, looked up at the eaves. The glasses did not fall off; they appeared to be stuck in the bridge of the nose.

As if a string had been pulled to unravel it, the doll's arms dropped away from the torso. The legs twitched once, splaying as the torso sank between them. Even as the rag doll collapsed into its component parts, the yellow rags fell too, forming a nest for the parts. But the strangest thing was between the rag doll's splayed legs: Betsy Cane McCall. Almost naked, shaved bald, and looking—well, parboiled. Her nudity was emphasized by the rigging of straps around her torso. It looked like an old braided silk belt and suspenders—very like the bird harness that I found in the drawer of the semanier that day with Roger and Grady, but without the egg. And stranger yet, she was all tucked up, her head down, her arms and hands crossed over her chest, her knees bent and tucked up to her belly. Like the drawing in the *Encyclopaedia* in the public library, I saw, like a fetus.

Fifty-seven

THE *water surged gently, very close to me. My cheekbone rested on damp sand. A ghost crab danced en pointe within inches of my face. Grass shook and shivered in the light air off the water. Slowly my breathing matched that of the waves washing the shore, and my heart beat with it and in counterpoint. A great tide of whispers fell over me, caressing me, tugging at me; retreated, releasing me, only to lift me again, draw me down, lift me, rock me, and the rays of the sun refracted through the water, lighting uncountable points of cold flame. The flicker licked at my eyes, stinging them with the fire inside each salt crystal.*

Listenlistenlistenlistenlisten

Someone hovered over me.

A rackety little fan stirred the air. The smell of the sea wafted in through an open window.

I was on my own bed in my crooked little room. The someone hovering was Cleonie. Her hand closed around mine on the sheet.

I didn't want to open my eyes yet. I wanted to take an inventory of myself, to see if I were all in one piece, and not bleeding, not bone-broke, not dismembered. I wanted to be sure of what I would see: Cleonie, my room.

One cool drop, two drops, fell upon my lips, from the warmth of Cleonie's other hand, close above my face. Two more drops of water: my lips unstuck. Her hand let go of mine and burrowed under the nape of my neck to lift my head a little and then there was the cool mineral edge of a glass, a sip of iced water.

She let me back down. I peeked quickly from under my eyelids. The reassurance in her eyes relieved me; I took a good breath and let my eyes open up. Cleonie sat on the edge of the bed next to me, a tumbler of water in one hand. *Whumpet whumpet whumpet*: So quoth the little electric fan on my dresser.

She shook her head in slow amazement. "Jesus save us."

Miz Verlow was coming down the hall. I closed my eyes, was afraid to see her. She tapped softly at the door and opened it to look in.

"She be restin'," Cleonie told her.

I stopped myself groaning. Why couldn't Cleonie have told Miz Verlow that I was asleep again?

Cleonie got up and Miz Verlow took her place on the edge of the bed, Miz Verlow's cool hand coming to rest gently on my head.

"Perdita says Roger found her on the beach?"

"We figgered for sure she be sunstruck, drown and daid."

"But you're still in this world, aren't you, Calley." Miz Verlow lifted her hand. "Open your eyes. I want to see your pupils." To Cleonie, she said, "Did you check her pupils?"

"Yes'm, Miz Verlow."

I stared up at Miz Verlow fixedly, in the hope that all she would see in my eyes was the state of my pupils.

"I'll sit with her, Cleonie," Miz Verlow said.

Cleonie went out.

Miz Verlow's face was oddly stiff on one side and she was hollow-eyed. She had had that root canal. Her whole lower face was braced against pain.

"Did you fall asleep on the beach or get a cramp swimming?"

"I don't remember."

"That's convenient. Someone's been in the attic. The door was open. Is that the key on that chain around your neck?"

Her words seemed to summon the chain and key into existence; I had not felt them before but now I did, half choking me.

She hooked one finger under the chain and against the skin

of my neck and yanked. The chain bit at me, and then it was gone, hanging in her hand.

It appeared to be the chain from the attic light, run through the hole at the top of the key.

"I was looking for a carpetbag to borrow. I'm gone to Tallassee," I lied. "I want to find Ford. Or one of my uncles. It's a good time to go, while Mama's away."

Miz Verlow nodded. "And how did you come to wind up semiconscious on the beach?"

"I don't remember. Maybe I fainted."

Miz Verlow glanced around, saw the water tumbler and handed it to me.

I took a mouthful and then another, amazed at how cool the water still was and how dry my throat felt.

Miz Verlow made a carefully neutral observation. "The heat up in the attic can be fierce, never mind how easy it is to get sunstruck on the beach."

I thought of all the times Mama and Miz Verlow and the guests remarked upon the heat, the lack of it, the wind, the rain, the drought, ad infinitum, and suppressed a giggle.

A speculative gleam appeared in Miz Verlow's eye. "Calley, you have been taking your vitamin, haven't you?"

My vitamin. Of course I was taking my vitamin. I couldn't imagine how taking it would prevent a swoon from the heat in the attic.

As if in answer, she said, "You could be anemic."

I didn't think that I needed to respond.

"Calley, you'd tell me, wouldn't you, if you thought you were pregnant?"

I could hardly believe what I heard—it's a cliche, but that's really the way I felt.

"You're too young to have a baby. And Grady Driver is experience and nothing more."

"Grady's my friend and that ain't 'nothin' more'."

"Of course," agreed Miz Verlow. "And a handy useful young man he is and entirely appropriate to screw."

My face burned all the way to the helices of my ears. She meant to shock me, of course, to show me that *she* was unshockable. And that I could keep no secrets from her.

"The footlocker is up there in the attic, the one they tried to stuff Daddy into and it's still bloody," I blurted. "Mama and I left it in Elba but it's in the attic, over our heads. It has been all this time. And I found something in it."

Miz Verlow's hand went swiftly again to my brow. I had risen bolt upright in my agitation.

"Lie down again, Calley."

Words continued tumbling out of my mouth without me knowing what I was going to say: "There was a *thing* in it."

Miz Verlow hushed me. "Shhh." She tucked a blanket up around me. "You're all shiver. Quiet yourself now, Calley. I'm going to get you something to help you sleep."

Cleonie must have been stationed just outside. She came in as Miz Verlow went out, to sit down and hold my hand again. In a very few moments, Miz Verlow was back, with the plastic lid of a small jar in her hand. In it were two homemade pills. For the first time and without knowing why, I was afraid of them. A depth of confusion that I had never experienced before in my life overcame me.

Yet my lips parted, my mouth opened, Miz Verlow put the pills on my tongue, and Cleonie held the water tumbler that I might drink. The pills went down like hard little dried peas. Immediately, I shook uncontrollably for several moments and then suddenly, a calmness came over me. I don't remember closing my eyes or falling asleep. When I woke in the morning, I remembered dreaming of sleeping with my eyes open. Lying there in my room, while Cleonie sang to me and the moon fell into the sea.

Fifty-eight

A few days later, just before sunup, I dislodged the collar of the light fixture in my crookedy closet and felt around above it for my tin box.

My fingers informed me of grit and lint and dust and then—a flash, as my arm went rigid with shock and sharp little points exploded into my eyes. The electricity hit me hard enough to knock me deep into the corner of the closet, and in doing so, broke the contact between my hand and the live wire.

For a moment I was dazed. My head felt as if it were going to explode. My first coherent reaction was fear that the little bits that had sprayed at me were glass. But I could see. I managed to bring my left hand up to brush at my face. Grit and lint and dirt. Above me, I could hear a tiny smolder of fire like little mouse teeth chewing something up.

My right arm ached deep into the socket; it lay slack across my torso. I could not lift it. Every other muscle was weak as dust. I'd wet myself. The closet was not only dark because the light was blown out; there was smoke in it. I coughed.

As quickly as I could, I sorted myself out and struggled out of the closet. My strongest emotion was one of disgust at my own stupidity; if this didn't prove that no one on this earth could be stupider than Calley Dakin, I didn't know what would. A small dirty cloud of smoke hung just below the ceiling of my room. The window was open; I turned on my little fan to help circulate the smoke on out and draw in the good air.

Taking the flashlight from my bottom drawer, I staggered

back into the closet. It was a huge relief to see no flame. I no longer heard the fire; apparently it had gone out.

I sniffed. Lovely. A bouquet of fragrant pee, ash and ozone smell. The flashlight beam showed me the electrical line and the top of the light fixture. Where the line joined the fixture, the insulation was gone. I knew at once that I had managed to touch a live wire, but the beam showed me where it was. The little tin box was wide open—and heaped with ash and fragments of burnt bills.

So much for storing up treasure in this world. I dropped onto my bed, pulled a pillow over my face and laughed into it until my stomach hurt.

I had a mess to clean up, and myself. I kept a supply of small waxed-paper sandwich bags for disposal of used tampons. With a couple of these in hand, as quietly as I could and with due care of the exposed wire, I collected the little tin box and its ashy contents. Then I played the flashlight again to make sure that I had gotten everything even remotely flammable. The light picked up a dark corner of something. I used the flashlight itself like a hook to move the object closer. It was a book.

Even before I turned the flashlight full on it, I recognized the most common size and shape of a bird guide. An odd thought intruded: *I don't see it. It's not there.* But it was, most assuredly. There. As gingerly as if it were electrified, I touched it with my forefinger.

Just a bird guide. Forget it.

A puddle of something soft draped over the book, and a lump of gold hung against the edges of its pages. The bird harness, the egg locket.

I drew the book toward me and gathered the loops of silk rope and the egg locket with the other.

The book fit my hand perfectly—that sort of book is *designed* exactly for fitting hands. Still, I felt an excitement kindling inside me that I could neither explain nor resist. A jolt. A blast. It was the way I felt when I heard Haydn for the first time, or Little Richard.

I remembered: I put the book there, when I moved into my crooked little room. *I didn't need it. I had other, more recent guides. Mama, someone, might notice that it was stolen, that my uncle Robert Junior's name was written on the flyleaf.*

But I had not hidden the other books that I had taken from Ramparts, and, in fact, Mama had never looked into any of them. Every book that I owned had somebody else's name written on the flyleaf.

Listen to the book.

My heart felt as if it were on one of those pull chains with the white knob at the end. Something yanked that chain, and my whole being seemed to light up inside me. One of my fingertips stung as if burned. The one with the scar on it.

And dreams that were memories opened like a book in my mind.

A long time ago, the ghost of my great-grandmama Cosima spoke to me, preparing me to meet a ghost named Tallulah Jordan, who vanished before anyone else saw her. And Tallulah Jordan had instructed me to listen to the book. The burning of my fingertip had identified the book as this one, my very first own bird guide, that was stolen goods from a dead uncle.

The cold gold egg locket in my palm had my name inside it, opposite a picture of a woman I thought must be my great-grandmama. She was dead before I was born. Why had she written my name inside the egg locket?

The household was only just beginning to stir. Mrs. Mank's Benz sportster was parked next to Miz Verlow's Lincoln on the kitchen side of the house. She had been expected; I'd helped Roger and Cleonie arrange her suite, and then heard her arrive shortly after I had gone to bed. I left the house barefoot, with the legs of my coveralls rolled up to my knees and pinned there. My hat in a pocket of my coveralls. I needed some light, some sun, and even the thin light of dawn was freshening. As I had done habitually since a little girl, I ran barefoot through the swash, northward, away from Merrymeeting.

The birds were about their business, and so were the critters that lived in the sand, damp or dry, and the ones in the vegetation beyond the first dune. The beach mice were snugging up to sleep away the day. No other human beings were visible on the great swathe of white sand.

The bump of the book in my overall pocket intensified the faster I ran, until it was spanking me, as if I were a horse that needed urging in some furious race. The other horses in the race were invisible to me, though, and I could not see a finish line. I slowed to a trot and then a stroll, veering across the beach toward the dunes. The finish line, it appeared, was my nest in the high grass, and there it was.

Still breathing deeply from my run, I took the book from my pocket and sank into panic grass and sea oats, to the patch my bottom had long since shaped for me. The coarse tall grasses made space for two when Grady was with me, but when I was alone it seemed to fill in cozily around me.

The bird guide was familiar to my hands. Thick for a small book, the paper of its pages as thin as the print on each page was tiny. Most of the dust had shaken off the book while it was in my pocket but the cover was still slightly dust-dull. I rubbed the book, back and front, and then the spine, on the thighs of my overalls.

With the spine up, my vision blurred as if I had gotten dust in my eye. I blinked rapidly to clear my eyes, and felt a few quick automatic tears leak. They sparkled in my lashes as I blinked, and were gone.

On the spine of the book, where the legend

**National Audubon Society
Field Guide to
Eastern Land Birds**

should have been, were the words

The Gnashunull Oddybone Sassyassidy Birdery

Once more, I tried to clear my vision with rapid blinking, but the legend remained the same. The absurdity of it made me laugh. I had no memory of altering it, and did not see how it could have been done. It took an effort to turn the spine away into the palm of my left hand, to look at the blank front. Then I flipped the book and looked at the spine again, as if to catch it changing back to what it should have been. It remained

The Gnashunull Oddybone Sassyassidy Birdery

I paged a leaf at a time: first blank page, the thin second blank page, the flyleaf, and instead of Bobby Carroll, the inscription was

Hope Carroll

And the title leaf read

The Gnashunull Oddybone Sassyassidy Birdery

When new, the guides are so firmly bound that they never just fell open, but the binding of this one, in the dry dusty space above the closet, had become loose. It fell open to the colored illustrations. Looking up at me was a cartoon of a loony woodpecker—loony not just in its expression, but its coloration, as it was all black-and-white as the common male loon is, and it sported a red crest (not that loons have crests, but woodpeckers do). Like many birds, the eyes of loons are red. The loony woodpecker clung to a cartoon tree trunk. It was identified as

Ivory Bill, the Woodpecker!
woodpeckerus nearextinctus

The loony woodpecker winked at me, double-drummed the trunk of the tree, and then cackled

Haha—hahaha! Haha—hahaha!

I dropped the book as if it were afire. The woodpecker's cackle ended abruptly in an offended squawk. The sounds were very like those of Woody Woodpecker, but harsher and more mournful.

Listen to the book.

Cautiously, I picked it up again and let it flop open.

A cartoon parakeet looked up from the page. The cartoonist had turned the yellow feathers of the parakeet's crown into a handkerchief wrapped around its head, and patched one eye piratically. The fluffy green feathers on its legs billowed into voluminous pirate's pants, tied about the waist with a string. It was identified as

Papaw Parakeet
conuropsis nocanfindus

The parrot screamed

Kee-ho! Keck-keck-kee!

I slammed the book closed between my palms. As with the woodpecker, the bird's call ended in an insulted squawk, in a much higher pitch.

I was listening to the book, but it was so bizarre, I could hardly give thought to what I was hearing.

I let it fall open a third time. It was a pigeon cartooned this time, in a threadbare morning coat with tails and a hobo's bindle under its wing. Its name was given as

Nestor Pigeon
ectopistes gonebyebye

The bird did not so much sing as fret

Wherewherewherewhere?

I stuck my tongue out at the cartoon pigeon. It pursed its beak—a cartoon bird can do that—and gave me a raspberry.

I closed the book and then opened it quickly, as if to catch the contents on the change.

The cartoon that looked up at me was of a Scarlet Macaw. It wore the traces of a harness.

Calley the Scarlet Macaw
ara macao calliope

Cosima, it rasped. *Cosima, Calley want a cracker. Calley want a cracker.*

The voice of this bird, I thought, was a real bird's voice. I shut the book gently, as if lowering a shade over a birdcage.

The book held tight in my sweaty, frustrated grasp. If it had something more to say, I wasn't at all sure that I wanted to listen to it. After a moment's fidget, I let the book fall open once more.

The cartoon on the page was of myself, with my ears exaggerated into wings. It was labeled:

Calliope Carroll Dakin
calliope clairaudientius

Calliope—Kalliope—is a Greek word; clairaudient, half-French, half-Latin. It was easy enough for me to understand. I had taken Latin as much for its use in taxonomy as for the foundation that it provided for all the other Romance languages, and English, and intended to take Greek as soon as I had access to instruction. But I did not need a spurious Greco-Franco-Latin tag to name myself, or my nature.

I waited. The bird's beak parted slightly and out came, whispered in my daddy's voice:

You are my sunshine

Tears ran down my face and I choked out a single sob.

Closing the book again, grasping the spine tight between the thumb and fingers of my left hand, I fanned the pages. I expected the faint breath of the pages on my face. Instead, there was an organ chord.

And from the closed book, in the voices of the cartooned birds that were pictured within, came a funereal hymn.

In the sweet by and by,
We shall meet on that beautiful shore;
In the sweet by and by,
We shall meet on that beautiful shore.
We shall sing on that beautiful shore
The glorious songs that are lost;
And our spirits shall sorrow no more,
Nor sigh for the species unwrought.
By the dark of the moon
We shall rise on that beautiful shore

> *From the ashes and ruin*
> *On great fiery wings shall we soar.*
> *Squawwwk!*

So endeth the reading, or the listening.

It was all so utterly nutty that I had to restrain myself from jumping up and pitching the book into the waters of the Gulf.

The pieces of the puzzle were in my head, however, and I could not help pushing them about.

Hope Carroll was the name of one of Mama's sisters, my aunts, the ones Mamadee had given up to my great-grandmama. I knew nothing more of her than she had had a sister, Faith.

What was I to extract from all this oddybone sass? The cartooned birds—caricatures of the ivory-billed woodpecker, the Carolina parakeet, the passenger pigeon—were of species known or feared to be extinct. The altered wording of the hymn first discouraged hope and then implied resurrection or rebirth. The phoenix, rising from its own ashes. Which told me exactly what? Nothing that my poor *bird*brain could sort out. That I was one of the last of the species? Scarlet Macaws weren't near-extinct. And they weren't North American birds either.

Despairing of comprehension, I tucked the book back into my overall pocket, and stubbed my fingertips on the egg locket at the bottom.

"I'm psycho," I told myself aloud. "Schizo. Somebody lock me up."

Calley the Scarlet Macaw
ara macao calliope

The Scarlet Macaw's name was Calliope, Calley, for short. She had been my great-grandmama's own bird. Mama had named me after her grandmama's pet macaw.

I might have laughed, had I not been knuckling tears from my face.

At least Cosima had loved her Calliope, or she would not have attached the egg locket to Calliope's harness.

As I emerged from the grasses, a darkness against the distance coalesced into the figure of a human being. I slipped down the dune onto the beach. A few steps confirmed my im-

mediate suspicion: Mrs. Mank was walking south on the sand.
As broad as the beach was, we were the only two people on it
and there was no way I could avoid her.

After years of not being sure how I felt, I knew then that I
did not like Mrs. Mank, but I did want the education that she
was offering, and I did not know how to get it on my own.

Mrs. Mank was dressed as informally as I ever saw her (until she was dying), in sandals, clamdiggers and a middy. In
splendid oxymoronic defiance of their purpose, the clamdiggers had a parade-ground crease in them. Every stitch she wore
was hand-tailored and looked it. I couldn't say what unborn
animal had been sacrificed to make the fragile leather for her
sandals, but it was likely the last one of whatever it was. She
wore dark glasses but no hat and the rising sun highlighted her
hair that was no less and no more silvery than it ever had been.

When she reached me, her hand fell directly over my right
forearm, which was still more than a little numb from electrical shock. The low sun behind her made a corona around her,
bright enough to make me squint.

"Calley, walk with me."

My legs were longer than hers, and I was a few inches
taller, forcing me to shorten my pace to match hers.

"You're going to be six feet tall," she said, as if I were a
prize ficus plant. She gave me an arch look. "If you stay here
any longer, I fear you will become pot-bound."

"That would be a metaphor."

"So the local school has taught you something."

"I hope so, ma'am."

"What's that great lump in your pocket? A book?"

"A bird guide."

"Which one. Let me see it."

Reluctantly, I gave it up.

The spine read:

**National Audubon Society
Field Guide to
Eastern Land Birds**

"This is ancient," she declared. "Don't you have a more recent edition?"

"Yes, ma'am. If I get this one wet or sandy, it's no loss."

The skepticism lingered in her face. Her elegantly manicured nails pried at the covers, but the covers seemed to resist. Her eyebrows veed in surprise.

"It's gotten wet so many times," I said, trying not to show my utter terror that she would either succeed in opening it or else throw it into the Gulf, "the pages stick together."

"Glued together, I swear," Mrs. Mank said. There was an edge of anger in her voice. "I can't imagine that you could separate one page from another without destroying both."

I produced my oyster knife and she looked down her nose at it and made a dismissive noise. She thrust the book at me, and I made it disappear into my pocket again.

"Merry Verlow has informed you where you will go to college and that you will live with me," she said, picking up the thread of her previous remarks. "I know that you would like to finish high school here but that's impossible. In order to succeed in the caliber of school to which you are going, you need to spend a year in a first-class prep school."

The thought of leaving Merrymeeting and Santa Rosa Island evoked a shiver of panic. I was not as ready as I thought.

Mrs. Mank squeezed my forearm insistently.

"It's the right time, Calley. Your mama is engaged to marry Colonel Beddoes. She is going to start a new life. Surely you don't want her to live the rest of her life alone."

"Surely, I don't. It's not Mama that gives me pause, Mrs. Mank. I was preparing myself to go, just not so soon."

She said nothing for a time while we walked on. My own thoughts were rushed, my emotions surging from panic to excitement. My whole body shivered with gooseflesh.

"When?" I asked.

"Not very long," was her placid answer. "Not long at all."

We were within sight of Merrymeeting.

"There is nothing like the sea air for spurring appetite," Mrs. Mank remarked. "I am *ravenous* for Perdita's breakfast sausage. Say nothing to Roberta Dakin when she returns, Calliope. Let her have the pleasure of her wedding planning."

We parted in the foyer, Mrs. Mank for the dining room, me for the kitchen.

I won't tell Mama, I thought. I won't tell anyone, not even Grady. And not just about leaving.

Fifty-nine

THE day we set out, Grady and I made Tallassee by dinner-time, but of course we didn't go Mama's crazy route through Elba. I told no one that I was going. Grady was always good at keeping his trap shut, so we had fixed our own day, borrowed the Edsel from Roger, and snuck off as soon as it was light enough to see.

Tallassee had gotten smaller, to my eye. That's the way it felt, though of course I knew that it was Calley Dakin who had gotten bigger.

The first thing we did was hit a diner that served breakfast all day and night. After we had filled our stomachs, we went looking for a service station to refill the Edsel's tank. The sight of a rusty red Pegasus sign sent my pulse racing. I took it for luck and it was: The gas station had a telephone booth with a phone book chained inside.

I checked Mr. Weems's phone number against the list in my lunar notebook and copied out his home address. The names in the phone book jumped from Ethroe to Everlake with no stop for Evarts. A careful study of the page that listed physicians informed me that Tallassee had more doctors than when I was a child, but that Dr. Evarts did not appear to be among them.

The listings for lawyers offered no Adele Starret, not even A. Starret.

"I'll write the Alabama bar," I told Grady. "Adele Starret would have to be listed with them."

"If she was for real."

When he said that, for an instant I felt as if he had decided that I had made the whole thing up. A certain mulishness welled up in me.

I checked that phone book for Verlows and Dakins too, in case of new listings or a mistake by the directory assistance. Not a one. I didn't expect to find Fennie Verlow's name but it seemed strange that a clan as big as the Dakins should have no listings. Surely some of them would share a party line with someone somewhere.

Grady occupied himself gawking at Tallassee. He hadn't ever been outside of a thirty-five-mile radius of Pensacola, and marveled at how strange it was to be so far north. He wasn't sure that he liked it, being so far from the Gulf or any other body of saltwater, never mind he didn't understand half of what anybody said to him.

Without a map, and depending on a small child's memory, I had more trouble than I expected finding Ramparts. We kept coming to the same block of recently built houses.

Grady drove us downtown, where I went into the old pharmacy. To my relief, Mrs. Boyer was behind the cash register and Mr. Boyer was visible in the back of the store, doing his pharmacist duties. They were both older than I remembered but not as old as I expected they might be.

"Mrs. Boyer," I said.

For a second there was a question in her eyes because she wasn't sure who I was.

"I'm Calley Dakin," I told her.

"Calley Dakin," said Mrs. Boyer. "Well, I never."

Mr. Boyer raised his head and peered at me.

I waggled fingers at him.

"All grown up," marveled Mrs. Boyer.

"Yes'm," I agreed, and laughed as if being grown up was just what I put down on my Christmas list. "It's been so long since I was here, Miz Boyer, I caint seem to find Ramparts!"

"Oh dear." Mrs. Boyer's smile faded straight away and she looked very unhappy.

Mr. Boyer came to the front of the store.

"Calley Dakin," he said, shaking his head. "Honey, Ramparts burned down, oh—well, years ago—it went for new houses. All those old live oaks, chainsawed right down."

To know Ramparts was gone was an unexpected relief, though I felt some regret for the trees.

"Oh." I put my hat back on and tied the ends loosely. "Oh, well."

"She didn't know," Mrs. Boyer said to Mr. Boyer in a pitying voice.

He shook his head. "Didn't know."

"Thanks," I said, and stumbled gracelessly out the door to the Edsel.

The Boyers looked out at me as I flung myself into the passenger seat.

"Ramparts is gone," I told Grady. "Burned."

Grady glanced at the Boyers looking out at us behind the plate glass of the pharmacy. He turned the key in the ignition.

"Shit," he said with notable cheerfulness. "Ain't it allus the way. I was looking ford to them umbrellas."

The Weems's house was at least still there, though it took three go-rounds of the neighborhood before we found it.

This time Grady went to the door with me.

A colored woman answered the doorbell.

I opened my mouth, intending to inquire politely if Mr. Weems was at home, but what fell out was, "Tansy?"

She stared at me through thick-lensed glasses and crossed her arms over her stomach. Her hair had gone all white.

I took my hat off.

She blinked rapidly.

"Hit Calley Dakin," she said, in an amazed mocking tone.

"Yes." I drew Grady forward to stand next to me. "This is my friend Grady Driver."

She gave him a cursory once-over that made it clear she didn't think much of my choice of friends.

I managed to ask then if Mr. Weems were at home.

"Mistah Weems allus at home," Tansy said. "Had hisself a stroke three years ago come Chrismus." With considerable satisfaction, she added, "He caint talk, caint walk, caint get out the bed. He's jes pitiful."

"Well, maybe I could see Mrs. Weems."

Tansy smiled grimly. "Miz Weems pass over. She loss her mine and Doc Evarts give her some pills to make her better and she took ever one of 'em all to onced."

"What about Dr. Evarts?"

"He don't live here no mo," she told me, again with seeming pleasure. "He divoice Miz Evarts and lef. She done got married up again to a fella in Montg'mry."

"Well, where's my brother, Ford?"

"Doc Evarts took him with 'm."

Though Tansy was telling me what I wanted to know, it was like begging for cookies and getting one at a time.

"Tansy, where?"

Tansy reached out and touched the tip of my nose. "What you done to your hair, gurl?" Then she started to close the door in my face. As the door closed between us, she said, "N'awlins. Hear tell they done gone to they Quarter."

Then the door was closed.

"Ain't got no address, do you?" Grady called after her.

Her voice came from behind the door, as if she still stood there. "Cracker wanna know? Ah know where they gone be someday," she said, "where's all the rest of them Carrolls, down to Hellfire Street, care o' Satan hisself."

I pounded on the door. "Tansy, I ain't done talkin' to you, open this door."

Amazingly, she cracked the door open wide enough to peer out at me.

"What's Rosetta's last name? Where's she at?"

"She at the colored boneyard. Her girls done bought her a big stone crosst, says *Rosetta Branch Shaw* right on it 'n' her dates. *Mama*. Real sweet."

We didn't say anything to each other until we were back in the Edsel.

"Dry hole," Grady said.

"Tansy's grave's gone be marked with a Dead End sign," I told him.

He laughed and then said seriously, "I caint take another day, even if she ain't lying and we could find 'em in a place as big as N'awlins."

"I want to see Daddy's grave and Mamadee's. We'd still have time to go to Montgomery and maybe find Miz Verlow's sister, Fennie."

He shrugged.

"After that, we make a U-turn for Pensacola, OK? By then

I reckon I'll have seen about as much of Alabama as I ever expected to," he said.

"Let's see that phone book again."

"For what?"

"Check the funeral parlors. Undertakers must know all the graveyards around here."

"That's right smart."

"Not that smart. If I'd thunk of it before, I could have called ahead."

Grady grinned. "Rattle them bones, Miz Calley."

It seemed important to keep the red Pegasus in sight from the phone booth when I called the funeral parlor with the biggest ad.

A breathless, elderly voice answered. I had to repeat my question twice, and have it repeated back to me.

Then I waited, while the phone transmitted the sounds of the elderly person moving around what was apparently quite a small office space, trying to get a file drawer open and eventually succeeding, and a rummage among paper, all while the elderly person hummed and talked to—himself, I decided.

On picking up the receiver again, he cleared his throat, a process that easily took three minutes, and had Grady in stitches when I held the phone to his ear.

"This is necessarily partial," the elderly man warned me sternly when he finally could speak. "Country folk bury folks anywhere, you know, and call it a cemetery." Then he read the list, haltingly and with much repetition as I asked for spellings and directions, and while he lost and found his place in the listing.

I had hoped that I would remember the name of the graveyard where Daddy was buried if I heard it but when he finished, nothing had twigged my memory. All I had, and I wasn't sure what the use for it might be, was how to get to the Last Times Upon Us Church Cemetery where Mamadee was supposed to be interred. I wasn't even sure that I wanted to go there.

"You reckon that old fart choke up a lung?" asked Grady. "Let's call him up again and see if we can get him to gargle up the other one."

At least he was entertained. He looked at the directions that I had noted down. "You recall any of this?"

I shook my head no. "Never been there, to the best of my knowledge."

It took stopping a deputy but we did find it.

Mamadee had come down in the world, for sure. The Last Times Upon Us Church Cemetery reminded me of the one where Daddy had been buried; if anything, it was grimmer. Some kind of mineral crystal winked in the sour dirt and among the dandelions and plantain that seemed to be the only green things able to grow there. Most graveyards, somebody lays out in plots. Nobody had done that in the Last Times boneyard. It was a crazy quilt, the rectangles of the graves helter-skelter, puzzle-pieced and shoe-horned in among each other. It was a weird contrast to the grove of spindly pines behind the graveyard, for the pines, making room for themselves by acidifying the ground beneath with their dead needles, were spaced as neat as tacks on a card at the hardware store.

Grady and I wandered around the chaotic boneyard for a good forty minutes before we found the grave. The stone wasn't even marble. It was a coarse, already cracking, cement bar set unevenly in the ground.

DEIRDRE DEXTER CAROLL
1899–1958

Grady made a face and shivered. "Cold. Brrr. She don't even get a Bible verse or an R-I-P?"

"There's two *Rs* in Caroll," I said. "I don't know why she hasn't climbed back out to fix it."

"Don't go putting any ideas in her old daid haid, now." Grady was not entirely joking. "I don't see how it's gone help find Brother Ford."

"Me either. Less blow this pop stand. I want to go to Banks."

"Banks? We stickin' some up after all?"

"Banks, Alabama. It's on the way back to Pensacola."

"What's in Banks? You tole me Great-gran's house burned down years ago."

"Might be a graveyard there."

Grady went back to the sedan, dropped in behind the wheel and shook out the tattered old road map that he had gotten from somebody he knew at some gas station on Santa Rosa Island.

I crouched quickly, wet the end of my finger and touched the dirt of Mamadee's grave. I tasted my fingertips. Salt.

"Banks," he said. And after a few seconds, "Bingo. There she is. That's not what I call dreckly back."

"It's only a couple hours from Pensacola."

He could see that, of course.

"Ain't nothin' there, Calley. Some railroad tracks and a couple streets. Probably nothing but graveyards there, on account of ever'body ever lived there is dead. Probably anybody even stays there overnight drops dead on account of there's so much nothin' in Banks, Alabama, there ain't even air."

He had a point. Finding a house that had burned down a decade or more ago was likely to be something of a chore, never mind the grave of my maternal great-grandmama, in the hope that I would learn something from it.

"You got the right of it," I told him. "Less gone home."

He chucked me under the chin. "I'm sorry, Calley. I wisht we'd found your brother."

Sixty

EXPECTING to help serve and clean up supper, I entered the house by the kitchen door.

Perdita glanced up at me from arranging portions on plates. "Miz Verlow waitin' you on the v'randah."

As I crossed the kitchen, Cleonie came in from the dining room with an empty tray.

She held the swinging door open for me and hummed low at me as I passed. It was a hum of warning.

The guests in the dining room were forking in enthusiastically.

I paused at the front doors to listen for Miz Verlow and heard not only her but also Mrs. Mank. They were in the little alcove where Adele Starret had read Mamadee's will to Mama.

The two women were smoking cigarettes. The beverage of choice, I saw, was bourbon, in thick crystal glasses. The decanter sat close at hand on the little table. A candle flickered next to it, providing the only light in the alcove. The amber liquid in the decanter glowed with the reflected candlelight, as if it had a small pillar of fire at its core.

The faces of the two women were shadowed. I had to draw a chair up to face them and sit before I could see them clearly.

"What did you learn?" Mrs. Mank said, in a flat voice.

I gave up the finding that I thought least useful. "Mamadee's maiden name was Dexter."

Of course it was. As in Dexter Bros., on the circus poster. Her daddy the Dexter who married Cosima, the bird lady who rode the howdah.

Miz Verlow raised her glass to her lips.

Mrs. Mank said nothing for a long moment. She took a long suck on her cigarette.

"And?" she said at last.

Tests. How many tests? Was I going to let these two women run my life and why did they even want to?

"Mamadee must have been ashamed of it, and if she was, then Mama is, and that's why Mama never told me."

Miz Verlow relaxed.

"Deirdre's father was nobody," Mrs. Mank said, with great satisfaction. "Deirdre tried to make herself into somebody by marrying a Carroll, but there it is, graven in cement."

Miz Verlow made a little chuckling noise.

"I knew Deirdre," Mrs. Mank said. "She ruined your mama and she would have ruined you. I was very glad to learn that your mama had taken refuge with someone whom I trusted entirely."

Mrs. Mank reached out to pat Miz Verlow on the hand. Miz Verlow smiled warmly at her.

"Perhaps," said Mrs. Mank, "one of us should have told you these things earlier. But you were a child. You've grown up on us and we were not prepared." She smiled at me quite warmly. "We must do something about your hair and you really must learn how to dress properly, Calley. You're going to go out into the great big rest of the world very soon!"

I could not help the bloom of excitement in my guts.

"Well." Mrs. Mank stood. "At least you were in time for supper. I'm quite hungry, Merry, and supper smells heavenly."

I wasn't hungry but I ate too, and then helped clean up.

I took up Mrs. Mank's cocoa for her.

I bathed and went to bed. Though I was tired, sleep eluded me.

Mrs. Mank had known Mamadee. She held Mamadee and Mama to be no-account. She had not just chosen me out of the ether or on the say-so of Fennie or Merry Verlow. She had come close to an admission that she had made some attempt to interfere before Mama would ruin me, whatever "ruin" meant to Mrs. Mank.

When? When had she made her observations and drawn her conclusions? Before Daddy was murdered? Before Fennie Verlow sent us to Merrymeeting and her sister, Merry?

Did it matter?

And where? I did not remember Mrs. Mank from the first part of my childhood in Montgomery and Tallassee. Given how young I was, the lack of memory more than likely meant nothing. Mrs. Mank might have known Mamadee for years and years, and just not been around when I was a little girl in my daddy's house.

Mrs. Mank had spoken of Mamadee with a distinct, personal disdain. Perhaps they had known each other in childhood, and that was how Mrs. Mank came to know that Mamadee's father was "nobody." What did the term "nobody" signify to Mrs. Mank? The snobbery innate to the term angered me. Grady Driver was nobody, and so was I.

If Mamadee's daddy was nobody, did that mean that her mama, my great-grandmama, Cosima, was *not*?

How was I going to get to New Orleans and, once there, find my brother? And before Mama returned. Before I could plan such a trip, I had to know more about where Ford might be in New Orleans or even if he were still there. It made sense to locate Dr. Evarts. If Ford were in college somewhere, Dr. Evarts would know. Surely he would tell me if I asked. I was Ford's sister, who had been a little girl when Dr. Evarts became Ford's guardian. Dr. Evarts could not believe that I was Mama's agent or that I had designs on Ford's money. Surely not. Oh, hell—yes, Dr. Evarts might very well think just those things about me.

All I could do was find the man. There must be some chance that if I did, even if Dr. Evarts would not tell me where Ford was, some clue might come my way. Why, Ford might be on break from college, and visiting with Dr. Evarts, and open the door when I knocked at it. That was hope, not wishful thinking, and hope was good, hope was necessary. Faith in myself, and hope for a good outcome. Faith and Hope, my aunties. I needed to think about Ford.

I was putting too much into the consequences of finding him. Likely it would turn out a wild goose chase. If Ford proved to be hateful, I told myself with what I felt was adult rationality, I would be free to walk away from childhood and the wreckage of my family. That's how young I really was.

Sixty-one

MRS. Mank's plans for me made me more determined not to be diverted from either seeking Ford or any information about my family that I could unearth. The trip to Tallassee had been a severe disappointment. It was here on Santa Rosa Island that I had remembered, and not forgotten again, the memories of the events of my first months at Merrymeeting.

On the shelf over my bed, the hallucinatory bird book had reverted to being an old edition of the *National Audubon Society Field Guide to Eastern Land Birds*. I put it in my overalls pocket again, along with my oyster knife, before going downstairs and helping myself to a key to the attic from Miz Verlow's key safe. Though she was in the kitchen with Perdita and might emerge at any time, I did not fear her surprising me, nor her anger if and when she discovered that I had taken the key.

When I turned the knob of the door to the attic, experimentally, though, it gave easily: It was unlocked. I dropped the key back into my overalls pocket. Once through the door, I closed it behind as quietly as I could.

I stood in the dark, waiting for my night sight. The whispers and shuffles of the small dark lives of the critters that lived in the attic reassured me. I felt more than a little bit like one of them, just trying to survive in a predatory world. And in the dark. The bird guide, my oyster knife and the egg locket weighted one of my pockets. If the critters did not frighten me, that thing in the trunk had, not so very long ago. Whether an oyster knife, a bird guide or the egg locket would be any protection was questionable, but they were what I had.

When I could see enough of the steps, I moved up them cautiously until I found the light chain and its cool white ceramic knob, seemingly hanging there waiting for me. A tug shed the filthy light of the row of bulbs above over the shrouded, secretive, and unreadable shapes crowding the nearly full space.

The snick of a key engaging the lock of the door at the bottom of the attic steps reached my ears. I heard no one. Mrs. Mank might be able to move without my hearing her, but no one else ever had. And she was not in residence. What noiseless someone or something had locked the door behind me?

Whatever the answer to that weird little mystery, I had a key in my pocket.

Slowly I began to explore the attic again. There was no way to do it systematically. Despite all the efforts that Roger and I had made over the years to store like with like and make everything accessible, it was almost as if someone came up and disorganized whatever we did—or else the miscellany rearranged itself.

The lights went out. I stood rigidly still in the dark instant. For all the light to go out, either someone or something had pulled the chain, which I had not heard, or had removed the fuse. I didn't have a spare fuse in my pocket, nevermind the fuse box was in the pantry. Again my vision adjusted, so I was not totally blind, and the light of day leaked in at the portholes in the eaves.

I groped my way to the one where the tarp that Roger and Grady and I had used was still spread out. The candle stubs we had abandoned had long since melted in the heat to an amorphous puddle, staining the tarp underneath. The wicks made black hyphens in the yellowed wax. I had no lighter or matches, nor had I planned well enough to bring a flashlight. I crouched over the melted wax and flattened it as best I could with my palm. Rolled into a crude cylinder around the longest piece of wick, it would have to pass for a candle. It only stood up because it was not tall enough to fall over.

Taking it with me, in hope of discovering a way to light it, I continued my exploration. The candle comforted me. I might be able to use it or not. But I had it. It might even light if I could find a lighter or matches. In the meantime, I wanted to find the old trunk, the scary one.

Stubbing my toe hard on the cast-iron base of an old sewing machine, I staggered against it. The thing was so heavy as to be unmovable and to my relief, held me up enough to avoid going flat on my face. My looks would not be improved with a Singer treadle pattern on my face, to say nothing of putting an eye out on the projecting ironwork. *Don't run with a cast-iron sewing machine stand in your hand, Calley; you could poke your eye out.* The ludicrous thought made me snicker.

Balance regained, I slid along the edges of dressers and tables, grasped the ears of chair backs, and fetched up finally near another of the portholes in the eaves. It was fabulously webbed and filthy, but I was not much cleaner by then, so I patted the screen in the porthole with the palms of my hands gently, to shake loose some of the accumulated grime. A clearer air wafted in, and I breathed of it gladly, even as it emphasized just how thick and dusty the air that I had been breathing really was.

I rested there a moment, savoring the hardly perceptible surcease of heat, and the access to the salt-tinged air. Reluctantly I moved on, promptly barking my shins on a crate, using a standing lamp to steady myself, and stumbling about until I was face-to-face with the totemic face of the old semanier. Something, at last, that I recognized. Recalling that I had not tried all the drawers, I began opening them from the bottom. Crap galore in them, from Masonic jewelry to a nice selection of little silk shorts—underpants, I realized as I handled them with my dirty fingers, from the twenties. Step-ins, Perdita called them. I dropped them back into their drawer and rummaged behind them. The rigid edge my fingertips stubbed up against proved to be a rusty little tin box, with a matchbook in it.

Fire! My heart leapt as if I were a caveman coming on a lightning-struck mammoth, split open to give me access to rare meat and steaming offal.

Soon I had my crude candle burning. I held it carefully, while peering around for something to put it in. It was frustrating to see nothing, not even an old ashtray that might be useful, when I had seen so many candleholders and candlesticks on previous visits. I considered the little tin box, but it was flimsy and rusty and might get hot to hold. Surely I could do better.

And I did. Gyrating slowly, holding the candle high to cast its light over the greatest area, I caught a glimpse of purple-blue glass on an open shelf of a shabby curio cabinet that had had the glass of its door broken right out. I reached careful past the shards still in the frame of the door, and brought out the cobalt-blue glass candleholder that Mama had bought in New Orleans, in the ticking antique shop. *Prop: Mr. Rideaux. The bell on the door jingling. The woman who looked at me. A wall of clocks lying about the time. Mama's lost Hermès Kelly bag that wasn't lost at all.*

Despite the nonstandard chubbiness of my candle, the glass candleholder married my candle as if the two objects were made for each other.

Holding it high again, moving carefully so as not to bang myself up any more, or inadvertently light up something flammable, I made better progress in my exploration. I was running sweat as if instead of the burning candle, I was doing the melting. My overalls and the man's undershirt that I wore underneath it stuck to me as wet pages stick to one another.

The thought reminded me of the bird guide. I touched it to reassure myself. It occurred to me that I ought to look at it, to see what state it was in—steady-state National Audubon Society Field Guide, or nutty oddybone.

I drew it out, picked out a nearby rug-covered chest with an end table next to it, and sat down. I put the candlestick on the table. Held in both my hands, the spine of the book read

The Odderbone Field Guide to Calley Dakin

I expected it to flop open but nothing happened. When I tried to open it, it seemed to be as firmly stuck closed as it had been for Mrs. Mank.

An insubstantial and mildly impatient voice said, enunciating each word clearly:

Listen to the book.

I stopped trying to open the book. I knew that voice. It was Ida Mae Oakes's. Tears welled over my lower lashes and I blubbered.

"I'm all ears," I said in a whisper. "Ida Mae, I've listened for you particularly. I wish you wasn't dead."

Me too, Ida Mae said. *If it wasn't for the Peace That Surpasseth All Understanding, I'd rather be alive. You stop your blubbering now. I had a nice easy passage, which is more than a lot of folks get. Closed my eyes for a minute during the second Sunday service, and woke up hovering over my own daid old carcass, and nobody even noticing, they was so many of them nodded off. It was a hot day and Brother Truman would drone, no matter how much the amen corner tried to work up a momentum. And I was so young. I wasn't but fifty-six. My mama is still alive, with sugar, cataracts, not a tooth in her head and don't know her own name most days. She married her third husband when she was fifty-six, and raised up three of his children that had run wild since their mama passed of a sudden. She earned a crown doing that, I am sure, but she's been in no hurry to claim it. She asks for me all the time, thinking I am still alive. I hear her, "Where my Ida Mae? Why don' she come see her mama?"*

"I missed you," I told her. "Missed you terrible."

I know, she said, in her old gentle way. *I held my tongue all this time for a penance for being put out with passing so all-of-a-sudden, but I would have spoke if needed. I kep my eye on you, darlin'. You don' know how many souls are keeping their eyes on you. Well, mayhap you do.*

"Daddy?"

You know it, darlin'.

"Tell me why he died—"

Hush, now. It was his time—

"No it wasn't!" I cried.

The candle wavered as if I had struck it.

"Revenge is mine, saith—"

"Yeah, you bet," I retorted.

Mind your manners, Ida Mae said sharply. *I'll hear no*

blasphemy from a child that still has breath in her lungs for to be grateful.

"I want some answers," I said. No, I didn't say it. I shouted.

Ida Mae made a very odd laugh. *People in Hell want sweet tea, Calley Dakin.*

"I believe I *am* in Hell," was my retort.

Gotta be a lot worse than you have been yet to get there. Ida Mae hummed briefly as if she were about to sing. *Listen to the book,* she sang softly, to the tune of "I See the Moon." *Listen to the book.*

The book fell open in my lap, to the flyleaf. It was inscribed: *Calley Dakin,* in my own handwriting.

Unlock the footlocker, the book said in my voice, with a little flutter of its fine thin pages.

"I don't know where it is."

Ida Mae's voice came out of the nowhere again. *You're sitting on it.*

Sixty-two

I jumped off and spun about, losing my grasp on the field guide and worse, nearly knocking over the candle. I dropped the book and used both hands to secure the candle. A fearful sweat was running from my hairline in rivulets, and from every pore, or so it seemed. I was breathless and my belly was knotted up like a fist.

With the candle safe and steady on the end table, I drew the rug away from the chest, and sure enough, it was not really a chest, but a military footlocker. Green and black. Padlocked. No key in sight. I sniffed the air but detected no odor of the abattoir.

The guidebook lay on the dusty wooden floor. I picked it up and put it in my pocket, and when I did, my fingertips encountered the key to the attic.

I drew it out and studied at it. It was a door key, the old-fashioned long-barreled kind, not the stubby key that a padlock would have. I pulled out my oyster knife. One of them was going to open that padlock, or else. I didn't know what the *else* might be, but I knew that I was serious about it.

I made a try with the door key. And, of course, it worked. It slid into that padlock like water down a thirsty throat. And I was thinking about water; I was thirsty by then. I turned the key and the padlock let go.

If I failed to actually open the footlocker, Ida Mae was going to speak up or use the guidebook for a megaphone—oh, how stupid I had been; of course that was exactly what the guidebook was, a ghost megaphone.

I bent my knees, unhooked the padlock from the metal tongues of the footlocker, and put my back behind my lifting of the lid of the chest. There was no resistance, only the unhappy shriek of its disused hinges, as it rose and then fell away with my immediate push. I looked down into the trunk, which was filled with neatly banded bundles of money. Sitting on top of the paper money was a silver dollar. Not a bill in a bundle would be dated later than 1958, I was immediately sure: It was the ransom that had not saved Daddy's life, and the silver dollar appeared to be my very own.

I put my silver dollar in my pocket. Seeing an old wicker laundry basket not far out of reach, I fetched it to the footlocker and emptied the ransom money into it. The hamper was less bulky, less heavy, and I could push it toward the steps, where there was luggage close at hand. After I had done just that, I went back for the candle, my oyster knife, and my guidebook.

By the light of the candle, I filled a well-used good-sized canvas suitcase with the money. I did it without excitement or anxiety. A million dollars was a lot of money back in 1968. Finding the silver dollar on top of it all seemed like a signal that the paper money was mine to dispose of as I wished. It was freedom; I could buy my own education and shed Mrs. Mank, Miz Verlow, and Mama, all in one go.

I closed the suitcase, *click-click,* and repressed a chortle. Whatever part of me was true-blue Carroll was deeply satisfied for the first time in my life. I felt for the door key. And did not have it, for it was on the floor by the footlocker, still in the open padlock.

Taking my rapidly diminishing candle with me, I turned to go back to the footlocker.

The heat was getting to me. Sweat set on my upper lip and my tongue could not keep up with licking it off. But I did lick at it reflexively, for it wet my mouth and throat. In a few steps, I doubted my direction. It occurred to me that I could die here in the attic, die of thirst or starvation or the heat. But, of course, I would cry out first and be heard. It was only being wrung out by the heat that even made it seem possible. The hell with the key, I told myself, I still had my oyster knife. I would find my way back to the steps and the suitcase.

Long moments later, I had not found my way. I crouched by one of the portholes and sucked at the air coming in through the screen, and berated myself for failing to bring water with me. And breadcrumbs, or white stones, anything to have used for a trail.

The candle's tiny flame breathed a little larger. It would very soon gutter in its own melted wax.

"I listened to the book," I said in a mutter. "A fine kettle of fish it's gotten me into."

Making myself breathe easy and concentrate, I listened closely, but Ida Mae did not speak. I listened hard enough to hear the babble beneath the water of the Gulf but no voice I knew emerged from it. I slid my fingertips into my overalls pocket to touch Calliope's locket, half-expecting some magic from it. But there was none, except the skin smoothness of the gold at the tips of my fingers.

Heat rises. Hot as it was on the floor, it was not as hot as it was at my full height. I crawled, awkwardly, what with having to hold the candle in one hand. The book bumped against my flank as if to remind me it was there.

Stopping in a crouch, I put the candle on the floor and took out the book.

As I held it in my hand, it said, speaking again in my own voice:

Point your finger. Follow it.

My forefinger, I thought, the one I burned in a candle flame the Christmas morning when I was seven.

So I stood up, shoved the book back into my pocket, picked up the candleholder with my left hand, and pointed my forefinger. It failed to sting or redden. I turned slowly, until it did. And it did. It felt just as if I was shoving it into the flame of my homemade candle in the cobalt-blue candleholder. A doorbell *caw-caw*ed far away. The sound came from my pocket, so I knew it was the book.

I moved in the direction that my finger pointed. The way was far from clear. I had to go over low things, and between things, and around things, and then point my finger again until the pain of burning confirmed the direction.

The beams as they sank toward the eaves forced me into a stoop and then a crouch. I could smell dead meat again. Finally I was on my knees, and the footlocker was in sight, against the low wall of the eave. It was not the same one, I told myself. The one that had contained the ransom had had plenty of headroom above it. A padlock was on the floor, open, no key in sight.

The closer I crept to the footlocker, the more the stench gagged me. The tongue of the footlocker hung loose. With one quick movement, I lifted the lid and flung it back. I let myself fall back in reaction to my own forward force, so there was some space between the footlocker and me.

The candle was just at hand. Its flame all but floated on the transparent melt of its wax. Lifting it slowly so as not to smother it by a sudden rush, I drew closer to the footlocker, close enough to hover the candle over the open footlocker. The bottom looked a long way down. The Calley effigy was sprawled there, with Betsy Cane McCall obscenely between her legs.

Unbidden, the thought was suddenly in my mind: I should set the rag doll aflame, and use it for a torch, to spread fire at every corner of the attic. When the house was on fire, someone would unlock the attic door. The rag doll looked up at me with its stony eyes. The flame of the candle raised a light in each one, and a tiny reflection of me. Its eyes pled with me; it so wanted to burn.

Bent over the open footlocker, I lowered the candleholder. A tiny unsteadiness in my hand spilled a clear hot drop of wax upon the rag doll's face, where it became a cloudy tear splat.

I moved the flame to her hair, which flared at once. The sudden flare of fire stung my hand like a whip. I dropped the candleholder into the footlocker. The hot melted wax spattered over the blackening rag doll, feeding the fire. Sooty black smoke bloomed from the flames. The rag doll writhed. It looked like a blackbird on fire. Poor Betsy Cane McCall blackened and fumed too; as it melted her polyvinyl mouth seemed to gape open, her eyes to widen, until she appeared to be screaming.

I dropped back onto my heels, then jumped up and kicked the footlocker with my bare foot. It felt as if I had busted every toe. But the force of my kick drove the footlocker back against the wall, and the lid dropped down, pinching a billow of smoke into my face. It was nasty and black, that smoke, and I got a mouthful of it that made me cough and wretch.

I crouched nearby, watching the footlocker, to see if it would catch. When it seemed as if at least an hour had gone by, though I knew it was only ten minutes or so, I ventured to open the footlocker again. Of course doing so released another cloud of the foul smoke right into my face. More coughing and gagging, this time until tears ran down my face. I knuckled the tears and smeared wet soot around my face.

After a moment or two, I could see into the footlocker. Fire out, starved of oxygen. The cobalt candleholder sat in the black mess at the bottom of the footlocker, like an unpolished gem in a tar pit. Like my own heart, sooty and hard, but unmelted. I felt no fear any more of the rag doll or the footlocker. I dropped the lid again.

When I stood up, I looked up, searching out the center beam of the attic. Once I was under it and could look in either direction, I followed it to the attic steps. I coughed a lot while I made my way.

Impulsively, I gave the light pull chain a yank, and all the lightbulbs came on. I could have done that before, when I brought the ransom money to the luggage, but had not, what with realizing that I had left the door key in the padlock. I might have had clear vision, if only I had done the simple and obvious thing: Try the light chain again.

There was only one way to turn the lights on, and that was the pull chain. I had not heard its distinctive catch and click, never mind anyone who might have pulled it. Knowing that it had not been the fuse still left me without answers that mattered.

I backed down the steps, with the canvas suitcase bumping on each step after me. When I tried the door, it was still locked. I used the oyster knife. It worked and I swore I would never be without it.

It was only midday, I realized, as I emerged into the hallway. I heard the sound of dinner from the dining room. The best place to temporarily stash the money, I decided, was in the linen closet. That highest shelf, where the Christmas decorations were stored, and no one ever ever looked, that was the place. In a few moments, the ransom was hidden, and I had gathered clean clothes and was locked in the bathroom.

The sight of myself in the mirror made me laugh until I cried again. I looked like a charred owl. I jumped into the shower to cover the noise I could not stop making.

When I went down the backstairs to the kitchen, Perdita was arranging dessert plates.

"I'll do those," I said.

She watched me do one to make sure that I did it right, and then she wrinkled her nose.

"I smells burnin'. Bin smellin' least a quarter hour. Nothin' boil over, though, nor burn on neither." The outrage in her voice made it clear that Perdita would not allow boil-overs or burn-ons.

I sniffed the air and shook my head in puzzlement. "Maybe somebody's campfire on the beach."

"If it is, Lawd save whomsoever be eatin' that mess!" Perdita said.

Miz Verlow did not seem to notice, perhaps because so many of the guests just then were smokers, and the smoke was always wafting in from the verandah. She did give me several puzzled glances, as if she could not quite remember who I was.

I heard her in the attic that night. She went straight to wherever she was going and stood there for a long moment.

And then, very clearly, she said, "It's too late, Calliope Dakin."

Sixty-three

MAMA came home with a new pair of tits. Her jawline was ten years tighter. Her eyes had acquired a slight and sexy tilt, like Barbara Eden's, while the shadows under them had disappeared. The suggestion of Barbara Eden was entirely deliberate; Mama was rigged out in billowing gauzy harem pants and a form-fitting short jacket that was meant to serve up her décolletage like a tray of meringues, and did.

She sashayed into Merrymeeting still wearing her sunglasses, so she could casually whip them off. She had to check the effect in the mirror in the foyer and on anyone who might be standing there looking. Everyone was, given she had timed her arrival for the cocktail hour, when the guests gathered to knock back a few drinks before supper.

Several of them were regulars who knew Mama. They knew that she was different but only a few of the women could have said how. Fewer of the guests were new; Mama had the greatest effect on them. One of the younger men even made a low whistle—very low and very short and ending in an odd, smothered yelp, as his wife stomped down on the toe of his sandaled foot.

Colonel Beddoes, bringing in Mama's suitcases, missed the byplay. He passed the luggage off to me to take up to Mama's room, freeing himself to put an arm around Mama's waist and nuzzle her ear.

Miz Verlow went through a little routine of being so attentive to one guest that she didn't notice Mama until she turned around at the kerfuffle of commotion and saw Mama getting her ear sucked by Colonel Beddoes. Mama had to swat him down mockingly, to keep her dignity in front of Miz Verlow.

Mama went out again with Colonel Beddoes after supper and it was late when she returned but I was still awake. When I heard her, I went to her room and knocked.

She had left the door ajar, which meant that I should come right in. She looked at me in her mirror, where she was sponging off her makeup.

"My feet are killin' me," she said. "Show me your hands."

I held them up so they were visible in the mirror. Then I picked up a bottle of her hand lotion and helped myself. My nails were fine but my skin was dry.

"That's expensive," she said, "don't waste it."

She had a cigarette burning up in an ashtray on the vanity and a glass of bourbon breathing pleasant airs. I picked up the cigarette and took a drag.

"Buy your own," she snapped.

I took a sip out of her glass of bourbon too.

"Calley!"

I dropped onto her bed, kicked off my sandals and flopped back.

Mama stopped to suck on the cigarette and knock back some bourbon. "I don't know what I did to deserve you."

I didn't say anything. She finished with her face, tied the sash of her negligee, took her cigarette and bourbon and went off to the bathroom for a quarter hour. I used the time to open her pocketbook and help myself to a twenty and then I turned down her bed for her.

Mama came back, glass empty, cigarette stub no doubt flushed down the toilet.

She handed me the glass and arranged herself on the bed. As I opened the jar of foot cream, she gave a great melodramatic sigh.

"It was hell," she said. "You cannot imagine."

I held her feet in my lap. Her new tits poked up the bodice of her negligee proudly. Her eyelids bore very thin but still visible red scars, and other scars were exposed behind her ears, where she had tied back her hair to do her face.

I worked the foot cream into her feet methodically.

"But," Mama said, reaching for the pack of cigarettes and a

lighter on the night table, "it was worth every damn cent and every damn miserable moment."

She went into some detail about the miserable moments, which were more miserable for her than anyone else who ever experienced them. When I was finished with her feet, she was still talking. I closed the jar.

She paused to take a hit on her cigarette.

"Good night, Mama," I said, leaving her with her mouth open, words ready to spill out and no one to hear them.

I closed the bedroom door gently.

*

IT was Miz Verlow's custom to sort the mail when it arrived, usually right after breakfast. Then she would give it to me to distribute. As a rule, her guests received very little mail; they were short-term residents, after all.

In the years that we had been living at Merrymeeting, Mama had received only communications from Adele Starret, an occasional postcard or note from some guest with whom she had struck up an acquaintanceship or, even more rarely, a billet-doux from a boyfriend. It was more common for me to receive mail, for I shared the interests of so many of our long-time guests. Not only notes and postcards arrived with my name on them, but books and records and tapes, and even the occasional feather, dried flower, or packet of seeds.

The day after Mama returned, Miz Verlow handed me a letter for her. She handed me that envelope with a curtness with which I was now familiar. Miz Verlow ignored me most of the time, since my last visit to the attic, but sometimes it was obvious that she was extremely displeased with me. I made an early decision to ignore any reaction from her, and stuck to it.

The envelope was lovely thick stock, with a Paris, France, postmark on it and no return address on it.

Mama was drinking coffee and doing her nails on the verandah. Once upon a time, she never would have done her nails in public or even semi-public. Miz Verlow frowned in Mama's direction when she handed me the letter. She said nothing but I could see that she was steamed at Mama about doing her manicure on the verandah.

I took the envelope to Mama, who looked right through

me, and waved one hand in the air to dry her nails as she studied the envelope.

"Paris, France," she said loudly, in case any other guests were in earshot. "Well, I caint imagine."

Mama wrinkled her nose. She didn't want to ruin her nails. "Open it for me, Calley."

I sat on the edge of the railing and slit the envelope open with my oyster knife. A single, folded sheet of the same heavyweight stock filled the envelope tightly. When I shook the folded sheet flat, a photograph dropped free. I caught it with my free hand. It was a black-and-white snapshot of a handsome young man on a sailboat, one hand on the rigging.

Ford. I knew him at once. Grown up, or nearly so, but still Ford.

With the snapshot in one hand, I read the letter aloud:

Dear Mama,
*   It has taken me a long time even to start to find you. Obviously as a mere child, I could hardly do it. As soon as I could, I began to search for you. Now I know that you are still alive, and where you are, I can hardly wait to see you again. I will shortly return from junior year abroad. It is not my desire to intrude upon your present life. Please come alone to meet me at the Ford automobile agency in Mobile at 3 in the afternoon of the seventeenth of August.*
Your loving son,

Ford
P.S.
Let me assure you that if you feel any shame at abandoning me, I know now why you did, and understand it, and forgive you.

Tears ran down Mama's taut face. I handed her the snapshot. She took it with trembling fingers. Wiping her eyes frantically, like a child, with the back of one hand, she stared at the picture of Ford.

"Ford," she whispered, "my baby."

Her eyes closed and she kissed the snapshot.

I let the envelope fall to the floor of the verandah. As silently as I could, I slipped away.

The young man in the photograph was of the age that Ford would be now. It was a shiny new snapshot. My first impression that the young man was, in fact, Ford seemed convincing evidence in itself of the authenticity of the photograph.

All that rummaging that I had done to find Ford had been a waste of time.

He had not mentioned me.

Of course, Mama *would* be more important to him.

I was curious to meet him again, grown up and all, but now there was no particular urgency. Mama would have what she thought was her due, Ford, and access to the fortune that she thought should have been hers. She might very well not marry Tom Beddoes, if Ford took against it.

Understandably, Mama was caught up in the realization of her dreams and desires. So much all at once—not since Daddy died, had so much come her way.

I felt as if a knot had been slipped. Maybe the last knot. What a marvel. Unanswered questions blown away like a dandelion head on a puff of breath.

I had a million dollars, plus one, in a safe place. Not the linen closet. That had been the most temporary of arrangements. Leaving was going to be easier than I had thought.

Sixty-four

THE waxing moon hung overhead like a scimitar raised high for the decisive blow. The night was too sultry to sleep inside. Even on the beach, I did not sleep, but sprawled on my blanket staring at the sky. Mrs. Mank's Benz hummed in the distance along the road to Merrymeeting.

I sat up and hugged my knees and waited. I heard a mouse rolling grains of sand under its paws as it streaked from one sheltered place to another.

Mrs. Mank came over the dune and walked toward me down the beach.

"It's time to go," she said.

I nodded. "Before we do, I want to ask a question."

Irritation sharpened her features.

"Why was Daddy murdered?"

"I have no idea," she said. "What a peculiar thing to ask me."

"You should have said because he had the bad luck to fall into the hands of two criminally insane women."

She took a sharp breath.

"Are you accusing me of complicity?" Her voice rang with incredulity and anger.

I looked past her, at the Gulf waters sprinkled all over with moonlight. I didn't answer her.

Instead, I asked, "Don't you want to ask me a question?"

Her expression settled into passivity.

"I may have to wrack my brains," she said sarcastically. "All right. What's the latest word from the dead?"

I smiled at her. "Justice."

She flinched as if I had slapped her.

"And who are you?" she asked. "Judge and jury?"

"No. I'm Calley Dakin, and my daddy was murdered in New Orleans in 1958."

"That's the past," Mrs. Mank said. "His life ended. Yours did not. You have to live the rest of it."

"Why in hell do you care?" I asked, in a near whisper.

She smiled crookedly. "I don't *care*. I want to know what you hear."

"Why?"

"Don't act as if you were simpleminded, Calley Dakin. You hear what no one else does. It might have driven you insane. I've gone to a great deal of trouble to protect you while you were growing up. I'll tell you a secret, shall I? But not until we're in Brookline."

This time I was not going to refuse, even if I had to go to Brookline, Massachusetts, first.

I rose slowly, gathering my blanket. I folded it with care. Mrs. Mank stood by, watching me.

Merry Verlow stood by the Benz. I walked passed her without a word and went into the house and up the backstairs. Mama's door was closed, of course. I went into my crookedy-room.

From the shelf over my bed, I took the old bird guide. On the spine it read:

**National Audubon Society
Field Guide to
Eastern Land Birds**

Just as it had when I took it out of my overalls pocket after listening to it on the beach. I was confident that the flyleaf was inscribed Bobby Carroll. I listened intently but the book was silent. Setting it aside, I stripped off a pillowcase and threw some clothes into it, and my lunar notebook, the old bird guide and Calliope's locket. I looked out my little window, at the view that I had seen when I first came to Merrymeeting. Every drop of water in the Gulf, every grain of sand on the beach, every molecule of air, was different and yet, it was all the same. Things change, but only into themselves.

Downstairs, outside again, and I went to the passenger side of the Benz and opened the door. Miz Verlow and Mrs. Mank kissed each other on the cheek.

I tried to take in the house all at once. It was shabbier. It creaked more in the wind and the verandah floor was splintery.

Mrs. Mank slipped behind the wheel as I closed the door on the passenger side.

Miz Verlow bent to wave at me, a small wave, and the swiftest quirk of a smile. There was something embarrassed in that smile. Merry Verlow knew that the secret I was going to learn would change everything and would do her no credit. She nodded and stepped back from the car.

"Go to sleep," said Mrs. Mank, "we've a long way to go."

Sleep? Not hardly.

I settled back in the seat to watch the Gulf as we sped along. Just past midnight, the dark insubstantial as the shadow, it was the time of night that always has felt least like night to me: neither night nor day but a suspension of time altogether. Water and sky surged into one black liquid pulse, the glisten of the moon like the blink of a bird's golden eye.

When the turn came, away from the Gulf and toward Pensacola, I looked back. The black water of the Gulf was already no more than a distant dark glimmering horizon.

Artificial light increased steadily as we left the island. Pensacola slept with open windows in the heat. Placid streetlight defined the leaves of trees and glistened on pavement. As the Scenic Highway climbed the western side of Escambia Bay, again, I looked back. The Causeway arched to the clot of darkness gridded with light that was Gulf Breeze, and the similar shape of Pensacola Beach beyond. Santa Rosa Island loomed as an uneven ghostly slash, pocked scarcely with lights and splotched with inky black vegetation, between the Gulf and the bay.

I didn't know where I would be when the sun rose. I only knew where I wasn't going to be. Nor did I know how long I might be away, but I did not expect to be very long. I would return; I had money to collect.

I felt stuck in the summer night like a bug in amber. In the silence between Mrs. Mank and myself, the clock in the dashboard of the Benz became notably loud.

Mrs. Mank shifted upward and the Benz surged. My stomach lurched and the forward motion pressed me back into the seat. The dashboard clock tsked loudly at me.

> *klikitpikitlikitrikitklikitstikitlikprikitlikitwikitwikit*
> *tell you a secret*
> *secret unshine*
> *otongotongotongoton*
> *unshine secret secret secret*
> *don't make me tell don't you tell secret hell sunshine*
> *see the cold moon sees me seize the dark sun seas me*
> *calliopecalliopecalliopecalliope*

I opened my eyes into a dazzle of oncoming light. I was blinded. And I saw. The light passed through me and was all around with a great noise that pushed and pulled at every cell of my body, like the slipstream of the wings of an enormous bird passing by. There was no heat in the light, and no cold, only its vibration resonating in the small dark space where I bowed my head over my knees.

I woke again, with a small jolt and the sensation of falling. My mouth was open and dry as if I had eaten a ghost, and its corners were damp with spittle. Mrs. Mank was only inches from me across the gearbox. The headlights splashed enough light back off the tarmac to show her like a shadow.

I thought: I am a shadow to her too.

I said, "I know a secret too."

Her gaze whipped right.

"Daddy told me, Daddy told me what you did, Daddy told me why!"

Mrs. Mank gasped as if she were running very hard. Her eyes were on the road again, her body crouched over the wheel as if to spring right through the windshield.

I closed my eyes.

Sixty-five

ROLLING gently over gravel, the Benz chuckled and cackled as if it were amused. My eyelids felt glued shut. The effort it took to open them had that protest of lashes tearing out.

The light was morning soft, and the world around was drunkenly green. A yawn forced its way out of me, and the flavor of all that fresh green washed into my mouth and lungs. My cells seemed to suck it up. I wondered if I would be green when next I looked in the mirror.

The Benz came to a seemingly inevitable stop, and settled heavily on the gravel. Mrs. Mank sighed as if she had made a great effort. I looked toward her, and met her gaze. It was calm and confident and more than a little smug.

I wanted to slap her face.

Some fierce glint must have shown itself in my eyes because she flinched.

"Calley," she said, "I'm trying to give you the world."

That was the secret?

"I don't want it," I said, without thought, and with plenty of adolescent pout in my tone.

"You have no choice," she said. "Debts have been assumed and must be repaid."

"Not by me." I opened the car door and unfolded myself from the Benz.

Inhaling lovely cool green air, feasting my eyes on the flawless depth of green lawn, I strolled away from the Benz to face the house squarely. If any question had risen in my mind that Mrs. Mank was very wealthy, the house in Brookline answered it definitively. It didn't have a name the way a Southern house would, but the double front doors opened wide onto a high-ceiling hall, and in that hall stood a grand piano. Not a baby grand, a *grand*.

I went straight to it, opened it, and let my fingertips caress each key reverently.

Mrs. Mank spoke over my shoulder. "It's not going anywhere, Calley."

And I wasn't, at least not right away. I wanted to explore. Mrs. Mank chose to behave as if I were going to go along with her plans, despite my defiance in her driveway. It was an attitude that Mama would have been right at home with.

The no-longer-quite-young man who had opened the doors as the roadster stopped in the drive came in with my bindle— my pillowcase. Mrs. Mank greeted him with the name Appleyard, and casually told him my name. Appleyard was an ugly man who wore a neat beard to cover acne scars. His eyes however were as beautiful as any I ever seen, the shade of violet once associated with the eyes of Elizabeth Taylor.

I was shown to the room that was to be mine, a room with its own bathroom, and an east-facing balcony with a tiny table and chair for civilized morning coffee. An assortment of new clothing hung in the closet or was folded in the drawers of the dresser. I liked the clothes that Mrs. Mank or one of her minions had chosen for me. For the first time in my life I did not feel like an orphan in a thrift shop.

The bathroom was furnished luxuriously as well, with the biggest bathtub I had yet to encounter, along with a walk-in shower. A terrycloth bathrobe sat folded on a stool by the tub. From soap to knickers, everything that I could conceivably need was provided.

So this was what it was like to have something.

The first thing that I did was drop my clothes and shower. After, when I sat at the vanity and picked up the comb, I thought: This is how Mama feels, like a grown woman. Tugging the comb through the tangles of my hair, I was surprised to see a fistful of my hair on its teeth. I went on combing, out of curiosity, and in a few minutes was looking at myself, entirely bald, in the mirror.

Mrs. Mank was unperturbed.

"It will grow back in," she declared.

She took me out after we breakfasted and bought me a copper-penny-colored wig, in a dramatically asymmetric style. For me, the extremes of fashion in the sixties are divided between Space-Age Stewardess and Thrift Shop Halloween Costume. My new wig belonged to the first category. Though Mama had accepted the Jackie Kennedy variant, Space-Age Stewardess Married To Airline CEO, she would have been horrified by the color and unfeminine style of the wig as too *too*, to say nothing of being inappropriate for a young girl still in school. The wig amused me almost as much as it did Mrs. Mank and Appleyard.

Appleyard turned out to be Mrs. Mank's factotum. He turned up sooner or later in all of Mrs. Mank's homes, of which she had, at that time, nine. The Brookline house had its own housekeeper, a woman addressed only as Price, and two mute, hearing-impaired maids, Fritzie and Lulu, with whom it was necessary to communicate in sign language. Since it was the preferred *lingua franca* of the household, I picked it up as quickly as I could.

With so little spoken aloud, the house retained a fundamental library quiet. It was a house without television but not without music. Often classical music filled the house, played from the hi-fi system that was connected to speakers in every room. Mrs. Mank's LP collection was enormous and, I would come to realize, immensely valuable in the number and quality of its rarities. I have found recordings there of which there is no public record, that must have been made just for her.

I was allowed free use of the piano. Without a day's lesson, I could and did play exactly what I heard. Mrs. Mank did not play the piano—people, money and information, interchangeably, were her instruments. She was incessantly on the phone, and heaps of discarded newpapers marked every place she sat.

Piano playing was not my only occupation. I immersed myself in a stack of books that constituted the summer reading list for my new school, the name and location of which I was not given. I amused myself by carefully not asking Mrs. Mank for that information. I did not intend to ever attend that school.

And I listened. Mrs. Mank knew that I was listening. She had brought me into her house, knowing that I would. Perhaps that is why she made so little effort to keep most of her secrets from me. For the time being, I chose not to remark upon what I heard. I waited. And listened.

By the end of the first week of our arrival in Brookline, I was still bald under the wig but stubble was emerging on my scalp. I wasn't sure but I thought it was the sand-color of my hair before Santa Rosa Island. When I reported this to Mrs. Mank, she was again unperturbed.

"How would you explain such a phenomenon?" she asked me.

I had been thinking about it long enough. "Miz Verlow's shampoo that she made for me."

Mrs. Mank smiled her secretive smile.

"I have made an appointment for you with a gynecologist, my dear. You will need a reliable method of birth control now."

Ah. Miz Verlow's vitamins. Thanks for letting me know, Miz Verlow. It might have saved Grady and me a few days of wretched anxiety. No wonder Merry Verlow had looked just a wee shamefaced when I last saw her.

My large and growing feet made shopping for shoes the most daunting task of all. One day in the second week of August, Mrs. Mank took me back to the shop where she had ordered specially fitted shoes for me. As I waited for her to pay for the shoes, a transistor radio babbled softly in the back of the shop. A change in the cadence of speech clued me in at once that a newscast was on but then the place names shouted at me: Gulf of Mexico! Hurricane! Gulf Coast! Florida Panhandle!

"There's a hurricane off the Gulf Coast," I told Mrs. Mank.

"Oh my," she said mildly.

The Benz sedan in which Appleyard had driven us occupied a parking slot a few spaces from the shop. Appleyard waited on the sidewalk to relieve us of the shopping bags as we reached the sedan. While Mrs. Mank and I folded ourselves into the backseat of the Benz, Appleyard whipped the bags into the trunk, closed it, and was there to close the door of the sedan after me.

When he was behind the wheel, Mrs. Mank asked him to turn on the radio and tune it to a station that would report on the weather. We were in Brookline and entering the drive to Mrs. Mank's house before we heard another report on the approaching hurricane. Appleyard turned up the volume and we sat in the sedan in the driveway, in the air-conditioning, while the radio told us that a hurricane named Camille was churning over the Gulf toward the coast of Mississippi. She was expected to turn toward Florida's Panhandle in the next twenty-four hours. All hurricanes are dangerous but Camille, according to this report, was extraordinarily powerful.

Mrs. Mank attempted in vain to reach Miz Verlow. Rising winds preceding the hurricane had already taken down the line and cut off Merrymeeting on Santa Rosa Island.

Camille's threat raised a storm of guilt in me at leaving without saying good-bye to Perdita and Cleonie and Roger and Grady. I did miss them. Still, I had not sent so much as a postcard, let alone written a letter. Every night I went to bed thinking that in the morning, I would leave, go back to Santa Rosa Island, collect my money, and find myself a school of my own choice. Every morning, I woke with the thought that it was the day that I should confront Mrs. Mank and demand the secret that I was promised, and then I would leave, at once. In her presence, though, I felt a certain amount of fear, enough to keep me hesitant. I told myself that I was playing a long game, and everything that I learned while I waited was worth the while. And damn, I was going to have a lot to tell Grady about living the life of the wealthy.

Writing after the hurricane would be pointless. No one on Santa Rosa Island would be getting any mail for a while. I lost myself in reading. When eyestrain blurred the words and headache locked up all sense, I prowled the house, trying to interest myself in Mrs. Mank's LPs or the books shelved in nearly every room. Mama was supposed to meet Ford in Mobile on the seventeenth. I hoped that the deterioration of the weather ahead of the hurricane had not trapped her on Santa Rosa Island, preventing her from the reunion she had so desired.

Camille never made the predicted swerve toward Santa Rosa Island and Pensacola. She struck the coast of Mississippi head on, over the seventeenth and eighteenth of August. Camille savaged Mobile, but it was Pass Christian she hurt the worst.

It was Pass Christian and not Mobile where Mama's body was found, floating tits up in a hotel pool. The hotel the pool once graced was gone.

Sixty-six

MAMA was not missing for long. Floating around in that swimming pool in the middle of the cement slabs on which a hotel stood two days previous, like a bug in a puddle in the middle of a cemetery, she would have been hard to miss.

Miz Verlow was able to contact us via marine radio on the nineteenth, so I knew that Mama had gone to Mobile. She had hired Roger to drive her in the Edsel. Why that old clunker? I wondered if she had thought that it might in some obscure way please Ford.

Finding Roger took longer because he was taken sick with pneumonia in a shelter set up in a little colored church in Mobile. He had no memory of how he had gotten there or what had happened to the Edsel or Mama. The last he remembered was he and Mama smoking cigarettes inside the Edsel, parked on the broken pavement that was all there was left of the Ford automobile agency once owned by Daddy, and debating whether they should find a hurricane shelter. Mama had wanted to wait for Ford who surely, she insisted, had *promised* to be there. The Edsel rocked from side to side in the blasts of wind, scaring the both of them, but when Roger decided that he was getting the hell out of there and started the Edsel again, he could see nothing outside. The Edsel began to roll seemingly on its own, with Mama shrieking in the back. Roger clung to the wheel. The elements became so indistinguishable, a freight-train vortex of wind and rain, that Roger thought he might for a while have actually flown the Edsel in it.

After the hurricane, the broken pavement was gone, replaced with the roof of a Chinese restaurant. The Edsel turned up driven halfway into the hull of a fishing trawler named *Katie* sitting athwart East Beach Boulevard, also known as Route 90. Dorothy and Toto were nowhere to be seen.

Mrs. Mank relayed the news from Merry Verlow to me, in the garden of the house in Brookline, just outside of Mrs. Mank's ground-floor sitting room. I had heard the phone ring and Merry Verlow's voice over the phone from where I was, stretched out on a comfortable chaise with a book in one hand. Mrs. Mank hung up and came to the French doors that opened from her sitting room into the garden.

"You know," she said.

I nodded numbly.

"Have you heard anything?"

From Mama, she meant. I shook my head no. I was not lying. She knew that I had been listening since we heard of Mama's disappearance. I had been listening for Roger too.

My brother, Ford, or someone so identifying himself, claimed Mama's corpse. None of the officials Miz Verlow queried had any idea where Ford had taken Mama's remains but she was told that he had made mention of cremation. Where and when the cremation occurred or if any sort of funeral had been held, or burial of an urn or scattering of ashes done, she was unable to learn. Colonel Beddoes's desolation deepened when he learned that he was not going to get back Mama's ring, for it was not recovered. Either the hurricane had taken it, or some other thief.

Camille beat up Santa Rosa Island as well, just not as severely as Mobile and Pass Christian. She tore off most of the verandah and punched Merrymeeting's roof through with seven pine boles and an Adirondack chair. The damage report from Miz Verlow, via Mrs. Mank, added that a school bus from Blackwater had been discovered half-buried in the dune fronting Merrymeeting. Its windows were sealed closed and it was full of water, and water moccasins.

Two days after Miz Verlow reported that Ford had claimed Mama's remains, the mail arrived at Mrs. Mank's. It was late morning, and I was in the garden again, trying to read and failing, for the desire to leave was very intense. Mrs. Mank was in her bedroom, with her masseuse. I heard the mail van on the gravel of the drive, and knew it was mail-time, but it was a surprise to have Appleyard emerge from the house with an envelope in hand. He presented it to me silently.

It was an ordinary greeting card envelope, addressed to me in care of Mrs. Mank at the Brookline address, and without a return address.

Inside was a black-edged card announcing that an interment service for Roberta Ann Carroll Dakin would be held in Tallassee, Alabama. The given day and hour were the morrow, the place a cemetery called The Promised Land. I recognized the name as the one where Daddy was buried, that I had not been able to remember when I returned to Tallassee with Grady. There was no RSVP number. No one to contact.

Later, when I showed it to Mrs. Mank, I said, "This is from Ford, obviously, and I want to see him."

She frowned. "It's a long way to go. How are you going to do it?"

"Take a bus," I said. Of course, I didn't have the fare. I would steal it, if I had to, or beg it at the bus station.

Mrs. Mank gauged my determination and shrugged. "We'll fly—"

"You weren't invited," I said.

She covered her shock with a cold little laugh.

"Yes," I said suddenly, "let's fly."

The flinch in her eyes was satisfying. "Don't be tiresome," she said. She crossed her arms over her bosom. "You're in no position to order me around."

"Never mind," I answered, turning toward the stairs. "I'll take the bus."

"No," she said, biting the word off sharp. "We will fly."

I smiled to myself and went upstairs to pack my brand-new luggage.

We were to leave early the next morning, the day of the service.

We dined by candlelight, just the two of us, as usual, in the formal dining room of the house in Brookline. Mrs. Mank had begun educating me about wine and food. I was surprised to discover that wine was well-worth drinking, and the knowing-about was only important to my palate, not to impress anyone.

Mrs. Mank had been pleased that I appeared to possess both an educable palate and a strong head.

At the end of the meal, Price set out the brandy snifters in their sterling silver cradles. Mrs. Mank poured the decanted brandy herself, and lit the spirit flames beneath the snifters with a long wooden match.

The wine that we had consumed during the meal had mellowed us both, lessening the tension over my defiance.

"Tell me about the Circus," I said, and made a little calliope wheeze.

Mrs. Mank laughed at my boldness.

"You've been listening," she said, with some pride.

Indeed I had. I did a little more calliope, and she laughed again.

"I use the term generically," she said. "Life's a circus, is it not?"

"Fat ladies and acrobats and lions—oh my."

"Indeed," she said agreeably.

"It means something more, doesn't it?"

"Of course." She twiddled the crystal balloon, so the candlelight gilded its contents. "I prize talent, special talent. People with special talents have special needs. Their talents need protection. People who stand out of a crowd," she said, "like excessively large ears on a Calley Dakin's head, draw the sometimes murderous hatred of all those sadly untalented people who make up the mob. Is there any more characteristic human behavior than the burning of witches?"

It was an assertion that I could not refute.

"My Circus provides a refuge for certain specially talented people. Now, it happens that the talents in which I am interested can and often do occur in families. Your great-grandmama, for instance—"

"Cosima—"

She nodded. "Cosima. What a gifted woman she was. To give credit where it's due, the idea of the circus as a refuge was hers. It isn't at all surprising to me that mere death had not silenced her. Personalities of Cosima's strength do not easily unravel. She married your great-granddaddy when he was a mildly successful proprietor of what he called 'A Traveling Show.' She made it into a real Circus. She drew talent like a magnet. She made him a wealthy man. He repaid her with infidelity. In turn, she took revenge by nursing him through his final illness, which was syphilis. Before the syphilis reduced him to a grinning toothless lunatic, he suffered her extraordinary kindness and gentleness. Forgiveness is a terrible thing, Calley. It wracks the guilty worse than hate."

"It's a point of view," I ventured. I wasn't about to commit myself to forgiving anybody, least of all Mrs. Mank.

"It's the truth," she said, straightening in her chair. "Cosima was a goddamned angel." Her tone was sarcastic. "She forgave *every*thing."

The brandy had loosened her tongue. I didn't want to interrupt her.

"Your grandmama had only her looks. Beautiful women are as common as sin, of course. Because the world so overvalues beauty in a woman, the beautiful woman often becomes an empty shell. I myself," she added, "am not beautiful."

I wondered if she meant the face that she presently wore, with its strong resemblance to that of the current Queen of England, or the one with which she had been born. Had she changed her face for strategic purposes or because she hated her original one?

"I have a particular talent, and that is to be able to recognize and use the talents the rest of the populace would gladly smother in infancy." She nodded toward me significantly.

She may have wanted me to thank her. I didn't.

She drank a little of her brandy and continued. "Your mama received only Deirdre's and Cosima's useless beauty. It brought her only grief, I can assure you."

"Speak ill of the dead," I said.

"If I wish." She pursed her lips. "Your mama's sisters had talents. Deirdre tried to kill them. She was enraged to be afflicted with them, the sort of people that she had fled in her marriage to 'Captain' Carroll." Mrs. Mank said "Captain" roguishly, mocking Mamadee. "Cosima saved them from her. Alas, your mama undid Cosima's best efforts. When she was in her teens and Deirdre was becoming jealous of her looks, she ran away to Cosima."

"It's a fairy tale," I said. " 'Mirror, mirror, on the wall, who's the fairest of them all.' "

Mrs. Mank smiled sourly. "Of course it is. Once in Cosima's house, your mama could not abide living with her own sisters, those ugly but talented young women. Did she mean to burn the house down and everyone in it except herself? Ask Cosima sometime, will you? Or your mama, if you can. It hardly matters. Faith and Hope were lost, and so was Cosima."

For a moment she sat silent, brooding. "I wanted to hate Cosima. I was never very successful at it. I had my jealousy, for I had neither Deirdre's beauty, nor talent of the kind that Cosima and your aunts had. Mine are talents far more common in the world. Jack Dexter's talents."

Her features sagged with dissatisfaction.

"Yes, I am Deirdre's sister. Your great-aunt." She looked at me with suddenly wide-open eyes. "I'm half-pissed," she said.

I laughed. "It's been fascinating."

She laughed as if she had been clever. "I bet. Look, I've been a fairy godmother to you. I expect some return on my outlay. Do we understand each other?"

I nodded as if in the affirmative. I needed her in order to get to Tallassee for Mama's interment.

I drank her brandy, and let her think that she was ringmaster.

Sixty-seven

THE flight was direct, from a private terminal at Logan to the little airport at Tallassee. Firsts for me, to fly, to fly on a jet, to fly on a chartered jet—I remembered the train from New Orleans to Montgomery, and it came to me that I would not run out of firsts until my death, and that would be a first too. Mrs. Mank slept the whole way, because she did not want to talk to me, but also because she was hungover. She took a pill of some kind and offered me one, but I declined. Her lips pursed at the realization that my head was stronger than hers.

The wardrobe she had provided me was short on black, so I wore a boxy Courreges stewardessy cobalt-blue dress that went only halfway to my knees. I was barelegged, but my shoes were black, black flats because Mrs. Mank said tall girls had to wear flats and she had picked them out and paid for them. One day, I promised myself, I would buy my own shoes, and own a pair of stiletto heels in black. My copper-penny wig covered the stubble of my new hair. Both my black beret and the pin that held it to the wig were borrowed, volunteered by Mrs. Mank from her own wardrobe. The beret bore the label of Elsa Schiaparelli, and for that reason alone, I accepted the loan of it. Wig and hat felt like two hats, but I didn't intend to make a habit of wearing the combination.

A car and hired driver awaited us. It was a black Cadillac, and the driver was a woman. She was a thin woman, the worn-out Southern kind, with huge eyes and sun-damaged complexion, bad teeth and cigarette-stained fingers. She did not have an ounce of flesh to spare, no chest, no fanny, and her hair had been burnt to rusty wire by harsh home perms and dye-jobs.

The first thing that she did was to introduce herself as Doris, and then express her condolences for the late Mrs. Dakin. Hers was a lunger's voice, breathy and harsh.

I wondered how Doris knew Mama's name. Surely Ford had not put it in any of the local newspapers. Perhaps Mrs. Mank had included the information with the address of the cemetery that was our destination.

Doris's eyes in the rearview mirror were curious but only for brief seconds; she drove skillfully, and never hesitated as to our route.

Mrs. Mank glanced at the Rolex on her wrist and said, "We're going to be a little late."

Doris stepped down on the accelerator. She did her best, but the country roads could not be driven as if they were highways, not safely.

The Promised Land shocked me, so closely did it match my memory. Its resemblance to a used-car junkyard was deeply disheartening. Someone had left a dusty Corvette at the verge of the road into the cemetery.

"Stay here, please," I asked Mrs. Mank.

She rolled down the windows and sat back. "Have it your way." From her purse, she took a flask.

Doris held the door for me.

"I'll just wait with Missus," she told me, with a flicker of her gaze toward Mrs. Mank. It was as if she didn't want to say Mrs. Mank's name.

There was no grass, just prickly weeds in patches. The weeds were rooted in coarse sand, amid pebbles with edges so sharp I could feel them biting the thin soles of my flats. Crumbling concrete marked out the sunken rectangles of the graves and all the tombstones tilted forward as if they wanted a better look at the man or woman or child or stillborn infant they commemorated. On nearly every grave a cracked clay pot or old milk bottle held dried-up old flowers. The few trees thereabout were all bent and scraggly and seemingly half dead. They looked like the paper trees we cut out in kindergarten for Halloween decorations, so the bats and ghosts would have some background beside the moon.

I looked for a crow. Not only were there no crows, there were no birds at all, and in Alabama, I recalled, there were always birds in the sky.

A casket waited on a mechanical frame in an open grave. There were no flowers. Nearby stood a big black funeral hack, its rear door open. Two men sat inside the hack, in the front seat, with the windows rolled down, and cigarette smoke whisping out. A white man in a black suit leaned against the body of the hack, smoking a cigarette. He wore a black fedora. He did not need to remove his sunglasses for me to recognize him.

He pitched his cigarette butt past the coffin and into the open grave.

"Let's get this gone," Ford said in a bored drawl.

The two men, the undertaker and the driver, got out of the front seat of the hack and assumed respectful postures next to it.

Ford hitched the hem of his suit jacket, which was silk and hand-tailored, and drew a small, thick book from a rear pocket. The jacket fell perfectly back into line.

He pushed his hat back on his forehead. He let the book fall open.

He did not look at it but intoned, "Dearly beloved, we are gathered here today to lay to rest the sorry remains of the late not very beloved Roberta Ann Carroll Dakin, relic of Joe Cane Dakin, the larger proportion of him moldering already just to my left. If you examine his stone—beg pardon, there is no stone, as Roberta Ann Carroll Dakin never got around to having one placed there. Let none of us doubt that she had a more pressing need, if she ever did recall that she had yet to perform this widow's duty, perhaps for cigarettes, or silk stockings, or makeup, that week. Allow me to substitute mere words:

> *Here lies Daddy,*
> *Soul still achin'*
> *Without a stone*
> *'Cause he was a Dakin.*
> *A Dakin, A Dakin, A no-count Dakin.*"

Ford took a mocking bow.

"To the task at hand."

He looked down at the casket. He spread his hands upon the polished wood of the top.

"Mama," he said. "Blame me. I had your bloated carcass drug here all the way from Pass Christian. I bought this here plot next to Daddy, just for you. Now your fine Carroll bones gone spend eternity right next to his Dakin bones. Most of 'em, I mean. Mama, I spent the last decade of my life thinking up the things I was gone say to you. But now we're here, I ain't wasting my breath."

He tipped his chin heavenward and closed his eyes behind the lenses of his sunglasses reverently.

"Ashes to ashes, dust to dust," he said mournfully, and then laughed. "Let's go get drunk."

"I'd like to sing a hymn," I said.

He tore off his hat and cast it roughly to the ground.

"I knew it," he said. "I knew you could not by-god-and-sonny-jesus keep that huge flapping mouth of yours shut."

Ignoring him, I sang, in my own tuneless voice.

I see the moon,
and the moon sees me
and the moon sees the one I long to see.
So Gobbless the moon
And Gobbless me
And Gobbless the one I long to see.

"Okay," said Ford. "Now shut up and let's go get drunk."

Sixty-eight

"I want a few minutes with Daddy."

Ford rolled his eyes. "He's deader than she is, Dumbo."

But he waited. And he removed his hat.

I stepped sideways to the sunken place that he had indicated was Daddy's grave. I felt nothing, no emanation, certainly, and no sense of peace.

"He's not here," I said.

"What I said." Ford smoothed his hair and stuck his hat back on his head, the same way, tipped jauntily back. "Better go tell Saint Peter."

Ignoring Ford, I started back toward the Cadillac. I was going to tell Mrs. Mank that I meant to go have a drink with Ford, possibly even get drunk, and she could go back to Massachusetts, but I didn't bother to tell Ford. He was full enough of himself already.

He strolled along behind me, though.

Doris stood next to the sedan, her eyes bigger than ever at what she had heard and witnessed. She opened the passenger door at my approach.

Ford stepped between me and the open door.

"You," he said to Mrs. Mank, in a mocking tone.

She flinched.

"That's right," he said. "Why don't you just get yourself out of this here Cadillac and dig yourself a hole in an unconsecrated ditch somewhere and pull the dirt in on yourself and die, Auntie? I won't help you either. I won't even throw the dirt on your face, old woman."

She snarled, but seemed unable to speak a word.

"She wants to make a confession, first," I said.

Mrs. Mank looked from me to Ford and back again. Her jaw twitched violently, nearly dislocating itself. At last she got it in gear.

"I am *owed* Calley. I knew it the minute that I saw her in that shop in New Orleans face-to-face. Deirdre promised me. Her stupidity cost me those two girls, Faith and Hope. The two of them weren't half of Calley, of course, not that Deirdre would admit it. She thought she was going to get Joe Cane Dakin's money too. Fennie sorted her out for me. You should thank me for that, boy. You two have no complaint against me. Old Cosima was charcoal before you were born. What could she do for you but interfere?"

Ford slammed the door hard enough to make the automobile shake.

Inside, Mrs. Mank hit the door lock. *Clunk*. Cadillac door locks always clunked.

"Let's go get drunk," he said. "I had all this I can take."

"What about her?"

"What about her?" he said irritably.

He strode toward the Corvette and with a glance back at Mrs. Mank's purpling face, I followed him. I guessed that I didn't have to tell her anything. I didn't have to account to her.

Ford did not open the car door for me. He went over the one on the driver's side, of course, rather than open it for himself. I did the same thing on the passenger side, no doubt showing my underpants to Doris, Mrs. Mank, the undertaker and his man. Those two fellows had yet to begin lowering the casket. They were standing there gawking, and who could blame them?

Sinking into the bucket seat, I unpinned the beret and took it off. I tucked it under my fanny.

Ford watched me quizzically.

"It's a Schiaparelli," I said.

He chortled. "Oh, Mama, you hear that?"

He drove just the way I expected he would, like an idiot. It was highly enjoyable, and I whooped and hollered and laughed along with him.

We came to a roistering stop outside a cement block roadhouse. It was properly low in every way, as a Southern bar should be, on account of drinking and everything associated with it is so sinful. The least a body could do was sin in as squalid a place as could be found.

We didn't actually stay. Ford bought a bottle of Wild Turkey from the old blind man behind the bar and we carried it away to his Corvette. A black limousine waited in the parking lot not far from it. Doris waved at me from behind the wheel. The windows were up, no doubt with the air-conditioning keeping Mrs. Mank cool, and so she was not visible to us.

"Is this against the law?" I asked Ford.

"Hope so," he said, throwing the cap away.

Handing me the bottle first was an unexpected, gentlemanly gesture that might have brought tears to my eyes, if Ford were anyone else but Ford.

"Krast," he said, letting his accent thicken ridiculously. "You growd tits. No much of 'em but that's about as much as I expected. You gone drink that whole bottle yourself?"

"You ain't changed a bit," I said, with airy contempt.

He sucked a good mouthful out of the bottle, swished it around like mouthwash and swallowed it.

"That's a lie," he said. "Now we're orphans, you best be kinder to me."

"You gone be kinder to me?"

"Maybe." He fingered the breast pocket of his jacket, withdrew from it a card, and passed it to me.

"Fred Hatfield. Damn," I said, "I'm getting all warm and gooey." I tucked the card into the pocket in my dress.

"Daddy set up a dealership to sell Fords to colored people," Ford said. "That was the last straw for Mamadee. Not that it matters. When somebody wants to kill somebody else, motivation is justification, that's all. So when Auntie offered to help get rid of Daddy and steal his money, Mamadee jumped right on. She should have known Auntie would double-cross her. Evarts and Weems and Mamadee cooked the books on Daddy. They were gone steal him and Mama blind. And did. But those loonies that murdered Daddy, they were tools. Tools for Isobel Mank, who felt about Daddy much as Deirdre Carroll did but was most anxious to control you. What you gone do about her, that old witch Isobel?"

I shrugged. Truly I did not know.

"What happened to all the Dakins?" I asked him out of left field.

He grinned and rubbed his thumb and forefinger together. "They accepted the kind assistance of Mamadee's agent, Lawyer Weems, to remove to California. I'll send you all the addresses of the ones that are still alive."

"How do you know her?" I asked.

"Same way you do," said Ford. "She bought me from Lew Evarts. He took the money and run. She told me right off that she was Mamadee's sister and my closest blood, next to Mama, who run off like the slut she was. She already had custody of you, she said, and you were in someplace for the feebleminded. She put me into the Wire Grass Military 'Cademy. It's outside of Banks, Alabama, about as far from anywhere as you can get and not be dead. It's run by some friends of hers, the Slaters, and it's a lot more like a prison than a school. First-class teachers, though. They'd all been run out other schools for some peccadillo or another, like picking their noses in church or being ex-Nazis or something socially iffy."

"There were other kids there?"

"Seventy-five, give or take. Juvenile delinquents, basically." Ford grinned. "I learned as much from my fellow inmates as I did from the faculty."

"Did you send Mama that letter, the one from Paris?"

"Yeah. I went from Wire Grass to Phillips Exeter, and then I got control of my money and split for France."

"How did you do that? Get control of the money?"

"Blackmailed Mank. I can connect her with Fennie Verlow, the morning that y'all skedaddled. I hear the Edsel plowing up the driveway and reckoned Mama was in a snit at Mamadee. So I came downstairs and there was ol' Fennie havin' a cozy chat with Tansy. Tansy tucked some cash money away real quick, so I wouldn't see it, but I did. Then Mamadee started squealing for her coffee and toast. A couple hours later, Mamadee had this thing on her neck I couldn't even see to start, and she was going batty. Tansy pretended to find fault with something and ran off, which made me a little suspicious. I poked around the kitchen and found the new butter thrown into the trash with just a little bit gone, enough for Mamadee's toast. It didn't smell like butter. It had a funny medicine smell. After she ran around town buying umbrellas, Mamadee went into her bedroom and didn't come out. I peeked in and by then that thing on her neck was visible, my God it was disgusting. I jammed an umbrella ferrule into the keyhole. Lew Evarts turned up and got the door open. I saw him touch that thing and then it exploded. She flopped around like a fish on a hook and then she was dead. I didn't see Lew Evarts do a thing to stop it. The blood. He just looked disgusted."

He paused for the cause and then resumed. "Anyway, that isn't the only thing that I've got on Madame Mank. Among other things, she twiddles currency, you know, and a lot of it she forgets to do legally. I'm a hell of a researcher, worse luck for her, and a very good thief"—he rubbed the tips of the fingers of one hand together—"and while I can't hear the way you can, Calley, I mastered the latest techniques in phone tapping at Phillips Exeter. Some of those rich kids come by dishonesty honestly. You ever smoke pot?"

I shook my head regretfully.

He looked at me. "You're gone enjoy college. What's your next move? You gone let Mank pay your way through school, and then work it off for her?"

I was still thinking about it. "How free am I, right now?"

"Free enough to say no. I'll pay your way through college, Calley. I'm a thief but I'm your brother too. Most of the money I've got was Daddy's, or Mamadee's, and we should both be heirs. I'll give you half. Take you to a lawyer today and sign it over."

The offer stunned me.

"I've got the ransom," I confessed.

Ford winked at me. "You do have some Carroll in you."

He watched me take another drink from the bottle and pass it back to him, and fidget, while I turned everything over in my mind.

"You think you can beat Mank at her own game?"

"You did," I said. "And maybe you'd help."

Now it was his turn to drink, fidget, glance at the limo, drink again and pass me the bottle.

"I'll be on the outside," he said, with a surprised unhappiness in his voice. "I gotta think about it. We're talking about your soul, you know."

Impulsively, I gave him a kiss on the cheek. While he was laughing and wiping it off his cheek, I climbed out of the Corvette.

Doris saw me coming and was outside of the limo opening the door by the time I reached it. I glanced back at Ford, before I folded myself into the rear seat. I thought I saw him give the briefest of nods, and then he threw me a double eagle.

Epilogue

ONE of my ghosts evaporated unexpectedly and with embarrassing ease. In a course on meteorology, taken to fulfill some undergraduate requirement, I discovered that the giant ghost in the fog was myself. Mrs. Mank's headlights had cast my own shadow onto the fog. It's called the Brocken Spectre. I suffered no chagrin. It happened when I was an ignorant little girl in strange circumstances. The discovery did, however, allow me to dismiss the occasional leakage of other memories of weirdness in my childhood as just as likely to be explainable in rational terms.

The ease with which I pick up languages and sciences, everything that I learned working in radio while I went through the various colleges that I attended, I built into a double-barreled career as a translator and radio producer. There were other schools that I attended under Mrs. Mank's sponsorship, schools that don't give degrees to hang on the wall. Under cover of translation and radio production, I have traveled everywhere in this world, gathering and absorbing information useful to Mrs. Mank and her superiors. I was more than a good servant, I was a brilliant one, and as much as I earned, I was never overpaid. I am proudest of the mischief to Mrs. Mank's interests that I was frequently able to trigger without her suspicions ever being raised. Ford and I between us put many a spoke in her wheels. Toward that end, she knew that someone was playing a long game against her, and that she was weakening and would eventually lose.

She believed that I was passing messages to her from her

mama, my great-grandmama, Cosima, forgiving her, giving her direction. Ouija-board stuff, really. *Mama, will I go to Hell? Mama, should I buy low and sell high? Mama, should I bet on this politician or that one? Mama, blah, Mama, it wasn't my fault, I've just had to do what I had to do, Mama. Deirdre brought it on herself, Mama, you know she did.* Isobel Mank, who scammed the world, let herself be scammed by Joe Cane Dakin's daughter, with a little assistance from Cosima. It was easy for me to speak in Cosima's voice, of course, but oftentimes I really was telling her something that Cosima told me to tell her.

I had the pleasure of being at Mrs. Mank's bedside when she died seven years ago. Cancer of the lungs had invaded her throat, and she had lost the power of speech. All she could do was caw *"Uhhhk, uhhk!"*

"Joe Cane Dakin wants to tell you something," I told her, as I sat at her bedside.

She didn't look good to start but the sound of his name coming out of my mouth, the first time since she took me away from Santa Rosa Island, made her look a lot worse. Like maybe something was sitting on her bony chest, sucking the breath out of her ravaged lungs.

"Uhk!" she cawed.

"He says there's a party waiting to start in Hell, and all your friends are waiting. Mamadee and old Weems and Doc Evarts and Tansy and Fennie Verlow and her sister, Merry, and Adele Starret and those two poor loonies you had her bamboozle into killin' him. Fennie and Mamadee won't sit next to each other, for sure, on account of that awkward little bit of Merry's poison Candle Bush that Fennie ground into Mamadee's butter and paid Tansy to put on her toast. But never mind. You're the guest of honor, and the main course."

Then, as she stared at me in horror, her eyes like bloody boiled eggs in their swollen sockets, I did her a kindness that closed out any "debt" that she might have imagined that I owed her; I emptied a syringe of morphine into a paper cup and pumped a bubble of air into her veins. It was as merciful a death as anyone might ask. The morphine did not go to waste either. I passed it to someone in pain who couldn't afford it.

Mrs. Mank left me everything—she didn't mean to do it, but she had no one else to leave it to and she wasn't taking it with her, so I made sure the will in her safety deposit named me explicitly.

The house in Brookline is the only one that I have kept. Appleyard lives there and will die there; I have promised him. It was Appleyard who saw to my sexual education. We have been friends ever since. Throughout my life, sex has been the servant of friendship, convenience, and sometimes commerce, and less trouble than it ever was for Mama. While I think of myself as heterosexual, the tenderest lover that I have known was a woman, and she was not the only woman whom I ever knew that way. My taste in men was firmly fixed by Grady Driver: sweet and not too bright. I have never been in love, whatever that means, and trust I never shall be. I have never married, or had a child, and never will now.

My spare time since Mrs. Mank's passing has largely been devoted to the dispersal of her estate to charitable causes, libraries and disaster relief and so on. I particularly enjoy giving to the Carter Foundation because of its attention to Africa. Mrs. Mank once remarked to me that AIDS was going to wipe out the population of Africa, and *entre nous,* the depopulation of that continent would be all to the good. She loathed charity almost as much as she did nonwhites. I have amused myself enormously doing with her money exactly what she would have hated done.

I did see Grady again, when he tracked me down by means of the simple expediency of asking Miz Verlow where in creation I was. On my return one winter day to Mrs. Mank's house in Brookline, my first year at Wellesley, I found him sleeping on the porch with the pair of mastiffs who were supposed to safeguard the place, and me, from what I did not know. Not Grady, in any case. Mrs. Mank was away, as was Appleyard. Price and the maids were off for the weekend.

With the place to ourselves, Grady and I drank Mrs. Mank's Moët et Chandon and smoked the high-quality bud that my generous allowance from Mrs. Mank afforded me.

Grady's most interesting news was that another child had come to live with Miz Verlow at Merrymeeting.

Fennie Verlow in person, whom I had never seen at Merrymeeting in my time there, had arrived one day with a little boy of five she called Michael. The child wore a sailor suit, which delighted Cleonie, causing her ever after to refer to him as Michael the Sailorman. How it was that Michael came to live at Merrymeeting, Grady, who had been summoned to unclog a sink, could not say but he met Michael sitting on the closed commode in the bathroom in question.

Michael had cut off most of his hair, it seems, with a pair of shears he had found in an old shoebox that he found at the back of a crookedy little closet in his room, the one that had been mine. With all those swatches of hair available, Michael had attempted to tape swatches of his hair on the crumbling old paper dolls also contained in the shoebox. When the project was finished, Michael then tried to flush his handiwork down the sink, causing it to clog.

Michael's curiosity was unsated; he wanted to watch Grady unclog the sink.

While Grady did so, Miz Verlow, having just been informed by Cleonie of what Michael had done, came into the bathroom to scold Michael.

"Paper dolls," Miz Verlow said scornfully. "Girls play with paper dolls. I cannot abide girls."

"You're a girl," Michael pointed out.

"Little girls," Miz Verlow clarified.

"You sound mean," said Michael. "I don't care if you like girls or not. I don't like you."

Flustered, Miz Verlow protested, "I am not mean."

"Sound it," Michael said. "Who died and made you God?"

Grady and I agreed the child must have heard the phrase from a grown-up; he was too young to have thought it up himself.

Michael became feverish later that day and what was left of his hair fell out. It grew back in but it wasn't the same, Grady told me. It was reddish-blond and thick as fur.

It was the last time I saw Grady, who left his bones in a rice paddy three years later.

Reports of Hurricane Ivan hitting Santa Rosa Island brought my time there to mind again, and thoughts of Santa Rosa's wild beauty insisted on being thought.

An e-mail was in the inbox of an online account that I use only for the most personal communications.

> From: FordDakin@FCD.com
> To: BetsyCaneMcCall@bcm.com
> Hey, Dumbo. I'm feeling sentimental in my old age.
> I'll be at Merrymeeting on Wednesday next.
> Affectionately,
> Ford Cane Dakin

I left for Pensacola the following Wednesday. The airport was open by then but the whole area was still in disarray, some five weeks after Hurricane Ivan had elected Santa Rosa Island and Pensacola as its bull's-eye. The Route 10 Causeway had fallen in several places and was still under repair. Undermined by storm surge, the Scenic Highway had broken up in numerous places. Everywhere there was still damage evident—the chainsawed trees, the heaps of wood chips, road crews, detours, and debris not significant enough for immediate removal. The easiest way to get to Santa Rosa Island was by helicopter. I had made arrangements ahead of time to charter one. It was waiting with its rotors spinning, the pilot already onboard, when my jet put down its wheels on the runway at Pensacola.

I made an immediate transfer to the helicopter.

Transit by chopper, of course, afforded a grand tour view of the hurricane damage. It is especially shocking to see a bridge collapsed that one has previously driven so regularly as to take it for a permanent feature of the landscape.

Despite the damage, from the air it was still apparent that there had been a lot of development since I left in the late sixties. Though the hurricane had destroyed a portion of that development, evidence of its existence remained in the debris. The chopper pilot spoke through the earphones that we wore, pointing out the beach that Hurricane Opal had created and some other places that had been damaged in previous hurricanes, repaired with beach nourishment and replanted vegetation, and damaged again by Ivan or other storms. The beaches had washed over the roads and after the hurricane, emergency road crews cut through the sand, so that what now existed looked like roads ploughed through snow.

North of Pensacola Beach, the sand covered the road in places and the water had drowned part of it as well. The wall of dunes that had defined the Gulf shore of the island was gone, the shoreline no longer a line at all, but a milky fringe. A shallow pass separated the Fort Pickens end of the island from the rest; Fort Pickens itself was flooded. I knew that it had happened and where it had happened, of course, but it was still stunning. And I had wondered years ago how much the island might be changed by the time I returned.

The roofline of Merrymeeting rose from the sand but its back was broken, and it looked like it might be the keel of the ark. It had long been abandoned. Each passing storm had frayed it or clawed it or kicked it upside the head, but Hurricane Ivan had reduced it to a broken roof.

Merry Verlow died in a hotel fire in Las Vegas. She has never told me why she was there but admits that she started it with a lighted candle that she left too close to a drapery.

How Fennie wept for Merry. Mrs. Mank and I went to Merry's funeral in Birmingham, where the Verlow sisters had grown up. Fennie's hair was still that unlikely color and still marcelled. She committed suicide after Merry's funeral, by overdosing on heroin. Thoughtful of her, Mrs. Mank had joked, as we were already in town for a funeral.

The chopper settled on the nearest solid patch of sand. The pilot let the chopper rotors come to a standstill. I jumped out and ducked away under the rotors.

Where once the sea oats and panic grass held the dunes in place and the shorebirds peeped in the swash, water flowed from the Gulf into Pensacola Bay. Eventually, if this little neonate pass did not silt up, sand would accrete on its corners and new beaches would be created. For now, the sand was a watery desert, strewn with detritus of every kind flung by wind and water. Here a sand-roughened cobalt-glass candlestick, there a sodden cigarette pack, and over there, a black feather. And at my feet, a fragment of cassia.alata var.santarosa. The source of so many of Merry Verlow's potions. And poisons. How easy it must have been to suborn Tansy to poison the butter on Mamadee's brioche.

I wondered about the beach mice. They were endangered even before this particular disaster. Still, they had survived so many other storms.

I looked up instinctively.

I see the moon.

But I did not. The moon was not in the sky, and would not be, until the wee hours of the day to come. As I habitually do, I touched the Calliope locket that hung round my neck on a gold chain, as it had for years. It had been my good luck charm, my comfort, all the while.

The pilot, my brother, Ford, came up beside me, his helmet in his hand. Ford brushed his hair back from his forehead with one hand. His hair was thinning. It had been some years since we had crossed paths in the flesh.

He grinned at me. "Calley."

He looked hale and hearty and prosperous. He looked like a man who enjoyed every bit of his life. No sullenness, no boredom.

I closed my eyes and listened. I heard Ford's breathing and my own. The water in its permutations, lap and lick, surge and suck, touch and go. The wind tugging and pushing, whistling and sighing. Wings striking in the air, the whip of fish in the water.

Deeper than that.

You owe me. Merry Verlow.

You owe me too. Fennie Verlow. The Echo sisters.

We'll settle this later. Isobel Dexter Mank.

We can contest it. Adele Starret.

Nothing from Mamadee. Said all she had to say.

So much for the Liars Chorus.

Lord my feet hurt.

You wore your shoes too small, Mama, and the foot cream I massaged into your feet every night kept you on Santa Rosa. Poor Mama.

Put your pants on and let's go get some more beer. Grady, laughing.

It was instantaneous, wasn't it, Grady? That deadly death hidden in the tender shoots of the rice?

A long silence.

You are my sunshine. Daddy, from very far away and very close at hand.

"She had him torn limb from limb," I said, "to make it harder for him to be heard."

Ford's lips barely made a smile.

"So I would have to listen harder," I went on.

Ford shook his head with incredulity.

"She didn't care what he had to say. She wanted to hear from Cosima."

"Well?" Ford rubbed his hands together in exaggerated anticipation.

"I might tell you someday," I said.

He grimaced. "Damn, Calley. That's not fair."

The water rolled something, rolled it toward the sand, end over end, gently, onto the quartz sand that once was marble, Alabama marble.

The wind moved over my face like a caressing hand. The living intruded: Cleonie and Perdita, both still alive though widowed, both still devout AME ladies, living with Roger and his wife and their pack of kids in Ontario. Roger hybridizes prizewinning daylilies. Roger kept the ransom money for me until he was threatened with the draft. When I found out, I had him take half the money and all his kinfolk and go to Canada. He maintained the rest in accounts that I could access when needed until after Isobel Mank's death. It was Cleonie and Perdita leaving that ultimately shut down Merrymeeting, as Merry Verlow never succeeded in replacing them with adequate help.

After a little while, I opened my eyes again and walked slowly toward the water of the new pass. Ford followed me.

The margin of water and sand was sloppy as unset Jell-O. The water advanced and retreated, advanced and retreated. The moon was in the water, I thought, but of course it could not be. Nonetheless, there it was, as if it had fallen into the water, and sat there on the sand, its belated headstone. How silly of me, I thought. The moon looked back at me from its one whole eye socket.

"Ford," I said.

He moved closer at once.

I poked a finger at the water. "Do you see it?"

His gaze followed the line of sight my finger drew. I heard the sharp intake of his breath and then he stopped to untie and remove his shoes. He stepped into the water, where he bent and with both hands groped below the surface. He raised the cold moon in his hands, and the water ran from its broken face. I thought I knew that face. I held out my hands and he put the skull into them. It had no jaw, of course; it could not speak. I raised the broken thing to my lips and kissed its brow that the elements had polished to perfection.

Ford made a crooking sound. "Who," he began and then stopped, dripping and overcome. "Daddy?"

"You are my sunshine," I whispered. "You make me happy."

"It's the beautiful shore," said Ford suddenly, as if he had just remembered. "You sang it at the cemetery."

A smart crack of wings startled me. I looked up: A blackbird branded itself against the sun. Out of the blinding sun fire came a drawn-out, rude laugh: *uuuuhhhk.*